DOUBLE BOOKED

'A laugh-out-loud rom com about what it means
to come out, not just to those around you, but
ultimately to yourself... a must-read.'
Red Magazine

'The queer rom com I've been waiting for.'
Laura Kay, author of *The Split*

'Whip-smart... has a real funny bone that
comes through in every page.'
**Abigail Mann, author of
*The Wedding Crasher***

'Brilliant... horribly relatable and so
perceptive. You will love it.'
Hannah Tovey, author of *Is This It?*

'A double whammy of wit.'
Helen Lederer

'Right up my street – hook it up to
my veins immediately, please.'
Laura Jane Williams, author of *Our Stop*

'Sweet, charming, and has left me feeling hopeful about the future.'

Matt Cain, author of
The Secret Life of Abert Entwhistle

'So fun and steaming hot.'

Mikaella Clements and Onjuli Datta, authors of *The View Was Exhausting*

'A big-hearted and beautifully fresh story of love and self-discovery.'

Emylia Hall, author of
The Book of Summers

'Literary crack. I am so on board it hurts.'

Leena Norms, booktuber and author of *Bargain Bin Rom-Com*

'Absolutely hilarious… deal[s] really thoughtfully with questions of identity and grief.'

Emma Hughes, author of
No Such Thing as Perfect

DOUBLE BOOKED

LILY LINDON

HEAD
of ZEUS

An Aria Book

First published in the UK in 2022 by Head of Zeus Ltd
This paperback edition first published in 2023 by Head of Zeus Ltd,
part of Bloomsbury Publishing Plc

9 7 5 3 1 2 4 6 8

A catalogue record for this book is available from
the British Library.

ISBN (PB): 9781801107587
ISBN (E): 9781801107594

Typeset by Divaddict Publishing Solutions Ltd

Printed and bound in Great Britain by
CPI Group (UK) Ltd, Croydon CR0 4YY

Head of Zeus Ltd
First Floor East
5–8 Hardwick Street
London EC1R 4RG

WWW.HEADOFZEUS.COM

For my dad, Robert Lindon

PART ONE

1

'Sorry, can't. I've got other plans.'

'Georgina!' scoffs Soph. Even over the phone I can see her sarcastic glare. '*You* know that *I* know that you *don't* have other plans.'

It's forty-two past three p.m. I've just taught my last piano lesson of the week and if I keep to my usual walking pace I'll make it to the Tube before peak hours, saving me a sweet fifty pence.

'It's Friday,' I recite, 'so I'll get a takeaway from Cod Almighty. One portion of fish and chips, ketchup on the side. Then I'll have a bath, one medium glass of white wine, and—'

Soph joins in, '—lie back and watch *Friends*. I *know*,' she moans. 'But you don't *have* to. You could change your schedule, come out with me and actually have some *fun*.'

'Genuinely, what could be more fun than watching *Friends* in the bath?'

'Oh, I don't know, *anything*?' squawks Soph. 'Like, literally what I'm suggesting right now? Come to London's best gay bar, see one of the most exciting up-and-coming indie pop bands perform live, and get all your drinks paid for by your generous and gorgeous best friend?'

I pretend to consider as I stride down the pavement. I remember to step over the dangerously wonky manhole cover, saving my most comfortable work heels from a scuffing. Well done, Gina!

There's a glimpse of spring sun this afternoon, a golden glow hesitating through London's usual gloom. To feel the warmth on my neck, I tuck Soph under my ear and twist my hair into a bun.

Then I see myself in a window and remember that I look *astonishingly* bad when my hair's up. It reveals my whopping jaw, the freaky freckles along my neck, the way my goofy ears stick out like a garden gnome's. As quickly as I'd tied it up, I let my hair down again, back into limp brown curtains. It's not great, but at least it hides the ears.

'Surely there's someone more suitable you should go with? Have you forgotten which of your friends you're talking to? I'm *Gina*, the one who is very boring, very plain, and very straight.'

'The lady doth protest too much, methinks.'

'Don't start that nonsense again or I'll accuse you of reverse conversion therapy. Why can't you go with Jenny?'

Soph doesn't reply. I try to hear her expression but I swear she's avoiding my eye.

I slow down. I'll be furious if I miss that off-peak discount, but I guess comforting my best friend is worth fifty pence.

'You *were* going to go with Jenny,' I deduce, 'but you've broken up again.'

Jenny is the kind of open-hearted, unaffected woman who'd wear her muddy Arsenal merchandise to her own wedding. She and Soph are in a perpetual on-off relationship. A real-life Ross and Rachel.

'Did she refuse to be in your *SophieSnob* videos again?'

Predictably, Soph explodes. I lean away from the phone to save my eardrum.

'I don't *understand*. Most women *gag* at the chance to be with me. I'm gorgeous! I'm funny! I'm smart! I'm famous! But Jenny won't even do a photoshoot with me.'

'Blasphemy,' I agree.

'Whatever,' she sighs. 'It's just a shame. Couples videos are really popular and I've never been able to do one... Oh well. Maybe being single is better for my brand anyway.'

Her glumness is infectious.

'If you'd be embarrassed to have Jenny there tonight,' I say, fiddling with the button on my outdated grey pencil skirt, 'then you certainly don't want *me* there. Your hideously plain chaperone.'

'You're not hideously plain.' She pauses. 'But I could give you a *tiny* makeover if you want?'

'I'm at the Tube now,' I lie. 'Good luck!'

'No you're not. You've still got one and a half minutes.'

Damn it! Damn her! Damn my routine!

I pick up speed.

'Why don't you go with one of your party lesbians?'

'Because I prefer you!'

I wait.

'And,' Soph admits, 'because they're all on holiday in a Berlin sex dungeon.'

'*There* it is. Goodb—'

'Honestly,' she says quickly, 'it's the best thing that could have happened. I'll take some quick footage, then we'll hide in a corner and judge the band. Just the two of us, Gee, like old times. *Pleeeeeese...*'

At uni, Soph and I fancied ourselves as talent spotters, going to all the gigs we could afford on student loans. She'd review them on her vlogs, I'd take inspiration for my own songwriting. Obviously, we haven't done that in years.

But salvation! I'm in sight of the Tube. I can taste my medium cod already. I'm about to hang up when a sudden softness in Soph's voice makes me stop.

'Please, Gee…? I know it's still difficult for you to—' She changes track. 'I wouldn't pressure you if I didn't think— I really do think we'd have a fun night together. I miss talking about music with you.'

And, for a moment, I close my eyes and allow myself to imagine it: sitting with Soph in a secret corner of a neon bar, all makeovered, sipping a cocktail, watching from the shadows as confident women laugh with each other, listening as the band starts playing and…

'Nope,' I say, shaking my head and striding towards my destination. 'Sorry, Soph, but I can't. You'll find someone else, some beautiful lesbian to go with, and you can tell me all about it on the sofa on Monday. Tonight, I am going to a wedding with my other *Friends*.'

My finger is a millimetre away from the button to end our call when Soph plays her trump card.

'Pumpernickel.'

I drop my phone. Some banker walks into my back, shouting profanities. I pick the phone up and hiss into it.

'*Really?*'

'Really,' she says. 'Pumpernickel.'

Pumpernickel is our blood pact, used for calling in favours. It started in second year of uni when Soph had a delicious but indigestible pumpernickel bread and ravaged our bathroom, just as her crush arrived at our door. I took the blame. Since then, 'Pumpernickel' has been used to bribe agreement. I Pumpernickeled her into starting standing ovations at my terrible early gigs, she Pumpernickeled me into dumping exes on her behalf and we both used it to write each other's essays. Pumpernickel cannot be denied.

Weirdly, reliefs flood through me.

Following Pumpernickel is like following the routine laid out for me in my calendar: it's not my choice, and it's therefore not my fault if something goes wrong.

'I'll be at yours at six,' I say. 'But I still want chips.'

After we've hung up, I update my digital calendar, deleting *Fish and Friends* and replacing it with a new event: *Pumpernickeled: going out-out with Soph.*

I stare at the screen, reading its instruction over and over again.

I realize I'm not just relieved.

I'm excited.

2

'It's five pounds for gays, eight pounds for straights.'

Good thing I remembered to bring change.

We're at The Familiar, a gay bar in gay Hackney Wick. It is indeed familiar to Soph, who practically moved in when we all came to London after graduation.

'You should just pretend you're a lesbian,' she says, handing her fiver to the butch on the door. 'Thanks, bab, how *are* you?'

While Soph has a heart-to-heart with the bouncers, the queue eyes her up. Soph is literally glowing tonight – the neon lighting casts artistic shadows on her dark brown skin, her sparkling black eyes are framed by glittery pink cat eyes, her short sequined dress gleams almost as much as her long, moisturised legs, and the gold cuffs on her braids glint like crystals when she moves. And *boy*, does she know it.

Meanwhile, no one gives me a second glance. Maybe it's because their functioning gaydars tell them I'm as straight as a very straight thing. Or maybe it's because, with my wall-paint white skin, mid-length mid-brown hair and 'I haven't been out in years and have nothing to wear at short notice' mid-length black dress, I look plainer than a default avatar. I was too self-conscious to allow Soph to give me that 'tiny makeover'. You can't nail-polish a turd, after all. I keep my eyes on the ground.

'Excuse me,' says a miscellaneous supermodel from the queue, 'aren't you *SophieSnob*?'

Soph curtsies and they all squeal. Oh, fresh hell.

'Oh my God, I've watched your channel since I was a baby gay!'

'Your sex tips genuinely saved my life.'

Thankfully, the bouncer shouts at them to get in line. Soph regally waves her camera and tells everyone to like, rate and subscribe.

It's weird seeing Soph in her lesbian habitat like this. Usually, when we're together, we slob out on the sofa, watching romcoms and gossiping about people we don't know. But here at The Familiar, everyone thinks she's a legit culture critic, a queer connoisseur – and judging by their stares, very fit. My inferiority complex flexes.

The bouncer pulverises my hand with a stamp.

'It's a cat,' says Soph, seeing me prodding at it. 'Like a witch's familiar. Cute, right?'

'You should get yours tattooed. You'd save a lot of money.'

'Genuinely, very good idea.'

She herds me down the ramp into a dark passage lit by neon-pink cobwebs and winking pumpkins.

'I don't get it,' I say, poking a slimy wall and wiping it on Soph's shoulder. 'It's February. What's with the spooky stuff?'

'It's The Familiar.' She shrugs, wiping the goo back on me. 'It's witchy. Get on board.'

At the end of the passage is a gothic arched door with the drawn outline of a massive witch. She's split in half: angelic blue on the left, holding healing flowers; demonic magenta on the right, with deadly potions. Soph takes footage posing in front of it. She tries to bring me in for a selfie, but I pretend not to hear.

The bar itself is even more saturated with camp Halloween decor. Ghost bunting screams at me. Glittering paper cats raise their backs. Silky bats flap into my eyes. Soph establishes us in a covert corner booth, under posters of a scantily cloaked hag. She returns from the bar with two signature cocktails, one blue Good Witch and one magenta Bad Witch. She hands me the blue one.

This irritates me. Just because I'm straight doesn't mean I'm boring.

I take a sip and choke. 'What percentage is this?'

Soph pinches my cheek. 'Thanks for coming along with me tonight, Gee,' she says.

I shrug. 'Thanks for emotionally blackmailing me when your cool friends were busy.'

'I promise I won't let any other queers bother you,' she says and winks outrageously. 'Unless you finally decide you want them to.'

I scratch my face with my middle finger.

Soph rolls her eyes and leans back, surveying her kingdom with satisfaction. Even hidden away in the corner, I swear passing eyes are drawn to her. Must be nice, to be attractive.

It's strange; when I (admittedly, very rarely) go on 'straight' nights out, I'd love to feel like random men weren't ever going to come over and bother us. Here, though, with no laddish men around, it hits differently to get ignored. Maybe it's because I trust women to have a better sense of taste? It's like getting unfavourably peer reviewed.

I don't want to let Soph down, but as yet another gorgeous

woman smiles at her, then sees me and swerves away, I feel like my presence is a massive cockblock. Bad choice of words. I need another drink.

Soph insists I go to the bar myself, regardless of how self-conscious I feel. It's even worse when I look up from the floor to see the bartender is offensively beautiful. She looks like Cara Delevingne, with a platinum buzz cut, dark eyebrows and hundreds of hooped earrings. Under her cropped vest, she has an eclectic patchwork of tattoos – a sun and moon, a howling wolf, something that might be a block of cheese (?) and a long sunflower growing down her side. Idly, I wonder how far down it goes…

God, it's hot in here. But, presumably because I'm neither gorgeous nor gay, the busy bartender keeps me waiting. What do I need to do to get served in here, tattoo a rainbow on my face?

A waft of Soph's Chanel. She leans on the bar next to me, nonchalantly nods her head, and instantly gets bumped to the front of the long line.

'A Bad Witch and a Good Witch please,' she says, somehow making a drinks order sound cool and seductive.

The bartender starts hurriedly flipping cocktail shakers.

'Actually, two Bad Witches,' says my mouth. 'And make them doubles.'

I immediately realize my mistake.

'They're cocktails,' says the perfect bartender, barely glancing up from scooping ice. 'They don't come in doubles?'

Soph laughs and I pretend to join in, but I know this moment will be replayed in my nightmares. I cower back to our booth with a non-double Bad Witch. Soph raises a smug eyebrow at me.

'Stop looking at me like that. I just wanted to try a pink one.'

'Whatever, bab,' she snorts. 'You don't have to justify your cocktail choice to me.'

Thankfully, a distraction arrives before I have to invent one. The bar lights dim and everyone turns to the stage. A spotlight follows a hooded cape, sashaying to the microphone. The cape is thrown off to reveal a buxom drag queen with a sparkly fuchsia gown, wig, and beard.

'Good evening, magical darlings,' she sighs, sultrily, 'and welcome to The Familiar. I am Polly Amory, your compère extraordinaire.'

The audience whoops. I gather they're familiar with her work.

'I have a spell to summon our first performer. But – oh no! – where did I put my wand?'

She pats herself down, enjoying the process immensely.

'Oh, I'm always losing things. My keys, my cards, my dignity. I'd lose my own head if it wasn't tucked in.'

She pulls a phenomenally long wand out of her knickers.

'Voila! Now I can summon a Drag King legend – and one of my many ex-lovers – Willy Nilly!'

I didn't know Drag Kings were even a thing. Turns out they are very much a thing in The Familiar. He's dressed like William Shakespeare and speaks in ye olde verse about how good he is in bed. He then does a striptease, seductively removing his ruff to reveal another underneath. When he finally whips off his pantaloons, his own little William has a little ruff too. For someone thrusting around a fluorescent green dildo in a paper skirt, he's pretty good.

With a pantomime wink, Polly says, 'Willy likes it ruff!'

The audience groans, then cheers Willy's retreating bottom.

After Willy Nilly comes a very sincere poetry reading about how straight people are complicit in the patriarchy. I chuckle a bit out of nerves until Soph kicks me.

'It's the interval,' announces Polly, 'so have a drink, a wee, a flirt, and be back in ten minutes for our headline act... I know they're why you're all here in your best outfits. We'll be blessed by the presence of everyone's favourite girl group, *Phase*!'

My head jerks to Soph. The audience are squealing like hungry pigs. She takes an innocent sip of her Bad Witch.

Urgh. So *that's* why she lured me here tonight. Soph has been going on and on about this band. She saw them a few weeks ago at the The Glory and raved about how much I'd love them. 'They're so original, innovative, sexy, yadda, yadda, yadda.' But they aren't available to listen to anywhere online. Not that I looked much, obviously.

I tap my chin, feigning indifference. 'Aren't Phase the band where all of their songs are about, like, woo-woo occult stuff?'

'No,' Soph replies. 'All of their songs are about *astrology*.'

I glare at her.

'Trust me,' she says, 'once you see them, you'll believe anything they say.'

'Oh, please. It's going to take more than some amateur pop singers to make me believe in horoscopes.'

'Horoscopes are very gay,' says Soph defensively.

'No wonder I don't get it, then.'

Soph raises a plucked eyebrow at me. 'I want to interview them for *SophieSnob* and help launch their careers. I plan to make them dedicate a song to me.'

'*Oh Sophie,*' I croon, in an improvised pop chorus, '*you're in luck, our stars tell me we're destined to fuck.*'

'Wow, you've still got it!'

My cheeks flush. I'm not used to drinking this much.

'You know,' says Soph more gently, 'you *could* just write your own songs again.'

I stab at the cocktail olive with my witches' broom-shaped umbrella.

'That was all a long time ago.'

'Oh wait,' she says, 'you've got something there.'

She picks at my collar and examines her fingers.

'Looks like... yes, it's... a massive chip on your shoulder.'

I push her off her bar stool. She just laughs.

'Seriously,' I say. 'It's not funny. I am not going to play piano again.'

'You are literally a piano teacher.'

'Exactly! Those that *can*, do. Those that can't, teach.'

'That's not what you said about your dad's teaching.'

It's a low blow. Even Soph seems surprised at her audacity. I pretend not to have heard her.

Instead, I stare at the stage, where a tall, handsome Black woman with short cornrows and a tight denim shirt is setting up a keyboard.

'That's Marsha Adomako,' says Soph. 'Phase's keys.'

My staring becomes intent. I bet she's better at keyboard than I ever was.

Offstage now, she's checking her phone and explaining something to Polly Amory. The others in Phase must be late.

Just as I think that, as if following some performer cue, three people enter through the side door, bringing in a surge of evening air. The whole bar turns to them.

They're the strutting popular girls in a high school film. They're the cowboys off to fight the sheriff. They're the superheroes arriving to save the day.

'They're Phase,' whispers Soph.

At the front is a curvy blonde who looks like Marilyn Monroe, but somehow *more* feminine. Elaborate blonde waves, snow-white skin, glossy lipstick. She's wearing a glamorous long red dress, cinched in at the waist with a buckled belt that matches her strappy heels. She carries her guitar case like it's a handbag. She reminds me of a Renaissance painting, or a vintage pin-up poster.

'The femme at the front is Isobel Evennett. Lead vocals and guitar. Behind her, with the pink afro, is Rudy Cooper. Bass.'

Rudy's curls are indeed dyed candyfloss pink. Her brown skin is heavily freckled and she's wearing baggy denim dungarees and a mischievous grin. Swinging her yellow bass guitar case, she does elaborate personalized handshakes with everyone she walks past. She looks like a Pixar character.

But my eyes are drawn to the person behind them. The third horsewoman of the lesbian apocalypse.

'*She* is Kit Tsuki.'

Kit is, quite simply, the most attractive person I've ever seen. Tall, toned, androgynous, she has smooth brown skin and messy black hair lying in an effortless halo round her face. She's wearing a battered leather jacket, ripped jeans, and well-travelled boots, with no accessories except a nose ring and a simple silver chain clasped round her neck. Her cheekbones are so sharp I'm bleeding just looking at them and her smouldering eyes are lined with rock-star kohl. They're like black holes, pulling me in. And she's looking right at me.

For one second, I swear, we stare at each other. In that second, the world stops. My stomach flips upside down. My cheeks flush. I abruptly look away.

Well, *that* was weird. Must be a bad reaction to the cocktail olive.

Everyone watches as Phase casually catwalk across the room. But just before reaching the stage, Kit hesitates. She casts a momentary, but definite, look in my direction.

'—like now!' squeals Soph. 'Don't you see what I mean?'

I realize Soph has been talking this whole time and I haven't taken in a word of it. I drag my eyes away from Kit to look at her.

'Whaddyasay?'

'Kit's looking at me *all* the time. *Don't look now!* Jesus, have some subtlety.'

Oh. Right. Obviously Kit was looking at *Soph*. God, I'm an idiot.

'Do you like her?'

'Like?' Soph emphatically tosses her braids over her shoulder. 'We're basically in love.'

I laugh. Soph doesn't.

'Kit and I have always had an understanding,' Soph insists. 'It's going to happen soon. We're playing sex chicken.'

Maybe Soph *has* talked about Kit. I never remember specifics amongst the long list of people she's 'basically in love' with.

'Kit's in a thing with Marsha,' says Soph, leaning in conspiratorially. 'Marsha says it's an "open relationship". Kit says they're "just fucking".'

I feel my cheeks redden again. The last glance we see of Phase before they head backstage is Kit casually brushing something from Marsha's neck. My own neck tingles. I claw it away.

Lights fade on the bar, rise on the stage. Polly Amory returns, sparkly gown, wig, and beard now all bright purple.

'Hello again, my pumpkins,' she says. 'I know you'll want me to keep this short. So please welcome to the stage, four of my favourite ex-lovers… Phase!'

Phase stride onto the stage, godlike. Lit by glitter curtains, starry bunting, disco balls and pink and blue lights, they sparkle with self-assurance.

Marilyn Monroe/Isobel slides her fingers round the microphone and smiles coyly up from it.

'Hello, loves,' she breathes. The audience stops breathing.

'Thank you for having us back at The Familiar. Have any of you heard us before?'

The majority of the crowd raise their hands reverently.

'I promise that even if you've seen us before, you won't be bored,' says Isobel, 'because we never play the same song the same way. We improvise and adapt our pieces in a truly live experience. So please, put your phones away and be in this moment with us.'

Even Soph, who once live-Tweeted during intercourse, submits her phone to her pocket. What dark magic is this?

'We are Marsha, Rudy, Kit, and Isobel, and together…' She pauses and bites her lip. 'We are just a Phase.'

Marsha starts to play the keyboard introduction to their first number.

Those first urgent notes are like a bullet straight to my brain. Way too late, I'm reminded why I shouldn't have come here tonight.

Because they're brilliant. Too brilliant. They're experimental, combining influences of jazz, rock, folk, blues, pop into a unique sound. It shouldn't work, but somehow, together, they make it perfect. They're exactly the kind of musicians I want to be. No, exactly the kind of musicians I *used* to want to be. And the jealousy and resentment and guilt and craving roars through me so hard that it winds me.

Phase sing out, steady and assured, in a hypnotic close harmony.

'I've always known that I was born on the cusp
I'm always too much or not quite enough…'

I know I shouldn't lose myself to it; it will just be more painful afterwards. But it's as if the music is holding my face underwater. Adrenaline courses through me and I really am struggling to breathe. It's so *embarrassing*. I remember myths of sirens, calling to sailors to jump overboard. I have a mad impulse to cover my ears, but I don't want Soph to see.

Their voices are so right together. It's all so right.

And so I let myself drown.

Marsha closes her eyes, spreading her hands along the keys, Isobel's hands cup the microphone, Rudy embraces her bass, Kit's toned arms gently circle over her drums.

Everything else melts away.

Please. Just one more chorus…

But the song comes to an end.

There's a heavy moment of total silence. I close my eyes, trying to save this moment to my internal hard drive.

Only one thought of my own remains: I wish I could tell Dad about them.

Then the crowd starts to scream and the world rushes in again. I'm shaken awake from a deep sleep, disorientated, out of breath, ashamed. I should applaud. I should whoop like the maniacs around me. Or at least tell Soph that she was right.

But I can't move at all, can't do anything except stay staring at the stage, desperate for them to play again and replace my awful personality with their perfect songs.

Isobel speaks softly into the microphone, at me.

'So tell me truthfully: when did you first accept your own desires? When did you first realize you weren't straight?'

I stop breathing.

'As a child,' she continues, tucking a blonde curl behind her ear, 'I wasn't taught about queer love. So I assumed that the intense feelings I had for a few friends was just the way everyone felt about pretty girls.'

The audience laugh and I remember I'm in a crowd. She's not talking to me. God, that was silly. The dangers of getting lost in music.

The audience are nodding and clicking their fingers. Clicking, it seems, is like gay clapping.

'Then, at my church, I heard two women sing about wanting to get married to each other and everything started to fit. That's why being part of a lesbian band is so important to me. I want to be a voice reaching out, giving alternatives to what happiness can look like. I will always be grateful to the community for welcoming me with open arms—'

'And legs!' heckles someone in the crowd. Isobel laughs and shakes her ringlets. Then, looking to the others first, she starts singing a slow, beautiful power ballad and I melt back into her voice.

'Another lonely afternoon,
For the Virgo in June…'

The song is so bittersweet my throat aches. The pain of the lyrics mingles with the tenderness of Isobel's voice. She's living every word and I'm there with her. I'm watching the person she loves kiss another, patiently waiting – longing – for her to change her mind.

The song ends and reality returns too abruptly again.

This time, Soph turns my face to her. After sharing a long look, she affectionately wipes the wetness away from my cheek. But we barely have a chance to compose ourselves before the mood of the room shifts completely.

Still in the aftershock of 'Virgo in June', Rudy leaps to the front of the stage, shouting an upbeat count-in and bursting into an electro-glitch-hop song. It has sounds of phone notifications in the chorus and keeps repeating something about a 'co-star', which I don't understand, but has the audience laughing even as they jump along. It's the kind of outrageously joyous, addictive song that makes you feel sure that everything is going to be OK. Soph pulls me to my feet.

When I've been 'out-out' in the past I've been too self-conscious to really enjoy dancing, but something about the room and the song – and the fact I'm completely sloshed – makes my inhibitions slide away. Soph and I dance in our dark little booth and when the song finishes with a bang of confetti, we're delirious, whooping like we're on a sugar rush.

Then Kit stands up from behind her drums.

The room freezes. Kit stalks to the front of the stage, pushing her hair back from her eyes, and taps the mic lightly to check it's turned on. It is. Just like everyone else.

'This one's called "Mercury",' she says. God, she's got a husky rock-star voice. 'And it's just about sex.'

I swear a girl in the crowd faints.

Rudy's bass squeals, Isobel and Marsha hit a staccato riff, and Kit, back at her drums, leads on a fast tempo.

'Don't make us
Come apart
Come over come over come over here…'

Kit sweats. The audience sweats. Just standing there watching, I sweat like I've never sweated before.

Finally Kit plays a last loud cymbal and closes her eyes, sticks held triumphantly in the air. She leans her head back, breathing heavily, as if savouring her exhaustion. She rocks forward on her chair, panting, eyes still closed, holding on to the built-up feeling for a moment longer. A blush spreads over my entire body.

But then Kit opens her eyes and the crowd explodes. They're shouting, weeping, passionately making out – sometimes all three at once – and I can feel Soph's eyes on me. I know I should turn and grin back at her, but I'm still glued to Kit.

She's going to go so soon and I know I'll never see her again. If I can capture the exact line of her jaw, the way the lights hit her face, her hair, her eyes, maybe I can still imagine…

Phase take a brief bow and leave. The stage is emptied of its magic.

'Well, folks,' says Polly Amory, 'it's the end of the show, but only the start of the night. See you out there!'

The lights return. The speaker system blasts Britney Spears. Everyone carries on as if everything's the same.

But I stand still. I feel like Dorothy, seeing technicolour Oz.

I want to be as talented as Marsha. As graceful as Isobel. As fun as Rudy. As… magnetic as Kit. I want to be friends with them. I want to be part of them. I want to *be* them. I want to be up on that stage, making people feel something. I want to smile back proudly at this adoring crowd, knowing that I belong here.

But I can't. It's time to go home.

I tell Soph that I'm going to the loo then leaving. I don't think she hears me, because she's spotted Jenny's football shirt across the room and they're doing some kind of make-up dance mating ritual.

Even though the loos are gender-neutral, the queues for the cubicles are bonkers long and I'm far from confident enough to wee into a urinal. But oh God, I'm actually bursting. Please, I can't wet myself in front of all these perfect women.

Drunken instincts make me waddle through the backstage door, searching for another loo. I press my ear to the Green Room door. Empty. I lurch through half-folded costumes and half-eaten snacks towards the en suite. *Hallelujah!*

But now I'm sitting down, I realize quite how much the world is spinning, how much I want to sleep. No, I must stay awake or Soph will think I've been kidnapped by lesbians with low standards. I try to concentrate on Phase's music, still playing loudly in my head.

'Don't make us come ap—'

Kit's voice, vivid as anything.

'Don't recycle those words on me!'

Wait, what?

'Marsha, calm—'

'Don't you *dare* tell me to calm down.'

I hold my breath. I intuit that now would not be a good time to step out of the loo and start fangirling.

'An open relationship doesn't work if we're not open with

each other,' Marsha says. 'I can tell you're hiding something from me. Who is she? Is she someone I know? Are you *in love* with her?'

'Marsha, you've misunder—'

'No, *you've* misunderstood. This is over. I'm not seeing you any more and I'm not playing in Phase any more. You're finally free to sleep around and never address another human being's feelings, or your own. Good luck with that.'

Shoes scuffle. Kit calls out. Door slams. Silence.

I sneak open the loo door, peek around it. All clear.

Wondering what that was about, I wash my hands, splash my face, look into the mirror with its nostalgic light-bulb frame – God, I look terrible – see Kit sitting on the floor, check my earrings are OK, try to pat my hair into some kind of reasonable—

I spin round. Kit stares up at me from under a clothes rail.

'I'm s-so s-sorry,' I stutter.

'No, no, it's—'

She wipes her face hurriedly. Oh crapballs, she'd been crying. I stay rooted to the spot like an awkward tree.

She coughs. 'Are you one of the other performers?'

'I'm a musician,' I autopilot, then realize what I just said. Crap! Change the subject.

'Er – I really loved Phase,' I say. 'Tonight was my first time hearing you and you were...' I search for the right words to express how much it meant to me. 'Good.'

Kill me. But Kit smiles weakly.

'Thanks, man. Sorry about the, er, encore.'

'Oh, God, no, *I'm* sorry.'

'Shit happens,' she shrugs. 'But I'd appreciate it if you didn't tell everyone.'

'I would *never*.'

'No,' she says, considering me. 'No, I don't think you would.'

She sighs, then jumps up and pulls a pack of cigarettes from her leather jacket. She offers me one. I shake my head instinctively. She shrugs, a little surprised.

'Bad habit,' she says, balancing one between her lips.

I stare as she lights up. I glance at the smoke alarm in the room, which has a plastic bag covering it. Normally Goody Two Shoes over here would have run away, calling the police and the fire brigade at the same time. But this feels like a test – a test I'm desperate to pass.

We stand in the quiet, watching the smoke drift out around her mouth. I make a mental note to take up smoking ASAP.

Then Kit holds out her hand to me.

'I'm Kit, by the way,' she says, cool as a cucumber.

'I-I'm Ge-Geor-Ge,' I say, stupid as a cucumber.

Her hot fingers grasp mine. I dare myself to meet her black eyes and my stomach backflips.

Kit is looking right at me, as if she knows me, and knows we're the same.

'It's a pleasure to meet you, George.'

I stumble back through the dance floor to find Soph. She'd barely noticed I was gone because her mouth was locked on to Jenny's.

'Soph, I need to go home,' I shout to their conjoined face. They come up for air and Jenny salutes me.

'I thought you were having fun?' whines Soph, breathless. 'Why don't we go meet Phase?'

'No! No, I need to go.'

'But—'

'Soph.'

'But—'

'Pumpernickel.'

She calls us a taxi.

And then there I am. Outside my flat, but with Phase's songs looping in my head. And a secret from Kit to keep. And the tingling feeling of her hand in mine. And the sound of her voice, calling me George…

George! No one has ever called me George before. Gina, usually. Ginny, by my parents. Gee, by Soph. But never, ever George.

George.

I think I like it.

Humming the tune of 'Mercury', I fumble around with my keys.

But then someone on the other side of the door twists the handle and yanks it open.

A tall, bearded, bespectacled man stares at me. He has freckled white skin, and auburn hair everywhere that's not covered by his knitted jumper. He's baring his teeth like a puppy expecting a treat.

'Gina!' he shouts, with a Scottish accent and no consideration for the neighbours. 'Welcome home! How were the lesbians?'

Then he picks me up in a bear hug and swings me all the way into our bedroom.

Ah, yes… This is Douglas. My boyfriend of seven years.

3

Truth is, my night out with Soph is the most unusual thing to happen to me in years – apart from a few oddly shaped vegetables I saw in Sainsbury's.

I live the stable, ordered, balanced life of being in a long-term relationship with a stable, ordered, balanced boyfriend. Our one-bedroom, one-bathroom, one-everything-else-room flat might not be the most glamorous in all of North London, but it's ours. (Well, as long as we keep paying the rent.) Like it says on our posters and drinks coasters and pillow covers and keyrings, Doug is the 'his' to my 'hers': my perfect other half.

That's why I will not be going to The Familiar again, or see Phase again, or be around a flock of gay strangers again. We already have our happy life planned. That other stuff is simply not in our calendar.

Seven years – well, very nearly seven years – into our relationship, I would say the secret to mine and Douglas's happiness is our shared digital calendar. I don't know what I'd do without it, except be late all the time, and one of the benefits of a digital calendar is the ease of adding in repeating events. I think pretty much all of my life is now on automatic repeat.

Still, on the first day of every month, Doug and I go through our calendars together. We spend the morning at our rickety kitchen table with our favourite matching mugs, chocolate Hobnobs, and phones at the ready. We used to do this to ensure we got quality time together. Nowadays it's mainly out of habit. That's the great thing about a regular schedule. When it's full enough, you don't have to worry about how to best use your time. It's all already there, for you to drift along ticking off the days.

Doug blinks through his tortoiseshell glasses at his calendar app and says in that lovely Scottish lilt, 'So, Mondays after work is still rehearsals.'

During the day, Doug is an account manager at a marketing firm. No, I don't know what that means either. We thought the job was only going to be temporary so I didn't get caught up in the detail, and now he's been there for so long it's too embarrassing to ask.

We thought it was only going to be temporary because – humblebrag – my boyfriend is an actual pop star. He plays bass in a band called Bronze Age. Remember them? Their debut single, 'Shy Guy', was the breakthrough sound of the summer a few years ago. The one that goes '*Sh-sh-sh-sh shy guy*'. Yeah, you've got it stuck in your head again now, haven't you? You're welcome.

'And for me,' I reply, 'after teaching Mondays, I sit on Soph's sofa.'

I hover affectionately over my repeating event, *SophieSlob*.

'Then Tuesdays are still exercise night with Bronze Age,' says Doug. 'We're going to try boxing this week. You should come!'

I raise an eyebrow. 'Can you imagine *me* boxing?'

He grins. 'I'm just saying, you're always welcome to join.'

But I know the offer is hollow. Not in a mean way – Doug thinks he's being kind to include me – but I know it would be weird.

I was actually a member of Bronze Age at uni, when it first began. But since I quit the band, I know they don't really want me at their 'socials'. I'm not one of them any more. I'm just Doug's girlfriend.

'No thanks, Tuesdays are my me time,' I say, hovering over my repeating grey calendar event. 'I'll have a bath and a glass of wine and watch *Friends*.'

'Haven't you finished it yet?' Doug teases. *Friends* is the only show we're not watching as a couple, so I binge it at my own pace. (A sprint.)

'The last episode I watched was a massive cliffhanger.'

OK, I have technically seen all ten series of *Friends* several times over, so it doesn't really count as a cliffhanger any more, but I've been on tenterhooks all week. I'm as stressed as if it was all happening to my *real* friends. (Friend.)

'Wednesday evenings are still free,' Doug smiles, 'for our Dougina date nights.'

I smile back, hovering over our mutual sky-blue evenings on Wednesdays. The colour of Doug's lovely eyes.

'For this week's date night,' he says, 'I thought we could play a board game.'

'Yes!' I shout. 'That sounds so fun!'

Doesn't it!

'Then Thursdays it's Bronze Age rehearsals again.'

'So Thursdays I go to Soph's sofa again.'

I used to worry Soph would get bored of our nights in

together, but I think she must like slobbing with me as a contrast from impressing her cool friends.

Some people, like Doug and Soph, are the kind of proactive, passionate people who decide what they want to do and do it. And then there are people like me who just slot their lives around the productive people's gaps.

Sure, it might not be the usual approach, but I'm grateful to them. They make organizing my time very easy.

'And Fridays,' I say contentedly, 'we have another Dougina date night.'

'Er...'

I look up at him over the sky-blue screen.

He mumbles, 'Last night's gig at Dane's went really well.'

Bronze Age perform at a pub called The Great Dane. Regulars call it Dane's, as if it belongs to a massive bloke from Denmark. Bronze Age definitely count as regulars.

'I think there's a possibility that they might want us to do the Friday slot every week... But maybe not. Mmm. You know what? Forget I even said anything.'

I release a breath I didn't realize I was holding.

'OK, well... Let me know so that I can plan my episodes.'

He puts his 'his' mug down carefully. I grip my 'hers' mug even tighter.

'Gina, you know we don't have to do this calendar ritual?' says Doug. 'If it isn't helping you any more. We can just fill them in separately as we go along. Your events don't have to mirror mine.'

'No, no,' I say, with my biggest smile. 'Sorry if I sounded grumpy. Whatever happens with your gigs, I support you. And I've got loads of stuff to do when you're out. *Loads*.'

He pats my hand. I smile even more broadly.

'So, Saturday afternoons, I ring my mum,' I say. 'And then Saturday evenings are still your regular gig at Dane's, right? And… are you sure you still want me to come watch?'

'Yes,' he insists. 'It's nice feeling like we're all back together again, once a week.'

'If you're sure,' I say, and dip a biscuit in my tea, astonishingly cheerfully.

'Mickey will probably want to go out afterwards,' Doug adds. 'You should join us?'

I leave my biscuit in my tea too long, and watch a chunk sink to its doom.

'I don't want to overstay my welcome…'

'You wouldn't be,' urges Doug. 'It would be like the good old days!'

But the good old days are long gone.

'No, it's OK,' I smile, not meeting his eye. 'I'd prefer to do my own stuff.'

Doug squeezes my hand.

'Sure thing. You're your own woman. But if you change your mind, you're welcome to join. Anytime.'

'So,' I say, trying to sound like my own woman, 'if you're going out with Bronze Age on Saturday nights, you'll want to keep our lie-ins on Sundays?'

Doug's eyes crinkle.

'We love our lie-ins on Sundays, don't we?'

I nod, and use a spoon to fish out the soggy biscuit crumbs.

'Then we'll go for a long relaxing walk,' says Doug, holding my hand, 'have a romantic pub lunch, come back, put on our joggers and our best of indies playlist, and batch cook for the week.'

I savour the sugar dissolving on my tongue and hover over the recurring Sunday all-day blue appointment.

'My favourite day of the week.'

'My favourite day of the week, too,' he says. And meeting his eyes, I know he means it. The knot of tension in my stomach eases a little and I reach over the table to kiss him.

'You know what else we do on a Sunday?' I wiggle my eyebrows at him and he wiggles his back.

Doug and I have not only mastered our calendar together, we have also mastered sex. Practice makes perfect, and we had three university years to practise *a lot*. Now we've got our sex routine, carefully equal, honed to a fine art.

Doug reaches over the table and kisses me more deeply. But not *too* deeply. After all, it's not a Sunday.

'And that's the Dougina calendar done for another month.'

In celebration he hands me another Hobnob, twisting it so the chocolate is on the top. I do the same. We cheers each other's biscuit and then simultaneously dunk and chew.

This choreography began in first year when we started going to each other's room after music lectures. We'd drink tea and eat Hobnobs, and soon realized that I ate them with the biscuit on the top, but he ate them with the chocolate on the top. Now, I actually prefer it his way. Oh, the mysteries of love.

'Maybe we should get a physical calendar,' muses Doug, 'like one of those family planners.'

'But we're not family planning,' I say, and we laugh overly raucously.

We're both twenty-six and I certainly don't feel ready for parenthood, but when you've been in a relationship with someone for seven years you have to make it *very* clear you're joking when one of you mentions children.

'We're going to get a dog before anything else,' says Doug. 'So really we'd need a Puppy Planner.'

We laugh too hard again.

'Maybe we should stick with what we've got,' I say, as if it's the most hilarious thing in the world.

'If it ain't broke don't fix it,' Doug roars, slapping his thighs.

We hastily bite into some more biscuits.

'Did I mention I love you?' he says.

I smile and say it back, then watch as he starts to fiddle with the plastic on the bridge of his glasses. Huh, that's weird – he normally only does that when he's nervous.

'Gina,' he says, 'shall we visit your mum soon?'

I freeze.

'I know you still find it tough,' he says hastily, 'being there. But last time you said you should go back more often.'

I gulp my crumbs. He's right. Mum's been up to London on day trips, but it's been months since I last visited home. Maybe even years.

'I'll be there too,' says Doug. 'And we'd get to pet Bunny. I'm sure your mum would appreciate it.'

That does it. My guilt at being a terrible daughter, usually squashed in the bottom of my stomach with the other piles of shame, can no longer be ignored. I nod. Doug kisses my forehead, and adds *Visit Greengables* as *tentative* in our calendar.

I text Mum to ask if she's free for us to come visit, knowing that she will be unless there's a special episode of *Gardeners' World*. She texts back instantly.

YESTHATWOULDBELOVELY!

Despite me explaining it a billion times, Mum still insists on texting in all capitals with a space in between each letter, like ransom notes.

IWILLGETPROSECCO.

Of course she will. One of Mum's frequently repeated life mottos is 'celebrate the small things'. 'Small things' – like her self-obsessed only daughter finally paying her a visit.

I text Soph about Doug wanting us to visit her.

She replies, *lol bb. wake up. dog obvs want 2 ask ur mum 4 ur hand in marriage.*

Oh my God.

Oh.

My.

God.

I watch Doug, making a bolognese, like he's a suspect in a murder mystery. Is he adding oregano like he's about to propose?

Don't joke about something like that!! I text back to Soph.

i am not jking. he is obvs going 2 pop the question. we new this was going 2 hapen 1 day.

And then a shrug emoji.

Shrug emoji? *Shrug emoji?*

I type back, *This is not a shrugging emoji kind of matter.*

Doug's dancing around to The Kooks. He sees me looking and grins, adding basil and an extra thrust. Is that the thrust of my future husband?

Soph is right, I should have known this would happen. I just didn't expect it to ever be happening *now*. But I guess some people do get married at twenty-six...

I have a vision of Doug and I after a Bronze Age gig, showing the gang our engagement rings. In my weird imagination, my mum is there too, celebrating with Prosecco.

Maybe it's the natural thing to do. Most people spend their whole lives looking for a relationship half as lovely and effective as ours. People learn that Doug and I have a shared calendar and a regular weekly routine and a sex schedule and I think they assume we're boring or sad. But they're just jealous. It's been perfect for us.

Doug brings over a spoonful of sauce for me to try. He blows on it carefully so that it isn't too hot. It tastes delicious. Exactly the same as always...

Swallowing it down, I realize that's the problem, isn't it? Our relationship is perfect *exactly* the way it is. Any change is a risk to our equilibrium. I mean, I got anxious when Doug tried to change our toothpaste brand. But marriage is officially life-changing, with new rules and expectations and questions. He'd start thinking 'Gina might be good enough for a girlfriend but is she really good enough for forever?' And I'd start thinking...

Well, I don't know what I'd start thinking. I don't want to start thinking. It's all too sudden.

How could Doug do this to us? How *dare* he want to marry me?

4

For four years now, Bronze Age have played the same slot, in the same pub in Shoreditch, to the same audience, every Saturday. They're such regulars that these events feel like a family reunion.

At The Great Dane, everything is brown – but like, a swanky brown. Exposed brick walls decorated with sepia postcards of dogs; too many craft beer taps, lit by dangling bare light bulbs; leather sofas imprinted by specific bums; polished wood floors, polished wood bars, food served on polished wood trays; smells of cologne and stale ale and gentrification.

Bronze Age always sit at the same table in the back. Mickey always says that the pub should instal a plaque on it, commemorating their custom and Poppy always replies that maybe they will when Bronze Age are actually famous.

Mickey and Poppy are technically my oldest friends. Along with Soph and Doug, we were in the same tight-knit music course. Apart from Soph (who is a decent singer and guitarist but more interested in being a critic) we all wanted to be *stars*. So the four of us formed a band together in first term: Mickey on lead guitar and vocals, Doug on bass and backing, Poppy on drums, me on keys. We played together in student bars as well as for our course exams, and we spent the rest of our time getting drunk, cooking mounds of budget pasta in tomato sauce, and fighting over albums to play to each other. Between her *Snob* videos and her gay socials, Soph always came along to cheer us on (and provide brutal 'constructive criticism'). We were inseparable.

The name Bronze Age was from a book of tattoos in Poppy's room. It was picked at random, but it stuck, and the design became our logo. Drunk after a gig two years later, she and Mickey even got it inked on their ankles. Doug and I didn't: too shy (slash too sober). With everything that happened later, thank Christ I didn't.

We scootch into our set places at Bronze Age's table – I have to steal a spare chair from a neighbouring table.

'So, Gina, how're the piano lessons going?' asks Jasper.

Ah yes. Jasper. Jasper is Mickey's brother and Bronze Age's keyboard player. Yes, maybe I was a bit strained with him at first. Who wouldn't be strange with their replacement? I've only really met him at these Saturday events, but he's nice enough.

Mickey and Jasper are non-identical twins, with the same flourescent ginger hair and fluorescent white skin. But where Mickey is short, stocky, and cocky, Jasper is tall, thin, watered down.

'Same old, same old,' I reply.

'Oh *Jesus*,' says Mickey, in his loud Dublin accent, 'let's not talk about *work* like we're all *dead*. Come on people. What's the *goss*?'

If Mickey was one of those pull-string toys like Woody from *Toy Story*, Mickey's phrases would be 'What's the goss?' and 'Hey girl, wanna shag a pop star?'

Everyone laughs, as usual.

'Poppy, any goss?'

Poppy shakes her head and then ties her long scarlet hair into a messy bun atop her head. If I tried that, I'd look like the last pineapple in the shop. Poppy, though, with her tattoos of snakes and birds painting her cream shoulders, pulls it off.

'What about that big guy who was hitting on you after rehearsals?' says Mickey.

'He was telling me how to play drums,' she says, in her Derry accent, 'having never touched any before.'

'Sounds like a real catch,' I say.

'He certainly seemed to think so,' she says, grinning at me.

Poppy's obviously gorgeous, but I never heard of her getting with anyone at uni. She's so private about that sort of thing. Soph used to think she was gay. In fact, I think we had a – in retrospect, problematic – five-pound bet on it.

'Gina. Goss?' asks Mickey.

'As usual, there is no goss from us,' says Doug, taking my hand.

Oh God. Now I'm looking out for proposal signs, I wonder how long we have been an answering-for-each-other kind of 'us'?

'Actually I *do* have goss,' I splutter. Everyone turns to me, surprised. Especially Doug.

'Er... Soph is back together with Jenny,' I improvise.

Everyone groans, kindly overreacting to my pathetic story.

'Next week you can tell us the incredible goss that they've broken up,' laughs Poppy.

Mickey finishes his drink with a belch.

'Time for one more before the show.' He slams the bottle down. 'Your round, Jas.'

'Usual?'

'I'm sure it's my turn,' I say, standing up.

'Don't you worry about it,' says Mickey, waving the offer away. 'We've a tab going from our other nights.'

'It's my treat,' I say, knocking my knees on the table.

'I insist,' says Mickey, pulling me down into my seat. 'You're our guest.'

I don't try again.

'So… usual?' asks Jasper again.

I know Mickey's trying to be kind, but every time I come to these Bronze Age drinks, I feel less and less a part of them. Just Doug's girlfriend. A groupie.

'*I* have goss,' announces Mickey. 'Becky's getting married.'

My shoulders tense.

'As in Becky and Pyotr from lectures?'

Mickey nods smugly.

'That's so weird,' says Poppy.

'Why is it weird?' snaps Doug. 'They've been together forever.'

I don't look at him.

Poppy scoffs, 'Mid-twenties is not marriage age!'

'Why not?' says Doug. 'I read an article recently which said women think the best age to get married is twenty-six.'

I choke on my drink. I could do without the worry that I'm actually getting too *old* to marry.

'But *we're* twenty-six,' splutters Mickey, 'and we're basically still teenagers! I haven't been on a successful date in months, let alone getting successfully hitched.'

'What's wrong with it,' says Doug, 'if it's right for them? My parents got married when they were nineteen, and they've been happy ever since.'

'Different generation,' says Poppy.

'Yeah,' says Mickey, 'your parents probably got preggo and needed to put a ring on it so they wouldn't get, like, burned at the stake. A wedding our age now is seriously weird. Unless you're religious and too horny to think straight. How could you be sure you want to stay together forever when you've barely shagged anyone else?'

Then he realizes who he's talking to. 'Er, no offence.'

'None taken,' say Doug and I together, in the same sarcastic tone.

Doug wiggles his eyebrows at me. I feel a bit sick.

Jasper returns with beers and the conversation moves on to Bronze Age 'business'. I don't usually contribute, so I just sit there, sipping my gin and tonic, imagining coming here every Saturday for the rest of my life.

'Please welcome, Bronze Age!'

Mickey slides to the mic. For a man who's five foot five, he really knows how to take up stage space. The bronze lights cast flattering shadows on his tousled hair and artful stubble.

'Wassup, Bronzers? Good to be back!'

I must have heard Mickey say his exact, long introduction hundreds of times. (Once a week for four years equals 208…)

Their warm-up song, 'Dance With Me', is one of their oldest. In fact, we wrote it together. It sounds like every other derivative pop song about wanting to dance with an attractive stranger.

Yet still, like an intrusive advert, whenever I hear those opening chords, my brain replays the night of the last gig I played with them…

★

It's the night after our final exams. We're headlining at a student union party, playing to swarms of elated third-years, drunk on cheap Prosecco and freedom. 'Dance With Me' gets them bopping away and 'Shy Guy' goes down a storm. Doug, Poppy, Mickey and I grin at each other, all glowing gold under the spotlight as the crowd roar for an encore. As a finale, we play my new song – 'I Choose You'. The crowd sing along to my lyrics, waving their lighters. When it ends and they're cheering and we're all hugging as we bow, I remember thinking – *knowing* – that it was the best night of my life.

Everyone says that your university days are your best days. But what that doesn't prepare you for is that everything after that is downhill. It's a bit sad, isn't it? When you realize you'll never be that happy again...

Thankfully, at this point I spill some of my drink down myself. Mopping up, I take a deep breath, plaster on a nice smile, and bury that memory safely down again.

The trick to getting through these Saturday gigs is to keep it all at arm's length, listen like it's background noise. Like I'm a stranger in the audience. Then, I simply think Bronze Age are an indie pop band with a brand USP that they're all ginger. (Coincidental, sure, but it definitely helped with their publicity, so it's all for the best I quit.) As a stranger, all I would know is that Bronze Age play the popular summery hit, 'Shy Guy', and that they have been 'about to make it big' for several years.

Their next song *is* new. 'One Shot'. I've heard Doug practising the bass line.

'I've only got one shot
With you

So I'll drink another shot
With you...'

The problem is, the lyrics just repeat and repeat. Soon the words 'one' and 'shot' have lost all meaning. I want to scream: 'It isn't one shot any more, is it? It's approximately two hundred shots.'

But the audience don't seem to mind. They're blithely bopping around.

God, I'm annoyed when Bronze Age are good, playing happily and successfully without me, but I'm also annoyed when they're bad. What's wrong with me? I remember Soph at The Familiar, picking at the chip on my shoulder. Maybe she's right. But it was *me* who quit, for God's sake; I have no right to be anything but supportive to Doug and his band.

When 'One Shot' finishes, I clap very loudly.

They've saved 'Shy Guy' for their finale. The loyal crowd has started to '*Sh-sh-sh-sh*' each other already. Their excitement, along with my heady combination of alcohol, guilt, and shame, propels me to dance.

'I guess I'm just a shy guy
But if you want to try
I could be your shy guy
I could treat you right...'

I look up at Doug, his hands running easily over his frets. He grins at me from the stage, and I want to shout to everyone in the room that *he* is *my* boyfriend, so they'll tell me how lucky I am. My boyfriend: a musician. My nearly-fiancé: a star.

There are friendly shouts of 'Encore!'. Thankfully for my sore-heeled feet, I know Bronze Age don't have one.

But Mickey looks into the crowd like it's Wembley. He

starts playing the opening chords to 'Shy Guy' again. The others look at each other, confused.

Are they really going to...?

They're playing the whole thing again...

'Sh-sh-sh-sh shy guy'

I try to keep up the energy to dance, but I've used up all my moves.

'Sh-sh-sh-sh shy guy'

I always said they shouldn't repeat the chorus there.

'Sh-sh-sh-sh shy guy

Yeah I'm your mister right'

I sing the final *'Shh'* too emphatically.

Then it really *is* over. Poppy sprints off, Mickey bows too many times for the amount of applause, Doug and Jasper, caught in the middle, shuffle off sideways. The microphone screeches until the barman cuts its power off.

Afterwards, I go to congratulate the gang as usual and kiss Doug on the cheek goodbye.

'Gina, come out with us!' says Poppy, her bare arm round my shoulders. 'The rum is on me?'

That was our spirit of choice, always on offer in student bars. Many an evening was spent holding back her long red hair as she threw it up.

But I know they'd secretly prefer it if I wasn't there. Plus, Poppy's looking particularly stunning tonight and it's making me feel even more of an outsider than usual. The blush rises to my cheeks and I make my standard excuses.

Then Doug surprises me by sliding his hand around my waist and telling the others he's not coming with them tonight.

'What, the Missus can't even let you be free for one night a week?' teases Mickey.

I cringe and protest, but Doug speaks over me.

'We've got an early start tomorrow,' he lies. 'See you guys at rehearsals.'

Mickey and Poppy strop performatively. Doug laughs and takes my hand. As we walk out, listeners wave goodbye to him and I feel like a groupie again.

But the fresh air is delicious. We walk down to the station in quiet public mode.

When sufficient distance is between us and Dane's that we won't be overheard, I say, 'But tomorrow is our Sunday lie-in.'

'It just felt like you weren't your usual self, tonight,' he says, stroking my head. 'Is something up?'

Damn, I hadn't realized I was showing it.

'Sorry...' I hesitate. 'I think... Well, I feel like I'm intruding. I'm not part of the band and I should stop clinging on.'

Doug squeezes my shoulders firmly.

'You *are* still part of the band,' he says. 'You were there from the beginning. Nothing can take that away. Honestly, we love it when you come to watch.'

I notice Doug is an 'us' with me, but a 'we' with Bronze Age.

We arrive at the ticket stile leading underground. I spin him round before he commits his card.

'Doug, thank you, but you should go out as usual.'

'But I want to spend the evening with you.'

'You can spend the evening with me tomorrow. As per our calendar.'

'There's no harm in being spontaneous,' he says,

misunderstanding the point of a calendar. 'I'd like to spend as much time as possible with you every day. Every day, for ever.'

Oh God. I know I should find that sentiment lovely, but alarm bells are ringing in my head. Alarm bells that sound like wedding bells.

'Why don't we flip a coin?' I say, desperately.

'You don't have to flip a coin if you already know what you want to choose,' he laughs and taps through the ticket barrier.

My Oyster card beep sounds worried.

When we're in the carriage, Doug keeps kissing the top of my head affectionately. *Too* affectionately. Is he about to get on one knee on the grimy Tube carriage floor? Surely he has more class than that. It would be OK for me to say no if the proposal was on the Victoria Line, right? Finally the doors open and I bustle him out as quickly as possible.

For the rest of the walk home, I keep the chat light-hearted to the point of banality.

'Gosh, it is getting dark at night-time isn't it?'

Doug looks around and nods as if surprised.

'Yeah, it is.'

'Would you say we're about, ooh, three minutes from the flat?'

'Three or four,' agrees Doug.

'Let's try to do it in two.'

When we're getting ready to sleep, he's still looking very serious. I try to avoid him, but that's difficult when you share a bedroom. I pretend to be distracted by our decorations, even though they're the same ones we've had up for years. There's a poster from the first-ever student gig we performed at as Bronze Age, which my dad made us *autograph*. A photo of the four of us from the same night, my face smiling out from behind the keyboard. There are postcards from Doug and me taking anniversary city breaks. Photos of us walking in Hampstead Heath each summer, getting imperceptibly older. Then, over on Doug's side of the room, framed awards for 'Shy Guy', posters of the line-ups for their professional gigs, and a group photo from last year where the face smiling behind the keyboard is Jasper's.

Eventually Doug turns my face away from the wall and points it towards his. We look into each other's eyes for a long time. He licks his lip and starts to say—

'Doggie,' I interrupt, 'I'm dying for a wee.'

He deflates.

'I'll be quick,' I say, and tap the bedside alarm clock. 'Seeing as you didn't go out, we could wake up earlier and soak some oats for breakfast.'

He nods, looking cheered.

I stumble to the bathroom where I open the window and splash my face. I feel like a hamster who has just realized her comfortable cage is locked.

My phone lights up.

i am ur maid of honour, rite? Soph types. *i'll start organizing ur hen do but only if i dont have to get u novelty items in the shape of a penis*

I avoid Doug's eyes when I go back in. Yawn loudly. Get straight into bed. Rest my head on the 'hers' pillow next to 'his'. Turn the lights off.

I lie awake, little teaspoon to Doug's big ladle. Normally I love the feeling of his arm around my chest, but tonight it's too heavy.

My calendar keeps flashing through my head. The uniform,

regimented repeating events. The same colours in the same pattern, day after day, week after week, year after year.

I don't understand why it feels like a nightmare. Ever since Doug first suggested we share our calendar, I've loved our little routines. I should *want* to get married, shouldn't I? Weddings are what women are supposed to want. It would mean even more safety and security with Doug, right? The natural next step, everything going to plan.

And it would make my mum happy. I suppose she'll be the one to walk me down the aisle.

But after the wedding planning, it'll be honeymoon planning. Then family planning, school planning, retirement planning, funeral planning, and... that's it. Life complete.

I thought having our calendar in sync meant we were in sync as a couple. I thought having my life tracked meant my life was on track. But... Is this really it? They lived happily ever after, The End?

Already?

This?

5

Weekend's over, we're back to work, and all thoughts of drastic life changes can be put on hold for five days. Doug wouldn't propose on a weeknight.

I teach private piano lessons at a private secondary school. It's called, apparently unironically, Liberty Secondary. Each wall, chair, piece of stationery and uniform is an orderly navy blue. Soph disapproves of me teaching at a private school, but pragmatically, it's a good job: the children are well behaved, the pianos are well tuned, and it was very much the only job I was offered. I was lucky to get it, honestly. I didn't really have the credentials, but I argued that, as my dad taught piano, I had an extra few decades of experience from him. Unfortunately, in practice, aptitude for teaching doesn't seem to be hereditary.

I spend my days in the oxygen-deprived Practice Room 3 in Liberty's Performing Arts Centre. Officially called The Play Space, it's a detached, soundproof building hidden in the back of the school grounds. In The Play Space, no one can hear you scream.

Every week my pupils play the same mistakes, make the

same apologies and say they'll practise for next time. Every week we both know they won't.

Mondays start off with Timothy Tucker. Soph refers to him as Fimothy Fucker. I remind her that he's an innocent thirteen-year-old boy, but she still finds it funny.

I wonder what Doug would want us to call our children...

'Miss?'

Timmy's pubescent voice comes out of a room I now realize has been silent for a while. I turn to his worried blue eyes and worrying red pimples. Oh well, I know my script by heart.

'You forgot the F sharps again.'

Timmy looks baffled at the keyboard, as if it's the first time he's seeing one. It may as well be.

'Sorry, Miss.'

'Don't apologize to me, Timmy. Apologize to Mozart.'

'Sorry, Mozart,' he mumbles.

'Maybe if you practise adding in those F sharps very carefully this week, then you'll remember them next week.'

He nods, fiddling with a spot. The bell goes, he lopes off.

'See you next week, Miss.'

'See you next week, Timmy.'

Hope Zhu is usually about three minutes late, so I look out the window and watch the children on the sports field, running round and round.

Three minutes later the door opens and a hopeful face pokes through.

'Sorry, Miss!'

'Don't worry, Hope, just try not to be late next time. How was practice this week?'

She smiles widely but doesn't meet my eye.

'Great!'

Non-existent then. She sits at the piano stool and adjusts her skirt.

'Miss?' she asks, tentatively twiddling a plait. Wow, this is new.

'I wondered if I could play you something of my own?' she says. 'I want to be a singer-songwriter.'

I look into her optimistic little face.

'That's a competitive business,' I say.

Hope nods her head.

'You'll have no job security.'

She nods her head even more eagerly. This twelve-year-old has more ambition than I do.

I consider telling her the truth:

'Trust me, it won't work out. Then you'll be a failure, and you'll watch the chosen few succeed, and become a bitter carcass of a human being. You'll start to hate music but realize it's all you have. So you'll find a teaching job and tell yourself that it's *almost* what you always dreamed of, and that it's all for the best really, because you were never good enough, and performing is inherently pointless, vapid and self-indulgent.'

I just about stop myself from saying that aloud. Instead, I say, 'I think you should stick to Mozart.'

So she plays 'Für Elise', the Grade Five piece I ask everyone to learn, makes her usual mistakes, and leaves three minutes early.

'See you next week, Miss.'

'See you next week, Hope.'

I can already hear the eager snuffles of my last pupil of the morning, Percival Worthington. Or as I think of him, Civil Percy.

Percy's been my pupil for three years and has passed four exams with distinction. He's working towards Grade Seven, which makes him the most advanced of my pupils – a success story that helps keep me safely employed. It's convenient, because Percy teaches himself.

'Good morning, Miss Green,' he says, rosy-cheeked. 'Pleasant weekend? Isn't it a glorious day?'

'Hello, Percy,' I say, looking out at the disgusting weather. 'Yes, it's lovely.'

'I've been looking forward to our rendezvous,' he says, pulling hefty tomes from his briefcase. 'I am besotted by these Bach fugues.'

Percy already plays his new piece at examination standard and I congratulate him appropriately, pencilling a few notes that slipped. He squints at them through rectangular glasses and nods gratefully.

I enjoy my lessons with Percy. He's proficient. To him, music is an equation to be solved. His squat pink fingers are programmed to play the required patterns and it's why I've always avoided giving him pieces by anyone wishy-washy – you know, Romantics or Moderns where the music 'means' something. That emotional nonsense should not sully Percival's repertoire.

'I have been perusing the options for my Grade Seven Examination,' he says, 'and believe I have my selection.'

He crunches back the spine of a book which looks suspiciously like—

'The third movement of Debussy's *Suite Bergamasque*.'

My body goes into fight or flight. 'Clair de Lune'. My dad's favourite piece of music. He used to play it before going to bed, like a lullaby. I haven't listened to it in years.

Before I can stop him, Percy launches into the first chord.

For just a second, I'm back in my dad's music room, in my comfiest lavender-washed pyjamas, drinking our nightcap hot chocolate. I see the back of my dad's balding head as he bows towards the piano, his limber body relaxed, his hands poised over the keys, and—

Percy clunks through with the emotional delicacy of a wrecking ball. Oh sure, the notes are correct, but this piece is meant to conjure moonlight, with fluid timing and graceful pauses. Percy's methodical playing is feeding delicate memories of my dad through a mangler.

'*Stop!*' I scream.

I don't slam the piano lid on his fingers. Just.

He twitches at me through steamed glasses.

'Frightfully sorry,' he says. 'Do you not care for that one?'

'Er,' I say, lowering my shoulders and smoothing my sensible skirt over my knees, 'forgive me, Percy, but I don't think you should play "Clair de Lune". No good for the school concert, it's too… Better stick with Bach.'

'Righto,' he mumbles. 'I'll come with different choices next week.'

'Righto, Percy,' I say, not able to meet any of his four eyes.

I watch the children on the sports field, running round and round.

In my interview with the Head of Music, Alexa Lang, I'd nervously joked that she must be only half as good a pianist as Lang Lang. She didn't smile and said it was therefore a good thing she was a violinist. I assumed I had not got the job. But four years later, I've still never seen Alexa smile.

Despite the fact that she's always trying to quit smoking, she insists that we have our daily bitch session in the Performing Arts Centre smoking area. So we're sitting in the ugly aluminium shelter, littered with butts, overlooking a plain brick wall.

Alexa's black bun is so tight it's making veins pop out on her forehead. Or maybe that's just with the effort of restraint.

'I need to surround myself with the temptation to smoke,' she reminds herself. 'That proves I'm stronger when I resist.'

'Right,' I reply. 'Is that why you still carry cigarettes with you?'

'No,' she says, frowning at me. 'That's in case I want a cigarette.'

It's a dull, overcast day, and I'm feeling the ennui of hearing the same bar of music played incorrectly over and over again.

'I don't think *any* of my pupils practise between lessons,' I sigh.

Alexa shrugs and opens a large bag of Liquorice Allsorts. The way that Alexa fights her addiction is by becoming addicted to other things. When she offers, I take a pink tube, knowing they're her least favourite.

'You're lucky you don't teach the group classes,' she says. 'They become so stupid trying to fit in. I don't think any of them even enjoy their little cliques, but they think they have to be in one.'

She munches on a blue Spog.

'Humans are better alone.'

We contemplate that wisdom in silence for a while. Then the bell goes. As we part, I see her hands move with a conductor's precision to scoop the rest of the bag's contents into her mouth, bin the wrapper, and start immediately on another.

At 4.30 p.m., a calendar notification pops up. It says: *Text your boyfriend :)*

I smile back at the smiley emoji.

This is one of the notifications that's been in the calendar for years. It was one of the first Doug put in, in those months after graduation, after Dad. Back then there were only a few events in there, more like reminders: *Drink a glass of water :)*, *Meditate for five minutes :)*, *You're the best! :)*. Most of them lapsed over the years (who has time to meditate?), but *Text your boyfriend :)* has stayed strong.

I start typing to Doug, *I love you :)*

As always, before I press send, I get a message from him. *I love you more! :)*

6

Friday night, Doug's performing at his temporary extra gig with Bronze Age so I get to have some extra me time. Cod Almighty wrapper's in the bin, bath's running, and I've snuck in an extra glass of wine because hey, I'm spontaneous.

I'm about to open up *Friends* when Soph sends me a selfie from The Familiar's witchy door.

not the same without u bab!!

Hmm. I wonder if she posted footage from last week. I open up *SophieSnob*'s channel.

I scroll past the replay button on her pinned video – *Ten Black Queer Icons! (Yes, Including Me)* – and see she's dedicated a section to her early sequence: *Should I Come Out? (To My Traditional Family)*, *How To Come Out! (To Your Traditional Family)* and *Why My Terrible Coming Out Story Shouldn't Stop YOU*. Oh Soph…

I'd only known her for one term when it happened. She'd told me, while we were packing up listening to Michael Bublé's *Christmas* album, that she knew her Jamaican parents had been brought up under homophobic laws, but she was sure they didn't really believe it. She'd kept her sexuality low-key growing up in Birmingham, not wanting to be the only out lesbian in her school, but had become so involved in the university's LGBTQ+ society that it felt like the right time to stop hiding. She said she was excited to finally unite the different parts of her identity over her mum's famously strong Sorrel Punch.

But her family did not react the way Soph hoped. Her parents said they'd never accept her having a girlfriend. Even Soph's younger brother Joshua, who she'd always been close to, said he'd sever all contact with her if she didn't choose 'the right way'. She had to choose between being a good daughter or being gay.

Soph chose to be herself. She packed back up, spent Christmas with her new queer friends, and almost immediately started making more defiant, personal, activist videos on *SophieSnob*. Said she wanted to be a supportive figure for anyone else without one. And so her fanbase grew, obsessively grateful.

Away from her Snobbers, Soph always said she was fine and didn't want to speak about it. Even when she spent Christmas with me at Greengables, she steadfastly kept conversations light. But sometimes when she was really drunk, or thought I wasn't looking, I'd see her open her old family's group chat on WhatsApp. I guess what I'm saying is, Soph's a far braver person than I could ever be.

I'm looking at her most recent videos now. I'm about to click on the *ARE YOU COMING OUT-OUT? (Best LGBTQ+ Nights in London!)* video when I'm distracted by her latest. It's called *Think You Might Not Be Straight? (Here's a Simple Test)*.

I blush.

Like a crazy person, I check over my shoulder.

I'm just being a good friend and a good ally. I'm just educating myself.

I click on the video.

Digital Soph is facing the camera, looking gorgeous in sponsorship eyeshadow and an aspirational bedroom of careful product placement. The guitar she used to play is hanging on the wall like a piece of artwork.

'Hi, Snobbers! So, I've had a lot of requests for this video. People find themselves on my channel looking for a sign about their sexuality. The thing that worked for me was asking myself, "Do I fancy women?" When the answer was yes, I thought, "Well, I'm not straight then".'

I glare at her through the screen. She gets *paid* for this content?

'But some people are less able to do that, for reasons I've discussed in other videos, including,' she points around her and links pop up, 'Lack of representation! Inadequate sex education! Internalised homophobia!'

She stops doing angry jazz hands and changes angle.

'So if you want a way to come out to yourself, I have devised a simple test. I'll get *straight* to it.'

Her face leans conspiratorially close to the camera. Blood pounds in my ears.

'If you clicked on this video,' she says, and it's like she's grinning only at me, 'congratulations, you're probably queer.'

I close the tab, delete my browser history, and snap the laptop shut.

Hump day evening with Doug. I don't mean we have sex, (that's Sunday), I just mean it's Wednesday. Board game night.

Doug asks which game I'd like to play. I dread making decisions as important as that, so I get out a coin. Then I worry about whether to pick heads or tails. I wish you could flip a coin to decide...

Anyway, I lose, so we play Risk, a game which stresses me out more than I can explain. Doug always wins games which involve luck. Today, though, he looks very unhappy about it. Instead of cheering or bragging, he coughs and says in a rush, 'Gina, I'm sorry.'

'It's OK, we can play Monopoly next.'

I'm good at Monopoly.

'No, it's...' He rubs the back of his neck. 'It turns out we did get offered that gig at Dane's every Friday.'

Numbly, I check our shared calendar. Sure enough, the sky-blue date events have been deleted from Fridays and now Doug's evenings are even more Bronze Age orange. My corresponding calendar space is blank.

'Th-that's great news,' I say. 'Well done.'

'Yeah! Yeah. It feels like a step forward, at last. We get paid a bit more, and it's a fun crowd, and... Oh God, Gina, I'm so sorry.'

'Don't!' I squeak, shaking my head uncontrollably. 'Please don't apologize.'

I'm so pathetic.

'I'm really proud of you,' I manage to say. 'I'm glad Bronze Age are doing well. I just...'

I just feel like I'm in my own private *Groundhog Day*, watching other people move forwards? I just feel like I'm bound to a calendar I don't even know if I enjoy any more? I just feel like I'd be happier if I was living a completely different life?

Don't upset him, don't worry him, don't be a bad girlfriend.

'I just used to like our date night,' I say, with my most natural smile. 'But it's fine. I'll find something else to do.'

I could say I'm going to watch more *Friends*, or buy some nicer bath bombs, or higher percentage wine – but my mouth opens without my planning.

'I had a good time with Soph before,' I say. 'If you're going to be busy with Bronze Age, I might ask if I can go along with her every Friday.'

Doug blinks at me.

'Do you… Would that be OK?'

His expression unfolds from crumpled to gleaming. 'Yes! Gina! That's a great idea. You definitely should!'

He ruffles my hair. He's supportive of me doing anything.

Before I lose my nerve, I text Soph.

Soph can I go out with you?

Hurriedly send another.

Lol I mean, not GO OUT with you!

Obviously

I mean come out

Urgh. I wish I could retract texts. I send another batch.

Not COME OUT come out!

Obviously

I just mean go out with you and your lesbian friends to gay bars every Friday?

7

Pre-drinks at Soph's. We're getting ready and listening to someone called King Princess, who, Soph says, is so mainstream for lesbians that even straights should be able to sing along. Fine in theory, but the song playing currently is called 'Your Pussy is God'.

She's tidied her flat, but it's Soph levels of tidying, so there's just about room for the two of us on the sofa, between empty takeaway boxes and unopened gift bags from firms who want their products marketed to the pink pound. I suspect that Soph would normally have loads of her party friends round for pre-drinks, but she's being kind to me on my 'official debut'.

'Soph, remember, I'm only coming because my boyfriend is busy.'

'Yeah, yeah, you're a dutiful girlfriend, I get it.'

I'm getting cold feet about the whole thing, and not only because Soph made me take off my safety tights. It was fine when it was me doing Soph a favour, but now we both know I *want* to go, the vibe's nerve-wracking.

She eyes me through her hand mirror. 'Want that makeover yet? You have so much potential.'

'I don't need to look good at a gay bar,' I blush. 'I already have a boy—'

'You'd sound more convincing if you weren't currently drooling over my denim jacket collection. Go on, try this one. It's been in the closet for a long time.'

She snorts, very pleased with herself. I concede to shrug it on. It's oversized and distressed, with big pockets and badges. When I glance at myself in the mirror, I'm taken aback by how much I love it.

'Fine,' I say, carefully casual, fiddling with a button which looks alarmingly like interlocked scissors. 'I'll wear it if I *have* to. For you.'

Soph pats my head. I grudgingly agree that she may also paint my nails. I pick Scorching Framboise to symbolise that I'm fun and independent.

'I can't believe your boyfriend is so traditional that he's asking for your mum's permission,' Soph says, untwisting the cap.

I breathe in the tangy smell. I feel very French, complaining about marriage over a manicure.

Between fluorescent brushstrokes, she asks, 'So do you *want* to marry him?'

'I love Douglas,' I say, watching her paint. 'I guess I'd always imagined that one day we'd move to the countryside and get a dog, and I guess that's basically marriage, isn't it? But one day was always years away. Now it might be *now* and I'm not so sure.'

She looks at me over the quivering brush.

'What changed?'

Oh balls. Do I really want to talk about this?

'Well... When I came with you to The Familiar last week, and saw Phase, I—'

Soph grins at me. She's painted a nail-polish wedding band on my ring finger.

'Might as well get used to it, bab!'

A scuffle while we try to wipe nail polish off on each other without staining her upholstery. I try to rub the nail-polish line off my finger. It spreads.

'I don't want to think about marriage any more!' I snap. 'Give me one night off, *please*.'

'You want a night off from your boyfriend at a gay bar?'

I roll my eyes at her, but she's much better at it than I am, so it's a bit embarrassing.

'Are there any bands playing tonight?' I ask, innocently.

'Gee,' says Soph, putting on huge false eyelashes, 'if you want to ask me if Phase are playing you can just ask me if Phase are playing.'

I pretend to struggle to get the top off the rosé, but it's hard to be convincing with a screw cap.

'As it happens, there isn't a show tonight' she says. 'But I suspect the members of Phase might be there drinking. And I know you're "not interested" in gay gossip, but I heard that Marsha and Kit broke up.'

I do my best impression of being simultaneously surprised and disinterested.

Soph lifts the wine to her lips again, but she's so excited to carry on she doesn't actually drink. 'Do you think that means I'm allowed to get with Kit tonight? Seven days is enough time to process, right?'

'You're asking the wrong girl. I'm not au fait with lesbian dating rules.'

'Oh, there aren't rules! Practically everyone's open anyway. But there's open – and then there's *open*.'

'Right, yeah, I understand now.'

She rolls her eyes. 'Watch my videos.'

'But aren't your videos for queer people?'

Soph looks at me for too long. Then she downs her wine. 'Watch this while I go for a whizz.'

She hands me her phone, on a *SophieSnob* video called *Opening Up About Open Relationships* and sashays away. I don't tell her I've already watched it.

'Hi, Snobbers, how *are* you!' she says, no trace of Birmingham accent. I skip forwards a few seconds. '… for some couples, an open relationship means anything goes, but for most people, openness is within certain parameters. In some, partners can have sex with someone else, but not an emotional connection. Some can date, but not more than a certain number of times. Open relationships have loads of rules.'

'Doesn't sound very open to me!' I shout, towards Soph's bathroom. 'Why can't you just do what straight people do and have affairs?'

'Cheating is tacky,' shouts Soph. 'Polyamory is queer.'

I skip to a part of the video where sparkling green letters say 'But what about jealousy?'

SophieSnob's now interviewing a surprisingly normal-looking woman.

'Jealousy stems from insecurity,' she says, 'and the false belief that happiness is a limited resource. In an open relationship, you take those negative jealous feelings, and you convert them into *compersion*.'

I chomp on crisps, incredibly disinterested. 'Why is she saying "compassion" with a weird accent?'

Patronisingly sparkly letters spell 'compersion'.

'*Compersion* is the feeling of happiness you get from seeing your loved ones happy,' explains *SophieSnob*. 'Imagine your friend had a nice brunch with another friend. You wouldn't be jealous, you'd be happy they had a good time. It's the same in an open relationship. But substitute the nice brunch with, for example, wild sex.'

'Problem is, Soph,' I say, as she returns from the loo, 'if you had a nice brunch with a different friend I *would* still get jealous. And as for the wild sex…'

She slaps my elbow and pours us more wine.

'Would Jenny be fine if you got with Kit? She'd be all compersion-y?'

'Jenny and I are not in an open relationship. We're just casual.'

'Right.'

'And no, she would not be fine, she would be jealous as fuck.'

'Right.'

'But the thing is,' she taps the side of her nose, 'Jenny wouldn't need to know.'

I hand Soph's phone back to her.

'Ri-i-i-ight. Clearly there's a lot of nuance about dating rules in the queer community.'

Soph grins at me and toasts my glass. 'Good thing you're a quick learner.'

I laugh to show we're joking.

Then, as if the idea just popped into my head, I say, 'If Kit and Marsha broke up, will that break up Phase?'

Soph's face drops.

'How had I not thought of that?'

She reaches for her phone as if expecting the BBC to have

sent out a news alert. 'Will Kit stay or will Marsha stay?' she flusters. 'Who's easier to replace, drums or keyboard?'

I darkly crunch more Monster Munch. 'Keyboard.'

But Soph's already tapping away on her gossip networks.

'We already know Marsha is going to leave anyway,' I say, 'because Marsha dumped Kit.'

Soph looks up at me and I realize my mistake.

'Issn't thawha yousay?' I slur, as a remarkably convincing drunk.

'Don't be stupid,' says Soph. 'It must be to do with one of the other girls Kit's seeing.'

I imagine a thousand gorgeous girls caressing Kit's toned arms.

'Like who?'

Soph turns to me fully. 'Gee, for someone who doesn't care about Phase, you're asking an awful lot of questions.'

I hold my hands up. 'Just trying to take an interest in your life!'

But Soph's had a thought.

'Oh my God! Maybe they'll hold auditions for a new member. Oh my *God*, if it's for keys *you* could audition.'

'Ha! Imagine that,' I say, as if I haven't been obsessively imagining that for the past week.

'They'd need someone gay, though,' says Soph.

Questions hang in the air like elephants on a trapeze.

'First I'm not ginger enough to be in a band, then I'm not gay enough?' I say, licking the pickle crumbs from my fingers. 'Good thing I'm sticking to teaching.'

★

'Five pounds for gays, nine pounds for straights,' says the butch on the door.

'You've raised the straight fee!'

The bouncer stares me down. I fiddle around for the extra coin and hand it over with an open hand so that Soph can see.

Down the ramp, through the bat tunnel, and into the Halloween party bar, Soph guides us towards a big table where her friends wave her over.

'Everyone, look, she finally agreed to come!'

I note they're half-checking me out, like they're checking if they need to check. They're all intimidatingly self-assured, and all wearing denim.

'You've met Jenny…' Jenny gives me an enthusiastic high five. She's wearing her red football shirt. I wonder if she washes it, or has multiple identical ones?

'And this is Lucy, she/her, Lin, they/them, Leighlah, they/she, and Lou, she/them.'

Good thing I don't have a speech impediment for the letter L.

Avoiding Soph's eye, I introduce myself as George. Then, fumbling, she/her. I realise that outside of The Familiar, I have never once been asked my pronouns.

'George, hi, I like your jacket,' says Lucy. She's very pretty in a Jack Wills sort of way, and being called George sends a thrill of excitement through me. It reminds me of how Kit looked at me when she said it. I complement Lucy's identical jacket.

I ask if anyone would like me to buy them a drink and am impossibly relieved when they say no. Except Soph, who makes devil horns.

The bartender who looks like Cara Delevingne is serving again. My stupid nerves make me joke.

'Two Bad Witches please,' I guffaw, 'and make them double.'

The bartender starts and looks up at me from cutting lime wedges. Her eyes are phenomenally green. She frowns.

'Was it you who said that, like, last week?'

My guffaw flops and is replaced by a painful blush.

'Sorry. Terrible joke.'

But then I realize she's smiling, wonderfully, lopsidedly.

'I love terrible jokes,' she says. I flush harder.

'A sandwich walks into a bar,' she recites. 'But the barman says—'

'"Sorry, we don't serve food here!"'

The bartender laughs delightedly, a laugh that sings above the bar music. That joke was a favourite of my dad's. The memory stabs until I meet her green eyes again. She conspiratorially pours extra rum into the two Witches.

'Doubles are on me,' she winks. 'But don't tell anyone, or they'll think I have favourites.'

This denim jacket must be magic. I skip back to the table, elated. Soph's L friends move up to let me sit.

Lin explains, 'We're just talking about my pussy.'

I nearly drop my glass.

'She's got a UTI.'

'I'm sorry to hear that,' I gulp. 'Have you tried cranberry juice?'

Soph rolls her eyes.

'Their *cat*,' she says. 'We're talking about Lin's pet *cat*.'

Lin laughs and nudges me in the ribs.

'Do you have a cat, George?'

I smile. 'I'm more of a dog person.'

Sudden silence. The table looks at me like I'm a holocaust denier.

'Well, I like both,' I say quickly, 'but I grew up loving my own pet dog, so…'

The Ls look at each other and then, as one, fight back:

'But cats are so cute! Glamorous – your equal – independent – little paws—'

'And bring you dead mice,' I play along.

They mob me.

'Dogs are violent – passive – needy – dorky – messy – loud – don't think for themselves…'

'You can like both,' I repeat, but now I'm not so sure.

They all start getting out persuasive photos of their cats.

I've already finished my Witch. Blonde Lucy places another in front of me. I look to Soph for reassurance, but she's cooing over Jenny's kitten.

'He's called Eric Catona,' Jenny laughs. 'Get it?'

Soph doesn't get it. No one here gets it. Jenny doesn't seem to mind, but Soph shuffles away from her.

More pressingly, Lucy keeps shuffling closer to me. I move up, thinking she wants more room, but her leg springs back firmly.

I mutter to her, gesturing to the one hundred and one tabby pictures, 'Do you always spend the evening comparing cats? I feel like I'm in an Andrew Lloyd Webber musical.'

Lucy shrieks with laughter and clutches my arm. I'm the first to admit that joke wasn't worth that reaction.

She says something but it's inaudible over the music.

I lean in. 'I didn't hear that.'

She leans closer still. Her thigh presses hard against mine.

But I still don't hear what she said, because 'I Don't Feel Like Dancin'' by the Scissor Sisters starts playing and she screams, 'Oh my *God*, I *love* this song!'

The other Ls laugh as she grabs my hand.

On the dance floor, Lucy's doing that excessive hair tossing thing that people do to flirt. Her skin looks very soft...

Stop it, pervert brain, don't objectify new friends.

I dance in an overtly platonic way. Lucy laughs and shimmies around me.

OK, sure, she's pretty. But that means I should compliment her, or feel jealous of her.

She puts her arms on my shoulders.

OK, she is... *very* pretty, and looking at my mouth, and stroking her thumb up the back of my neck...

I don't stop her.

Unoiled gears clunk around in my head.

Lucy leans forwards, until her mouth is right next to mine and I can taste the sugary cocktail in the air between us...

Then Soph pulls me away to the smoking area.

What the fuck was I doing? Reality rushes in, and the guilt and confusion rushes to my head. I gulp at the fresh air.

Soph gestures wildly at me.

'Gee-Gee – or is it George now? Why are you suddenly hiding things from me?'

I just shake my head. God, my stomach hurts. It's been hurting for weeks now.

'You know you can tell me anything,' she says.

Soph tilts my chin up, but I can't look at her, can't bring myself to say it, because saying it would make it real. How can I tell someone something I barely accept myself? But Soph strokes my cheek, and hugs me tight. She smells like Chanel N°5 and pickles.

We've always been there for each other. Through constant calls and nights on the sofa and Pumpernickel favours, through her family rejecting her and that summer after finals when I quit the band, Soph knows me better than I know myself. She's been trying to help me realize something all this time, but I'd always refused to listen...

The world sways around us and I whisper into her shoulder, 'I think I'm not straight.'

The panic rises in my chest. I feel like I've exposed myself in public but Soph just gently pets my hair.

'Welcome to the club,' she whispers back. 'I'm proud of you. It's going to be OK.'

My stomach sags with relief. Now I've said it out loud, it does seem a bit less complicated and secret and awful. But...

'The problem is,' I continue, 'I'm not a lesbian, either.'

Soph chuckles.

'You know, there *are* other options?'

I pull back from her.

'Bisexuality? But I thought that was a bit of a...' I don't want to say 'phase', but it's definitely the word on my lips.

'Wow,' scoffs Soph, 'here's a unicorn telling me unicorns don't exist.'

She takes a deep breath. I can tell she's about to go into *SophieSnob* educational mode.

'Bisexual people are the largest group within the LGBTQ+ community! But they're routinely erased. They get boxed into one side or the other and stereotyped as like, "indecisive", or "confused".'

'Oh God, Soph, but I *am* indecisive and confused! If I said I was bi, everyone would think I was letting the side down.'

'Individuals shouldn't have to represent a whole community,' she says.

There must be another get-out clause.

'If I really am this "bisexual" you speak of,' I say, 'why haven't I fancied women before?'

Soph raises her eyebrows. 'Are you *joking*? You blush whenever a hot girl looks at you.'

I blush. 'OK, but that could just be jeal—'

'What about all your "girl crushes" which you insisted were completely different from "normal crushes"?'

'OK, but—'

'And remember in first year before you got with Douglas, and I Pumpernickled you to come for that LGBTQ+ meet-up?'

I'm outraged. 'You *can't* be talking about Emilia agai—'

'You and Emilia were flirting harder than I have ever seen two people flirt in my life,' she squawks. 'I had to practically *restrain* you from moving in together right there and then. I've never seen a more textbook example of a lesbian U-Haul.'

'Emilia knew I wasn't gay so—'

'She did *not*,' says Soph. 'We were at a queer event and you were hitting on a lesbian. That's quite a gay thing to do.'

'When you put it like that...'

'My gaydar is never wrong,' she says. 'You give off bi-fi signals. Why do you think we became friends in the first place? I fancied you.'

I pull the straw out of her mouth.

'You bloody *what*?'

'Sure,' she says, calmly taking the straw back.

I gawp at her. 'You don't still...?'

She throws her head back and laughs for longer than is strictly necessary for my ego. '*God* no. That was before I got to know you. Now I find you as sexy as a slug.'

'Shut up!'

'*You* shut up.'

We punch each other again.

'I guess,' I admit, 'there may have been a few clues that – that I was – somewhat repressing...'

'Bab, ever since you and Doug got together, you've done all you possibly can to lock yourself up in that closet, like you do with all the emotions you feel ashamed about. But now the doors are off and Narnia is calling. You have to accept yourself – *all* of yourself.'

I stare at her.

'Look, it's lovely that Aslan and Mr Tumnus want to meet me, but at the end of the day it doesn't matter if I'm...' I mouth the word 'bi'. 'Because I have a...' I mouth the word 'boyfriend'.

Soph guides me to a bench in the yard.

'Bab, everything is fine. There's no rush. You don't need to declare anything about yourself, or do anything you don't want to do. Now, I'm going to get us some water. Just stay here – *and don't snog anyone.*'

I'm still smiling when I feel a tap on my shoulder.

'That was quick,' I say, but it's not Soph. It's Kit.

Every part of me turns into blancmange. She's wearing her black leather jacket, her hair's slightly wet, and she has a cigarette behind her ear.

'George, right?'

Oh my God, she remembers my name! Oh my God, do I smell like Monster Munch?

She sits on the bench next to me and we look out in silence for a moment, then seem to remember Soph will be back soon and start talking at the same time. We smile and look away, and then back again.

'I heard your girlfriend,' says Kit finally, lighting her cigarette.

'She is *not* my girlfriend.'

'Oh,' shrugs Kit, 'then why aren't you allowed to "snog" anyone?'

I watch her cheekbones turn as she blows the smoke away from me.

'I...'

Her face is so close. I can see the smudged layers of her kohl eyeliner, traces of past nights like rings in a tree trunk. From here, her irises aren't black but mahogany, their depths flickering with gold. Her pupils are cavernous, staring into mine unwaveringly. I think of birds of prey, sharp eyes looking right into the lens. And I'm her rodent. But in a good way?

She blinks. Crap, I'd forgotten to speak.

'My friend was joking.'

She taps the ash from the end of her cigarette, looks back at me, head tipped.

OK. OK. So maybe I should accept I *am* bi. Maybe I'm bi, and fancy Kit. Maybe I'm bi, and fancy Kit, and nothing else in my life seems to make sense any more, but I would really, really like to kiss her, and if I just lean slightly—

'Kit!'

Soph is holding two plastic pints of water. Just seeing them sobers me up enough to feel a wave of guilt.

'Hi,' says Kit, friendly enough, but I have the distinct feeling she doesn't know who Soph is.

'I was *so* sorry to hear about you and Marsha,' she says, in a blatant lie.

Kit looks at me sharply. I start to shake my head.

'I bumped into her and she told me,' Soph continues, 'But I haven't told anyone else. Your secret is safe with me.'

Another blatant lie. Kit takes another drag.

'What are you guys going to do about Phase?'

'Don't know,' says Kit, dropping her cigarette even though there's still half left. 'See you around.'

As she walks away, I can't help noticing how everyone else's faces in the yard turn to watch her and several people toss half-inhaled cigarettes to follow.

Soph rounds on me.

'I leave you for one second! *Why* did Kit come over to you?'

I guess I could tell Soph about our first meeting now Kit's secret is out. But for some reason I find myself shrugging and saying, 'Asked if I had a lighter.'

We both stare at the exit.

8

I wake with such a violently disgusting stomach that I assume I must be dying, until I check my phone. Texts from Soph:

hey bb bi!!

here 2 chat whenever u want

love u

do u wanna come out again this weekend?

i mean 4 drinks lol

also lucy wants ur number

should i give it to her?

lol only jk

... unless?

also

hav u already come out 2 doug?

Horrible, horrible hangover mixes with horrible, horrible guilt.

What the hell is wrong with me? I've barely glanced at another man since being with Doug. But as soon as I was with Kit I started pouting.

It would be different if I was a *proper* gay. If my whole relationship with Doug was a lie and I'd been forcing myself to be someone else, I could have this moment of epiphany and triumphantly come out and damn the haters, run away to the lesbian circus like Soph.

But I'm not gay. I have a boyfriend – practically a fiancé – who I'm in love with, and who loves me. So what would be the point? Coming out would only confuse things. Upset him, upset my mum, upset everyone. And over what?

I'm not saying that *all* bisexuality is a phase, but for *me* it is. Natural pre-wedding jitters.

I just want everything to stay like it was. So I can't come out to anyone else. If I carry on as normal, I'm sure it will go away nicely.

I text Soph back.

No. No. No. And No.

And turn my phone off.

I wake Doug to a nice fry-up in bed. We go for a nice walk. We have nice sandwiches for lunch. Well, actually, I absent-mindedly messed up the sandwich fillings, but we have a nice joke about it.

When did I start living a life where the height of excitement is mixing up sandwich fillings?

'Gina…' says Doug, putting down his cheese and peanut butter sandwich, 'is something up?'

When I look at him, I realize I haven't looked at him properly in ages.

The sun through our kitchen window catches on his glasses, his kind eyes, the copper flecks in his beard. I see him again, suddenly, as a real living human being with his own complicated brain. I used to know everything that was going on up there. He's been my wonderful boyfriend for seven years, and in return, I'm being utterly crap. Guilt, guilt, guilt. I should be honest with him.

'Sorry, Doug, I've been distracted.'

I put down my cucumber and jam sandwich. He takes my hand and strokes my knuckles.

'How can I help?'

He'd be fine with it. Surely?

'I'm...'

But just by telling him it changes the dynamic between us, doesn't it? Coming out to my boyfriend also admits I fancy people who aren't him, implies I've met someone I fancy enough that I feel the *need* to tell him. And admits there's a world that I belong to – a world of butches and femmes and horoscopes and cats – that doesn't include him. Couples are meant to share everything, but *he* couldn't be part of the queer scene.

I think of how it feels for me, not being a part of his band any more. I never want to make Doug feel like that.

'I think I'm just a bit tired,' I say. He stops nodding.

I know I owe him more truth than that. But how can I risk all that we have together over a hypothetical? *'By the way, if we weren't together, I might get with a woman?'* It's obviously not worth it.

I swallow and say instead something else that feels true.

'I don't know who I am at the moment. And whoever it is, I don't think I like that person very much.'

Doug's face creases in pain. Now I feel a hundred times worse.

'No, no! I'm sorry, I'm fine, I just... Do you ever wonder if you're happier in a parallel universe? Being someone who actually does the things you've always wanted to do?'

'Like what kind of things?' he asks.

'Oh, I don't know. Something for myself?'

He was about to squeeze my hand. Now he hesitates. I continue hurriedly.

'Not that I don't love *you*, or the stuff we do together. You know how much I love our calendar – I *need* our calendar, it's just, recently…'

I trail off. I don't want to hurt his feelings by articulating myself badly. This man has shared my life for nearly seven years. When I was at my lowest, he helped me to stand on my own feet again. How can I say that I'm starting to think it wasn't *my* feet I was standing on at all, it was his and that now I might be strong enough to live my own life again I don't know what to do with his shoes?

It all sounds so selfish, so unromantic, so cold. And I'm not sure the metaphor makes sense.

So instead I say, 'I suppose I don't feel very fulfilled.'

'Have you tried playing piano again?' he says, offering me a corner of a Hobnob. 'Or writing songs? Just for yourself?'

I retract my hand from his to wipe my eyes.

'What are you scared of?' he asks.

He doesn't get it. There's too much there to be scared of: realising how much I've missed it, discovering how bad I've become, bringing back memories of my dad…

I just shrug.

'What would you say to your pupils?' asks Doug.

'Don't put gum under the piano lid?'

He laughs, a real bark that always makes me feel better.

'What would your dad have said to you? If you were one of his pupils, scared to play?'

I don't have an answer.

Doug gently, gently kisses my forehead.

'I'm here for you, Gina, you know that. Anything you need, I'm your boy.'

I think of the things that have helped me when I've felt sad in the past. Routine. Familiarity. Distraction.

'I'm sure I'll feel better once I'm at tonight's Bronze Age gig.'

The smell of craft beer, the sound of male banter, the colour brown. We're at the usual table at Great Dane's.

'So Gina,' asks Jasper, 'how's work?'

'Jesus *Christ*,' says Mickey. 'No work chat at the pub. What's the *goss*?'

Honestly, I could copy and paste this evening, except tonight they play 'Shy Guy' first, last, *and* for an encore.

I try to rub the imprint of The Familiar stamp off the back of my hand.

After the gig, I sit in my spare chair at the Bronze Age table, watching them all pack up.

Doug comes back first, buzzing, his post-gig excitement spilling over into public displays of affection. His hand is around my waist, spilling lower. I try to send messages through my bum into his hand to keep it away. It doesn't work.

'Poppy, I loved your solo in "One Shot",' I say.

'It hasn't changed,' she replies, watching Doug's hand.

I flush. Jasper brings post-show drinks over and calls to Mickey, who whispers a goodbye into the ear of a leggy blonde.

When he saunters over, Poppy says, 'I am not playing "One Shot" again until it has changed a *lot*.'

'I'll redo the lyrics,' laughs Mickey.

'Not enough.' Poppy turns to me. 'Gina, what do you think?'

I choke on my tonic. I'd been thinking that they should add a different chord in the verse progression, a counter-harmony, and at the very least a bridge, but I wasn't going to actually tell them. Who cares about the opinions of a Grade Three piano teacher?

They're all staring at me now.

'Umm, I don't know. You could—'

'How about a bridge?' says Doug.

'That's such a good point, mate,' says Mickey. 'Let's add a new bridge.'

Doug squeezes my knee under the table.

'We smashed it with "Shy Guy" though, right?' asks Mickey.

'We always smash it with "Shy Guy",' smiles Jasper.

'Oh my God,' cringes Poppy, 'we should not have done the encore! What happened to leaving them wanting more?'

I nod, but then catch Mickey's eye. My neck prickles with embarrassment. He must think I'm a groupie with delusions of grandeur. I should remember I only *used* to be a musician. I only *used* to be one of them.

I need another drink. I know better than to offer a round, so I just wander off. They probably don't notice. Trying to catch the eye of Big Jeff, the bartender, I can't help wishing that he looked a little more like Cara Delevingne...

'You're always running off without saying goodbye,' says a Northern Irish accent, close behind my shoulder.

Poppy's hair smells strongly of coconut shampoo. It makes me imagine her applying it in the shower. Bloody hell, I need to chill out.

'What can I get you?' she grins. 'Rum?'

'Oh,' I fluster, 'umm, no, no thanks, just a half-pint.'

She looks a bit put out, but then effortlessly gets the barman's attention and reels off the table's order.

'I'll get these,' I say, quickly.

She bats the offer away. 'Put it on the Bronze Age tab, please, Jeff. Oh, and if Mickey asks for tequila, don't give it to him, yeah?'

'Yessir,' says Jeff, winking back.

Why do my friend's interactions with bar staff always leave me feeling emasculated? Still, surely Poppy came over to me for a reason? I regret not taking her up on the rum, but I'm always surprised when she remembers things like that. I feel so out of Poppy's life now. At uni, we knew the minutiae of each other's timetables, slotting in rehearsals, drinks and hungover coffees before lectures. But this is already the longest I've spoken to her in years. I wonder if we'll ever be close again. Maybe I could try...

'So, Poppy,' I say, trying to lean casually on the bar, 'umm... How you doin'?'

She looks at me sideways. 'Pretty depressed, to be honest.'

My elbow slips. She fiddles with her beer label.

'Did Doug not tell you?' She smiles back at the table. 'No, I guess he'd think that was my business. Oh, I don't know, Gina, I guess I don't think Bronze Age are doing so great at the moment and they're all I have in my life. I always imagined I'd be doing more by now.'

'But you guys are doing amazingly,' I say. 'You've been asked to do another regular gig.'

'But it's not *going* anywhere,' she says. 'It's just "Shy Guy". I didn't think our creative output would stop at the first song we recorded.'

I try to hide my wince. They recorded their famous single only a few days after I quit the band. Didn't even tell me. I heard it on the radio that summer, someone else playing my keyboard parts.

'We've been playing it for so *long*,' Poppy's saying, 'over and over and over again. We still have nothing else that sets us apart.'

'No other band is all ginger.'

She winces. 'Urgh, I hate how obsessed Mickey is with the ginger thing. Why can't it just be about the music?'

I shrug at her sadly, but I don't think she's really asking me.

While we were away, Mickey somehow procured tequila. Smiling at his brother, he says, 'Your moustache does look so fucking gay, mate.'

Jasper rolls his eyes but laughs. 'I'm comfortable in my masculinity, dickhead.'

'Sure, bet you'd be comfortable balls-deep in some masculinity, if you know what I—'

The two of them scuffle, putting each other in a headlock.

I take a huge gulp of my drink. I know I should say something but...

'Stop it, you big Nancy!'

'*You* stop it, you big poof—'

Doug's voice cuts through their scuffle.

'Not cool, guys.'

They freeze, midway through a masturbatory gesture.

'Doug, it's just a—'

'No man, it's not OK for you to say stuff like that when you're some of the biggest straights in the world. Be better.'

'Are you gay, Doug?' slurs Mickey, thinking it's still a joke. 'So Gina, you single now? Want a proper shag for a change?'

I'm about to say something, unsure what, when Poppy stands up.

'Apologise to both of them, or I quit.'

What the hell is going on?

Mickey is so pissed he can barely sit upright. He's dribbled on his performance T-shirt. Realising his mistake, his eyes well up.

'Um soggy evree unn.'

Doug nods and grasps Mickey's shoulder.

We disband quickly after that. I try to nod goodbye to Poppy and Jasper, but they're busy cleaning up Mickey.

On the Tube back, Doug and I squeeze each other's hands in silent conversation.

'That was unexpected,' I say eventually.

'Yeah, I'm worried about him. I know he doesn't mean that stuff, but still, it's not cool. You shouldn't be making homophobic jokes, especially when—'

He looks at me, bashful.

'Especially when what?'

'Well,' he says, 'especially when certain friends of his might be, y'know, struggling to come out.'

Oh.

The carriage rattles past a tunnel. The impassive faces in another carriage judder past.

I'm such an *idiot*. All this time, I've been so worried about coming out to Doug, but of course, it's like with Soph. He already knows.

I grip the rail and take a breath.

'How long have you known?' I ask, eventually.

'I've had my suspicions since we met.'

I swallow. Build up the courage to look at him. The corners of his eyes are creased in his lovely smile.

'Has Soph ever spoken to you about it?' he asks.

'At The Familiar the other night, actually, yeah…'

'Huh. I'd always wondered if something could happen with Soph.'

I laugh loudly.

'Nah, Soph's just a friend.'

'Yeah, I guess they're just not each other's type. She might be bi, I don't know. But every man at Dane's has hit on her and she's never responded to it. So maybe she's, you know, full gay.'

There's a pause. Very slowly the clogs click into place in my brain.

'Oh. You mean Poppy.'

'You think she's full lesbo then?'

I choke. I can't stop shaking my head.

'I— Yeah. Sure. Maybe.'

I stare at the patterns in the Tube seats. 'How would you feel about that? Poppy being gay? Or bi? In theory?'

Doug tilts his head at me, rubs the plastic on the bridge of his glasses.

'Nothing to do with me either way, I guess.'

He looks a bit embarrassed, but not openly homophobic. Seems positive. This would be a good time to tell him. I could just come out really casually right now.

Or now.

No, there are loads of weird drunk men around, they might get violent if I say I occasionally fancy women.

I'll tell him at the next Tube stop...

OK, the moment's gone a bit, but I'll bring it back up on the walk back.

When we get home...

But when we get home, we have our nightly Hobnobs, get into our matching monogrammed pyjamas, rest our heads on our 'his' and 'hers' pillowcases, and cuddle. And even though there are a hundred moments I could bring it up, I don't.

'Well done on a good gig tonight, pet,' I say into his big spoon bicep.

He kisses the back of my head and snuggles in tight. And I think: it feels so nice here, in bed with him; maybe I'm straight after all. How could it get better than this?

9

My parents moved to Greengables cottage in the Sussex countryside when they got married thirty years ago. Dad joked that it would help the postman remember where the Green family lived.

Even before I came along they were accompanied by a sausage dog. My mum, lover of dachshunds though she is, harrumphs when she sees someone else with one, as if we invented and patented the breed.

Dad was one of those people who finds puns genuinely funny and always gave them terrible sausage-related names.

The first was Porky. Porky did indeed get plump. When Porky went to the great kennel in the sky, they filled the sausage-dog-shaped hole in their lives with another golden long-hair. Mum refused to accept the name Mustard ('What would we shorten it to, "Tardy"?'), so Dad called him Ketchup. The nickname for Ketchup ended up worse. In my early teens when Mum would lose the dog in the park she'd scream, 'Have you seen Ket anywhere?!' The village still thinks she's addicted to Class B drugs.

Ketchup was also my first experience of death.

On my fifteenth birthday, I blew out the candles and,

sneakily under the table, gave Ketchup a mouthful of cake. A week later, he was put down. Weeping over the long, thin, rectangular hole in the garden, my parents tried to comfort me by confessing that he had been ill for months. But I still blame myself and that forkful of forbidden frosting.

When Ketchup walked his last walk (/was murdered by me) we grieved for a few months. But soon – perhaps because my parents were desperate to stop me from crying every time I saw cake – we were blessed with another visit from the dog stork. Our smooth, black and brown dachshund puppy.

Dad got creative. Inspired by hot dogs, Dad called him In-A-Bun. Mum and I call him Bunny. Bunny used to love chasing after his namesake, but now he's in his stubby twilight years, he prefers the bread version.

Doug keeps talking about how excited he is to see Bunny again, I think to distract me from thinking about being home. But getting on the usual platform at St Pancras, I already feel sick. This time, there's not just the anxiety of being back and the inevitable vertigo of sadness and guilt that will come from seeing reminders of Dad. That's bad enough. But now there's this additional Doug-asking-my-mum-for-permission-to-marry-me thing. He bought Mum a suspiciously large bouquet from M&S.

On the train, I must look like I'm about to throw up, because Doug reaches across the table and takes hold of my hand.

'You're going to be OK,' he says, stroking my fingers. I swear he lingers over the fourth of my left hand.

I pull away. You don't own it yet, pal.

But he still smiles sympathetically at me, his eyes overflowing with affection. He gets out his earphones and passes me one string, playing the Beach Boys song, 'Wouldn't It Be Nice'.

Yes, it's a cliché, but it's our song. One of our songs. When we got stressed during revision, we'd sit and listen to it, imagining how wonderful life was going to be after graduating.

Doug leans his head against the window and closes his eyes. I watch him for a bit. (It's not creepy when you're in love.) God, he's lovely. I don't want to hurt him. What on earth would happen if he proposed and I said, 'No, because although I do love our routine, I also can't stop thinking about snogging girls?'

We'll stay happy if everything stays the same. We will, I *know* we will.

So how can I stop him proposing? Let's see…

Doug's traditional. If he doesn't get Mum's permission, then he won't. We'll be delayed until the next time he can see her. And I can make sure that never, ever happens. So, all I need to do is prevent him from speaking alone with my mum.

The song ends and I open my eyes, cheered by my plan. Doug's looking back at me. Looking at me like he wants to marry me.

Not today, motherfucker.

Mum honks from the car outside the train station. As we walk over I'm filled with trepidation.

'Hello, hello!'

Watching her unfold from the car and let out Bunny from the back, I think about how Mum is a bit like a sausage dog. Surprisingly tall and lithe, but with stubby legs. (Don't tell her I said that.) She's dignified yet playful, takes things at her own pace, has her habits and creature comforts – and does not like change.

To be honest, probably more than I care to admit, she looks similar to me. We have the same skittish brown eyes, and the same archetypal haircut. When I was a child, she used to cut our hair over the bath into the same shoulder-length shape, and even though hers is now salt-and-pepper, neither of us have ever deviated from that style. (Can you call a straight line a 'style'?) We've got different ears, though. I've got my dad's big ears.

Doug gives Mum a hand up and a big hug. His mouth is close to her (small) ear. Crap! He could be whispering secret messages to her already...

'Hey, I want a go!'

I break them up violently and bear-hug my mum. Mum seems pleased by the unnecessary scuffle.

'Oh Ginny,' she says, standing back from me, 'why are you wearing those manly trousers? You look so much better in frocks.'

Mum's wearing a flowery blue maxi dress which is older than I am – literally, I've seen it in her maternity photos. I'm about to start a fight when Doug gets the flowers out of the gift bag at his feet.

'But these are lovely!' says Mum. 'What's the occasion?'

'Nothing,' I say, brightly, before Doug can answer.

'Just pleased to see you again, Maggie,' he adds, smooth as a snake. 'Celebrate the small things.'

Mum giggles. I glare.

'Bunny's happy to see you both.'

He barks on cue. I rub his ears through the window. He's the only one I trust around here.

Then with a showman's flourish, Doug pulls deluxe dog treats out of the gift bag and rattles them. Bunny suddenly couldn't give less of a damn about me. He slobbers over Doug's petting hand, writhing with desire. Oh Judas, is this how you betray me?

I need to up my game.

I could have told you what conversations would come up on the car journey back to our house, and, if it weren't for the more pressing proposal crisis, I'd have been dreading them.

First, Mum asks Doug how Bronze Age are doing and keeps saying how talented and wonderful they are. Then she says I should start writing songs again. All the while, she studiously avoids any mention of why I quit, or indeed anything associated with that summer of finals.

I remember doing this exact journey from the station when Dad was the one driving. He'd always have a Classical music CD on, way too loud, and just wave back at anyone else's road rage. The thought of it makes me smile, and then feel sick.

'Just round this corner,' says Mum, and in my head I finish the sentence along with her, 'are the *daffodils*!'

To be fair, our village is at its best in the spring, with these first flowers rising from freshly mown front gardens. Daffodils, daisies and dandelions line the banks between the butcher's, church, and three pubs.

'Ooh, Maggie,' says Doug warmly, 'those daffodils are *lovely*. Like lovely yellow trumpets.'

'Yes, lovely yellow bobbing trumpets,' agrees my mother.

They're both gormlessly smiling out the window, bobbing their heads.

'Bob bob bob,' sings my mother.

'Bob bob bob,' sings my boyfriend.

'Bark bark bark,' sings my dog.

'I need to get out!'

The car slows enough for the safety catch to come off. I stumble out. We've stopped in a country lane and I run up to lean my forehead against a cold tree. Doug and my mum clamber out in concern.

'I just need a bit of air,' I yell, waving at them to keep away.

They stop and stand by the car, muttering to each other. Damn! I'm not meant to leave them together.

'Actually, do come over here,' I shout, waving my hand the other way.

They both start towards me again.

'Only one of you!'

What is this, the hokey-cokey?

They look at each other, weighing up which of them is the right person to hold my hair back while I throw up.

'Just Mum,' I say, feeling mean.

Doug flops a bit. Well, it's his fault for wanting to spend the rest of his life with me.

Mum rubs my back. I look deeply into the crevices in the tree.

'What's wrong, Ginny? Oh, my little girl...'

Oh bugger, she probably thinks I'm pregnant. The one thing that's *not* going on right now. I can't let her get all excited about being a grandma. Maybe I should come clean and tell her why I'm really feeling sick. But why am I? Is it my fear of coming out, or confusion over Doug proposing, or the anxiety of seeing Dad's left-behind belongings?

A car honks, stuck in the lane behind us.

'I need to go and reverse out, Ginny, but I'll come straight back, OK?'

I stay in my insane crouch. Mum heads back, but I then realize Doug is sitting in the car. Crap.

I run past her and get in, protesting their protests.

'Honestly,' I pant, 'I'm fine, I'm fine. Let's just get home.'

Eventually we pull up to our cottage. Home. The mismatched flowers and muddy gardening shed; the green door that Dad also thought would help the postman. The paint's a bit cracked.

I try to take deep breaths of nostalgic countryside air, but my gulps are erratic. Doug squeezes my elbow until I calm down.

'I'm going to pop to the little girl's room,' says Mum, trying to sound light.

'Me too,' says Doug. 'Well, to the little boy's.'

'I'll come with you,' I say quickly.

They both look at me and then at each other.

'I mean, er, I'll go after you.'

They go to the lavatories at the opposite ends of the house. I lean back against the wall, listening at Doug's door to ensure they don't communicate anything through the pipes.

On the wall in front of me is the canvas family photo taken when I was about sixteen. One of Dad's adult pupils was a portrait photographer and offered a free shoot. I remember Mum got so nervous about which of her accessories to immortalize, but in the end my dad picked her a fresh flower from the garden and tucked it behind her ear. She's still blushing happily in the photo, sitting on the left of our living-room sofa. I'm in the middle, wearing a baggy T-shirt with diamante stars on it, arms crossed self-consciously. And on the right is my dad, wearing that piano tie I always used to find so embarrassing, his arm proudly round the both of us.

Bunny is stretched over all our laps and the four of us are smiling toothily at the camera.

Mum and I are now sitting on that same sofa. We sip our tea in silence, not looking at the seat to our right. But Mum's always on the move. After barely tasting it she says, 'You both make yourselves at home. Bunny and I are going to water the plants.'

'I'll come,' says Doug.

'I'll come too,' I sigh, looking longingly at my cup of tea.

'It's just to let Bunny have a wee,' says Mum, but we all march out together.

With the three of us looming over him, poor Bunny gets performance anxiety and only does an embarrassed dribble. We wander around the garden, Doug and I taking it in turns to compliment the flowers we know nothing about.

Mum never used to be one for gardening. That summer, when no one was tending it, it became a barren wasteland. But now she loves it. She's been slowly nursing the bulbs back to health and this spring white buds are starting to glimmer through again, along with a handful of early daffodils.

'Nice trumpets,' says Doug, nudging my mum's elbow. 'Bob bob bob.'

'Turns out I've got Mrs *Green fingers* after all,' she jokes, for the hundredth time.

I say, 'Our tea's getting cold.'

'You can go back in,' offers Doug.

'No,' I say, '*all* of our cups of tea are getting cold.'

'Ginny,' says Mum, 'why don't you play some piano?'

'I don't want to bring my work home with me. And I said our *tea*.'

'Those poor old notebooks, accruing dust.'

'They're not accruing dust,' I mutter, 'you clean them every day.'

'Never give up hope,' she says. 'How about you play some piano while I make dinner?'

'May I help you in the kitchen, Maggie?'

'I was counting on it! My sous chef!'

'Can I be your trois chef?' I cut in.

I'm infamously bad in the kitchen.

'Oh,' says Mum, frowning at Doug. 'Of course, sweetie, but the kitchen isn't really big enough for three of us.'

'And I can't play the piano accompaniment,' says Doug.

'Neither can I,' says Mum.

'Neither can I,' I insist. 'I don't play the piano, I only teach it.'

'*Please* Ginny?' says Mum. 'I miss the sound of it tinkling away while I'm chopping up the veg.'

Dad and I always used to practise our scales before dinner. Sensing my weakness, Mum squeezes my elbow and firmly steers me to the music room door.

It's shut. Dad always left it open, unless he was teaching. I haven't been in since he died and the thought of seeing it covered in dust is even worse than seeing it empty.

But Mum doesn't give me a moment to stop her. She pushes open the door, pushes me in, and leaves.

It's clean and tidy. The window is open and a light breeze from the garden ruffles the curtains. Our battered upright piano is against the wall in front. Two chairs are against the right wall: I still think of them as his teaching chair and my listening chair. Every other surface of the small room is bookshelves with stacked piles of music books and scores. On one wall are framed certificates of my piano music grades (if you *must* know, I passed all of them with Distinction), and on the wall behind me are Blu-Tacked Thank You cards.

The room is almost exactly as I remember it, but the differences are immediately obvious. The tall vase on the table is new, full of stiflingly perfumed white lilies. My songwriting notebooks, which used to lie open across the top of the piano, are now tucked in a closed cardboard box. And worst, the piano stool is tucked in.

Dad *never* tucked the piano seat in properly. Like when men leave the toilet seat up, it was one of Mum's pet peeves. She'd see it through the open doorway on her way out of the kitchen and aggressively tuck it in, only for my dad to come in, do a few riffs, and leave it jutting out at a jaunty angle again.

I don't want to even touch the piano, but I can hear Doug and Mum starting to talk in the kitchen and remember I need to stop them.

I pull the stool out, sit down, tuck in, swallow. Press the foot pedals.

The last time I saw Dad here, we raced each other through complex jazz scales, playing in unison on different octaves. Now even a C major scale feels insurmountable.

But I take a deep breath. Come on, Gina. He wouldn't resent you one scale, surely? For Mum?

My right hand thumb presses middle C.

Then C to C, up and down, both hands. Over and over again. Bland, repetitive scales, as loud as I can make them, to drown out their chance to talk and my own thoughts.

After a while, though, my fingers can't resist breaking out. They play snatched melodies, a strange meandering medley of songs from my old notebooks, Bronze Age, Phase…

I stop myself from playing anything for long enough to be recognizable, as if I'm giving myself a get-out clause. I think of recovering alcoholics smelling liquor, ready to indignantly brandish the untouched bottle if accused.

My fingers are clumsy. Dad would have been shocked to see how out of practice I am. He said that teaching and playing were two sides of the same coin and always kept his hand in both. But teetering on the edge like this feels too dangerous. I'm remembering how easily the music comes to my fingers when I let it, how much I love it. Despite knowing how my songs ruined everything – how I hurt so many people – how hard it was to rebuild my life afterwards… The more I let myself play, the harder it is to stop.

A song starts to come out of my scales, a song that sounds suspiciously close to Phase's 'Cusp'. My throat tingles with its lyrics, singing along in my mind. I could hum it very quietly…

'Din-din's done-done!'

Mum's voice from the doorway makes me start. I could be ten again. I twist to her guiltily, pulling my fingers from their chords, wondering how long she's been watching me.

It's only when I tuck the stool neatly under the piano that I realize something. The piano is in tune. Mum must have organized to have a piano tuner come round recently. In the hope that I would use it? Out of habit? Or because she can't bear to leave it untended?

'To your good health,' Mum toasts with the Prosecco, 'and your happiness.'

I'm about to raise it to my lips when she continues.

'And to *love*. I'm so glad that you are settled together. It's such a comfort to me, alone out here, to know that my precious daughter has a lovely young man to look after her. I hope that she looks after you too.'

Is Mum practising her wedding speech already? I need to stop her from going and putting on a big hat.

'To many more bottles of celebratory Prosecco,' smiles Doug.

They both toast. I just drink.

Doug's finished brushing his teeth and tries to squeeze into the room past Mum, who likes to stand in doorways. He smiles amiably and attempts to fold his broad body into the narrow gap. Mum, flushed with Prosecco and embarrassment, can't cope.

'Why don't you two use the big bedroom? Really, really?'

Ah yes, of course, I'll just push my ageing mother out of the bed she's slept in for thirty years. Why do Mums offer things like that?

'Mother! We're absolutely fine. Thank you.'

'Maybe we should convert the music room into a spare bedroom?' she mumbles, and then blushes harder. We both know that's never going to happen.

I hug her sternly and she squeezes back. Doug comes and hugs around both of us. We're only like that for a second, but it's nice. Really nice. I try to save it to my brain's hard drive of cosy memories.

'Night night, Ginny-Gin.'

'Night night, Mummy-Mum.'

'Night night, Doggy-Dog,' Mum experiments, tipsily.

'Night night, Maggie-Mag,' says Doug, beaming with pride.

The next day it's easier to keep Doug and my mum from being alone in a room together. Maybe he feels he's lost his moment, or maybe they're both trying to keep me from randomly crying again, but either way it works in my favour.

Doug fries us tomatoes and onions from Mum's garden and eggs from her next-door-neighbour, Sheila.

'She looks like her chickens,' jokes my hungover mother for the third time this morning.

Doug examines the egg he's about to crack into the pan. 'Do you think she laid these then?'

Mum giggles away, as if it's her he's about to propose to.

We're all feeling as fat and content as Bunny when we take him for a walk through the nearby fields. I keep strictly in the middle of Mum and Doug and we stroll through country lanes, Mum pointing out the hedgerow berries and telling us how many pots of jam she's made from each. Sheep bleat at us from behind kissing gates and in the distance, between rolling hills, we can glimpse the sparkling sea. After London's endless grey, it really is beautiful. However distant I've been since graduating, I don't think this view could ever stop feeling like home.

Then Bunny, in a burst of youthful vigour, catches sight of a squirrel.

'I'll get him!' I shout, and run after him. It doesn't take very long to catch up with his tiny legs. He's slobbering at the base of a tree, his tongue lolling, only one ear raised. He truly is the best thing in the whole world. I get my phone out to take a picture.

Raising my camera, I see three things at the same time. One: a text from Soph asking *hows Operation Crash the Wedding?* Two: Mum clasping a delighted hand to her mouth, looking in my direction, and then enveloping Doug in a huge hug. Three: Bunny doing a wee on the tree.

I take the photo. I suppose it'll be good in the wedding slideshow.

10

'Timmy. F sharp.'

'Oh yes,' he says, then plays it wrong again. I don't bother to correct him.

Hope has stopped asking me for advice about her own songs.

I tell Percy he will pass his Grade Seven exam with good marks, which he will.

Alexa has grown tired of liquorice and is now experimenting with peppermint balls. We stare at the smoking area brick wall and sigh in unison.

'Did you ever think your life would end up different?' she says.

I crunch on a mint.

'No, this is exactly what I always dreamed of. Hearing Fimmy Fucker play the same F sharp wrong over and over until I die.'

I hear a dog bark in the distance and remember, Pavlovian, about Douglas, and how I'm meant to be more grateful for him.

'I'm very lucky, though,' I splutter. The dog barks again louder. 'To have a secure, steady life.'

The dog starts to howl.

Alexa turns to me, poker-faced as ever.

'Right.'

She picks out another peppermint and sniffs it dubiously. 'I used to want to be an architect,' she says. I look at her in surprise, not so much at the revelation, but at the fact of her sharing something.

'I wanted to make an impact, I suppose. Skyscrapers. Surely I could have done better than the Gherkin.'

She crunches the mint to dust. 'If my childhood self had seen what my adult life would look like...' She shakes her head, 'I wouldn't have bothered to give up smoking.'

It's 4.30 p.m.

Text your boyfriend :)

The smiling emoji stares into my soul.

What would happen, I think, if I didn't text him today? I know he wouldn't *really* mind. But...

It doesn't matter either way, because as always, before I press send, I get a message from Doug.

I love you more! :)

And it does make me feel better. Definitely.

I'm at home tidying our board games when Soph forwards me a text:

hi guys!!! sorry for the group message <3 PHASE is looking for a new keyboard player!!!! so if you know any cool groovy fun lesbians *who play piano… drop us a message!! we're doing more auditions at familiar 2nite!!! thanks!!!! ru xoxo*

Oh God!

Just for a second, I let myself imagine it: I'm a cool, groovy, fun lesbian who plays piano – and I'm in Phase. I look over at my dusty keyboard, take a deep breath and pull one edge of the seat out.

Suddenly I'm back in Dad's music room and I stop. I usually stop there. But maybe playing those scales at home broke some kind of seal, because today – today I start up again. I sing the first thing that springs to mind.

'I guess I'm just a shy guy'

I map out the chords, feeling the familiar spaces.

'But if you want to try'

It all starts to come back. Turns out teaching piano every day has kept things ticking over after all.

'I could be your shy guy'

Maybe I could play, just secretly, for myself. That would be OK, wouldn't it?

'I could treat you right'

I used to accompany Doug while he was practising Bronze Age bass lines. Honestly, there was a time when I was the more advanced musician. But look at us now: he's getting paid to play live gigs twice a week and I'm barely a music teacher. My only connection to creativity now is him and *his* friends, and they're all fine without me.

'Sh-sh-sh-sh-shy guy'

That last gig we played together, when we were up on the stage under those golden lights, performing 'Shy Guy' to cheering friends… I wonder if I would have done anything differently if I'd known it was my last ever gig?

'Yeah I'm your mister right'

Did I not have any inkling of doubt, when I was up there on that stage? Was I so caught up in myself and my inflated ego that I didn't realize how pathetic I was? Did I really think it was *that* important to play my vapid little pop songs?

'Shhh'

The most damning part is, I think I did know. I think I knew exactly how selfish and pointless I was being. But I sang along anyway.

I turn the keyboard off, mind made up.

You'd better learn the piano quick then babes, I text Soph. *I'm obviously not going to audition. Also, I'm poorly tonight so I can't come for drinks with you. Sorry bye.*

I even do a fake cough, alone in my room, because I feel like Soph will be able to tell.

I try to atone (and distract myself) by watching some more *SophieSnob,* but her feverish video about the legendary, ironically exclusive, and subtly named Pride gig GAY FEST makes me start having vivid fantasies about performing there with Phase. I abruptly remind myself that is impossible on multiple levels and skip it. The next in the line-up is *Top (or Bottom) of the Pops: Sexiest Music Dykons,* which literally includes a clip of Kit signing a fan's cleavage.

I close the laptop and stare at the wall for a bit.

I'm so stupid for having even attempted to play again. When will I learn that I'm only OK when I stick to routine? That's why routines are there, for heaven's sake, to protect you from ruining anything else.

I wish that Douglas was home. I always feel so much more comfortable in my own skin when he's around. I put on one of his shirts, spray myself with his cologne, grab some chocolate

Hobnobs and eat them his way, with the chocolate on the top. I clear up the dirty socks he's left on our bedroom floor, reminding myself I have one part of my life that's sorted and happy and that should be enough.

The doorbell rings. It's Soph, dressed in one of her sparkly going-out minidresses.

I attempt to bring up some non-existent phlegm.

'Nice try,' she says, grabbing my arm and pulling me through my front door.

'Soph, Soph please,' I beg, but she won't listen. I aim for her Achilles heel. 'At least let me get changed?'

But she eyes up my slouchy joggers and Doug's button-up shirt.

'Just put on that denim jacket. You're a natural.'

So before I know it, I'm back at The Familiar, drinking a Bad Witch.

'Soph,' I say firmly, 'I'm sorry for any offence or confusion caused, but I'm not bisexual. Please let me go back to normal.'

'Can you hear that?' she says.

'Hear what?'

'Someone knocking?' She starts looking around, under the table, under her chair. 'Mmm. It's as if there's someone trapped in a closet?'

I glare at her.

'Soph, please! I just—'

'I *know* you,' she snaps. 'I know you, and I know you were telling the truth when you came out to me. Can you please stop hurting yourself like this?'

Horribly, I can feel tears welling up. Soph wipes them away. Her acrylic nails nearly scrape my eyes out, but it's still nice.

'You're welcome to hang out with my gal pals,' she says, gently. 'And, I don't know, you can come with me to more queer gigs, or go to football with Jenny – you know she runs that LGBTQ tournament, the Beautiful Gay-me? And I think you've already started watching my videos?'

It's exhausting having a best friend who is always right.

'Thing is, Gee-Gee, you need to work out whether you're going to be satisfied with just being a part-time member of the community. When you accept your full bi identity, can you accept that you might go your whole life without having had any queer relationships? If not, then you're going to have to think about whether you're ready to marry Douglas.'

I cringe so much at the m word that I nearly fall off my chair. 'But I'm all settled with Doug...'

'Really? Are you settled? Or are you settling?'

'Ouch, good one.'

Soph points at me threateningly.

'If you keep repressing your emotions, it'll hurt even more. You keep pretending that everything's fine, but what I'm worried about, Gee, is that soon you won't be able to tell the difference any more, between the brave face you put on and what you're really feeling. I know things were shit after your dad died, and I'm not trying to minimize how much it still hurts. But you can't keep on like that. You have to stop doing what you think you're *meant* to want, and start doing what you *actually* want. Stop holding yourself back.'

I stare very hard at a crack in the table. I realize the irony of suppressing tears after what Soph just said, but...

'I don't know *how*,' I whisper.

'You're not bound to anything that happened in your past. Think of that version of Gina as only one bit of you. There are so many parts of yourself that you're not living. There's *so* much more.'

I sip on my drink, trying to take in her advice. Gina is only one part of me...

'Start actually listening to your gut,' Soph says. 'If it was your last day on earth, what would you regret not doing?'

'Jesus,' I say, 'that's pretty intense.'

But my treacherous brain starts imagining a person who lives in the moment. A person who could be a musician without hating herself for it. Who could be with someone who loves her for different reasons to Doug. Someone who morphs into Kit, on a stage, looking at my mouth...

'No one else is going to live your life for you,' Soph says. 'Stop compromising. Have it all. I'm aware I sound like a motivational Instagram account, but I'm serious. YOLO, bitch!'

She pokes me hard in the chest. 'And you know what you're going to do first? You're going to audition for Phase.'

That wakes me up. I push her hand away.

'Soph, stop! Even if I wanted to – which I don't – I can't. I haven't practised enough.'

'Good! Phase would hate it if you were too rigid. They're all about improvising.'

I itch to strangle her.

'Isn't my coming out a big enough drama for you?' I say. 'I can't do the whole keyboard thing too. When I quit Bronze Age, I promised to quit playing full stop. Can't you just let me stay repressed about something?'

She grabs my face in her hands and forces me to look right at her.

'Georgina, you've got to move on. You've stopped yourself from being yourself for too long.'

She nods my head for emphasis.

'You're a musician, but not living that part of yourself. You're queer, but not living *that* part of yourself. Phase. Are. A. Queer. Band. In. Need. Of. A. Pianist. It's the perfect start for you. What more do you need, a sign from the stars?'

That's when Isobel, Rudy, and Kit appear in the doorway behind Soph. I can see the outline of the witch on the door behind them. Soph turns back to me and grins wickedly. Before I can stop her, she waves for them to come over.

So then Phase are walking over to us, looking tired but curious. What the hell is happening?

Kit's eyes lock on mine, like they had in my imagination a second before, and my breath catches. If I'm going to start hanging out more at The Familiar, I need to get an asthma pump.

'Phase,' says Soph, 'I'd like to introduce you to George, your new keyboard player.'

Oh. My. God.

'I-I'm terribly sorry,' I say, putting a restraining arm around Soph. 'Sh-she's on hallucinogens.'

But Kit's frowning at me.

'When you said you were a musician,' she says, her voice like smoke and pillow talk, 'I didn't realize you were a pianist.'

My head explodes, with delight that she remembers our conversation, and horror at what I'd said.

'Well,' says Isobel, looking from Kit to me, tucking a blonde curl behind her ear, 'we just wrapped up a lot of auditions...'

'But the room backstage is free for the rest of the night!' squeals Rudy. 'Come and play something! What's the worst that can happen?'

I'm in the Green Room, wishing I could hide in the loo again. Soph has thrown me to the lions and abandoned me.

'We've been asking people to play anything they'd like to,' says Isobel, gesturing to the keyboard like a polite executioner.

It's the same Yamaha I have at my flat. Out of an old habit, I switch it onto one of the softer voice settings.

And then – urgh – I don't know if it's because I'm drunk, or because of Soph's carpe diem pep talk, or because the tune has been stuck in my head for weeks, but I start playing the song they'd opened with, those weeks ago: 'Cusp'.

I can't remember all the ways they varied it, but I remember the chorus like it's seared into my synapses. I establish the chord progression with my left hand, then riff with my right, going where it leads me. First more wistful. Then playful. Then urgent…

Isobel starts to sing along with me. Her voice is even lovelier, quiet like this. I add in a counter-harmony beneath her. She runs her elegant fingers along the top of the keyboard, her lipstick forming into a Hollywood smile. She sings and I answer. We switch over effortlessly.

I'd forgotten how wonderful it is, to play live like this.

A light catches my eye. Rudy is filming on her phone.

Shit!

My fingers stumble. Flustered, disorientated, I fall out of the flow and clash with Isobel. I style it out, just about, but now I'm playing consciously, my brain is getting in the way. I fumble an ending.

I sense the three of them looking at each other, but can't bring myself to look up. I'm dizzy, embarrassed, boiling, humiliated. Wish I'd never allowed Soph to bring me here. Wish I'd never seen Phase. Wish I was back home, safe.

Then applause.

It's Kit. She's looking right at me, clapping, and for a moment I think that she's being sarcastic and want to die. But no, she's clapping for real.

'That was fucking incredible,' she laughs, joshing my shoulder.

Maybe I *have* died.

Kit, Isobel, and Rudy exchange a grin, nodding, and then Isobel reaches out a hand to me.

'George, welcome to Phase.'

A group of giggling queers happily give Kit their table in the quieter bar area at the back of The Familiar. Isobel buys us Jägerbombs.

'To George!' she says.

'To George!' Kit and Rudy answer.

I'm giggling hysterically. Thankfully the others are too. The Jägerbomb is even sweeter than I remember from when I last had one (what, ten years ago?) and goes to my head instantly. I can feel the sugar on my teeth, smell the same sweetness on the others' breaths.

'Tell us everything,' says Isobel, resting her pristine chin on the back of her delicate fingers. 'Who are you? Where have you been hiding?'

'I'm a piano teacher,' I say, overwhelmed. 'I teach beginner's Mozart to disinterested children.'

'I work with disinterested kids too!' laughs Rudy – Soph told me she was a TV presenter for a children's crafts show. 'Isn't it *the worst* when you're hungover?'

Neither Kit nor Isobel volunteer information about their jobs.

'I can't believe you're not a full-time musician. You played "Cusp" like...' Rudy clicks her fingers in the air. 'From memory? By ear? You're a genius!'

'Where did you learn to play?' asks Isobel.

I try to sound breezy.

'My dad taught me. C major scale when I was four. Wrote my first song when I was seven. It was awful, obviously. Something about how complicated I was and how no one understood me.'

Everyone laughs and my heart soars.

'Is your dad a musician?'

My heart splatters to the ground.

'A piano teacher,' I say carefully.

'Like father like daughter,' smiles Isobel.

No, I think to myself, because he was a *good* teacher. But I just smile and nod.

'Isn't this crazy,' says Rudy, patting my hand. 'My brother is a teacher too!'

'Ru, that's not crazy at all,' scoffs Kit. 'You have four brothers. All have different professions, and wives with different professions to that. Everyone you meet seems to have the same career as *one* of them.'

Rudy grins back.

'I'm the youngest,' she explains to me, 'and we all had

music lessons on different instruments. I think my parents were trying to create a whole mixed-race orchestra.'

When she laughs, her candyfloss hair bounces.

'The basic instruments had been taken by the time it got to me, so I chose the bass because it was so massive. They said I'd grow into it. Still waiting for *that* growth spurt.'

Kit laughs and lays an affectionate arm around Rudy's tiny shoulders. I try to squash down my jealousy. Maybe one day that could be me...

'How did you guys, umm, start playing?'

Isobel and Kit glance at each other, telepathically agreeing who will go first.

'I sang in the school choir and my church,' says Isobel, fiddling with a loose curl. She seems defensively blasé. 'They kept inviting me to do solos because I was young.'

'Don't be falsely modest,' says Kit, poking at Isobel's dimples. 'They made you do solos because your voice is heavenly and because you look like a literal angel.'

'Don't be sarcastic,' snaps Isobel, but her dimples have become even rosier. She turns back to me.

'Kit-Kat, of course, was kicked out of the choir because she kept skiving rehearsals to smoke or make out with her curious classmates.'

Kit-Kat? I bet no one else in the world calls her that. Jealousy blends with curiosity. So they went to the same school together? That means they've been friends for longer than even Soph and I have. No wonder they act like an old married couple, bickering all the time. Does that make Rudy their little daughter? And me the distant creepy uncle?

Kit rolls her eyes but seems pretty pleased with the

description. Reminded of cigarettes, she slips a hand into her leather jacket and starts to lay out papers and tobacco.

'They wanted to expel me but, thank the Blessed Lord,' she says, crossing herself, 'I discovered my true calling in the music room, granted salvation by—'

Isobel fills in. 'Hitting things with a stick.'

Kit pretends to be indignant, hand to her chest.

'I hit things with *two* sticks.'

Rudy snorts so hard that her Jägerbomb comes out of her nose. Seeing her frothing nostrils nearly sends me to the same fate. I glance at Kit – the neon light on her confident cheekbones, a filter dangling from the corner of her lips – and am startled when she looks up, right at me.

'George,' she says. 'Why aren't you already in a band?'

I stop laughing abruptly.

Even though her voice is low and quiet it cuts through the bar noise. I meet her dark eyes and have a terrible compulsion to tell her everything. I'd spill my guts on the floor if I thought she'd find them interesting.

'I was in a band at uni,' I say, but stop myself giving any details. I don't want my new friends defining me by Bronze Age, or asking me too much about why I quit. I remember what Soph said about Phase being a new start for me, a new life. I don't want to lie, but maybe, here, with them, I can say different things than I normally would?

I say slowly, 'Once our final exams were over, I couldn't stay with them. There was too much history.'

Phase groan sympathetically. Huh. That worked better than I thought it would. I lick hopefully at the top of the Jägerbomb glass.

'I guess, if I'm being honest, I'd secretly hoped that I could play again one day. If things could feel different enough. If I could be myself, without... I dunno... Without feeling guilty?'

Phase nod back at me, very sincere. Oh no, I've made them think I was part of some horribly homophobic band. I should feel bad for misleading them, because really, it wasn't Bronze Age's fault, it was all mine. But, I remind myself, I'm trying to start a new life here. I don't need to be accurate to Gina's past.

'Anyway,' I say, 'enough about me. I want to know about—'

Isobel waggles her manicure at me.

'You don't get away that easily. What about your love life?'

Oh. Crap.

Phase is a lesbian band. They auditioned for lesbian pianists. *Phase can't know about Doug.* I don't want to lie, but those other little white lies worked pretty well...

'Well?' demands Rudy. 'Do you have a girlfriend?'

My tipsy cheeks flush.

'No,' I say carefully, 'I don't have a girlfriend.'

'Do you want one?' she replies, batting her eyelashes.

The blush spreads rapidly through my whole body.

'Only joking!' she winks. 'I have a girlfriend. But what's your type, huh?'

Without my permission, my eyes slide to Kit. I can't believe my body parts are betraying me like this. Bastards.

'I-I don't really have a type,' I say.

To avoid their gaze, I glance at my phone and almost faint. Rows of missed calls from Doug.

'How the *fuck* is it midnight?!'

The others laugh that midnight isn't even late. I start fumbling around.

'Look, guys, this has been a wonderful – and surprising – evening.'

Rudy's giggles have turned into hysterical hiccups. Isobel rubs her back maternally.

'I'll see you to the door,' says Kit, exchanging a glance with Isobel. Kit seems the least tipsy, or maybe she just doesn't show it in the same way. She helps me shrug my jacket on. When her fingers brush the inside of my arm, everywhere gets goose pimples.

'So excited to have you with us,' hiccups Rudy, giving me a generous hug.

'We'll message about rehearsals,' says Isobel, kissing my cheek and then wiping at the red smudge she's left. She kisses Kit's cheek too, even though she's only going a few metres away to the door.

They're all very touchy feely...

Then Kit is holding the door open for me, her hand on my elbow, carrying my bag. The cold evening air slaps my face like a fish as I call a cab, panic rising in my stomach. How am I going to explain this to Doug? He's probably filed a missing person's report.

But Kit offers me some gum, and as we chew in silence under the bright moon, I forget about all that.

One minute until the taxi.

'Thanks for waiting,' I say. She doesn't answer. I steal a glance at her.

She's looking at my collar. I look down, worried I've got some gross stain on it. But she comes closer to me, standing so close that I can almost taste her Extra Cool Breeze.

She fingers my lapel. I've stopped breathing. I look into those cavernous eyes, only inches from mine. Closer.

'Shirts suit you,' she murmurs.

I vow to never wear anything but shirts ever again.

She slowly fiddles with the lowest button on my shirt. Undoes it. Her fingers brush my navel. Shivers run down my torso and my legs. Even slower, Kit rebuttons it.

'I have some shirts,' she says, 'which I don't wear any more, but I could give you, if you like. I think you'd look... very...'

For a moment we stay there, her fingers still looped round the lowest button of my shirt. Then the taxi honks and we jump apart like startled rabbits.

I climb in, she shuts the door, and neither of us blink as I'm driven away.

11

Soph has been screaming her head off for minutes.

'Didn't I *tell* you you'd get in? You're *welcome*!'

Was that a tinge of jealousy? I'm skipping out of Liberty to the Tube, too giddy and hungover to concentrate on whether I'll make off-peak.

'There's this WhatsApp group with the three of them and they messaged this morning suggesting a weekend jam!'

'Jam?'

'Jam!'

We both repeat 'jam' for a while, at increasing levels of hysteria.

'I genuinely can't believe this,' sighed Soph, 'You've only been queer for five minutes and you're already in the in-crowd? No fair.'

'They still have time to chuck me out,' I say, remembering to be humble.

'Yeah, that's true,' says Soph, which was unnecessary. 'But you'll be my in. I'll interview you all for *SophieSnob* and make Kit fall in love with me. Success! Where was Kit during all of this, by the way?'

Ah. I might have left the Kit bits out of my retelling of

last night. I don't want to hurt Soph by making it sound like there's a *thing*. I'm doubtless imagining it, anyway. Kit probably fiddles with all her friend's shirt buttons.

'She doesn't exactly talk much.'

'True,' says Soph, 'but she says so much with her silence…'

I nod deeply, then thank the Lord that Soph can't see me down the phone.

'What happened with you and Jenny?'

'Had mind-blowing sex for four hours, she told me she loves me more than life itself, then I asked if she'd be willing to say that on camera, and she dumped me again.'

'So, same old?'

'Exactly. Stop trying to distract me, bab. Have you told Doug yet?'

I trip over the wonky manhole cover. Damn it.

'Umm, not completely.'

'Gee!'

'I got back so late,' I say. 'He was already in bed. So I just apologized and said I'd tell him everything tonight.'

'*Everything*? As in, everything like you've told me?'

I don't hesitate.

'Everything. Just like I've told you.'

I've prepped Doug on the sofa with a mound of Hobnobs, our favourite matching mugs, and a tissue box nearby. (Pessimist or realist?)

'I wanted to formally apologize,' I announce, 'for being back late last night and making you worry.'

Doug smiles like a Labrador. 'Apology already accepted. I'm just curious!'

'Well, talking of "curious"…'

Oops, that wasn't planned. But Doug blithely dips a biscuit into his tea. Back to the script.

'I was having a drink with Soph, and—'

'Isn't it funny that you resisted going to The Familiar for so long and now it's your favourite bar?' He shakes his head. 'Imagine all the fun you could have had if you'd gone with Soph years ago!'

'Talking of fun I could have had years ago…'

Doug smiles at me uncomprehendingly.

'There's two pieces of news, really.'

'Good news first, please!' he chirps.

Coming out to your boyfriend doesn't exactly feel like *good* news? So I go for the easier one.

'I ended up drunkenly auditioning for a band last night – a-and I got in!'

Doug stares at me in stunned silence. I race on.

'They're an indie pop band – well, alternative – a mix of everything – and they're *amazing*, though I'm not sure if they believe in horoscopes, but that's not important right now and, yeah, we're going to start rehearsals on Saturday and I'm excited but also so nervous I feel sick.'

I stop for breath. Doug's still looking at me, unmoving.

Then his whole face splits into a grin. He crushes me in a huge hug and spins me around until my feet knock over our IKEA tea table.

'Gina! This is *incredible*! *You're* incredible. This calls for Prosecco!'

Mum has us well-trained. We always have a bottle in the fridge in case of 'small things' to celebrate.

I laugh, exalted. 'But we're both still hungover!'

'Hair of the dog,' he says, ruffling his own hair.

That must be the fiftieth time I've heard him make that joke, but I still love it. He removes a bottle from amongst the fridge's Tupperwares of bolognese and peels off the foil.

'I don't know if we should celebrate,' I say. 'I mean, they could still change their minds.'

'Excuse me,' he says, 'are you Gina Green?'

I frown at him.

'I think so?'

'Then there's no need for you to have imposter syndrome.'

'Oh my God,' I laugh, 'so many dad jokes today.'

A second of awkwardness because of the D word, but Doug carries on almost seamlessly.

'There's no time for your self-doubt, Gina. What's the band called, can I look them up?'

'They don't have any social media,' I say, grateful that Doug doesn't know I searched for a *long* time, trying to find photos of Kit.

Doug scratches his chin.

'Hmm... good for intrigue, I guess, but you're going to need *something* online if you want to build a wider geographic fan base, right? I'm sure Soph could advise. Anyway, what's their name?'

'Phase?'

He nearly drops the bottle.

'Phase?!'

'Oh, have you heard of them?'

I'm secretly thrilled, but that also means that he might know—

'Of course I've heard of them! They're hot stuff! We've

never played on the same line-up, we're hardly the same vibe… Gina, aren't Phase all gay?'

This is perfect. I simply need to say, 'Yes, but that's fine, because second piece of news, I'm bi.'

Doug looks up from the Prosecco bottle, holding the cork just before it pops.

'Yes, but that's fine,' I start.

The cork pops. Doug laughs in delight as the froth bubbles over into our 'his' and 'hers' champagne flutes.

'Of course it's fine! To my beautiful girlfriend Gina,' he toasts, 'the only straight pianist good enough to be accepted into a lesbian band.'

I splutter on the bubbles.

'No!'

Doug pats me on the back. I swallow the bubbles down – and my news along with them. Look, he's happy for me being in the band. That's enough news for one day. I can tell him about the whole bi thing another time. It's reasonable to take things one step at a time. Soph is always saying that no one should be pressured to come out anyway. Right?

He wiggles his eyebrows at me. 'I expect you'll be adding a new colour to your calendar.'

It feels like I levelled up.

Sky blue for time with Doug, navy blue for work, purple for Soph, green for calling Mum, grey for time alone. Phase rehearsals will be, I decide, an unabashed pink.

Sipping Prosecco, I smile at my busy schedule. A full calendar equals a full life.

12

Early Saturday morning I'm so nervous about the Phase rehearsal that I can't sleep. I tiptoe downstairs to practise and lose myself playing through variations on 'Cusp'…

A plate of Hobnobs slides into my peripheral view, along with a bearded man, kissing my cheek. I flinch, disorientated. Then I shake my head, slide my headphones off, try to dislodge gay musician George's thoughts from Doug's girlfriend Gina.

'Thank you, Fluffy,' I say, robotically.

He smiles at me proudly.

'They're going to absolutely love you,' he says.

That's the plan.

I'm still deciding what to wear when my mum calls me. Crap, how did it get so late? I'd meant to make sure I had our usual call-time spare, but it's taken me longer than expected to work out what a lesbian should look like for a band rehearsal.

None of my usual clothes felt right, so eventually I washed an old tartan shirt from the depths of the laundry basket – it's been out of circulation for so long I've no idea if it's mine or Doug's – to wear under Soph's denim jacket. I should have asked her advice, but she might have asked why I was trying *quite* so hard.

I look at the calling contact picture of my mum and Bunny, both sticking their tongues out at me.

Damn. I haven't not picked up on her in years, but I haven't yet told her about Phase, and I don't want to have to rush it because I need to get the wording right...

I text her to say I'll ring later. Immediately she sends me a flurry of panicked texts.

AREYOUOK??!

I type back, *Yes!*

LETMEKNOW!!!

Yes, really, I'm fine, just busy, speak soon.

AREYOUSURE??!

I type back, *YES*

It's 2 p.m. at The Familiar. The pub is closed, but they let Phase – I mean, *us* – rehearse in the stage space. It feels weird not to see the bouncer with her cat stamp.

The Halloween decorations leer at me down the passageway, even more uncanny in the working-day lighting. Was it really only a few weeks ago that I was here for the first time? I take a selfie in front of the witch door, sending it to Soph with the caption *Jam!!!*

Isobel is the only one waiting. She's sitting primly on the edge of the stage, wearing a white turtleneck jumper, high-waisted jeans, and bright-heeled boots, reapplying impeccable lipstick. I tug at my shirt, feeling like a scruffy urchin.

'Hello?' I say.

Isobel squeals, skips over and kisses my cheeks. I think I kiss back too many times, but we giggle enough to cover it up.

'It's such a pleasure to have you with us, George. I keep watching Rudy's video of your audition and it still blows me away. And compared to some of the others we had in?' She widens fluttering eyelashes.

Past-Gina's stomach cringes in sympathy for those poor girls. New-George thinks: fuck 'em.

Rudy bursts in holding four coffees and a huge tray of doughnuts. Her pink curls and yellow Doc Martens bounce in excitement.

'George! Aaah! It's so nice to see you again. I picked us up a little snack…'

Half an hour flies by with the three of us chatting about London and music and baked goods. But still no Kit. Isobel follows my train of thought.

'Kit has no concept of time,' she tuts. 'Keeping appointments is something that mere mortals do. She comes and goes as she pleases.'

'You'll have to start escorting me from my bedroom, then,' says a low voice from the door.

There she is, hotter than ever, in a crumpled grey T-shirt and lazy bedhead. Isobel pouts, but stirs two sugars into Kit's coffee and hands it over. Kit's eyes crinkle.

'Thanks, Isy.'

Kit turns her eyes on me, lips hovering over the lid.

'George. I've been looking forward to working with you.'

My heart dances pathetically.

'Let's crack on,' says Isobel, clapping twice like a Victorian headmistress. 'George, the only rule of rehearsals is that we're a team of equals. Though we each have songs we lead on, the songs belong to all of us. That's what makes them unique.'

Bronze Age have never credited me for my part in their songs. They're just attributed to Mickey. And I know they don't think of them as a free-for-all, because they never played the song I led on, 'I Choose You', after that last gig.

'We'll want you to lead on a song as soon as you're ready,' says Isobel.

'Oh, no, no, no, I don't write.'

I may have just about got over the thought of playing piano again – in this new George persona of mine – but composing my own songs is a whole other kettle of fishy memories.

'Don't worry,' says Kit, squeezing my tingling shoulder. 'If you're nervous, I can help.'

Hang on. Me and Kit, writing songs together? Alone? That would be… different enough from old Gina's past, surely? Make some *new* memories…

'There's no rush,' says Isobel quickly. 'We'll work on our old stuff first. But add your own George twist!'

I don't have time to worry about how I'm meant to add a George twist when she's only existed for a fortnight because we dive right in.

There's no written music, no timetable, no metronome. We just listen to each other and respond, playing by ear and then learning lines by heart. It should be frustrating and unprofessional and a complete mess. But instead it's… effortless. No time passes, just a flow of music and emotions.

With each song, I feel I'm getting to know them better. Kit is virtuosic in songs with a fast tempo, like 'Mercury' or 'Co-Star', but in 'Virgo in June', she barely experiments at all, only playing a quiet hi-hat, as if scared to mess it up. Isobel, on the other hand, inhabits all her lyrics so deeply, except for 'Mercury', where she shies away from the more explicit lines. Rudy brings a chaotic randomness to the proceedings, sometimes adding in brilliantly original riffs, sometimes taking a back seat with a dependable accompaniment. She seems equally comfortable in either role, though her energy fluctuates depending on her sugar levels.

I wonder: while I'm starting to understand them like this, what are they learning about George?

The only moment there's any bump is when we start rehearsing Rudy's song, 'Co-Star'. As much as I love the song, I feel as though I can't improvise around it when I don't know what the hell it's about.

When I confess, Rudy looks at me open-mouthed then says, 'I am about to change your life.'

Turns out Co-Star is an astrology app. It gives you 'accurate daily horoscopes'.

'They get the data from NASA,' she reassures me. Why the accuracy of the star positions would affect the insanity of the premise, I don't know.

But still, she asks for my phone to set it up for me. I hurriedly put it onto airplane mode before handing my phone over, in case Doug texts me or a calendar notification comes up. I pat myself on the back for having already had the forethought to change my wallpaper to something more neutral than Doug kissing the camera. Boyfriends really do get everywhere…

Rudy asks for my date and location of birth.

'Are you planning identity theft?' I joke, not that I'd know whose identity they were stealing at this point.

Everyone gathers round to read my horoscope.

'Ooh,' says Rudy. 'Looking at your chart is like looking at you naked.'

I wonder if I could look at Kit's.

'I *knew* you were a Libra,' says Isobel. I'm about to say that it's easy to know once it's written in front of you, but her face doesn't indicate any irony.

'Libra. The scales,' says Rudy. 'The sign of balance and imbalance. Always torn in two.'

'You're indecisive,' reads Isobel. 'You hate choosing sides.

'You'll do anything to avoid conflict,' adds Kit.

I fiddle with my shirt buttons.

Oh, come on. Gina doesn't believe in this! It's just ambiguity and confirmation bias!

But… what does George think? I still can't tell whether the whole 'queers believe in horoscopes' thing is serious, or an elaborate joke. Is it part of lesbian initiation? Like, one day you'll be scissoring and she'll whisper, 'Yes, it's all fake, don't tell the straights?'

'You got me,' I say, holding my hands up in mock defeat. 'I'm a contradictory people-pleaser, and I'm also good at weighing recipe ingredients.'

Rudy laughs and Isobel smiles. Kit carries on studying my chart.

Pretending to accidentally brush my arm against hers, I click onto my horoscope reading for the day.

It says: *Stop lying to yourself.*

All too soon, the door opens and the tattooed bartender I still call Cara Delevingne in my head looks apologetically at us.

'Sorry, guys, time for me to set up the bar.'

'Gracious, already?' says Isobel, like a ditzy starlet.

The bartender smiles lopsidedly, then spots me and waves. Remembering about the double cocktails, I wave back and am about to get my best terrible jokes ready to tell her. Dad used to do one about a failed opera singer who became a pirate. Why? To finally hit the high Cs.

But then Kit starts talking to me and I forget everything else.

'Hungry?' she asks. 'You free to get food?'

I mentally check Gina's calendar and confirm that Doug is out tonight before agreeing.

I know I said I'd ring my mum back, but I can hardly say to my cool new band, 'Oh, sorry, can I go talk about vegetable growing and my dog's bowels for an hour?'

So I leave Mum's texts unanswered. I stop feeling too guilty by promising myself I'll ring her tomorrow.

Damn, that means I'll have to ask Doug to move our Sunday routine around. God, knock-on effects are *stressful*. I feel like a butterfly flapping up a distant hurricane.

But twenty minutes later, we're sitting on the ground of a dodgy park in Hackney Wick, eating chips and battered onion rings. (I'm so used to Ferdinand at Cod Almighty knowing my order that I forgot to ask for my sauce to be on the side. Old Gina would be devastated.) The park is grotty and there are pigeons with mangled feet pecking all around us, but with Phase, it feels like heaven.

'So,' I ask, incredibly casually, 'how did you three meet?'

They all grin and look at each other in that way that couples do, working out who is going to tell the origin story.

'Coincidence, really,' says Kit.

'Fate,' corrects Isobel.

'We were at this mahoosive house party in Vauxhall,' says Rudy.

'One of Kit's ex-girlfriends was dating one of Rudy's ex-girlfriends,' explains Isobel, 'and they said we *had* to meet.'

I'm deeply alarmed by the queer habit of staying close with your exes.

'Our friend happened to have a few guitars at their house, so we started to play. And we had a lovely time—'

'But then *Marsha* turns up,' says Rudy, dramatically.

'I think Marsha's ex invited her too,' says Kit, sipping her Coke.

Isobel nods a single nod.

'Cassia,' she says. 'With the teeth.'

She steals one of Kit's chips. 'Anyway, without asking or anything, Marsha joins in. And she starts ordering us around.'

'"We're playing in A Major",' mimics Rudy, '"we're going to play in three, and it's going to be at eighty-three beats per minute".'

The three of them laugh, startling the mangy pigeons.

'But it worked,' shrugs Kit.

'Yeah, it did,' agrees Rudy. 'And then the whole party is calling for an encore and Marsha's like, "Give me your numbers, we are going to make this a thing".'

'Because she wanted to sleep with Kit, mainly,' says Isobel, disapprovingly.

Kit rolls her eyes. 'Stop being such a Catholic.'

Isobel tuts, but steals another chip from Kit's lap.

'And that was – ooh,' Rudy squeezes more ketchup, 'nine months ago?'

'God,' starts Kit, 'that's a long time.'

'A full pregnancy,' agrees Isobel.

'We've made a baby together,' swoons Rudy.

They all look lovingly at each other. I nibble at my spork.

'When Marsha left,' says Rudy, 'we didn't know if we'd carry on.'

'We could have stayed as a three,' says Isobel. 'We don't *need* a keyboard. Loads of bands just have lead guitar, bass, and drums.'

I nod, and then stop myself. Don't agree with them, idiot, they'll get rid of you.

'Then you showed up,' says Kit.

I look up and they're smiling at me.

'Your audition was like that party all over again,' says Rudy.

'Stars aligning,' Isobel agrees.

Kit's eyes gleam in the evening light. She raises a chip.

'To George. And the next phase of Phase.'

We all toast our chips together, repeat the phrase, and laugh.

Maybe I *can* belong here.

'When will we four meet again?' I ask. 'Do we have a standard rehearsal schedule?'

'Oh, Kit would never be able to commit to something like a routine,' teases Isobel.

'How about Wednesday?' Kit says, stretching luxuriously back on the grass.

But Wednesday is Gina's date night with Doug...

I'll have to apologize to him later. I'm sure he'll understand. Some change is good, anyway. Right? Mix things up.

I add it into our shared calendar.

'Wow, George, your calendar is *so* busy!' says Rudy, seeing my screen loaded with Douglas's calendar on top of mine.

'No, it's just me!' I stutter, 'I mean it's just *me*, that's just what I'm like. I put *everything* into my calendar, even chores...'

'Classic Libra,' says Isobel, winking.

But Rudy's frowning at my screen and I'm terrified that a notification from Doug will come up. God, I know I need to tell them about him at some point, but I don't want that to be the way they find out. If Kit saw a reminder pop up on my screen saying *Text your boyfriend :)* I'd die.

I surreptitiously go to my calendar settings.

I could just turn the notifications off... Doug wouldn't know, and it wouldn't affect me still being able to check it. I don't need the reminders any more anyway. I've been doing the same Gina routine for years. I know it all by heart.

So for the first time since Doug linked our calendars when we moved in together, I turn off my shared calendar notifications.

In the second afterwards, I half expect some kind of divine retribution. An earthquake or, at bare minimum, an eclipse. I think that's what Gina used to think would happen, without her calendar, in the months after her dad's funeral.

But nope, nothing. Just a crow, clapping its wings.

'Yeah,' I laugh, sliding my phone back into my jacket. 'Classic Libra.'

That night, I make sure I get home before Doug.

I take off my denim jacket and baggy shirt. I slip on my prettiest silky nightdress, the one Doug got me as a fourth anniversary present all those Aprils ago. (The theme for a fourth anniversary is silk and linen. I got him a sausage-dog tea towel). I go and get a plate of pre-bedtime Hobnobs ready and nestle into my spot in our bed.

When he gets back, he asks me how my rehearsal went and I say brilliantly. I ask him how his gig went, and he says brilliantly. We drunkenly waltz around the room and then fall into bed and have brilliant, unscheduled sex.

We do our favourite positions, in our favourite order, and, like always, finish together. We fall asleep smiling.

13

It's Wednesday, 4 p.m., and my last lesson of the day. Mousy Matilda Jennings.

I don't call her that because of her looks, although she does have mousy brown hair in two short bunches, bright white skin, and a (frankly adorable) gap between her two front teeth. No, I think of her as Mousy Matilda because she's the quietest living being I've ever encountered. She touches the piano so gently that it doesn't actually make a sound. It's a shame, because I think she might be quite good, but she can only be heard by certain species of bat.

As she cowers at the keys, I'm reminded of a pupil of my dad's. This girl was so terrified that I thought she'd been kidnapped and forced to play piano as an inventive torture weapon. But at the end of one hour with my dad, she was giggling and bashing away at the keys, making up for lost time.

Old Gina would have squashed down a memory like that and carried on with Matilda in silence. But now, since joining Phase and everything, I feel... Maybe I can change things for the better? Not just myself, but those around me too?

'Matilda,' I say quietly. She jumps. 'Did you know that the original Italian name for a piano is a *piano e forte*?'

She stares, wide-eyed.

'Do you know how to translate that?'

Matilda opens her mouth silently.

'I didn't catch that.'

'Soft and loud?' she lisps.

'That's right! Well done! So I think you've really mastered the *piano*, but how about you try a little more *forte*? Try playing one chord, as loudly as you can.'

She shudders.

'Go on, deafen me.'

The corners of her mouth point slightly upwards. Then she tenses her muscles and presses a chord.

It's *almost* loud enough for human ears to hear.

'Now *fortissimo*!'

She presses it again, pianissimo.

'And crescendo!'

Slightly louder.

'Crescendo!'

Slightly louder.

'Crescendo!'

Matilda slams both hands down in a loud, full, rich chord. Startled pigeons flap past the window. She plays it again, in a decadent arpeggio. The echo of it sings round the room for a long moment afterwards. I look at Matilda in amazement. She giggles one tiny giggle.

And for the first time in my life, I think that I could love teaching.

After Matilda leaves, I consider running to tell Alexa, but maybe she wouldn't approve of all this 'trying new things for the benefit of the kids' nonsense. I sit with the happy news by myself.

I became a teacher, not only because I couldn't perform any more, but to feel connected to my dad. But I haven't even been trying. If I want to be like him, it can't just be in name – it needs to be in how I teach too. I realize I've been so obsessed with how much I miss performing, and how much I miss him, I made it all about me. I'd never once thought about the impact I was having on the kids.

God, I'm always so selfish. He wouldn't be proud at all. He'd be disappointed.

Happy mood shattered as quickly as it came, I stare out of the grey window thinking: I should have stuck to the routine.

Kit brushes sweat from her forehead. We're in the final bars of 'Mercury' when she catches me looking. She holds my gaze across the rehearsal room, smiles lazily, spins her drumsticks in the air and brings them crashing down hard on the cymbals.

I take a long gulp of water, trying not to explode.

When I'm being George, I forget all my old doubts and shames. When I'm playing with Phase, I can't believe I've been denying myself this pleasure for so long. It feels so… natural.

But all too soon, the buzz-cut bartender is opening the door, telling us it's time to pack up. It helps buffer the disappointment of ending the rehearsal, to see her colourful crop tops and lopsided smile. In the back of my mind, I start planning how I'm going to phrase my drinks order joke to her…

'So, George,' says Isobel, when we're sitting in a booth

later that evening, 'now that you're officially part of the team, is there anything you think that we should improve?'

It feels like that bit at the end of an interview when they say, 'And do you have any questions for us?'

'Well,' I choke on my Witch, desperately searching my brain for inspiration. It lands on what Doug said the other day. 'Yes. About Phase's online presence. I get wanting to keep things live, but it's missing an opportunity. People want to be able to relive moments, share the songs with friends outside of London. You – we – could grow a fan base. It feels worth the compromise.'

The bar feels suddenly quiet.

'Or not,' I say.

But Isobel nods.

'I hadn't thought about it that way. It does make us inaccessible.'

'Also, we're super cute,' says Rudy, chewing the lemon from her drink. 'We'd get *loads* of girls following us.'

We look at Kit, the deciding vote. She shrugs.

'Let's give it a go.'

Looks like having a boyfriend could help me in Phase after all.

Watching Rudy create the Phase profiles, I thank my stars that Gina's social media accounts are private and difficult to find, because she's a teacher who doesn't want to be cyberbullied by her pupils. There's no fear of being discovered.

I also realize this is probably the first Wednesday evening I haven't spent with Douglas in four years.

Kit's knee brushes against mine under the table. Is it OK for me to brush back? Platonically?

I brush back.

Her whole leg is against mine…

'Hellooo?' repeats Rudy, 'Earth to George?'

'Sorry?'

'Are you a gold star?' she grins.

Is that another horoscope thing?

'We all are,' says Isobel.

'Well,' I bluff, 'you saw my Co-Star chart.'

Kit's knee against mine hesitates.

'Oh,' giggles Rudy, 'I missed the bit where it said that you've never slept with a man.'

I spill my drink down myself.

They all laugh as I dash off to the bar for a towel.

Great. Now I've managed to lie to my boyfriend about being straight, and lie to Phase about being a lesbian.

I'll go back and confess. Say, actually, I'm bi, and I have a boyfriend, and that's that. Clear up multiple messes at once.

Unfortunately, asking for a tissue is not the conversation I'd planned to have with the bartender, so I have no bad jokes prepared on the topic. But when I catch her eye, she smiles.

'Oh, hello Doubles!'

Then she blinks her big green eyes in shock and covers her mouth. 'Oh my God, I'm so sorry! It's just that I don't know your name so I… I'm so embarrassed, please forget I said anything.'

'No! No, it's…'

I can feel my usual blush forming, but in delight. I'm about to tell her that I have given her a nickname in my head too, when – thankfully – I stop myself just in time. Obviously, giving people a nickname related to their order must be something she does for all of The Familiar's customers. God, could my ego *be* any bigger?

'It's fine,' I say, giving her a truly cringeworthy thumbs up. 'Good customer service!'

Her smile falters.

'Right, right,' she says, looking around as if wishing there were other customers to give her an excuse to leave. There aren't. With no other option, she turns back to me.

'I'm Cara,' she says, and my jaw must drop.

'No way?'

Cara blinks a few times, then says, 'If you're making another joke, I don't get it.'

'No! No, it's just mad because ever since I first saw you I've been thinking about how much you look like Cara Delevingne.'

We look at each other uncertainly again, and then she smiles that adorable lopsided grin.

'I'm George,' I say, more confident than I feel, reaching over the bar to shake her hand. 'But you can call me Doubles.'

Cara laughs and is about to take my hand when she must realize her hands are sticky. In the time it takes for her to wipe them strenuously on her apron, Kit appears at my shoulder.

Surprised, I remove my hand from mid-air over the bar. In the same moment, Cara reaches out hers. With mine gone, she retracts it again, trying to style it out like she was picking up a glass, but there's no glass there.

Oh God. My blush returns with vengeance. I wish I could evaporate.

But Kit didn't seem to notice. She asks, nonchalantly,

nudging the bar stool with her foot, 'George, do you want to come to mine? Pick up those shirts?'

I glance back at Cara, who is not looking at me, but pointlessly moving a lemon to a different compartment. I'm sure she heard.

Umm... Is Kit asking me back to her place? Cara takes her lemon to the far other side of the bar. Kit ruffles her hair, a hint of her pine cologne reaching me. I turn my full attention to her, wondering how I can say yes without saying yes.

'I live very close by,' she adds, dark eyes glittering. 'I can get you there in fifteen seconds.'

Flashes of her singing the sexually explicit chorus to 'Mercury' flash unhelpfully in my mind.

'I'm not *that* gullible, Kit.'

Kit confidently reaches her hand out towards me to shake on the bet.

I scoff and take it. A distant lemon falls to the floor.

Kit holds on tight and drags me away, knocking over a bar stool in our wake.

'Fifteen,' she shouts, 'fourteen, thirteen...'

She pulls me across the dark road laughing, barely stopping to check for traffic.

'Five, four, three...'

There are no houses here.

'One,' she says, triumphant, placing my hand on the bonnet of a large silver van.

'A van? No fair!' I laugh, panting. 'That's cheating!'

She shrugs smugly and pulls keys from a ring chain clipped to her jeans. She opens up the back doors.

'Home sweet home.'

*

I don't know what I would have expected if you told me Kit lived in a converted van, but it wouldn't have been this.

It's a bohemian Tardis. Everything is covered in a patterned rug or cushion, each in seemingly authentic abstract prints from across the globe. It smells of Kit's pine-tree cologne and weed, and breathing it in makes me feel high, though I'm not sure which part.

One wall is a tiny kitchen, with sink, cupboard and mini fridge. But the majority of the space is taken up by the bed, which is covered in fur blankets and scattered pillows. A handmade cross hangs above it. I wonder if that's a gift from Isobel?

'Renovated it myself,' Kit says, knocking on the wood affectionately. 'I like feeling that I can move around. Not settle anywhere for too long.'

I thought that now I was in Phase, I had plenty of time to get to know Kit. You know, to slowly become good, comfortable, platonic friends… But looking around I realize she could take off with no warning.

'How long have you been in London?'

She blinks, trying to work it out.

'Couple of years, now, I guess,' she says surprised. Her fingers fidget to her cigarette pocket. 'Since Phase started, I've basically stuck on this street. Jeesh.'

'Where were you before that?'

'Isy and I lived together for a bit after college.' She smiles to herself. 'It was like being married to your most annoying mate.'

I wistfully imagine living with Soph. At uni we'd made sure

to be in adjoining rooms near the rest of the Bronze Age gang, but when we moved to London it felt like the natural, grown-up thing to move in with Doug.

'Why move out then?' I ask Kit. 'Why the van?'

'Privacy, I guess,' she says, not meeting my eye. 'Independence. I felt like I couldn't invite people over.'

I flush.

'And I was blocking her from meeting, like, a saintly nun to marry. So I moved out.'

She doesn't continue, so I prompt, 'Do you prefer it? Living like this?'

'Sure,' she says exhaling smoke. 'We have more freedom now. But...'

She glances at me and exhales, deciding whether to say something or not.

'Recently I've wondered if it would feel good to have someone... Someone that made you feel more settled. Put down roots. Make a home.'

She swallows hard. My breathing hitches.

'George,' she says, mahogany eyes flickering at me, 'I know we only just met, but... I feel like I can... I can talk to you about...'

'You can tell me anything,' says George quietly. 'Anything.'

Her eyes meet mine and, for a moment, I think I understand her. I think she's saying that she feels this thing between us too, and suddenly sleeping around with no strings attached doesn't seem as appealing. She's saying, maybe we could be different.

But then it's as if she loses her nerve. She shakes her head.

'I'm glad we're mates,' she says, and puts out her cigarette.

She gets up and stalks around the van, half-heartedly tidying away a mug, a plate. She only has one of each. I'm left reeling from her confusing confession – does she want us to be *more* than friends, or more strictly *just* friends?

I want us to be friends, I remind myself. I'm not *allowed* the former.

I ask, platonically, 'Does your van have a name?'

Kit looks at me sideways.

'It's a Ford Transit.'

'No,' I snort, 'I mean, like, a pet name.'

'Oh...' I still don't think she gets it, but she says, 'What do you think I should call it?'

'Van Morrison?'

There's a split second where I think I've put my foot in it forever, but then she laughs. Like, an actual giggle. I feel delirious.

Platonic platonic.

'Van Morrison it is.'

Kit kneels by the bed, pulling out a storage drawer. I see everything she's collected, like a monster under the bed – battered maps and zines, unzipped bags and tangled wires. She rummages for shirts.

'Kit, are you sure it's OK for me to have these?' I say, trying to brush her arm casually against mine. 'It's very generous.'

'It's nothing. I never wear them. Some of them aren't even mine.' She examines a crumpled top and shakes her head. 'No idea who left this here.'

I will burn that.

She unceremoniously passes the pile to me.

'Do you want to check they fit?'

'What, here?'

It's an open-plan metal box, there's nowhere I could exactly change behind.

She raises an eyebrow at me.

'I could turn around?'

'Oh, sure.'

I wish I wasn't so flustered.

'You'd look good in this one,' she says, picking out a short-sleeved flannel.

She turns her back and I unbutton Doug's shirt. What if Kit turns around while I'm in a state of undress? (What if she doesn't?)

I leave hers unbuttoned for a second longer than strictly necessary, in case she does want to turn around and look at my best bra.

Nope.

So then her shirt is on. I feel like I'm trying on a prom dress in front of my date. I cough nervously. She looks around.

Her eyes roam slowly from my face down my body. Then her fingers reach delicately towards my neck. She takes both sides of the fabric round my collar, pulls them together, looks into my eyes, and does my top button up.

I can't breathe. Her proximity, her cologne... And the shirt is too tight. It's choking me quite a bit, but I don't say anything. My hair is still tucked in, so I reach to pull it out, but Kit gently stays my hand.

'It looks good short,' she says, surveying her handiwork. 'You look more *you*.'

14

'Soph, I want a makeover. Make me look gay.'

She screams down the phone.

'A dykeover! *Finally!* Oh, you are lucky you know me! This is going to be so fun. We can have a consultation about your vibe, your budget, your pain threshold, and – wait! Is Douglas OK with all this? How did it go speaking to him?'

I barely miss a beat.

'Everything is fine. What should I do to prepare?'

'First things first,' she squeals. 'You get to have your First Gay Haircut.'

I end up at a unisex barbers full of sincere hairdressers with pronoun badges and shaved heads. I've never really trusted a barber who has no hair themselves but I ramble for a preposterously long time to my bald hairdresser, Zee, about the kind of person I want to look like. About how I need to look with Doug, with my mum, with Liberty, and with Phase.

'So...' Zee squints at me. 'Half the time you want to be a goody two shoes professional straight girl, and half the time you're a creative-scene lesbian?'

'Er. Yes,' I say. 'Exactly. Have you ever made someone look like that?'

Zee switches on an industrial razor.

'All the time, honey.'

An hour later, I pay Zee a lot of money and then cry in a nearby loo.

I sneak home – wearing a hat – and examine the damage in the mirror.

Thing is, I've had exactly the same straight shoulder-length hair as my mum all my life. I know it's silly, but even getting a couple of inches taken off the bottom would have been pretty traumatic. And this is quite a bit more than 'a couple of inches off the bottom'.

But the more I actually look at it, the more I think I might *like* this haircut. Both of them.

Because Zee has, through barbering wizardry, given me a haircut with two completely different modes.

The Gina style is a simple, straight, fringed bob, stopping just below my chin. It's feminine but fun, fresh and youthful. My mum is going to hate it at first, obviously, and take it as a personal affront, but I think in time it will get her grudging acceptance. I look *pretty*.

Lift up the bob, tie it up into a messy topknot on the top of my head, and see that the entire underneath of my head is shaved, clippered to about ten millimetres, like stubble, and the back of my hairline is buzzed into a sharp V, pointing to the line of freckles and moles I used to be so self-conscious about. This is The George.

I take two post-haircut selfies: one Gina, one George.

I send the former to Doug and my mum, the latter to the Phase group chat. The only person who gets to see both is Soph.

She types, *omg u just levelled up in gay. like, u didn't even get one queer haircut, you got TWO!*

Everyone except my mum replies immediately, saying they love it – though I wonder how Doug will react when he discovers the shaved undercut. I can't keep that a secret from him forever. Unless I insist he never touches my head again? Pretend I have nits? Always?

Then Mum calls me and I know I have to pick up or she'll ring the police.

'Ginny? Hello? Are you having a breakdown?'

'Hi, Mum,' I say, checking again that I didn't send her the photo of George's undercut. 'No, I'm not. Are you?'

'I barely hear from you in weeks and then you cut all your hair off? A bob? A *bob*? What on earth is happening to you?'

Oops. I've now missed our usual weekend calls a few times. Truth is, I've been scared about ringing her, because I don't want to accidentally reveal anything to do with my George life and have to come out to her.

But this bold haircut is giving me new-found confidence.

'I do actually have some news…'

'Oh no,' she says darkly, 'I hate news.'

'It's not bad news.'

'All news is bad news to me,' she sighs. 'Oh, go on then, rip the plaster off.'

I try to inject fresh pep into my voice. 'I'm in a band!'

'Oh! Oh, that's *wonderful*! Bronze Age asked you back?'

'No, Mum, not Bronze Age. A girl band! In fact, it's a les—'

'But Douglas is still in Bronze Age?'

'Yes, Mum, Doug is still in Bronze Age, and I'm now in a different band, called Phase.'

'Fazed? As in disturbing? It's not one of those heavy metal bands, is it?'

'No, Mum. Phase as in, you know, a cycle. Like the moon. Something that changes.'

'Like that phrase "Just a phase?" Like they say about *bisexuelles*?'

This throws me. I wasn't expecting her to be the one to bring up queerness, nor for her to know about that cliché, nor indeed, for her to pronounce 'bisexual' like it's a kind of disease.

'Umm,' I say, trying to analyse her tone, 'yes, kind of?'

'But Fazed are not actually bisexuelles?'

'Umm,' I hesitate, 'not exactly. But Mum, it's not pronounced like that.'

'Fine, fine, *Phase* then. Ginny, are Phase these modern BLT types?'

Panic rises in my throat. She definitely, definitely sounds critical. I think of Soph crying into my shoulder about coming out to her parents, how she's never seen them again.

I don't want to do that to myself, and I also don't want to do that to my mum. I'm the only family she has left. Well, apart from Bunny. But Bunny isn't being relied upon to give her grandchildren.

I can't do this. I can't come out to her.

'No, Mum,' I lie, 'they're a-a normal band.'

She rambles on, not noticing my huge locked closet.

'I still don't understand why you quit Bronze Age. You

seemed to enjoy it so much. They could have waited for a few months for you to – to sort yourself out, surely?'

Mum knows, I'm certain, why I quit the band – how could she not? – but it's like she can't stop herself from guilt-tripping me.

'At least you're still connected to the band through Douglas,' she continues. 'That's *something* to remind you of happier times, isn't it? It's such a relief for me to know that you have someone so constant in your life. It's a blessing to have another half, like him. You stay grateful for him, you hear me?'

Shame shame, guilt guilt – I make up an excuse to hang up.

Instead of saying goodbye, she says, 'Don't worry, pumpkin, hair grows back.'

On Thursday afternoon in the performing arts smoking area, I want to provoke a reaction from Alexa, so I turn to her and flash the shaved undercut beneath my new Gina bob.

Her expression doesn't change. She just carries on chewing her strawberry lace.

'Did you and Douglas break up?'

'No.'

She continues on her infinite lace.

'It doesn't look as bad as I'd have expected,' she says, offering me a sweet. When I shake my head, she consolingly offers me a cigarette instead.

'Have any of the kids seen it?'

'Yes, actually. I accidentally tied it up when the room got stuffy and Timmy called me Sir.'

'Problematic,' agrees Alexa.

'He was very embarrassed afterwards. I quite liked it.'

'Maybe I should tell Year Nine to call *me* Sir,' she ponders. 'They might respect me more.'

'The others have only seen the bob. Percy said I looked "very modern, if I didn't mind him saying so".'

'Of course he did.'

'And Matilda said she liked it.'

'*Mousy Matilda?*' gasps Alexa, lace hanging from her mouth in shock.

'Yeah.'

'I thought she was a mute.'

'It's the first time I've heard her speak without significant prompting, certainly.'

'Huh,' says Alexa.

'We actually had a really good lesson. She played louder than mezzo.'

'Huh,' says Alexa, a strawberry lace still hanging from her lips.

The bell goes. Alexa lifts up a hunk of my hair and examines the undercut, then lets it flop down again.

She slurps up the end of the lace and gives a final 'Huh'. We part ways.

'Keep your eyes closed!'

Soph guides me to stand in front of her full-length mirror, after a full day of shopping and prepping.

'Ta da!'

Soph's tied my hair up into its messy topknot and revealed the undercut. I'm wearing new glasses instead of my usual contacts: they're those huge, round, silver-framed ones that every hipster wears. In the end, Soph removed my basic make-up, but somehow combed (?) my eyebrows (?) to make them look cooler (?). She also removed the nail polish from my nails and clipped them short. New piercings, still stinging, are ranged along the cuff of my left ear. I'm wearing Kit's navy corduroy shirt (I didn't tell Soph the origin), new 'boyfriend' jeans (ignore the irony), and Soph's old black Doc Martens.

Finally. Here she is. Here is George.

'I *love* her!'

'You don't have to talk about yourself in third person,' says Soph, squeezing my bun.

We go for a drink at The Familiar to celebrate. For the first time, I don't pay the straight fee.

Two of *SophieSnob*'s fans come up to us, and when they show us pictures of their pet cats, I find them genuinely cute.

I order both of us 'double' Bad Witches from Cara, and she seems to have forgiven me for leaving her hanging when we introduced ourselves the other night. In fact, she notices and compliments each part of my new look. I compliment her tattoos in return, patting myself on the back for recognising the pansexual flag colours she has in a heart shape under her collarbone. I'm rewarded with her lopsided grin.

Finally, I feel like I belong in a gay bar.

I have perfected the art of getting home just before Doug.

I carefully put my shirt, jeans, and Docs away. I change my sports bra and boxers for lacey pink lingerie, and put on a flowery blue 'going out to Dane's' dress. Put my contacts in, my make-up on – and straighten out my bob to completely hide the shaved undersides.

Looking at the transformation in the mirror I know there must be something wrong with me, because I honestly can't tell which one is the true me.

'Doug!' I squeal happily when he gets back.

'Gina!' he squeals back.

Then we have brilliant unscheduled sex – and I definitely think about him the whole time.

Double lives are fun!

15

Double lives are not fun.

It's Saturday night, and I'm planning to go to The Familiar with Soph and her L friends.

I message the Phase group chat to ask if they'll be there, looking forward to showing Kit my new lewk. But Rudy replies saying that they're busy: they're all going to see Kehlani. Rudy apologizes about how they booked the tickets ages ago and it's now sold out or they would have invited me, but I'm not so sure. It's like Bronze Age all over again. I wonder if Marsha will be there instead of me...

Later, drinking our Bad Witches and idly watching Polly Amory do an unusual trick with her magic wand, the question of whether Kit and Marsha still sleep together takes me out of the Ls' conversation. I tune in when I hear Lin say, 'Bi people are the most privileged queers.'

They shout over the rest of the table's boos.

'It's just a fact. Privilege is about choices. Bisexuals by definition have more choice than fully gay people. They can opt in on heteronormative privileges. A lesbian can't choose *not* to get assaulted in the street for kissing her girlfriend.'

'But what if a bi woman falls in love with a woman?' says Leighlah.

Lin shrugs. 'She can just change her Tinder settings.'

'Wow, romantic,' says Soph, then goes into *SophieSnob* mode. 'Stop erasing bi-erasure. In the media, at least they're starting to normalise gay and lesbian lives. But bi characters are still the same one-dimensional, hyper-sexual, "greedy" cheaters. Usually sociopaths. Or not there at all.'

I wish *I* could be not here at all. I sip at my half-empty Witch, pretending to be absorbed in Willy Nilly's camp soliloquy with a rainbow skull. As usual, I'm sure the others don't notice my absence from the conversation.

It's all so confusing. Before I came out of my own closet, I thought of myself as a good ally. Through Soph, I thought I knew the woke points of view I was meant to hold. But the more time I spend in queer spaces, the less I'm certain about. Some think *everyone* is bi to varying degrees, some think no one is, because the word implies only two genders. Some think queers are 'born this way', others think identities are constantly in flux. Some want to be treated the same as straights, some want to preserve queer difference. Campaign for gay marriage, overthrow marriage completely. And they all seem to feel so *passionately* about it all. Meanwhile, I'm just a stereotype of an indecisive bisexual, not even sure I'm allowed to call myself that.

'Let's not play a game of who is the most oppressed,' moans Lucy. 'Can we *please* give ourselves one night off having to be so bloody earnest and self-aware? Let's have a dance!'

'Loads of people must be out there,' says *SophieSnob*, ignoring her, 'with these queer identities they don't even realize because there aren't role models. They think they must be one or the other because the world's so obsessed with binaries. Even in the queer community.'

'Len, you're non-binary,' says Leighlah, 'it makes no sense for you to be biphobic. Just because your ex is now happily dating a dude.'

Lucy catches my eye across the table. She rolls her eyes at the conversation and tilts her head invitingly towards the dance floor.

So then we forget the theory and we dance. Platonically, obviously. And Tegan and Sara is playing, and the lights are flashing pink, and I think maybe the evening isn't going so badly after all. I even attempt a head-flick-hair-toss – though given that most of George's hair is shaved, the effect is probably more like a violent twitch.

'Drink!' shouts Lucy into my ear, but doesn't go get one. Hmm. A basically engaged girl probably shouldn't be buying a drink for another girl in a gay bar. But I *happen* to spot that Cara's on duty, and swear her green eyes are watching us from across the room.

'Back in a second,' I shout, and Lucy replies with a seductive shimmy.

'Hey, Cara.'

She carries on wiping the bar. If I didn't know better, I'd think she was in a strop with me. Is she still cross about me not shaking her hand when Kit surprised us?

'Hey, Cara,' I shout, louder.

'What do you want?' she snaps.

'Oh, right. Sorry. Two Bad Witches?'

I don't dare to make the usual doubles joke. Cara, seemingly in response to its absence, starts to throttle the cocktail shaker.

'Cara, are you—'

A slinky arm wraps around my shoulders. Lucy says breathlessly into my cheek, 'What's taking you so long?'

Cara slams the glasses down on the bar.

Lucy seems not to notice, clinking our Witches together and perching on a bar seat. She taps the one next to her.

'Enjoy!' Cara spits.

What have I done wrong? What am I about to do wrong? I want to apologize to everyone and everything, but I'm not quite sure what for.

I'm desperate for some kind of deus ex machina to save me. The opposite happens. Over Lucy's eyelashes, I see in the doorway, an unmistakable flash of long red hair and creamy, tattooed arms.

Poppy. Poppy is in The Familiar.

Shit fuck shit fuck.

Instinctively, I hide my face with my hand.

What's she *doing* here? Soph couldn't have seen her here before, or she would have told me. At the very least, she would have wanted to claim her five pound university bet on Poppy's sexuality.

But I don't have time to be curious about whether Poppy's here as an ally or on the pull. She cannot see me looking like George. She'd tell Doug. Not that I'm doing anything wrong exactly but...

Lucy giggles and removes my hand from my face.

'There's no need to be shy,' she says.

I imagine being Poppy, walking in to a gay bar to see my old, practically married friend, in a 'gay disguise', drinking with a girl in a rainbow miniskirt. Sure would *look* like I'm doing something wrong.

I grip Lucy's shoulders to use her like a human shield to block the view between me and Poppy. Lucy misinterprets, giggles happily, and mirrors the gesture. She tilts her face and closes her eyes.

Behind the bar, a glass drops onto the floor.

Damn it, damn it, damn it, why can't I do anything right? Maybe I *am* a greedy, cheating sociopath – without even getting to snog anyone.

Poppy walks behind a group of leather butches, disappearing from view. I've got to make a dash for it. I'm about to sprint away when I see Cara's face in the mirror behind the bar. Her crushed expression. Did *I* really do that? I've messed up everything, again.

'Sorry, Lucy, I can't do this,' I say loudly and try to leave. But Lucy snatches my hand.

'Why?' she demands. 'Soph told me you don't have a girlfriend.'

Long red hair resurfaces at the other end of the bar, coming towards us.

'I—'

I need to go *now*. But Cara's eyes catch mine and a blush forms along my neck. I feel so ashamed about lying to her (and Kit and Soph and Doug and Lucy and Poppy), but I don't know how to say it in a way that's quick or truthful enough.

So I just say, 'Sorry, I have no idea what I'm doing.'

And then I run away.

This is when I make another idiotic mistake.

I should have just got a taxi, but normally Soph and I

share and, seeing as it wasn't late, I find myself walking to the Tube.

I try to buoy myself up from the shock of seeing Poppy and generally being a contemptible person by listening to an upbeat *SophieSnob* playlist: 'LOUD N PROUD'.

I'm entering the carriage when I suddenly realize why I'm still on edge. I've never been outside of queer safe spaces looking like George. And boy, do strangers look differently at George than they do at Gina.

George's shaved hair, double denim and Docs, lack of make-up, self-assured posture and glittery rainbow badges are being stared at by a pack of drunk men. One nearby, with a black eye and jiggling leg, openly eyes me up and down. Like I'm a freak.

The hairs at the back of my neck prickle. I sit as far away from them as I can and pull out my receptionless phone, turning off my music but keeping my headphones in as some kind of pointless armour. I can tell that they're talking about me, but not exactly what they're saying.

There's a pair of women at the far end of this carriage, but would they do anything if something happened? I don't know if it's my imagination, but the group of men seem to be circling closer to my seat.

The tracks rumble, my heartbeat pounds in my ears.

At the next stop, I casually get up and walk out, feeling all their eyes on my back.

I weave through the crowd. Then I step back, into a carriage that's empty except for texting teenagers.

I let down my hair, so that the bob curls round my red cheeks, shove my denim jacket into my bag and undo the buttons of my shirt to show my black bralet and navel. I rummage for dangling earrings and red lipstick, which I apply shakily but thickly. I can't tell if I'm closer to crying or shouting or throwing up.

When Gina steps out to the escalators, a man with a black eye and a jiggling leg eyes her up and down and wolf whistles.

At three o'clock in the morning, having not slept, my phone lights up. I squint at it through puffy eyes. A private message from Kit.

btw your hair looks really good short x

I read, reread, and re-reread the message. Then I gently place the phone back, face down, on my bedside table, and snuggle into Doug's sleeping warmth.

It's all been worth it.

16

'Gina?' says Doug. 'Gina.'

I look up guiltily from my phone.

'Sorry, sorry, I was just – checking with Phase about – about what we have planned for rehearsals next week.'

I mean, I kind of was. I was texting Kit about her horoscope.

It's Sunday night date night and Doug's trying really hard not to look annoyed with how little attention I've been paying him. I put my phone face down on the table away from us, and resolve to make more of an effort.

Doug's even using the fancy silver service set Mum got him as a joke. He lifts one of the domes to reveal home-made spaghetti meatballs. I squeal.

To think I almost cancelled Dougina's date night to go to the pub with Phase! Ever since Phase went to that gig without me, I've felt this panic about not being present enough in Kit's mind. We've been texting a bit, sometimes on the group chat and sometimes on a private one (!), but she still hasn't seen George's new look in person, and I'm increasingly desperate to know her reaction.

Meanwhile, Doug's meatballs are delicious. Have I no

shame? He's also chosen for us to watch Disney's *Lady and the Tramp*. I know it's not exactly the most challenging film in the world, but those 2D dogs tug at my heartstrings more than any 4D human ever could. It will always have a special place in my heart because…

'This is the film we watched on the night we officially got together.' As I speak, Doug puts on the 'Bella Notte' song from the famous spaghetti kiss scene. I laugh along.

'Do you remember, we had spaghetti that night too? Because we were talking about how difficult it would be to recreate that kiss, and then you tried and spilled it everywhere.'

Doug offers me a fork of spaghetti and at the end of it, he kisses me. Just like he did seven Aprils ago.

'Happy Seven-Year Anniversary,' he says.

My mouth falls open, revealing half-eaten pasta.

His blue eyes crinkle and he clinks his wine glass to mine. No.

No no no no *no*! I do *not* forget things like this. My calendar sends me reminders.

But I turned off notifications so they wouldn't pop up in front of Phase.

And I haven't been checking my calendar because I thought I knew it by heart.

Oh, shit!

Doug is holding another of the fancy silver domes.

'For the seven-year anniversary, the traditional theme is Wool and Copper, so…'

He lifts the lid to reveal a beautifully wrapped present in copper paper, tied with wool.

Oh *fuck*, why is he so nice?

He's watching me attentively. I take the parcel and unwrap it. It's a thick, soft, copper-coloured scarf.

'I knitted it for you,' he says, his glasses fogging up bashfully. 'I've been doing it on my commutes so that you wouldn't see. It took quite a long time, but I wanted to make sure it was cosy enough.'

He lifts it out and ties it around my neck.

'It suits you,' he says, using it to pull me towards him.

I think about Kit, buttoning my shirt.

Doug strokes my cheek in a line so habitual I find it almost painfully comforting.

'Thank you,' I say. 'I'll never take it off.'

I kiss him for a long time, partly because I'm enjoying it, partly out of thanks for my gift, and increasingly because I'm trying to buy more time.

When we pull away, Doug looks at me expectantly.

'Well...' I should tell the truth. Lies are bad. 'I am so sorry, Fluffy, but...'

He looks crestfallen. It's like kicking a puppy while wearing steel-toed boots. I can't do it.

'... your present hasn't arrived in the post yet.'

OK, he still looks like a kicked puppy, but now only while I'm wearing sandals. Lies are good.

'Luckily,' I add, madly, 'it's not the only thing I got you. I also wanted to give you... something... Which is in the bedroom.'

'A sexy thing?' says Doug, hopefully.

'No,' I say, then curse myself. That would have been a lot easier to fake.

'Actually yes, there's some of that. But I need to give you something physical too.'

Doug cheers up.

'Yes please, you can give me something physical!' he calls, while I'm running up to the bedroom.

Oh God, it's our seven-year anniversary, *and* I'd forgotten that we missed our sex slot last Sunday because I was so sick from my hangover. I've been way too distracted by George's life. I need to get back on Gina, back on my calendar, back on my boyfriend.

I look desperately around the bedroom. Why the hell did I promise him something from here? The problem with everything in our bedroom is that we already own it.

Fuck fuck fuck.

What was it Doug said? Wool and copper. Wool and copper. Wool and... copper!

I hastily pick up an old jewellery box Mum gave me ages ago, containing a family ring. I chuck the ring into a drawer, but keep the bed of cotton wool. Then I grab my wallet and transfer the parts while I'm running down the stairs.

'I followed the wool and copper theme too,' I gasp. 'We are so in sync. Happy Seven-Year Anniversary.'

I hand him the ring box. My desire to overcompensate almost makes me go down on one knee, but I manage to stop myself.

He looks at me curiously, then opens the box. Inside is a two-pence coin.

He says after a moment, 'Well, you didn't bankrupt yourself.'

I'm sweating.

'Do you remember when I used to always flip a coin to help me make decisions?'

Doug nods, frowning.

'This is the coin I flipped, to decide whether or not to ask you out. It's funny, it, er, it actually came out tails. The coin said I shouldn't. But I flipped it again, because I knew I wanted to ask you out anyway. Best decision I ever made.'

Doug is still looking down at the coin. He's seen through me. It's literally worthless. *I'm* literally worthless.

'This is the most wonderful gift I've ever been given,' sobs Doug. 'Thank you.'

Oh no. This is worse.

'I love you so much,' he says, and kisses me again.

I'm never, ever going to tell him that I can't tell the change in my wallet apart. I might have given that specific coin away years ago, who knows. Please, God, let that gift coin be minted over seven years ago.

I excuse myself to the loo. My stomach is all twisted, like the spaghetti has got all tangled up in there; guilt in many different flavours.

Kit's sent me a meme of a cat playing the piano. My face still blank, I respond with two lines of 'ha ha's. I wonder if Kit has ever celebrated an anniversary with someone...

When I return, Doug has brought out pudding: a plate of seven chocolate Hobnobs with the number 7 iced on them. He snuggles into me on the sofa and starts the film. He's going to sing along to the Disney theme music.

There it is.

I wonder if Kit likes Disney – maybe ironically?

Doug kisses my nose. I think about how Kit would never kiss my nose.

Doug picks up two biscuits, different ways round, and passes one to me. I turn mine upside down so that the chocolate is on the top and cheers his. I think about how—

Stop thinking about Kit, for *God's* sake! I have the most incredible person right here in front of me, and he's *mine*, and he *loves* me.

So why do I care so much about some stranger's opinion of me? Isn't it basically cheating, to be thinking about her so much? And does that mean I shouldn't be with him any more? But how could I be so cruel and stupid as to leave him when he's the perfect boyfriend?

Then the film is over and Doug is asking me what on earth is wrong, and I have to pretend that I'm crying because of the sad pound scene from the film and Doug nods and starts crying too.

'Let's not do any of the sexy anniversary stuff tonight,' sniffs Doug. 'It would feel disrespectful to dogs who are put down.'

I nod.

'We can save it for next year,' he jokes.

He puts the coin I gave him into his wallet, next to a photo of me taken six years ago. I hang up his scarf in our closet.

17

Before I know it, it's the day of our first Phase performance, at The Familiar (of course). What if I get stage fright? What if I forget how to play? Worse, what if I look ugly?

Doug's already out with Bronze Age. It's a new kind of synchronisation, to both have gigs on the same night like this. But it's weird that, apart from seeing Poppy across The Familiar, I haven't seen Bronze Age in weeks. (Soph refuses to believe Poppy was there, thinks I made her up as an excuse to run away from Lucy. Maybe I did?)

After The Night of Mickey's Homophobia, I retreated from Bronze Age's Saturday gigs because I wanted to leave them to work it out between themselves, stop intruding. But then Phase started filling my time. I've even 'temporarily' removed the weekly Dane's trip from my side of the calendar.

Sure, it's a weight off my shoulders, to not sit through the memories inspired by their gig every week. But it's sad they clearly don't miss me. I wonder if they even notice I'm not there any more.

Mum messages.

AREWECALLINGASUSUAL?

Is it 'as usual' when I've missed it for a month? I'm scared she'll start criticising 'bisexuelles' again and I won't respond in the right way. I don't know what the right way even is, so I make up another excuse and add it to my growing pile of guilt.

I go back and forth, trying to decide which of Kit's shirts to wear for the gig. Approximately two hours later and I'm more unsure than when I started.

I open up the Co-Star app for advice.

My horoscope reads: *Today is today.* Thank you so much, NASA.

I scroll down to the list of advice:

Do: Wear that pink corduroy shirt / Be honest / Question things

Don't: Pussyfooting / Zorb / Question things

Spooked, I pick out Kit's pinkest shirt – a blushing rose colour that looks OK as long as I don't actually blush. I don't have any plans to go Zorbing today, which is a relief. Then I question what pussyfooting means (I'm careful to avoid Urban Dictionary). OK, so I shouldn't be 'non-committal or avoidant'.

Perfect.

'See you after the interval folks,' sings Polly Amory, to the whooping crowd. 'You won't want to miss our Headline act – or ogle their new debutante!'

Standing at The Familiar's backstage side entrance, their new debutante is about to throw up.

Pre-show anticipation didn't always feel like this, did it? George's stomach is fluttering with a whole butterfly sanctuary of pent-up nerves and excitement and thirst to prove herself. But Gina's remembering her final Bronze Age performance, how, the last time she performed, she vowed never to do it again. George's happy butterflies are drowning in Gina's waves of dread.

How did I end up back here? After all this time, am I still that self-obsessed show-off, debasing my morals to prance around on a stage? What would my dad think?

Rudy squeezes my shoulders. 'George, you have no reason to be nervous. Once we're playing, you'll forget everyone else.'

She reaches out her little finger in the air between us. The others roll their eyes affectionately, interlocking pinkies. I drag my sweaty hand up to meet theirs.

'Repeat after me,' says Rudy solemnly. 'We are not just a Phase.'

'We are not just a Phase,' we say, with varying levels of sincerity.

'We are a family,' says Rudy.

I swallow down the lump in my throat and meet their eyes.

'We are a family,' we say.

'A cool and sexy family.'

We all laugh and break away, joshing each other. Kit stamps her cigarette out and, with a final flick of her curls, Isobel pushes open the door.

'It's showtime, girls.'

The three of them catwalk into the bar. Then there's me, in my new undercut and glasses, Soph's Docs, and Kit's shirt. I feel like a gay Frankenstein's monster. The whole bar turns to watch us. I trip multiple times.

Then it all happens so quickly. Queen Polly is introducing us and we're stepping onto the stage. Blinded by pink spotlights and the shimmer from the glitter curtains, I can't see anyone in the crowd, only writhing shadows. I remember how Phase had looked like divine spirits that night I first saw them. Do *I* look like that now? Or do I just look ill?

Isobel walks up to the microphone, smiling benevolently.

'Hello, loves,' she says. 'We are Phase. I'm Isobel, God's favourite Virgo. Over there eating something is everyone's best friend Rudy, and on the drum kit is our handsome pet, Kit.'

The dark dance floor screams. Blood pounds in my ears.

'Most exciting of all, I am honoured to introduce our new keyboardist and your new obsession – George!'

Walking to the front, I'm greeted by a tsunami of cheers and the dopamine crashes through me. Gina's hesitations disappear. It's like at school concerts, university recitals, Bronze Age gigs, or even just for my parents in our music room. Instinct takes over.

I step up to the mic, too tall for me after Isobel and her heels, and perform the line the others helped me write.

'Hi, I'm George,' I say and grin. 'I'm gay, I'm single, and, most importantly of all, I'm a Libra. Thank you so much for having me.'

Someone heckles, 'I'll have you anytime!'

'Call me,' George shouts back, and everyone whoops.

Everything is brighter, more colourful. The curtain at the back of the stage is sparkling like the ocean at sunset, Isobel's hands cup around the microphone, Rudy adjusts her bass, the muscles in Kit's arms flex softly and our eyes meet... I can't believe I'm really here. On the other side.

Oh God, I'm really here! Isobel counts into 'Virgo in June' and panic flares up again in my stomach. What if I forget how to piano? What if something goes wrong? What if something terrible happens after the gig to punish me? What if—

But then we're playing and I stop thinking. I'm just there, in Isobel's bittersweet lyrics, sharing bass lines with Rudy, guided by Kit's pulse, listening only to each other. In this beautiful limbo together, like floating in space, or deep-sea diving. Effortless.

We play the final chord and for a second everything is perfect.

Then the song ends and my oxygen cord snaps; I gasp for air in the real world.

The audience are going *wild*. The others are grinning at me proudly. The pink lights are glittering in my eyes and I'm finally alive again.

I did it! I did it! I didn't mess up!

Soph is cheering at the front of the audience, her necklaces and sequins catching the light. I wiggle my fingers at her. Then I worry that people will think she's my girlfriend, so I tone down the wiggles. I needn't have worried; as I watch, Jenny's red football shirt dances up behind her and they wave at me in couple's unison.

Each song goes like that: the fall into lucid dreaming, the awakening to reality, the elation of the cheers.

How did I go so long without this? Every song is a blood transfusion.

Then the crowd is screaming for an encore, but Isobel just winks at them and tells them to follow us on social media. We bow, once, and leave out the back. Then we hug and hug and hug, and I realize that this is the happiest I've been in years.

I think – no, I *know* – that it's the best night of my life.

In a flash, I'm back four years, walking out from the golden lights and cheering crowd of the final student gig and hugging my Bronze Age friends. Not knowing, yet, about the missed calls. About what I've done.

But no, that all happened to Gina. Not to George.

It's *George* who's backstage now, celebrating with her band. George, laughing and elated, breathing in pine cologne from her drummer's neck. George, the musician.

Nothing's going to go wrong this time.

I always thought Bronze Age were hopelessly unrealistic and also icky when they talked about groupies. But, honestly? There's nothing like having played a corker of a gig for women to pay attention to you.

When we head back out to pack up, my body still vibrating, groups of girls are loitering by the stage, failing to look nonchalant. Phase walk over like graceful monarchs. I follow behind, also failing to look nonchalant.

Quickly, Isobel is surrounded by strong, short-haired butches. Kit is surrounded by lithe, long-haired femmes. Rudy goes off to dance with her girlfriend Amie, leaving me as an awkward third-wheel in Kit and Isobel's popularity contest. I'm surrounded by people welcoming me to the band, sure, but I'm certain no one is flirting with me.

It doesn't matter anyway, says Gina in my head, because I have a boyfriend.

But thoughts of Gina's boyfriend evaporate as I watch Kit. The more a pretty girl hits on her, the more I want to take their manicured nails and put them into their eyes. Not very feminist of me. Is she trying to make me jealous on purpose, or is she not thinking of me at all?

When we were playing 'Mercury' tonight, I could have sworn Kit was trying to tell me something through the music. Pushing the tempo, taking risks, like she wanted permission to go further. I'd really thought that tonight we might...

Isobel's squidging one of her admirer's biceps and, not to be out Alpha'd, Kit lifts up one of her admirers and spins her round. I can't stand it.

She probably doesn't even notice me run out to the smoking area for air. Meanwhile, I'm breathing hard, sat on the same bench where I pouted at her all those weeks ago, knowing I can't go anywhere without thinking of her.

Soph's texted me.

Omg baaaaaab!!! U were AMAZING!!!

Soon u'll b headlining GAY FEST!!!

Seriously tho, can't tell u how proud I am 2 c u where u belong

I'm heading home w Jenny (lol) but speak soon

Dog could come next time?

And Mum's texted me.

BUNNYMISSESYOU.

I'm a terrible daughter, terrible friend, terrible girlfriend. I can't reply to either of them. I can't do anything except think about Kit. Kit's black eyes watching me across the stage. Kit stroking the back of my neck. Kit's late night drunken messages. But it was all just in my head. My stupid, egotistical imagination.

Like I've summoned her, she's there. Walking into the smoking area, pulling out a cigarette, frowning, upset.

Our eyes meet. The hand flicking her lighter fumbles. I look away, worried she'll be able to see the hurt on my face. But then she's crouching in front of me.

'George.'

I don't look at her.

'George, come on. Let's go talk.'

She nods towards her van and reaches for my hand. Phoebe Bridgers is playing from inside The Familiar. I let Kit pull me up and, as she walks me across the street, she clasps my fingers in hers.

It's only when we're round the side of Kit's van and she lets go to get out her keys, that I stop her. To delay what I think could be happening here. What surely couldn't be happening here...

'Let's talk outside.'

Kit looks right at me, her mahogany eyes unblinking.

'George. We both know I didn't mean *talk*.'

The air around us becomes very still. I've forgotten how to breathe.

'I want you,' she says, stepping closer. 'You know I want you. And I know *you* want me.'

She smoothly slides her arm around my waist, under the base of my shirt. The ridge of her key gently cuts my side.

I can feel the damp of her stage sweat on her arms, the warmth of her legs pressed against mine, can almost taste the nicotine on her lips.

Her head tilts. Mine automatically tilts in mirror image.

What if the wrong decision is the right one?

'No. Kit, I can't do this.'

Her mouth stops millimetres from mine.

'Why not?'

I have a boyfriend, is what I should say. No pussyfooting. Or even 'because my friend Soph fancies you and I can't hurt her'.

But that isn't what I'm thinking. Right now, the truth is, I don't want to be like Marsha. Or any of the other girls Kit sleeps with but doesn't care about.

'I've only just joined Phase,' I whisper. 'I don't want to mess things up.'

Kit chuckles and starts to kiss down my neck. Each one burns.

'It wouldn't mess anything,' she soothes. 'Just – casual. We don't need to ever tell anyone.'

Maybe she's right.

Maybe we could…

Doug would never need to—

'No,' I say.

Her hands stop immediately and she steps away, making me lose my balance.

Standing out of arm's reach, she looks like I've slapped her.

Oh God.

I chose wrong.

'Kit—'

But she's walking away, back to The Familiar.

'Kit, please—'

She doesn't look back. I stand by her van, making promises with the universe about what I'll do if she changes her mind and returns.

After an embarrassingly long time, I accept she's gone.

I'm in the back of a taxi, wishing I could giddy up the driver. I've sent every apologetic message to Doug I can. But it's weird, he's read them, but hasn't replied. Seven years we've been together and Doug has never once ignored my messages.

Guilt swirls deep into my stomach. As soon as I get home, no matter what, I'm going to tell him everything. Everything.

Nearly there. Doug still hasn't replied.

Kit hasn't messaged either. Not that it matters. Not that I'm not wishing she would call me and demand that I drop everything and go back her van right now. Not that I would.

I leap out of the taxi at home, trying to close its door silently so I don't wake my sleeping prince.

But a light is on in the bedroom. Maybe he left the light on accidentally. Maybe he fell asleep reading *Sapiens*.

Hurriedly, I let George's hair down into The Gina and undo my shirt into something more feminine. I turn the door key.

I can hear sounds from upstairs. Voices.

I creep upstairs trying to work out who it is. Does Doug have guests? At gone 1 a.m.?

But it's tinny, I realize. Aha, he's listening to music on his phone. It's familiar but I can't hear it well enough.

Assuming he's awake, I decide to go for a playful apology. I call, as if he's the family dog, 'Who's home? Who's home?' Normally when I do that he leaps up and comes to give me a slobbery kiss.

No response.

I swing open the bedroom door. Doug is sitting upright on the bed, fully dressed, looking at his phone. He doesn't look up at me.

I finally realize what he's listening to.

It's the Phase performance from earlier. He's on our social media page. He's watching all the videos from my first gig…

'Hi, I'm George,' I'm saying. 'I'm gay, I'm single, and most importantly of all, I'm a Libra! Thank you so much for having me.'

He rewinds it. Watches it again.

Then he turns off his bedside lamp and turns away.

PART TWO

18

I think Doug dumped me last night, but that doesn't break our routine.

Sunday mornings we tidy the house. It's built into our muscle memory. So yes, we might be about to separate, but we still have to load the washing machine...

We go about the rest of our solo chores in agonising, avoidant silence. But then it's our shared duty to strip the bed.

I remove my 'hers' pillow case, he removes the 'his'. Doug grimly strips the duvet of its old cover and holds the corners of the duvet up. Not looking at him, I pick up the corners of the clean cover and climb inside it, like a ghost. Usually I make spooky wailing sound effects and pretend to haunt him for a bit. Not today. When I go to grip the duvet, our hands touch through the fabric. We drop it in shock. When we both bend to pick it up, we hit heads. I trip over the hem of the cover and fall backwards. Doug stands and watches me wriggle inside the cover for a bit, then leaves the room. The ghost quietly wails.

I need to apologize. Explain. Persuade him to give me a second chance. But how? Oh God.

The final step is a reward cup of tea. I put the kettle on,

anguished. Putting our usual biscuits on our usual plate and sitting on our usual sofa seems blasphemous.

The kettle starts to bubble. Shaking, I pull out two retired mugs from the back of the cupboard. Christmas gifts from parents. His says 'Keep Calm and Play Bass,' mine says 'Dream Big Princess'.

Doug sits on the sofa facing away from me. I take a breath and, quiveringly, offer the tea.

He takes one look at the ugly mugs and starts to cry.

I leap up, slosh the tea into our usual mugs, and grab three biscuit packets, apologizing again and again. He sobs loudly into his sleeve. I return in seconds and sit there, rattling the Hobnobs at him pathetically. He sobs louder.

'Pet, pet, I'm so sorry! Please don't break up with me. I'll do anything.'

'What?' He sniffs. 'I thought you were breaking up with *me*?'

I gawp at him.

'Why on earth would I break up with you?'

He howls. 'Because you're a lesbian!'

I howl back. 'No, I'm not!'

Doug squints at me.

I say, with embarrassed jazz hands, 'I'm bi.'

He doesn't react, except a bit of snot drips from his nose.

'I'm really sorry, pet – about not telling you, not about being bi – although, to be honest, that has been an emotional and logistical nightmare so far, so—'

'How long have you known?' he asks, mouth obscured by tissue.

'Umm, I think in some ways, forever? And in other ways, about a month?'

We search each other's eyes.

Then we both start laughing. And crying. There's a lot of tears and tissues and snot.

Finally, I tell Doug everything.

Well, OK, not *everything* everything.

I don't tell him about Kit almost kissing me the other night. In fact, I generally leave her out of the story. I need to be factual, not sadistic.

'You know, it does make sense,' says Doug, eventually. 'Like your "girl crushes" at uni, or like, how you and Soph have always had some connection I couldn't grasp.'

I peel crumbs off a Hobnob.

'Does me being bi make a difference to you?' I ask. 'To us?'

His lovely blue eyes turn on me, but, unusually, I can't read his expression.

'To be honest, I feel pretty weird. That you kept this big secret from me.'

My stomach tightens back into complicated knots. I'm going to be dumped. I'm going to lose everything that makes me feel safe. Our calendar, our past, our future together...

'Why didn't you talk to me earlier?' he asks. 'Did you not trust me?'

I scratch at the stamp on the back of my hand.

'I just... didn't think it mattered enough, at first. And then it felt like it mattered too much. God, I don't *know*. It felt like it was all happening to someone else. I didn't want you to think I was being automatically unfaithful.'

He nods, hesitantly.

'So... just to check, you aren't cheating on me?'

'No! Of course not! What, all bisexuals are cheaters? That's biphobic! Cheaters are cheaters! Regardless of sexuality! I haven't kissed anyone else except you and Bunny for the past seven years! Have *you*?'

I have a tendency to turn defensiveness into offensiveness. Doug is used to this and just carries on sipping his tea.

'Gina,' he sighs, 'obviously I don't care about you being bi. I mean, I do care, because it's a part of you. But it doesn't affect the way I feel about wanting to be with you. For a long time…' He meets my eyes. 'But does it make a difference to you wanting to be with me?'

'No!' I shout, even louder, not meeting his eye. 'Fucking hell, of course not!'

Doug reaches out to me and pulls my head into his shoulder. It's such a relief to be back in physical contact with him, with his cosy jumper. I bury my face in.

'I don't know.'

He strokes my hair.

'Gina, is it homophobic if I want us to stay together?'

I look up at him from his armpit.

'*I* want us to stay together,' I reply. 'Oh Doug, I know it sounds awful, but I want both. I want to stay with you, exactly how we've always been, forever. But I also want to know what it's like to be in a relationship that's… Where I don't have to be ashamed that I belong to that world. I know, philosophically, it shouldn't matter if I've never had a "queer" relationship, and maybe it doesn't, but how can I know if I've never tried?'

We sit staring into our mugs. My mind is whirring with thoughts of The Familiar and Phase. Wondering what Soph would say.

That's when I remember her videos. It suddenly clicks. The

simplicity of the solution makes me laugh.

'Pet. Pet.' I say, slapping his elbow. 'We *can* have both. We could open up our relationship.'

There's a little pause. Doug takes off his glasses, fiddling with the metal bridge. 'You know, usually when people tell their partner they want to stay together forever, they suggest, like, getting a mortgage.'

'But Doug,' I clutch his hands, 'it's perfect! We're *so* in love, and *so* stable and *so* committed with each other, that we should snog other people.'

Doug frowns at me like I'm the mad scientist in a disaster film.

'It makes so much sense, don't you see? It would benefit you as well. You could play the field while you're still young. We are each other's only ever committed relationship and it's like – you know how you love me, but you also fancy, say, Saoirse Ronan?'

'Yeah, but we've always said if I had the opportunity...' He scowls at me. 'Do you want a free pass with Saoirse too?'

'That's not what I... Actually, yes please. But what I meant was, what if we had free passes with obtainable non-celebrities too?'

'A free pass?'

I'm out of my depth, reaching for the end of an equation I haven't quite worked out yet. I try to remember Soph's lectures on open relationships.

'I don't mean a *free* free pass. There would be rules. Strict rules. And communication. Constant communication. We could trial it. Say, for one month.'

Hmm, that's an ambitious timescale to find someone to sleep with.

'Or six months. Or a year.'

Doug scratches his beard.

'The only person I know who is "polyamorous" is that guy Dave, from the uni jazz band.'

We both grimace.

'He was really weird.'

'Yeah. He was really weird.'

We both consider.

'I'm not suggesting we act like Dave from Jazz In My Pants. He was, palpably, a strange individual. But he doesn't represent all polyamorous people. And we don't have to be polyamorous to be in an open relationship. The thought of you falling in love with someone else is…'

I look at his lovely freckly face. I'm remembering the first time he ever told me that he loved me. He literally made me a cassette mix tape where the first letter of each song spelled out 'I Love You.' I still have that tape, in my overflowing 'box of memories' in our bedroom.

We reach for each other's hands at the same moment and squeeze hard. I don't want him falling in love with someone else. He's *my* perfect boyfriend. What if I'm making a terrible mistake?

But Doug's now got on board with the idea.

'You mean like we have friends with benefits?'

'Maybe,' I say, still clinging onto his hand.

'Huh,' says Doug, dunking a biscuit. 'You know, I love *you*, and I'm very happy just sleeping with *you*. But I guess, if you were *encouraging* it… While we're still young… I'm not *against* the thought of sleeping with Saoirse Ronan's sister…'

'You're not serious, does she really have a—'

He chucks my chin.

'Gina, do you really think an open relationship is going to work if you're jealous at a hypothetical?'

'Soph has a video about turning jealousy into compersion. We'll research. And I don't know… Do *you* think an open relationship could work?'

He strokes my cheek. He's quiet for so long I'm sure I've ruined everything.

'This is a lot to take in at once,' he says eventually. 'First my girlfriend is a lesbian, then she's not. Then she's half a lesbian. Then she's not. Then she wants to become a *consummated* half-lesbian—'

'The word really is bisexual.'

'Yes, sorry. I just… Look, I'm honestly not trying to make this about me, but it does affect *us*, doesn't it? And what if we go open and our balance is thrown off? Or one of us meets someone else? But if we *don't* go open, I feel like I'm some horrible patriarchal oppressor, denying you from half your identity. So… say yes, and potentially mess up our relationship? Or say no, and potentially mess up our relationship…?'

I nod, deflated.

'I know, I'm sorry…'

'Gina, you don't need to apologize. But we shouldn't rush into anything. We need to think and talk, take it nice and slow.'

I blink at him over my half-eaten Hobnob.

'S-so you'll consider it?'

'We'll both consider it. And talk again in a few days.'

We laugh nervously and toast each other's biscuits.

'Right! Sure! Nice and slow.'

★

The problem with nice and slow is Kit. She hasn't messaged me since last night and I'm too scared to reach out to her. But I remember her reaching to my waist, pulling me in to her warmth, her hands, her mouth....

If Doug and I *are* going to open up our relationship, it would make sense if it was, you know, soon. Say, before I next see Kit, in case there's an opportunity to apologize for not kissing her last night. Apologize, say, with a snog.

What would be wrong with that?

I message, instead, on the Phase group chat.

Hey gang, we all recovered from the hangover yet lol? When are we next hanging out?

Little dots form over them all typing.

Rudy: *last nite was SO fun!! U guys were making some sweet moves on the dance floor ;) Im free 2 rehearse WENEVA!!!*

Isobel: *Ha, yes, I confess my head does hurt a little today! I'm busy the next couple of days, but how about Wednesday?*

Kit: *i want a break*

I bury my face in my hands. It's worse than I thought. She's avoiding me. She hates me. She's going to force me to leave Phase.

No one asks Kit why she wants a break, thank goodness. But we agree to meet Wednesday next week.

That basically gives me a week. A week to open up my seven-year relationship and win back Kit.

Easy.

I start dropping little hints to Doug.

'Cereal or toast?' I ask over breakfast. 'Or *both*?'

He blithely pours himself some muesli.

I consider putting in a calendar event to *Talk about open relationship :)*, but I don't want to look pushy. Instead, I start reading articles about open relationships, especially whenever Doug is in viewing distance of my screen. My main takeaway from these articles is: why are people so obsessed with sex? Is it really *that* big a deal? Really?

Other than that, I'm disappointed that there isn't much practical advice about going into an open relationship. There isn't, for example, a suggested timetable to download. They just keep going on about openness, trust, and honesty.

Blah blah blah. Doug and I already nail all of that. Seven years in, we haven't had any secrets from each other. Well, apart from my sexuality, I suppose. Oh, and about Phase not knowing I have a boyfriend. Oh, and my not-strictly-friendly feelings for Kit. Oh, and Doug being about to propose to me. But other than that, zero secrets.

What I'm saying is, we're already completely open in our relationship. This would be a *sensible* next step for us. It's easy to open a door if it's already unlocked.

I try telepathically saying this to Doug before we head off to work, but he doesn't seem to catch on.

19

Wednesdays at Liberty Secondary are a treat at the moment: korma for lunch with roly-poly for pudding, and a lesson with Mousy Matilda, who has started to play her Chopin 'Sostenuto' through beautifully *and* at an audible volume.

I give her a solo round of applause and she gives me one of her rare gap-toothed grins.

'Thanks, Miss.'

'No, thank you! I know, in the past, you've been nervous about performing, but I really think you should play in the end-of-term concert.'

I hesitate, watching her face, but she doesn't wince the way she used to.

'It will be just like one of our lessons, except a few other people will get to enjoy your playing too. What do you think?'

She looks at her music book and for a moment I think I've pushed it too far.

'Yes please, Miss. I'll bring my parents.'

We both smile at her music book.

'OK,' I say casually, as if this hasn't made my year, 'I'll book you in. How about you open the second half?'

A privileged spot, and we both know it. Matilda nods,

glowing with pride. Then she looks like she's gearing herself up to say something.

'Miss?'

'Mmm?'

'I was reading about Chopin and... Was he gay?'

I blink.

'Umm... Yeah, he might have been. It's difficult to be certain.'

She nods.

'I'm gay too,' she says.

I freeze. Her huge eyes blink rapidly.

Oh...

A student has never come out to me before. To be fair, a student has never said anything personal to me before. But did she tell me because she knows I'm queer too? Is it this bob? How many kids would come out if I wore my hair in George mode?

I want to thank Matilda for telling me, to say that I'm honoured and that I understand. But am I even allowed to come out as a teacher? Would parents find it inappropriate?

'That's nice,' I say, rather lamely.

Matilda nibbles at her lip.

So, in a rush, I add, 'Tchaikovsky might have been gay too. And Schubert. And Handel. Of course we can be more sure with modern composers like Britten, Poulenc, Copland... As for gay women, they're doubly written out of the narrative, but... Would you like to try playing something by Ethel Smyth?'

She smiles at me shyly and she says she'll look her up. I surge with pride.

I feel that this was something my dad would have done.

Maybe not with such a specific interest in lesbians, but still. And it feels good. *Really* good.

Maybe teaching isn't so bad?

Alexa is staring at the smoking area wall so hard that her temple vein is throbbing.

'Is everything OK, Alexa?'

'Everything?' she blinks tersely. 'Everything in the entire world? OK? No, I don't think it's very likely that everything is OK, is it? There's the climate crisis, for one thing. Global inequality.'

I watch her profile, wondering whether she's forgotten her sweets or her cigarettes.

She says something but her mouth is so tight that I can't hear it.

'They want to change the timetabling again,' she says. 'When will these people learn that just changing something isn't going to fix it? They come in with their big ideas and think they're the first person to think of compulsory music classes or banning the arts completely. But they don't think about what those changes are going to do to the kids' actual education.'

Her fingers twitch, flicking imaginary lighters.

'But Alexa…' I say, after a while. 'You don't care about the children's education.'

She continues to stare at the wall.

'No, obviously not.'

Her vein still throbs.

'I've got some chocolate Hobnobs in my bag,' I offer.

But she says she's fine.

★

Sunday date night. Doug and I are making batch bolognese. When it's simmering, Doug tops up our wine more than usual and turns down the volume of his favourite indie pop playlist (titled BANGERS!).

'Gina,' he says, and I know immediately what the topic is. He takes a deep breath and my hand and says, 'I think if you're serious about going open then I'm serious about it too.'

My stomach lurches.

'You are?'

'I am,' he says. 'If you think we can make it work, then I do too.'

There must be something wrong with me, because Doug has never looked more handsome than in that moment.

'You do?' I ask quietly.

'I do.'

The phrase, and his bright blue eyes, and the sombre mood, makes me do something a bit mad.

I kneel in front of Doug, on one knee, and I take his hand.

'Douglas Wright,' I say.

Oh God, why did I do this?

'Would you make me the happiest girl in the world, by doing me the great honour of being in an open relationship with me?'

Doug closes his eyes and I can't read his expression. Then he says, 'I do.'

We kiss for a long time. His thumb traces its usual pattern along my cheek tenderly. We pull apart and stare at each other sombrely.

Then our faces split into grins. For some reason we start dancing around, holding hands, giggling madly.

'Let's open some Prosecco.'

Doug looks back at me from the fridge door.

'Do you know what this means?'

I finish the sentence for him.

'We need to add "seeing other people" into our calendar.'

20

'*George: keyboardist, here to advertise my fingerwork...
look up Phase to find our next gig! bi / open relationship /
libra*'

'*Douglas: Shy Guy. Take me for a walk? In an open
relationship, but not in a creepy way.*'

This is normal, right? Writing your boyfriend's dating app
bio?

Doug and I chatted about open relationship rules and
agreed about everything. Officially: 1) We will have open
communication, tell each other everything, and alert each
other *before* anything happens. 2) Secondary partners must
know we're in an open relationship and not looking for
anything serious. 3) No falling in love.

Well, OK, we didn't agree about *everything*. I argued
that a secondary partner didn't need to know about our
relationship because, by definition, if it wasn't serious you
wouldn't be discussing your long-term boyfriend, would
you? But Doug was adamant that the partner should know
the other exists. I couldn't push it too hard in case I looked
guilty.

So I would only be able to 'legally' get with Kit if I told

her about Doug... I mean, she blatantly doesn't object to non-monogamy, but how could I tell her about *him*? It's so off-brand.

But anyway, Kit shouldn't be important. What's important is that I have this chance to trial being in a legal gay relationship so I should make the most of it. And a successful hook-up would surely help me forget Kit anyway. (Or give me ideas for if Kit and I ever... Stop it!)

Thursdays, we agree, is the night officially open for dates with other people. We prioritised Dougina date nights, so that our relationship doesn't get imbalanced, but it does mean I have to remove one of my usual Slob nights with Soph. I'm sure she'll understand, though. I mean, me and Doug opening our relationship was practically her idea.

Doug and I are, therefore, in an unspoken competition to get a date for Thursday.

Everyone knows that dating apps are horrific, but the experience should be better for us. I mean, I'm essentially looking for a mistress. If someone doesn't swipe right on me, I can just go and hug Doug.

And yet, it *is* awful. I don't know which is worse, liking someone and not matching with them, or the ennui of not liking anyone at all. I spend twenty minutes swiping left: no to funny 'Abi, 28' because her favourite musician is Ed Sheeran; no to beautiful 'Neela, 30' because her entire personality is advocating fruitarianism; no to cool 'Kylie, 25', because of her gross boyfriend ('Looking for a unicorn to spice things up!').

Looking at Doug, merrily swiping right, I realize I need to lower my expectations. I can weed people out at the messaging stage. But in my pitiful handful of matches, no one messages. And when *I* message someone, there's no response, *and* I've degraded my hierarchy on the global dating scene.

I cuddle into Doug on the sofa and we compare screens. Occasionally the same person comes up and our minds are blown. We're detectives for London bisexuals now. Maybe I could ask them about their own double lives?

The next girl on mine is 'Blaire, 26'. She has short hair, a long glare, and her bio says she's a 'resting comedian'.

'She seems fun,' says Doug, leaning over to go through her pictures and then refreshing his screen. 'Shame she seems to only play for the gays.'

Oh, great. My boyfriend and I have the same taste in women.

I swipe yes to Blaire and am greeted with a cartoon pop of success. Doug and I high five.

Blaire messages me. A wave emoji. Hot!

I send her one back and scroll through more faces on the loo, waiting for her to reply.

I'm suddenly confronted with photos of Isobel. I nearly drop the phone down the toilet.

Isobel: Virgo seeks Hollywood romance. Cottagecore before it was cool. Take me to Church x

Her photos are masterpieces: singing with her guitar in a chapel, at a bar laughing with Rudy, in a retro-style swimsuit on the beach. Then, with Kit.

Oh Christ.

The photo looks like the cover of a *Perfect Weddings* magazine. Kit is in a dark navy suit and white shirt, with a couple of buttons undone to reveal her silver chain. Isobel is in a red dress, the wind blowing her curls out of her crystal eyes. Kit is handing her a glass of wine and they're looking at each other intently. I can't stop staring at it.

Then I realize that if I can see Isobel's profile, she can see mine. Crap! I shiftily edit my profile to remove the words 'bi' and 'open relationship'. I'll add them back in once I tell Phase everything. Which will definitely be soon.

Meanwhile, seeing Kit's face there is enough to make my brain explode.

I put the phone down on the floor and sit on the loo for a while, head in my hands. I'm suddenly exhausted. The open relationship, the apps, the girls – it's all too much. This is a *huge* mistake. I can't just hide my feelings for Kit by trying to find a replacement. I haven't seen a single person on here who makes me feel a fraction of the way that Kit does.

Doug knocks gently on the door.

'Gin, you alright in there? You need a Rennie's?'

'No, no, all good.'

Through the door, Doug stage whispers, 'I've got a date.'

I force out a squeak of excitement and wash my hands while Doug tells me about her. She's called Adelaide, she's a software engineer, and they're going to go for a drink at her favourite Soho bar next Thursday.

I make enthusiastic sounds, but my face in the mirror is terrified. Is this going to be OK?

'Gina? Is this going to be OK?'

Phew. We have the same hesitations. Maybe we should just call this whole thing off?

But Doug continues, 'What if she doesn't like me?'

Oh. I open the bathroom door. He's looking at me like a puppy with a huge stick it can't keep carrying.

'Of course she'll like you. You're the best guy in the world.'

He kisses me. A deep kiss.

I pull back and look at him, grinning. He cocks his head. I check my watch. We're a little early but...

We giggle our way to the bedroom. It is a Sunday, after all.

I'm excited about having *news*. I want to show off to *everyone*.

But not my mum, obviously. Or anyone at the school. Or Phase, yet. So, in reality, the only person I tell is Soph.

As an apology for postponing our Thursday slob nights, I told Soph I wanted us to do a big gay day out. We've just been to Gay's the Word, where I browsed for books about open relationships for Doug but didn't have the nerve to ask if the bookseller had anything targeted at straight people. Now we're in an upcycled vintage shop, looking for more denim jackets.

I tell Soph my news casually while she's in the changing room.

She pulls back the rail, half-dressed, to gawp at me.

'You and Doug are going *open*? In what way? A break-up way? Or a married-swingers-putting-car-keys-in-a-bowl way?'

'Car keys.'

She stares at me. Other shoppers gawp at her and her provocative bralet.

'*You*? And *Douglas*?'

'Yes,' I say defensively.

'But you've only been *out* for five minutes!'

Hmm... I get into the changing room with Soph and pull the curtain over.

'Do you think it's a bad idea?' I whisper.

'Open relationships aren't inherently a bad idea,' she says, absent-mindedly pulling on a skimpy top. 'I mean, loads of my friends find it works well for them. It's just – you guys don't exactly fit the classic open relationship mould. Normally it's gay, for a start.'

'I thought you said our relationship *is* gay.'

'Well, I mean *double* gay then.'

I sigh in the mirror.

'Why am I never the right amount of gay?'

'Bab,' she says, adorning me in an awful denim vest, 'there's no reason you *shouldn't*, it's just that most relationships *start* open if they're going to be open. Everyone I've known who was in a closed relationship and then opened it up? They were basically opening it for one specific person. And I'm like, that's not an open relationship, baby girl, that's cheating, but showing off about it.'

Soph laughs. I do not. She spins round.

'Wait. You don't have someone in mind, do you?'

I pretend to be interested in trying on one of her jackets and head into the next-door dressing room. No good, Soph follows me.

'Who is it? Lucy?'

'Let the Lucy thing go.'

'Then who?'

'No one,' I say, pulling the curtain violently between us. She wrestles it back. I need to distract her.

I put on my pleading face. 'Soph, please will you wingwoman me?'

She squeals, all doubts forgotten. 'Yes! Let's go somewhere new to celebrate. Find you some fresh blood to practise on.'

We go back into the shop floor with renewed vigour to find an outfit.

'Soph,' I force myself to say, over Hawaiian shirts, 'one more thing... I haven't told Phase about Douglas yet.'

Soph buries her head in a pile of novelty knitwear.

'Not more secret-keeping? The stress messes with my bowels,' she moans.

'Please, Soph, I'll tell them when I'm more established.'

She burrows deeper into the Christmas jumpers, groaning.

'Can't you see? If I were to walk in there now, when I've only done one gig with them... I'm not asking you to *lie*, I'm just asking you not to say anything.'

She emerges, a glove on her head.

'I don't like it, Gee, I don't like it at all.'

'Please? Very pretty please?' I wheedle. 'It benefits you too. The longer I stay in Phase, the more of a groupie you can become...'

'But what happens if I'm flirting with Kit and then she asks—'

'Pumpernickel.'

Soph and I stare at each other over a reindeer cardigan.

'Really?'

'Really. Just for now. I need to take things one step at a time.'

'OK,' she says, dragging it out. 'You Pumpernickeled *me* that I won't tell Kit about Doug. But I want a Pumpernickel of my own. *You've* got to help me and Kit get together.'

Shit.

'Soph, we're not children,' I snap. 'What could I do, ask her out for you?'

'Don't pretend you don't know what I mean,' says Soph, an

edge to her voice. 'Kit and I make *sense* together. She's not like Luddite Jenny, she'll understand my career, my lifestyle. And Marsha told me Kit had a bad coming-out experience too. That's why she lived with Isobel's family for a while.'

My heart flops.

'I know Phase is a big deal for you and I won't get in your way, but don't you see? Kit could be perfect for *SophieSnob*. Just imagine us, filming couple videos.'

And I do see it. As much as I suspect Soph is more in love with the idea of Kit than her reality, she does make more sense with her than I would. Lesbian Casanovas don't fall for lesbian virgins. I was an idiot to think someone like Kit would ever want someone like me.

Regardless, Soph should come first. Mates before dates. Bros before hoes. Best friends before open relationship secondary partners.

'Of course I'll try to help,' I say to her. 'Anything for you.'

Soph puts her arm around me.

'Perfect. Now let's both find some ladies to snog.'

Apparently gay bars don't *need* a Halloween theme?

It's 8 p.m. and we're sitting at one of the side tables in an already heaving Royal Vauxhall Tavern. Amidst chaotic strobe lighting, I nibble a chip and admire the sexy crowd. Punky art students do shots next to power-suited couples, bearded bears dance around moustachioed otters, and everyone smells of not-quite-hardy-enough deodorant. Rainbow stickers bedeck everything, from a glamorous drag queen's wheelchair to a twink's bare nipples. But I only spot a handful of Familiar faces. Goodness me, there are a lot of gay people in London.

And when did I start using words like 'twink'?

'Gina and Douglas in an open relationship,' Soph says, shaking her head over our dripping burgers. 'God, you have no drama for years, and now you have it all at once. So. Finally. What's your type?'

'I don't know! I've always just chosen my partner by which man said he was interested in me.'

I was with my first boyfriend Adam for two years, a long time when you're a teenager, but the only reason we'd ended up together was because we sang a duet in the school musical. It took two years for me to realize that I didn't actually fancy him. He wasn't even a good duet partner. What a waste of a hymen.

I arrived at university ready to live a life of titillating one-night stands like TV said I would. Instead, I met Doug in Freshers Week, paired up by our university as 'Buddies'. Seven years later, here we are.

Soph crosses herself to ward off patriarchal energy.

'Look around you,' she says, a kindly pimp. 'Who stands out?'

I try to stare in a subtle way. But as I look around at the people here I realize the fatal, if rather obvious, flaw in my elaborate open relationship plan.

'What does it matter?' I say, shrugging my jacket back on, 'No one will fancy me. This is humiliating. I'm going home.'

Soph rolls her eyes, pretends to pull piles of chips from my shoulder and pulls my bum back onto the chair.

'Excuse me,' Soph says to a random woman walking past, 'do you fancy my friend?'

The woman looks from Soph to me.

'Her?'

Soph smiles and nods.

'No, not really. No offence.'

While my soul leaves my body in shame, Soph and the random woman exchange numbers. When she walks away, Soph smugly tosses her braids over her shoulder.

'Great wingwomaning,' I say. 'Thanks.'

'Bad example. Next time.'

Three abysmal attempts and a couple of Whore's Handbags later, Soph changes her tune.

'Gee,' she hiccups, 'sometimes even the most wonderful, funny, kind, talented person in the world can walk into a bar and not leave it with their soulmate. You can't expect to simply look around and suddenly there's Juliet falling in love at first sight with you.' But she looks round the bar just in case. 'I mean, I've been on the dating scene for my whole *life*. I've tried every app and every bar and every YouTuber convention and still nothing. And *I* look like *this*.'

I put ketchup on a chip and feed it to her.

'I know you think Kit is hot,' I say, casually, 'but wouldn't someone like Isobel make a better girlfriend for *SophieSnob*? Imagine the two of you together. All that femme energy. *That* video would go viral.'

Soph squints at me.

'Isobel's a goddess,' she says, 'but she's a prude, right? Never goes further than a first date. She's famous for it.'

'Maybe she's waiting for "the one". But *you* could be "the one".'

Soph doesn't immediately shoo away the idea, so I think there's potential in this plan to transfer her affections. While she's in the loo, I try to arrange myself for pick-up like she does. I am in an open relationship. *Someone* must want to get with me.

No? No one?

Oh my God, wait! Someone has come up to me. I look up flirtatiously.

At Marsha.

She's looking more confident than the first time I saw her, in a strappy top and flared jeans, her hair in tight lines of cornrows. She juts her hip.

'Well, look who it is,' she says. 'The replacement.'

I bristle, but she breaks the mood by laughing.

'I'm not here to start a fight. I saw you at the last gig. I liked what you did with "Mercury".'

I mumble a thank you, but keep my arms crossed.

She sighs. 'I know Phase aren't exactly my number one fan any more. I wouldn't blame them if they've been talking bad about me or whatever...?'

'They never mention you,' I say, like one of the Plastics.

Marsha's veneer slips.

'Oh. Right.'

I flush. I don't like playing that character.

'Sorry, Marsha, I'm being weird.' I can't tell if I'm too drunk to talk to her, or too sober. 'I'm – I'm worried about being compared to you, I guess.'

Her face lights up when she smiles.

'It's OK, man; being in a band can make you feel like you need to pretend to be someone else. I'm glad if you're having a good time.' She shakes her head. 'I wish I'd stayed honest to myself from the start. Belonging to something shouldn't mean you have to change to fit in.'

Oh blimey.

I have this urge to tell her everything. To ask why she fell out with Kit. Or at least ask whether she has a recording of 'Cusp', because it's *still* stuck in my head. But I overthink my words and the moment passes.

She smiles.

'Good luck, George.'

As she's leaving, she turns back and winks at me.

'Nice shirt, by the way. It looks better on you than it did on me.'

Soph and I leave, with the random woman Soph picked up. I've no idea what her name is. Hopefully Soph does.

In the front of the taxi, listening to them snog and feeling sorry for myself, I end up messaging that Blaire girl from Tinder.

I *think* we're getting on well, but sometimes it's difficult to read her tone.

i'm serious, she types, *i'm a resting comedian.*

I reply with laughing emojis.

what's funny?

You, presumably, I banter back.

because i'm a comedian?

... Yes?

i'm resting from being a comedian though.

Did you need to take a break from being amusing?

no, just doing the stand-up comedy work. it was very tiring

Haha

?

That's not what being a resting actor means

but i'm not an actor i'm a comedian

I have no idea whether we are bantering splendidly, or whether she is a comedian with no sense of humour. But I carry on talking to her, mainly because she's one of the only dating app conversations which have lasted longer than 'top or bottom'.

While resting from her high-intensity comedy career, Blaire's working in an obscure chain called Pizza Pasta Piazza. I feign an interest in mediocre Italian food, framing it as an obvious invitation to ask me on a date.

She suggests Friday. I insist on Thursday. We'll meet at Pizza Pasta Piazza at six.

SCORE!

When Doug returns home, I tell him the news and we tipsily make-out in celebration.

21

It's Wednesday. The first Phase rehearsal since the night Kit tried to kiss me. I still can't believe that wasn't a wild cheese dream.

But somehow Kit feels even more off-limits than when I was straight and about to get engaged. Doug's open-relationship rules mean I could only get with her if she knew about him, which I do think would be an irredeemable turn-off (no offence, Doug). *And* Soph Pumpernickeled me to help her get with Kit. I can't think of any loophole that therefore condones me kissing her. Regardless, Kit took my rejection so badly, I don't think she'd give us another chance. Which is definitely a good thing.

So let's not talk about the fact I'm wearing one of Kit's soft old shirts. Or that, when I arrive, I barely listen to what Isobel and Rudy are saying because I twitch every time there's the slightest noise, like a dog expecting the postman.

Eventually Isobel sighs and stretches her boots. 'I'll go and escort our royal highness from the camper.'

At which point Kit stumbles in through the door, looking all sorts of hungover. I wonder who she was drinking with and whether she was pretty. We avoid each other's eyes. Isobel tuts.

Kit looks for the coffees. I'm standing by them. Kit walks over, leaving a large force field around me. I decide to try handing an olive branch. I take Kit's now-cold cup and pour in her usual two milks. Savouring our proximity, I stir in an extra sugar. When I hand it over to her, our fingertips brush; Kit holds her fingers there for a second too long and, in my overactive imagination, our repressed tension reheats Kit's coffee like a microwave.

'Nice shirt,' she says, croak in her throat. That's *her* peace gesture.

Looking up, I meet her eyes. My face immediately flushes (the bastard).

Isobel calls for us to hurry up.

I'm impossibly thankful that our playing together is unaffected. If anything, there's a further deepening, an additional complicated undercurrent. In today's version of 'Virgo in June', Isobel seems to intuitively pick up on my feelings – her lyrics become about apology, about longing to kiss someone but missing the chance. Whenever Kit makes suggestions, I blush harder. Does she realize she's flirting with me, or is it all subconscious?

All too soon, the door rattles, and Cara comes in. She taps her watch at the others, but clearly avoids my eye.

Oh no, another gorgeous woman I've offended. When I've been replaying the night when Poppy came to The Familiar, I swear Cara was jealous of Lucy. Then I tell myself to stop being astonishingly self-absorbed. She was probably annoyed about some other bartender business. Why would she care about some customer who makes occasional terrible jokes?

Still, when we pack up our instruments I feel doubly

self-conscious of my limbs, wondering whether Kit and/ or Cara are watching me. I drop my reusable water bottle a hundred times. The metal casing clangs impossibly loudly over and over again.

Rudy, adjusting the straps of her lilac dungarees, makes a questioning drink gesture at me.

I have a date with Doug tonight. I've cancelled on him too many times for Phase and I promised I wouldn't skip another. But I can't tell them about that, so my mind jumps to *tomorrow's* plans...

'No, I can't stay tonight, sorry,' I say, my answer carrying across the room. 'I've got a date.'

'Ooh,' pouts Isobel, 'who is she?'

I don't dare to look if Kit or Cara are listening.

'We just met on an app,' I say. 'She's a comedian.'

'Oh my God, that's crazy,' says Rudy, 'my brother's a comedian!'

The three of us giggle together.

'Tell us all how it goes,' says Isobel, applying another layer of velveteen lipstick.

'Put her best jokes on the chat!' adds Rudy.

Kit and Cara do not join in.

'Well, you never know,' I say. 'Just... seeing what happens.'

I dare myself to wave a quick goodbye across the room.

Kit does a brief, almost conciliatory wave back.

At her side, Cara waves back too, in the same appeased way.

As I turn to exit, I see them notice each other's wave.

Doug and I play Monopoly and then get an early night.

*

Thursday after work, on my way home from Liberty to dress for my First Date with Blaire, I ring Soph for advice.

'This Blaire woman had better be worth you ditching Slob night,' she grumbles. 'Well, what do you normally wear on a date with Douglas?'

Doug and I haven't been on a 'date' in years. After about our second anniversary, we realized we prefer cooking our own pasta in the comfort of our own home and pyjamas, thanks very much.

'A dress? And… earrings? But that feels wrong for George.'

'Wear whatever you feel confident in,' says Soph eventually.

'Wow. A revelation.'

'Just don't wear stripes – you'll get mistaken for restaurant staff.'

I open the bedroom door to strewn ties and a manic, topless Doug.

'Hello,' I say, awkwardly. 'Getting ready for your date?'

He grins sheepishly. Neither of us know the script for getting ready for dates with other people.

'How about your blue jacket?' I mumble. 'You look lovely in blue.'

We get ready alongside each other. It's like when we get dressed every morning, except instead of unconsciously dancing around each other, we're now hyper-aware of each other's every move and keep colliding.

Doug has now seen me dressed as George, but it still feels… unnatural. (I suspect *SophieSnob* would have a lot to say about that.) I silently remove my make-up, replace my contacts with my glasses, and tie my hair up into George. I put on Kit's dark-green shirt, black corduroy trousers, Docs, and denim jacket, trying to ignore the feeling that I'm a murderer revealing my methods.

I catch Doug's eye in our mirror. He makes no comment, just heads to the bathroom and shuts the door.

Now I'm worried about undergarments. Not that I anything is going to *happen* this evening, but 'just in case'. Doug isn't exactly a connoisseur of underwear. He gives his approval – if that's the right word – to anything. He thinks my Marks and Spencer multipacks are fancy because they have a bow on them. But surely a fellow gal would be more discerning? Oh my God, what if we match? Will it be like when people wear the same dress to a party and one of you has to go home in shame?

And never mind the underwear. What about the – you know – under-underwear? After years of worrying about grooming with Doug, I defiantly said that I was only going to shave when and where I wanted to. He agreed that not only was that completely my choice, but also he didn't care or notice. I was furious. All those wasted hours and pounds to smelly Veet. Surely women don't expect each other to get a wax, out of sisterly solidarity?

Of course, if I *did* change my habits, Doug would know exactly why... I don't want him to begrudge me making more of an effort for a stranger than I do for him. Or to think I'm a hussy.

I'll take my favourite course of action: avoid making a decision, leave as is. I couldn't have done anything anyway – Doug's been in the bathroom for ages.

He emerges, smelling of an aftershave I don't recognise. Oh, I bought him that tie. He hasn't worn it for me in years...

'You look lovely.'

'So do you.'

We look at each other for a moment. He moves to kiss my lips at the same time I move to kiss his cheek.

'I hope your date goes really well,' I say, in the doorway.

'Well, not *too* well.'

He hesitates, then smiles. Ish.

'Yeah. You too.'

Pasta Pizza Piazza only looks like an authentic cosy Italian bistro if you blur your eyes a bit. The tables are made of plastic wood, the candles on the table are electric tea lights, even the napkins are rubbery.

Unfortunately, Blaire also only looks like her Tinder pictures if you blur your eyes a bit. Her orange lipstick doesn't quite suit her olive skin, and her smile doesn't quite meet her eyes. It's not that she's not pretty. She just – doesn't do it for me.

Damn it all. Me, finally out the closet, on my first-ever date with a woman, and I don't even bloody fancy her.

Regardless, I should give it a chance. Maybe I'm still repressing.

So, initial greeting – are we meant to go in for a hug, handshake, or full on snog? I go for a peck on the cheek, but she turns her face, so I actually kiss her left eyebrow.

My opening word on my first date in seven years is, 'Sorry!' Not a great omen.

Desperate to say something, I gesture to her black-and-white striped T-shirt.

'You'll blend in with your colleagues!'

She looks down at herself as if to check she has clothes on.

'This is our uniform.'

'Oh... I hadn't realized you were working here tonight.'

'I told you. I said I'd sit with you when I'm not busy.'

'I thought you were joking...'

She looks at me like I'm an idiot, and then takes me to a badly positioned table. I sit. She remains standing.

'Drink?' she asks.

'*Definitely*. Would you like to share the house red with me?'

I read a list of dating tips that recommended sharing a bottle. Her face scrunches like I've suggested something insane.

'Obviously I can't drink while I'm working.'

'Oh, of course, right, right, sorry, right. Umm, I'll just have a glass then. Extra large.'

She notes it down. I see her write the full sentence in cursive. 'One Glass Of House Red, Extra Large, For Table Ten.' Then she storms off.

I feel like I've been stood up. It would be better if I had.

I fiddle with the plastic candle until she returns.

I rather madly toast to her good health. She accepts this with a regal nod. I take an extra-large gulp.

She reels off the specials list.

'—and we're out of margherita pizzas.'

'What? You're called Pizza Pasta Piazza and you're out of margheritas?'

'Why, are they your favourite?'

'It's not that I'm particularly attached to plain tomato and mozzarella, it's just... Don't you see why that's...'

Nope, her expression is blank. I trail off.

'I'll get a pasta.'

'You can get a different kind of pizza?'

I'm losing my mind.

'How can you make another kind of pizza if you can't make a margherita? How about I order a pepperoni with no meat on it?'

She wipes her too-long fringe out of her too-big eyes.

'If you don't want salami, you could get a fungi? That's my favourite.'

'Because you're a fun guy?' I force a laugh. 'I get it. Very funny.'

'What?'

Looking up at her stupefied expression, I lay down a napkin like a white flag of surrender.

She writes 'One Fungi Pizza For Table Ten' in careful calligraphy, then off she goes again.

I take a deep breath and try to reset. Yes, we're not exactly hitting it off, but it's definitely me. I'm out of practice meeting new people. It's not Blaire's fault that she's working, I was the one who insisted on Thursday.

When she finally sits down, I pour her apology water.

'I'm sorry if I'm a bit off,' I say, 'I'm just nervous. I haven't been on a date in – in a while.'

Blaire smiles at a point a few metres above my head, and says, 'It's OK!'

I smile back gratefully and try to sip my wine in a casually flirtatious way.

'So, what's it like working here?'

'Yeah,' she says, 'it's OK!'

After a while, I swallow. She smiles back.

'Right! And, er... how's it going being a resting comedian?'

'Yeah,' she says, 'it's OK!'

My wine has disappeared. It's like being stuck next to someone at the bad end at a dinner party.

When Blaire's checking where my pizza is, I see a text from Doug.

Hey bae, we're going to stay for more drinks if that's ok? Hope you're having a great time too! xxxxx

I analyse my feelings. Jealousy, definitely. But it's not so much that I'm jealous he's off with another girl having an incredible time, it's more that I'm with another girl and *not* having an incredible time.

Have fun but don't forget you love me most xxxxx

He doesn't see the message.

Blaire hands me my fungi and watches me eat, which I do as quickly as humanly possible.

How to get away without being rude...

We stare at the tablecloth for a few minutes until I say, 'Well, this has been nice, but—'

'My shift finishes in fifteen minutes,' says Blaire. 'Shall we go to a bar?'

I stare at her and she stares back, holding my gaze and raising an eyebrow in what I can only assume is an attempt to look seductive.

Am I so out of touch that I can't tell how well a date is going? Is this what passes for a good time?

OK. I know *I'm* not enjoying this, but Blaire seems to be. And, more importantly, I don't want Doug to have a better first date than me.

'Take me to your favourite place,' I say. 'I'm sure I'll love it.'

*

It's strange, holding a girl's hand. Mine and Blaire's don't jigsaw at all, and she's gripping so tightly that my fingers are starting to go numb. I'm worried that everyone is staring at us with hate crimes on their mind. Thank God we've ended up in gay friendlier Soho.

Wait. Soho. Aren't Doug and Adelaide in Soho?

No, it's fine. There are a hundred bars in Soho. It's a busy Thursday night. What are the chances of seeing Doug?

Blaire walks us into Soho Theatre Bar and I immediately see Doug.

He's leaning forward over a candlelit table. He's mid-laughter, engrossed by the storyteller with her back to us. She has smooth brown hair, the same length mine used to be. In fact, seeing her profile, gesturing animatedly, she looks remarkably like a better version of Gina.

I yank Blaire's hand to swivel us out of the bar.

'I hate this place,' I shout. 'Too many thespians.'

But Blaire either doesn't hear me or completely ignores me, and continues into the bar. Actors glare at me with such convincing hatred that I reluctantly follow her in.

I try to wheel us to a booth in the back corner, where we'd have less chance of being seen, but it's rammed. There's only one empty table: an unequivocally, patronisingly empty one, horribly close to Doug and Adelaide's.

Blaire sits down at it. She glares at me across the room.

I mouth that I'll get our drinks.

At the bar, I try to work out whether to run away or masochistically stay to watch Doug's happy date face. Maybe he's less likely to fall in love with her if I'm there, centimetres away, staring at him?

A waft of sweet floral perfume. The woman who looks

like a beautified version of Gina squeezes up to me in the queue.

The bartender immediately goes to serve her.

'No, this person was here before me,' she smiles, gesturing at me. 'Oh, I love your shirt.'

Damn it all. Compersion is *hard*.

Looking back at the table, I see Doug is texting. I check my phone, but nothing... Must be no reception in here.

Adelaide glances at her phone as it lights up. She laughs beautifully at his message.

Compersion, compersion, compersion...

Well, if Doug is going to see me here with Blaire, I at least want to look like I'm having as good a time as he is.

I head to the table with our drinks and sit down feeling like a vengeful ghost.

Doug doesn't glance up from his phone.

Blaire says something I don't hear.

'Hahahahahaha! Oh my God Blaire, you're so *funny*.'

She nods in agreement. I stare at Doug, resting my face in a delighted, open-relationship smile. But he's engrossed in Adelaide returning to their table.

Doug's wearing his best flirtatious expression. He's looking up at Adelaide over the top of his glasses, one eyebrow slightly raised, his smile lopsided, biting his lip slightly as he talks. I haven't seen that expression in... years.

'I need to get out of here,' I tell Blaire.

'Would you like to come back to mine?' she asks.

That distracts me. I stare at her, mouth flopped open. Does she really think this is working? Or maybe whether you connect or not doesn't matter? Maybe sex is better if you don't fancy them at all?

Over her shoulder, I see Doug laughing at Adelaide's story. He looks so, so happy.

'Yes,' I say to Blaire, still watching him. 'Let's do it.'

I stand, definitely not stumbling, and slot my arm into my jacket hole, definitely not missing.

Striding past them to the exit, I trip and fall into Adelaide.

Blaire tries to catch me, but misses. I apologize madly and try to jerk away. But Doug has finally noticed me. The laugh freezes on his face.

'Oh, hi,' I say to him, as if he's a colleague I met once. 'I'm just off back to hers, if that's OK.'

Blaire and Adelaide look between us.

'Er,' says Doug, wide-eyed in panic. 'OK.'

I give him an emphatic thumbs up.

Then, desperate to get out of here before I cry, I grab Blaire's hand, and pull her away.

Walking to the tube, Blaire's hand feels like a manacle.

I'm not ready. I'm definitely in too vulnerable an emotional state to sleep with someone for the first time. I don't even *like* her. But suddenly we're at Oxford Circus station, about to tap in.

'Blaire,' I stop her. 'I-I'm very flattered but I-I have work early tomorrow and...'

Commuters jostle us. She continues to frown at me, not catching on.

'I don't want to have sex with you tonight,' I snap, 'thank you.'

A passer-by raises his eyebrows.

'Oh.' She looks at the floor. 'Did I do something wrong?'

'No! God no! It's all me.'

'How about next time?' she says, and in my awkward nervousness I say, 'Yes! Anything!'

Wait. What did I just sign up for?

'Well, goodbye then,' I say.

She licks her lipstick.

Oh, God. The parting kiss.

I haven't kissed anyone that isn't Douglas in seven years. What if I've forgotten how to?

My first queer kiss. What if this kiss unlocks my true lesbian calling and changes everything?

Conscious of all the people bustling around us, I look down at Blaire's mouth. I'm not used to leaning down to kiss. I clumsily cup her soft cheek with my hand, thinking about Doug's bristle.

I tilt my head. She tilts her head in the same direction. I tilt the other way, so does she. I bluff one way, and then swoop in the other, putting my mouth on hers.

Nothing. I feel absolutely nothing.

Until our teeth bash. When I flinch away, I realize with a start that her eyes were open, staring at me the whole time.

'Sorry,' I say, in parting.

Back at home, surrounded by Doug's discarded clothes. I take off my George date outfit and put on my oldest Gina pyjamas. Getting into bed, conscious of Doug's cold half, I eat through a pack of biscuits.

I'll admit it, I'm pretty fucking disappointed.

Yes, maybe a secret part of me had wondered if I was really a lesbian who had just accidentally ended up with a boy and, never knowing what real love was, lived a half-real version with a man who should really be a best friend. There seem to be so many stories of people, married with kids, who have a surprise gay affair later in life and are reborn. But a gay woman just put her lips on mine and I felt nothing.

My dad used to say that you can't call yourself a musician if you don't make music. Can I really call myself queer if I haven't consummated it with at least one toe-tingling, mind-numbing, body-inflaming kiss with another queer?

Meanwhile, my 'boyfriend' is clearly having a fantastic time dating someone else. What if he ends up falling madly in love with Adelaide and leaving me? When we were planning to open our relationship, why didn't I think of that?

Sitting here in a pile of snotty tissues and Hobnob crumbs, I can't help but think *I'd* go for Adelaide if I was him.

I hug a pillow that smells like Doug's anti-dandruff shampoo and watch a *SophieSnob* video about *What To Do If Your Boo Breaks Up With You.*

Eventually I hear the key in the lock and Doug tiptoes in, flushed with excitement.

While we brush our teeth, he talks about how lovely the restaurant was, how lovely the bar was, how lovely Adelaide was. My teeth are very clean by the end.

'But more importantly,' he says, finally squeezing toothpaste onto his brush. 'How was *your* date, Casanova?'

I spit.

'Not great. We kissed once. We didn't click.'

Doug removes the brush tentatively from his mouth.

'Oh... Neither did Adelaide and I. You know, thinking about it, I think she was a bit *too* perfect, you know?'

He pats my shoulder.

'Next time, eh?'

22

Doug and I both thought that being in an open relationship would mean convoying sexy people in and out of our bedroom. In reality, nothing much has happened. It's been over a month since our first dates and neither of us has done anything more than a goodbye kiss.

I've been on a couple more. Freya was... fine. Candice was... fine. Half-hearted texting culminated in half-hearted drinks and half-hearted goodbye kisses. But there was no spark, and clearly they felt the same way.

Doug went on a second date with Adelaide and returned glowing. I'm now dreading the moment he tells me he's going on their third. Because third date is code for sex, right?

Scheduling open-relationship dates into the calendar was relatively straightforward, but the logistics of having sex with someone else is an entirely different matter. Doug and I live together. We would be very aware if one of us was out of our bed, and even more aware if someone else was in. We have a night-time routine, favourite sleeping position, and shared alarm clock. And the thought of sleeping here alone, while he's out big-spooning someone else, or of him sleeping alone here without me... It's practically and emotionally impossible.

So we agree that we'll only share a bed with someone else if we're already away from home: if one of us is on tour, or a work trip, or something.

But for weeks, our calendar remains static. I can't tell if Doug has wanderlust too.

Summer Bank Holiday Sunday. Best day of the year. Doug and I embark on our favourite walk on Hampstead Heath. We've done it each year since moving to London and have each detail down to a fine art. Or at least, Doug has. I just follow him and worry about where the next toilet is.

I'm sweating already. I squint up at the blue sky in appreciation but also wishing I'd remembered my sunglasses.

Doug pulls my sunglasses from his bulging rucksack.

'Thought you might forget.'

I kiss him on his downy ginger cheek. Doug dollops sun cream on me, taking extra care of the newly exposed skin on my neck. When he's done, we wordlessly swap over.

While walking, we play our game, 'Dog Bingo'. The rules are: spot a dog, squeeze the other's hand and say 'Bingo!' It's very competitive.

'It will be lovely to be by the sea again,' I say, and then interrupt myself to point out a thick-coated Chow Chow. 'And to see your – Bingo! – parents again.'

Doug nods.

'They're looking forward to cooking you your favourite – Bingo! – Guinness pie.'

Since Bronze Age formed, we've stayed at his parents' house in Edinburgh for a week in the summer. Doug and I normally go a few days early to see his abnormally normal parents. They then go off camping and the rest of Bronze Age arrive. It's been slightly stranger, the past few years, since Jasper's been there. I prepare them meals, read in the garden, wait for them to finish, feel sorry for myself. Sure, they offer for me to join them, but I can tell they don't really want me there. Why would they? The ghost of pianos past, haunting their rehearsals...

What will our dynamic be this year? I haven't seen them in months. I'm in Phase. They're going to be busy practising for a festival they're playing at, the Scottish Festival of Love. (I remember going with the Bronzers in second year, dreaming that we'd play there one day...) Will I be treated more like one of them, now I'm a musician again, or will being in gay Phase make me even more of an outsider?

Holding Doug's hand, I ask casually, 'Did you and Poppy ever talk about whether she is, you know – Bingo!'

'No,' he says, missing a Labrador rolling around in the grass, 'she's always pretty cagey about feelings. She doesn't really let anyone in.'

I look at his thoughtful expression behind his glasses.

'Maybe I can try and find out when we're in Edinburgh.'

Doug looks out across the lake. Sighs.

'Aren't you looking forward to having some time off work?' I ask.

'Yeah,' he says, as if trying to convince himself. 'It's always nice pretending we're full-time musicians. But...'

We sit down on our usual bench by the lake, overlooking clear reflections of trees and clouds. After a moment, Doug turns to me and says, 'Do you ever feel like you're living a double life?'

I freeze.

'I have my musician night life with Bronze Age,' he says, 'but then I have my sensible day job at the office.'

My shoulders untense.

'Sometimes it's good,' he continues, 'to feel like you have two lives. If something is going badly at work or whatever, it's nice feeling like that isn't your only shot.'

'I've only got, one shot, with you,' I sing. He doesn't join in.

'But sometimes it's exhausting,' he says. 'And confusing. I don't know which I'm better at. If I concentrated on one, I'd get twice as far. You know, I could get a promotion by Christmas if I worked at it. But if we all quit our jobs for Bronze Age, maybe we could actually *make* it.'

'At least if you're split in two you keep your options open,' I say, not sure if I believe it.

'Yeah,' he smiles wryly. 'But what if keeping your options open ruins both of them?'

We watch the sunlight flicker on the lake. Ducks dive their heads under the surface.

'And now we're in this open relationship. To be honest, I'm struggling to find the time. Our calendar seems so full all of a sudden. You know, Adelaide messaged the other day, but now she volunteers with terminal cancer patients on Thursday nights and I can't fit her in anywhere else, so...' He sighs, shakes his head. 'It just feels a bit much, sometimes. Like good things are slipping through my fingers because I'm not on the ball. You know?'

'Yes,' I say. 'I know.'

'Thank God I've got you,' he says, kissing my hand. 'The one constant in my life. My anchor.'

We look out at the ripples on the water.

★

Doug and I reach the top of a hill, where a large oak tree shields a bench. We took a picture here on our first trip to the Heath, and now repeat the tradition every year.

Doug's hand around my waist, waving cheesily to the camera.

Scrolling back through the album on my phone, I realize that, unintentionally, I'm wearing the same outfit that I wore four years ago: a blue dress with a pink flower pattern which is a particular favourite of Doug's. But it's the first photograph where I'm feeling the breeze through my new Gina-George haircut.

Looking out at the beautiful rolling hills and happy dogs, I think about how this is one of our favourite places in the world, and how, if Doug were going to propose, he might do it right here under this tree.

Doug runs back and fiddles with the camera. Then he takes a deep breath and starts rummaging around in his rucksack. His back to me, he's trying to hide the contents.

No.

He's getting down on one knee.

'*Stop!*' I scream.

Doug's face jerks up at me.

He's applying a blister plaster to the back of his foot.

'What's wrong?' he asks, immediately stopping his surgery to check on me. 'What's happened?'

'I... Can we retake that photo? I was blinking.'

Doug sighs affectionately.

When we're ruminating over which of these identical photos is best to add to our bedroom shrine, Doug slips his arm round my waist and says, 'One day, when we take this photo, maybe there won't just be the two of us... there'll be someone else very special there too.'

My blood runs cold.

'Someone small,' he says, 'and cute, with tiny little feet.'

He bends down to kiss me. But I don't *want* his babies right now?

'Maybe someone perfectly sausage-shaped?'

Oh, a *dog*.

I kiss him properly in reply. He breaks away, checking his watch.

'Time to head back, put the bolognese on, and listen to some bangers.'

The perfect Sunday – as always. I squeeze his hand hard, even though there isn't a dog in sight.

'Bingo.'

Bank Holiday Monday, Doug's with Bronze Age all day.

I lie in bed, doom-scrolling.

I have this generalised desire-slash-paranoia about someone texting me.

But then Mum texts me, asking if I'd like to have a phone call, causing me to groan into the pillow. I'm scared to even make small talk with Mum in case I let something about George's life slip, and she realizes I'm 'bisexuelle' and disowns me. So I don't reply.

Then Soph texts me, but I'm scared she'll ask for a Kit-Pumpernickel update, and I'll have to decide whether to attempt lying to her. So I don't reply.

Then Doug texts me from rehearsals, but I don't want to

get into a big discussion about Bronze Age Edinburgh plans, which is making me feel anxious already. So I don't reply.

The other person who keeps texting me – constantly – is Blaire. Every so often I force myself to reply, despite having zero interest. I know that makes me sound like a terrible person, but really, how many times can I think of a different answer to 'what are you up to?' before wanting to end it all?

After lunch, Rudy messages the Phase group chat. I collapse with relief. It's a picture of a cat saying 'Freddie Purrcury'. Isobel messages back.

Ru… you're better than that. X

im absolutely not!!!!!! Lololol ;) xoxoxo

Then Kit types, *shall we get a drink guys i'm bored out my mind*

My heart beats in my ears. I need to type before the conversation moves on and I miss my chance.

Sozzie im making cookies with my brother!!!! hes a baker!!!! :) :)

Crap, I need to send a message *now* before the trip is cancelled. I carefully use all lowercase like Kit does.

i'm bored too I type.

Great, now if Kit rejects me it's going to be apocalyptic for my ego. I add, *i had drinks on hampstead heath yesterday, might go again today*

Kit can still reject me with that. I add a get-out clause.

if i can force myself out of bed

I stare unblinking at the little dots in the bottom corner.

mind if i join you types Kit.

In bed?!

can drive to heath in like an hour

Oh my God. Be breezy.

Sure!!!

So breezy. And damn it, I forgot the lowercase.

isobel, you joining? I add hurriedly.

u have a church thing right? types Kit.

Yes! Have fun, but not too much! X

So it's just me and Kit and a sunny Hampstead Heath. Like normal, platonic, pals.

Two hours later. Kit still isn't here. My phone battery is going to die. The knowledge that my phone will notify me if she messages does not prevent me from checking it every three seconds.

My phone goes off unbearably loudly and I drop it on the pavement. Smash.

'No!'

There's a crack right down the middle. Worst day of my life.

But there's also a message from Kit. Best day of my life.

It says, *look up*

I look up, and there's Kit, strolling towards me from the sun's rays, like an angel taking me to pearly gates. She's got a pack of beers in a plastic bag over her elbow, and is holding two Mr Whippys. All is forgiven.

Side by side under the dappled light, eating our fast-melting ice creams, I feel like we're the only people in the world.

Silence with Kit is not the same as silence with Doug. With Doug, it's two companions who know everything the other is going to say already. With Kit, it's filled with anticipation and expectation, the anguish of trying to seem laid-back but never boring.

Kit grins at me.

'You've got a bit of ice cream,' she says, pointing to my cheek, 'right here.'

Feeling the stickiness on my cheek I look at her coquettishly, hoping she'll wipe it away. But she's not looking at me any more, she's seeing how far she can throw her ice-cream napkin into the trees. I surreptitiously wipe my cheek myself.

There's a phenomenally cute corgi, wobbling past. I stop myself from saying Bingo, but I squeal, 'Oh my God! Look at that ickle woofer!'

Kit nods without passion. So Kit doesn't like dogs. Could probably have predicted that one.

We walk behind a gaggle of svelte women with tote bags. They're daring each other to take their tops off at the Ladies' Pond.

'Let's go,' says Kit, pushing me forwards.

It's busy in there, but we find a patch on the bank, close to the water's edge. I kick off my shoes but keep my socks on in case I have weird feet.

Kit lights a cigarette. I try to ignore the signs discouraging smoking.

We lie down next to each other on the grass. Do I dare to lie on my side? It would surely be unbearably intimate to lie looking at each other at this distance. I stay on my back.

I've started to sweat and redden with sunburn, but I don't want to spoil the moment by moving. Kit is so at home in the direct blaze, her skin bronzing almost before my eyes. I wonder if she's going to get a tan line around those sunglasses. If anyone could make awful tan lines into a fashion statement, it would be Kit.

She grins slightly. I wonder what she's daydreaming about.

'You're staring,' she says.

Crap, I thought she had her eyes closed. I flush beneath my already pink skin, looking like an uncooked sausage.

'How are you not sweating?' I ask her.

'It *is* pretty warm.'

She kicks off her trainers and socks. She has effortlessly unweird feet. Then, in one smooth movement, and to my repressed astonishment, she takes off her jeans. She's wearing black Calvin Klein boxers. I make a note to buy myself an identical pair. She lies back down, arm behind her head, white T-shirt catching slightly on one side, revealing her hip. The angular bone next to her soft navel is too much for me to bear. I stare out at the water, trying to cool down.

'You going for a dip?' she asks.

I look at her incredulously.

'I don't have a towel. I don't have a swimming costume. And unlike you, I don't want to strip off in front of people.'

'If no one else was around, would you swim?'

'I don't know… Maybe?'

Kit stands up, gesturing for me to do the same. I feel like this is another test and I want to pass, so I do. That's when Kit picks me up, puts me over her shoulder, and runs towards the pond.

I'm screaming and battering her back, unsure whether it's with delight or terror or both, bafflingly concerned about whether I'm heavy. The whole crowd watches. And Kit is carrying me through the garden, and I'm kicking and screaming in her arms and Kit is throwing me into the – *shit! Is she actually going to—*

Sudden freezing cold. Muffling silence. I try to enjoy the shock but my heart is racing. Opening my eyes under the surface, I thrash, trying to move with the water. The sunlight's streaming through and it's not blue under here, it's green and grey and orange. It's beautiful, it really is. But it's also murky and full of weeds and creepy crawlies and people weeing and what if I drown down here and—

Just before I think I might actually die, I break the surface. Kit whoops, the crowd cheers, the lifeguards reprimand. Floundering to the steps, self-conscious of my clinging shirt and sodden shorts, I'm elated and ashamed.

Kit charms her way out of us getting told off too much. It probably helps that she looks as if she's from an underwear catalogue. She promises not to do it again and leaves a crisp bank note in the donation box.

Kit puts her arm around me and steers us away. I'm laughing rather hysterically. We leave the ladies pond, collapse on the first bit of secluded grass, and look at each other, bright-eyed. Then Kit covers her mouth in sudden shock.

'George,' she says, 'I forgot a bottle opener.'

I laugh even more hysterically and she smashes the bottles against a rock with practised success. We toast the bottles together.

Kit gets out her phone and takes a picture of us. One single photo. I have a split second to arrange my face. She looks effortlessly roguish. I look like a newborn rat. But somehow, the laugh still on my face, George looks like a *good* newborn rat. Like a rat having fun.

Kit asks permission to post the photo online and I nod, thrilled at the thought that she wants to share this moment with anyone. It also means, I think happily, that I will have proof of that photo, and can admire it (/her) whenever I want.

Kit captions it: *george accidentally fell into a pond. she was definitely not pushed by kit*

I contentedly sip, trying to unstick my shirt from my bra.

'Do you want to take that off?' she asks.

'Absolutely not, you pervert!'

'Oh come on, can't you be comfortable in front of your mates?'

I look at her for a moment too long. We fill the silence with drinking.

'Shall we go back to my van?'

Umm… Is she inviting me back to her sex van 'as a mate'?

'We could dry you off a bit,' she says casually, 'find you another of my shirts. Finish these beers, listen to some music…'

That *would* all lead to snogging, right? I'm not imagining this?

I sip to give me time to think. Doug's rules say I need to tell him about her, and tell her about him. *Plus* Soph's Pumpernickel means I need to tell her about *her*, and tell *her* about *her*. So why is it that my main concern right now is that if Kit and I kissed, she'd probably expect more, and I'm scared of sexing wrong?

'Maybe another time,' I say, hating myself.

Kit's eagle eyes squint at me, and she shakes her head.

'I can't work you out, George.'

I look away.

'It's like you're never fully *here* with me. I never know what you're really thinking.'

She reaches over to me and gently strokes away a stray hair clinging to my cheek. It reddens.

'What is it that you really want?'

I try to laugh and regretfully shrug her off.

'I don't know,' I say. 'I'm just a Libra.'

I walk home.

Doug says he's glad I had a nice time in Hampstead Heath with Phase. He rubs aloe vera onto my sunburns. Guilt embeds itself even deeper in my stomach.

23

Before Timmy has even sat down his memory-foam hands stretch to play the wrong F sharp.

'Timmy.'

He freezes.

'What did I do wrong?' he says.

'Nothing.'

Yet.

'But I wondered if we should try something a little different today?'

He retracts his hands, face incredulous. Wow, OK, so the kids are aware of how samey my lesson plans are.

Timmy's like a girl my dad taught. She got so in her head about one note she kept playing wrong that the problem expanded. What started as one bum note became a bum bar, then a bum piece. So my dad tricked her.

'Let's leave that piece alone for now,' I say to Timmy. 'Try some scales instead.'

Timmy's so relieved he nearly falls off his chair.

I play a few exercises and ask him to repeat them. We jolly along like this for a while, moving up and down the keyboard. G, F, G. G, F sharp, G.

'Play that twiddle again, Timmy?'

He does so, amiably.

'You just played the F sharp bar.'

He's so flabbergasted that he turns to look at me while his fingers play it again. I'm a guru!

In a moment of mad euphoria, Timmy and I high five. Then we remember who we both are and slouch back. But the high-five mood remains.

'I'll practise this week, Miss. I actually will.'

I get that same rush of energy and benevolence as when I helped Matilda. This must be what teaching is meant to be like. My dad must have felt like this all the time. No wonder he used to glow after lessons and get so many Thank You cards, and wear that stupid piano tie with such pride. I wish I could have talked to him about us both teaching...

Maybe being a better teacher really would make him proud of me. Help him forgive me...?

Hope arrives her usual three minutes late, but I don't do our usual script about timekeeping.

'Hope,' I say, 'you're already playing "Für Elise" well enough for the end-of-term concert. But... Do you still want to write your own songs?'

Her smile ignites.

She plays a simple melody in a major key that reminds me of a nursery rhyme. Just what you'd expect from a girl wearing smiley-face hair clips. She starts to sing.

'*Nobody sees the me deep inside*
Don't know who I am except what makes me cry...'

She repeats that a few times, starting to sob.

'*Shatter my ribs,*' she rasps, '*Break my heart,*
I was already broken from the start.'

She takes her hands off the keys and turns back to me, smiling sunnily.

'What do you think?' she asks.

I think I need to call her parents.

I blink a few times and say, 'Wow! There's a lot of good stuff there. Avant garde.'

Hope beams.

'But I wonder if it might work even better if you make the lyrics and the melody... fit together?'

So we get to work. She has other disparate ideas and I show her how to piece parts together into a unified whole. For the first time, our lesson overruns.

'Thank you, Miss,' she says, packing up with a spring in her step. 'I can't wait to play you more next week!'

I'm looking forward to it too. I like Hope's emo punk side.

I'm particularly excited to work my magic on Percival.

'Good morning, Percy,' I say heartily. 'Isn't it a simply glorious day?'

'Oh! Quite!' he says, surprised to find another soul in agreement.

'I wondered if you'd had more thoughts about the end-of-term soiree?' I ask, getting caught up in Percy's voice. I lean in confidentially. 'Your offering is always a particular highlight of the proceedings.'

Percy's dimples are delighted.

'That's awfully kind of you, Miss. I confess, I have still been playing Debussy's "Clair de Lune"...'

My good mood deflates instantly. I want to be a good teacher, but I'm allowed to preserve my own sanity, aren't I? Just a little? How can I teach someone the emotion of a piece that haunts me to my innermost core? Listening to Percy frogmarch through 'Clair de Lune' every week will be like watching him urinate over my dad's gravestone.

Percy must notice my face drop, because he says, 'But no, I quite understand that I'm not proficient enough for the illustrious bergamasque. No matter. I have selected another piece. Something, I think you'll agree, quite different to "Clair de Lune".'

He goes to the last piece in the Grade Seven Syllabus. Last place usually means it's the most modern. Oh God. Percival doesn't want to play one of those 'quirky, postmodern' pieces, does he?

He puts the piece proudly on the piano stand.

It's called 'Honk Honk Honkytonk'. It describes its own tempo as 'with a funky groove, man'.

I almost stop him there. But, I remind myself, let him have a go.

Percy has a go. It's worse than I'd imagined.

'*Stop!*' I scream after five seconds of the torture, my desperate voice echoing off the walls.

'Awfully sorry,' he twitches. 'Was I fluffing it?'

'You're playing the rhythm *straight*, Percy. But it's honkytonk! It's jazz! It needs to be *swung*.'

'Swung?'

'Swung! Yes! You know, a swinging rhythm?'

He squints at me. I nearly ask how he has reached Grade Seven without ever playing anything other than a straight rhythm, but then I remember it's because I took a great deal of pain to ensure it.

I try to explain it in a Percival way. 'Straight rhythm is exactly how it's written in the book. Every beat is the same length as another. If a beat is divided into two – say here, with these quavers – then each takes up an even 50 per cent. You follow?'

Percy nods.

'Well, in swung rhythm,' I say, 'the beat is divided unequally. It's looser. The first half is slightly longer than the second half.'

'How much longer?'

I squirm.

'It depends. There's no mathematical rule, exactly. You've sort of got to feel it.'

His face falls again.

'Are there any techniques you'd recommend to master this swunging?'

I have a vision of trying to teach Civil Percy about jazz, syncopation and the concept of 'chilling out a bit'. I don't know if I *can*. I'm not exactly the grooviest cat on the block myself.

'I'm sorry,' I mumble. 'Maybe you should stick to Classical composers.'

The worst thing is that Percy doesn't fight back. Just nods, disappointed in himself for disappointing me.

'I'm dreadfully sorry,' he says, at the door. 'I'll play Bach in the concert. He doesn't need me to feel anything for him except profound respect.'

Percy salutes me sadly, knocks his head into the door frame by accident, and then walks away.

I stare at the piano.

My dad would have loved 'Honk Honk Honkytonk'.

God, I'm such an idiot.

I haven't been doing what my dad did so well for me: make piano something I *wanted* to do. I realize I've been viewing being a teacher as a kind of punishment and making the pupils feel that too. But in truth, finally letting myself think of memories of my dad in these lessons has made me feel closer to him than anything else since he died.

I thought the pupils wanted to simply pass exams and play in concerts without trying too hard. But – and it seems skull-bashingly obvious now – teaching music shouldn't only be about helping children play correctly; it should be about helping them to just *play*.

I rush to the door.

'Percy!' I call after him. 'For the school concert, I think you should play both of them. "Honk Honk Honkytonk", and "Clair de Lune". Let's work on them next week.'

Percy's face splits into a grin.

'Righto!' he says, and gives me a double thumbs up.

I can't help but give him a thumbs up back. As I go back into my music room, I hear some boys snicker 'Piggy' at him.

Percy snorts affably at them and walks on, a funky groove in his step.

Isobel brings a luxurious fruit platter to the next Phase rehearsal. She eats strawberries while Rudy laughs for a solid five minutes over the photo that Kit sent from the Heath. Emboldened by this confirmation of my friendship with Kit, when it gets to twenty minutes late I say that *I'll* chaperone her from her van.

I wait a second outside, mentally practising my knock and imagining the moment where she opens the door and smiles at me.

With a surge of adrenaline, I knock in the rhythm of 'Mercury'. A muffled croak comes from inside.

'Isy?'

'George,' I say brightly. 'I've got your coffee.'

There's a slow ruffling and the door unlocks. It's dark, warm, and heavy in here, the piles of patterned pillows haphazard. My head swims with Kit's pine cologne. She's squinting at me, wearing just a crumpled black T-shirt and grey boxers, her hair sticking out on one side of her head in a huge cowlick. I implode.

'So you'll only come into my room if I'm already in bed,' she grumbles. 'Chuck me a shirt?'

I throw her the white T-shirt which looks closest to clean. Without hesitating, Kit takes off her shirt. Instinctively, violently, I look away, then stare at the floor, hating myself.

Once I hear her go to the sink, I allow myself to continue staring. She splashes her face and brushes her teeth. Seeing Kit being domestic is absolute catnip to me. Finally awake, she looks at me with more alertness, more affection.

We grab a couple of drum bags each and both go to pick up her coffee cup. Our hands touch and we laugh. I carry it for her, feeling like her girlfriend.

'Thanks, Jeeves,' she says.

Girlfriend, butler, same difference.

When we walk in, Isobel picks up a notebook and, passive-aggressive, starts writing an agenda.

'Shall we finally start? "Virgo In June", "Co-Star", or "Mercury"?'

Kit picks up a kiwi, testing its ripeness.

'We've been playing the same songs for weeks now. Let's do something new.'

'We don't *have* anything new,' snaps Isobel. 'If you want something new, you should write it – but unfortunately that would require you to spend some of your time awake, sober, and away from other people's vulvas.'

Rudy stifles a giggle. I, too, try to pretend it was a joke. Has Kit been seeing someone else?

'Jesus Christ, sorry, Mum,' says Kit, cutting her kiwi. 'What about "Cusp"?'

Isobel clicks her pen.

'We're not playing that.'

'Why not?'

'Phase is about living in the present. We shouldn't play songs that aren't relevant any more.'

'What happened to this band being a democracy?'

Isobel throws down her notebook.

'Why do you want to play Marsha's song that much? Are you still in love with her?'

Kit stares at Isobel, mouth parted, each hand holding half a kiwi. She looks around the room at me and Rudy, but we don't say anything – I want to know the answer to that question too. Kit throws her hands up.

'Obviously not. I was *never* "in love" with her, for Christ's sake.'

Isobel crosses her arms. I cross mine too.

'"Cusp" wasn't good enough anyway. I barely remember it,' she says and rounds on me. 'George. How are you getting on with writing *your* song?'

I try to stay calm, sensing my opportunity to be the peace-bringer. The Libra. I pick up an orange.

'Yeah,' I say easily, peeling it. 'I have drafts. It needs work but we could build it together?'

Isobel smiles at me, finally, and I get that feeling like I've pleased the teacher and I'll get a star.

I offer Kit a segment. She takes it and shrugs her agreement.

'That's settled then,' says Isobel, taking an offered segment too. 'We'll start working on it next rehearsal.'

Rudy pops her segment in her mouth and bares it like a fluorescent smile.

'Can't wait to hear your songs for the first time!'

Yeah, I think. Neither can I...

We sink into the collective daydream of rehearsing. But today, it's fitful. 'Mercury' used to feel like an anthem celebrating lust, now it's more complicated. There are more clashes, uneasy dissonances. The chorus's lyrics change to '*You make us come apart / Don't come over it's over it's over.*' Don't get me wrong, the song sounds great: it's more raw, more questioning. But... Is it because I keep saying no to Kit's advances?

Then the door shuffles open and Cara shuffles in.

It's a confusing sensation: on the one hand resenting her for breaking the musical spell we're all weaving and preventing me from sleuthing on what Kit is really trying to say to me, but, on the other, I've become more and more excited to see her.

She's wearing a summery pinafore today, bizarre tattoos on proud display. I force my eyes not to slide down to examine them too closely.

She starts to walk over, directly to me.

I sense, more than I see, Kit turn to see my reaction.

Another test. I need to show loyalty.

Slowly, deliberately, I turn away from Cara, to Kit. In my peripheral I see Cara change direction to pick up our empty rehearsal glasses and feel momentarily guilty. But I've got so much guilt in my stomach these days, I barely notice a little drop more.

'Staying for a drink?' I ask Kit, in a low voice. But she shakes her head.

'Not tonight,' she says, twisting the chain at her neck. 'Need to clear my head. I'm going to drive out somewhere, out of London.'

Isobel applies another round of lipstick. 'Oh, we get it, you're very deep and mysterious.'

'Isy, if you want to come—'

'Wouldn't want to get in the way of you sleeping with some dairymaid.'

Kit rolls her eyes, but doesn't deny it. Just raises a hand in goodbye to the room.

'Text me if you want,' she says.

I know the invitation is personal.

I spend two hours drafting my text to Kit. At around 6 p.m., I send her *hope ur journey was/is ok?*

And check every hour in the night to see if she's replied.

Oh my God, finally, at 10 a.m., she's typing!

I hide my grin and open it, praying for a question or at least something I can work with to continue the conversation.

ha ha yeh

In the shower I think through every detail of our conversation and everything I have done wrong. I stay under the hot water for way too long, burning every inch of my skin.

Look, I know I'm pathetic. But knowing that doesn't stop me spending the rest of the morning – while Doug potters around me, cleaning – trying to think of a way to resuscitate this conversational dead horse.

Eventually I type, *you playing drums to some cows?*

Kit's 'online' button flashes up at midday. She reads my message. She doesn't reply. She goes back offline.

Oh God. Oh God. I meant practising in the countryside, but reading it back, could I sound like I'm insulting some women she's with?!

She hates me.

Or there's something wrong with my internet.

I turn my Wi-Fi off and on again. Turn on my roaming data in case there's a problem with Giffgaff. Nothing.

She hates me.

So I have to make The Choice about whether to double-text.

I know, I know. I shouldn't. But I will.

I scroll through the list of possible in-jokes: horoscopes, cats, short haircuts…

Wow, everything I view as special to mine and Kit's relationship is literally a cliché of lesbians. Does she have the same conversation with every girl? (Cows!) Do we have *anything* unique?

Eventually I send Kit a link to the song 'Caravan' by Van Morrison. Playful! Fun! And there are loads of ways that she can reply! You're welcome, Kit.

Kit comes back online. The tick on my message shifts to 'read'.

There's a pause. Though not long enough to mean she listened to the song I sent.

y hav u sent me this

My cheeks burn.

like we spoke about in ur van? I type. *ur van is called van morrison? remember? and then it just came up on my old playlist and i thought of you?*

She's messaging back! We're in live conversation! Thank you, God!

oh right yeh

I type and send, trying not to overthink:

can't believe you forgot that you silly sausage
i would never forget a pun you made!

I instantly regret the 'silly sausage'. But it's OK, she's typing!

yeh haha but ur more invested in this chat than i am

I read the message three times. The blush tsunamis my face, neck, shoulders, my whole body. I slam the phone screen down on the table.

I pick it up to read it again, then slam the phone down harder. A new screen crack.

She's not allowed to say that! Like, obviously both of us know it's true, but you can't *say* it.

How am I meant to respond? Am I meant to just leave it? Won't that look like I'm in a strop? But I *am* in a strop!

I'll give her the silent treatment.

I check my phone approximately three times a minute.

Doug cooks us a lovely meal and we chat about something about his work, I think.

I go to the loo constantly to check my phone without offending him. After the fourth time in twenty minutes he asks if I'm OK. I pretend I have diarrhoea.

He brings me tablets and gently rubs my tummy. I am a terrible person.

The next day, I text Soph asking if she's free to have a SophieSlob night in. Maybe devising plans for Soph to get with Kit will help me get over her. But she replies saying she thought I was too busy. She's got tickets to go to a gig with Rudy.

So while Doug's out, I watch *Friends*, have a bath – and a whole bottle of wine.

24

It's the middle of June before we have plans to sleep in separate beds. Doug is taking a long weekend off work so that Bronze Age can go to a Lake District cottage to write new songs. In the days before he leaves, I'm itching for the chance to invite a lady friend over.

But when he's standing by the door, guitar and travel bag by his feet, I just want him to stay.

'Text me before *any*thing happens, OK?'

Doug nods sombrely. 'You too.'

'And ring me afterwards. As soon as sexual etiquette allows.'

He ruffles my hair. 'I'll ring you mid throes of passion if you like.'

'Yes please.'

'Gina,' he says, chucking my chin, 'it's incredibly unlikely that anything will happen. I'm away for three nights. It's not a long time to charm someone. I'll probably just be hanging with the guys anyway.'

I wave to him out the window, blowing him kisses until his taxi drives out of sight.

Then I tie up my hair into George's bun, put on a shirt, and get to work.

Because Doug's right. We don't have much time. I need to find a queer who wants to sleep with me, ASAP.

I text Soph to put in some time out-out tomorrow. Saturday. For some reason, a vision of Cara pops into my mind. Could we ever…? No, idiot, stop aiming so unrealistically high. I still can't tell if she has a soft spot for me or hates me. Anyway, she's such a fixture of The Familiar that if we *did* get together (highly unlikely) and I was terrible in bed (highly likely) it would spread round The Familiar like chlamydia. My first should be a stranger.

I scroll in a frenzy on dating apps, but I'm not optimistic about my chances of turning someone from match to sex in three days. Unless…

Blaire! Hi! Sorry I've been bad at messaging back. Are you free this weekend? Or… tonight?

That night, with my snazziest Kit shirt, denim jacket, and new boxer shorts already riding up my bum, I'm at Blaire's flat. I've got it all planned. She's going to appear in the doorway, I'm going to say 'Where were we?' in a husky voice, and then I'm going to passionately snog her and lady sex her.

I'm about to turn my phone off and ring the doorbell, when I see a message from Doug.

I can still hardly believe this, he types, *but the sexy artist in the next-door cottage just asked me over to hers for a 'welcome drink'! Am I ok to go and maybe… do some sex? Good luck with Blaire!!!! XXXXXXXX*

Perfect!!!!! I reply, freaked out. *So in sync x*

I'm going to take this as a sign that I'm doing the right thing. Don't overthink it. And don't think about whether this 'artist' is better at doing sex than me.

I ring Blaire's doorbell. I put on a winning smile and prepare my best husk. The door opens.

'Where were—'

Blaire's wearing a frilly pink blouse which clashes with the orange lipstick. As she comes towards me for a kiss, I know for certain that I don't fancy her. But Blaire seems to have the opposite reaction. She eyes me up and down, shivers in lustful anticipation and says, huskily, 'Where were we?'

We're about the same height and when she curves her arms around my neck and presses her chest against mine, I feel our boobs jostle for space. She jabs her tongue into my mouth. I jerk back instinctively, then remember I'm meant to be kissing her. I look at her open mouth, where her pink tongue lies in wait, twitching with expectation.

Oh God...

'Do you mind if I use your bathroom?'

'I have an en suite,' she says seductively, and leads me upstairs.

I splash my face, dry it on Blaire's towel (hoping it's not her body towel, although I guess if I'm about to have sex with her it doesn't really matter).

'You *are* attracted to women,' I remind my reflection and go back into her room.

'So...' she says, from the bed. 'Where were we?'

Sweet mother of God. She's wearing a rubber banana costume.

A horrible silence.

Eventually she says, 'Ta da. It's my stand-up outfit. Isn't it funny?'

When I don't reply, she stands and wobbles over

'It's a joke,' she says, trying to kiss me again.

To be fair to me, I do stop her there.

'I'm sorry,' I say, the furthest from aroused I've ever been, 'your stem is poking me.'

She peels her banana skin off. What I had not foreseen is that this leaves her in just her bra and pants. Fresh horror.

Her underwear is different to mine, which is a blessing, I guess. But it's red and lacey with bits of mesh in unlikely places. It all screams 'sex' in a way I'm finding deeply alarming.

'Actually, could you put the banana back on?'

'What?'

'Don't worry.'

I take a deep breath. Come on, George, it's now or never.

Blaire's still standing still, in her underwear, staring at me.

'Could we maybe put some music on?' I ask.

She shrugs and gestures to a CD player she has in the corner. (My chest twinges with a memory of my dad playing music too loud in the car... Oh for Christ's sake, don't start remembering Dad *now*.) Blaire has six CDs in a neat pile. Coldplay, and *Now That's What I Call Music* compilations. This is even worse than the banana costume.

I pull out my phone, put it in Blaire's 'Funny Feminist' mug to amplify the sound, and play a *SophieSnob* playlist called *Classic Sapphic*: Hayley Kiyoko. Marika Hackman. Arlo Parks. Christine and the Queens. girl in red. The Japanese House. Phoebe Bridgers.

Their yearning, angst-filled lyrics fill George. She lies

there on Blaire's bed, listening, letting the musicians' desires empower her own. I feel replenished, reconnected to my body.

As the sapphists sing, I conjure Kit into the room. Imagine her so clearly I can hear her breathing. I dim the lights and return to her, lying on top of the sheets. I close my eyes and, along with the music, trace my fingers slowly along her soft side. I feel the goosebumps rise underneath them, feel her quickening breath. Her getting turned on turns me on in turn, and I guide her hands to unbutton my shirt, to slide my trousers down, to pull away at my top...

I'd thought this was going to feel so different, compared to the sex Gina's used to. And it does feel a little different, I suppose, softer, smoother... It's less practised, less linear, less targeted towards an end goal. We meander, linger in the heat. But I needn't have worried that I wouldn't understand the mechanics. You don't need a different manual. Sex is sex, I realize, just with a different person, someone who's discovering you for the first time.

The problem is the gap between songs. In the sudden silence of the bedroom, the illusion of Kit breaks down. Blaire's too-long hair flusters me. I become aware that her sighs and gasps are too... Blaire. George loses connection with the pent-up feelings in her body. All of it evaporates and I'm suddenly just me again, fumbling, not knowing how to touch this person I don't care about, don't even *like*.

I feel gross. It's unjust, unkind, all-round unacceptable, to be physically sleeping with this person but mentally with another. Surely Blaire can tell. Surely she knows I'm not really here with her.

So why does she keep saying yes? Why do I?

I *am* about to stop her, when the next song starts. King

Princess's 'Holy'. And George is back, and Kit is back, and she kisses along my legs, and I don't stop her at all.

Afterwards, Blaire wants to chat. She starts telling me one of her long, punchline-less jokes about someone's pizza order. I don't reply. I stare blankly at her bedroom wall, feeling like the kind of disgusting bloke straight women complain about.

What have I *done*? I shouldn't be here. I should never have been here. God, I hate myself. I hate myself, I hate myself.

I get out of bed, mumbling an excuse, fumbling George's clothes on. Blaire tries to kiss me goodbye, but our timings are all off again and, as I leave, I trip over her banana skin. Only she laughs.

I'm in the taxi when Doug rings. I consider whether I could not pick up, but then remember *he* just had sex with a stranger too.

'How'd it go?' we say in unison.

I try to analyse whether he sounds sexually satisfied or not.

'It was... different!' he giggles. 'Fine!'

Different?! Fine?! Is he breaking up with me or not?!

'Was she better at humping than me?'

'Gina, don't be silly.'

'So she *was*?'

'No! Worse than us, obviously, but still an experience.'

'To be fair to her,' I say, slightly consoled, 'we have had a lot more practice.'

He hums happily.

'How was Blaire?'

I take a moment to consider, then decide it's safest to just repeat him.

'It was... different! Fine!'

'Your first time with a woman and it was... fine? How are you feeling?'

'Oh, I don't know...' I say. And I really *don't* know. 'It wasn't the best experience of my life. It wasn't like with you.'

Doug clucks. 'Sorry to hear that.'

'No, you're not.'

'Well, no,' he laughs. 'I'm relieved I've still got a chance with you. Even with my dongle attached.'

'We need to get a better word.'

I imagine his eyes crinkling at the corners.

'Gina,' he says. 'I'm not sure if a one-night stand with a stranger is going to do much for me, to be honest. It's fun as a novelty, but it mainly reminds me that we're not missing out on much. It reminds me how lucky I am to have you.'

'Wow,' I joke, 'was your sex really that terrible?'

But now I'm not sure whether I'm more concerned about the thought of Doug finding someone else, or him closing our relationship before I've had a chance to sleep with a woman I'm really attracted to. Even if Kit is off limits, there's got to be others who are suitable surrogates, right?

We sit in silence for a bit. I feel like Doug is biting his tongue about something too.

'Let's talk about open relationship stuff again when I get back,' he says.

'Definitely,' I say. Fresh worry twists my stomach.

'Well done us,' says Doug.

When we hang up, I send some garbled messages: telling Soph I've consummated my sexuality, guiltily texting Mum goodnight to balance out my straight world and replying to a message on the Phase chat.

A message pops up. From my private chat with Kit.

ur up l8 she types.

I blush. It feels dirty to be talking to Kit when I've just had sex thinking about her. I feel sure she must be able to tell, somehow. Like your ears burning when someone talks about you, but not your ears.

so are you I type back.

cant sleep. wuu2?

I type, *on my way home from my first lady sex, which was physically satisfying but emotionally confusing, wbu?* then delete it.

just been on a weird date I send. *in taxi back to my place*

Her typing cursor beeps for a moment.

wanna hang out?

Am I just in the headspace to see sex with Kit, or is that an invitation?

Twice in one night? Who *am* I? But, I've got my date pants on. And Doug is away. And I'm feeling sexually confused. I might never have a chance like this again…

Message from Doug pops up. A row of love hearts.

Good night gingerbread xxxx he says. *Really proud of us xxxxxxx*

My stomach churns.

I delete the message I had typed out to Kit and send instead: *ah i'm back at mine now. going to head to bed*

I imagine her sharp eyes on mine as she asks me again why I keep running away from her. From what we could be. Oh God.

After a split second of deliberation, I add:
another time

'But Gee-Gee, how was the actual sex?' says Soph, slamming her fist on the table. 'Blow by blow!'

I cringe and gulp my Bad Witch. It feels good to be back on Familiar territory, but I'm not enjoying recounting my date. I can hardly tell Soph it was only good when I thought about Kit.

'I don't know. W-we weren't... matched up.'

'Matched up?'

I put my head in my hands as I tell her how awkward it felt when the music wasn't playing.

'It sounds like you got in your head about it, bab. You weren't in the moment, with her.'

'Yes!' I say gratefully. 'And I was paranoid that she must be out of it too, because I couldn't believe we could be feeling so differently.'

Soph nods sagely. 'You dissociated.'

I bang my head on the table. Soph puts her hand between my forehead and the table so that I hit her palm repeatedly instead.

'Maybe I'm not bi after all. Soph, what if I got this all wrong and I've just been claiming this word when I'm not allowed?'

Soph pushes me upright and flicks my cheek, hard.

'Don't start that again. Gee, you haven't been with someone other than...' She looks around and mouths Doug's name, 'in seven bloody years. And you've *never* done one-night stands. Only lengthy boyfriends.'

She shudders. She always makes a big show of hating the thought of long-term relationships.

'You need to understand the realities of sleeping around. I'd have been flabbergasted if you had an amazing time first time.'

'*Doug* did,' I say.

Soph's eyebrows raise so fast they almost fly off her face.

'*Doug*,' she mouths. '*Doug* has slept with someone else?'

'Yep, on the same night as me.'

'Jesus, you guys are *too* coordinated.'

I poke at the funky paper witch's hat in my cocktail.

'Gee-Gee,' she says, taking my fiddling hands in hers, 'it was your first time and you put a lot of expectation on it. It's natural to feel underwhelmed. And at the end of the day, I don't think you fancied this girl. If Blaire had been a guy, would you have slept with him?'

I cringe guiltily. Shake my head.

'She keeps texting me wanting to meet up again,' I confess, 'and I don't know what to do. I feel terrible about sleeping with her, but I never want to see her again. Her, or her fucking banana costume.'

I'd kept that bizarre part of the evening out of my retelling to Soph, and immediately regret letting it slip.

'Sorry,' she grins, 'her what?'

But thankfully a squeal comes from behind me. Rudy, Isobel, and Kit have arrived. As they come over, I still feel utterly astonished that these people are my friends.

As I catch Kit's eye, I blush remembering her text from last night. Will Soph be able to sense that I nearly broke her Pumpernickel?

Fortunately, Soph's distracted with someone else. She must

have listened to what I'd said about Isobel being good for *SophieSnob*, because she lingeringly kisses her rouged cheeks.

'Isobel,' she says, in her most luxurious *SophieSnob* voice, 'You look divine.'

Isobel blinks in surprise, but instinctively air kisses her back. 'Oh, why, thank you.'

They start fluttering their eyelashes at each other. Yes! Perfect! It's so convenient! I feel genuine pre-emptive compersion.

I try to catch Kit's eye, but she's staring straight at Soph and Isobel, as if deliberately avoiding me.

Rudy, wilfully oblivious to the dynamics, eats the lime from my drink. 'What were you guys talking about that was making George bang her head against the table?'

I look at Soph in panic, hoping she'll make something up. But she's busy comparing rings with Isobel.

'Basically,' I say, not knowing what will come out of my mouth until I say it, 'a girl I slept with wants to see me again, but I don't know how to tell her I don't want to, without being a complete dick.'

Rudy squeezes my shoulder. 'Get a coffee, go for a long walk, chat through all of it, allow time to process, say you still mean so much to each other but—'

'Rudy, you're too much,' Kit interrupts, shaking her head in astonishment. 'George, you don't want to be "friends" with this girl, right?'

I shake my head.

'It's not her fault, we just didn't... We didn't spark.'

I dare myself to look right at Kit.

'What would *you* do?'

She looks away, rubbing the back of her neck.

'Uh…'

'People know what they're signing up for with Kit,' says Isobel, listening after all. 'One night in the pleasure van and then you're out on the road.'

'Better than a date with you!' snaps Kit. 'Where some innocent girl will fall in love with you and you only give them a peck on the cheek and a passage from the Bible.'

Isobel calmly takes Soph's drink from her hand.

'People are free to do with their bodies what they will. But I want to save mine for someone special.'

'Amen,' says Soph. I nearly fall over at the audacity of this, but Soph doesn't meet my eye. She just asks if Isobel would like another drink.

'I'm sure *George* will volunteer to get them for us,' nudges Soph.

Everyone turns to the bar, where Cara is on duty. I swear she was looking in this direction, but turns away quickly when she sees us staring.

'Oh my God!' squeals Rudy. 'You and Cara? *Yes!* That would be so cute! My brother's a bartender!'

I roll my eyes, but I'm delighted. First Blaire, now Cara: somehow I'm managing to look like a competent lesbian in front of Phase.

At the bar, I'm so nervous about whether she'll be friendly or not this evening that I say, 'How *you* doin?'.

Her green eyes turn on me suspiciously.

'Was that a *Friends* reference?'

'Er, no?'

She grins lopsidedly.

'Doubles, you don't have to lie to me to try and seem cool.'

The blush sizzles my cheeks, but for some reason I like that Cara sees straight through me.

'OK,' I confess, 'so I know it's deeply unfashionable and hasn't aged well, but I used to watch *Friends* every Friday. Alone. In the bath. With wine. Quoting along.'

George suddenly realizes how utterly tragic that sounds. But Cara says, completely earnest, 'Honestly, that sounds incredible. I wish I'd been there.'

We both realize about the bath implications at the same time and become flustered again.

'I mean,' she says. 'Not in the bath... If you didn't want... I just. Look at this.'

Before I know what's happening, she's lifting up her top. What the hell?

Oh, I see. As well as her – frankly very hot – bra, she's also showing me an awful *Friends* tattoo of the sofa from the opening credits.

'No fucking way,' I say, unable to resist poking its abysmal wobbly lines. Her skin radiates heat.

'I know! From when I was like, seventeen. Could it *be* any more tacky?'

I splutter.

'It is very, very bad. Do you regret it?'

'Of course not,' she says, suddenly sincere again. 'All my tattoos are a part of me, and they all celebrate something I love. Why on earth would I regret that?'

A woman from the now exceedingly long queue behind me tuts too loudly for us to continue. So, regretfully, I just say a rather awkward 'laters' to Cara, and teeter back to the table with drinks.

Kit mutters, 'Finally.'

The jealousy I detect there is worth the extortionate amount of money I spent on this round.

Soph toasts, looking at Isobel. 'To Sappho!'

We all toast back and I chide myself for having worried that Soph being here would mess with the Phase equilibrium. All my best friends, together round one table. How could it be any more perfect?

Looking around, at Isobel, Rudy, Kit, and Soph, all laughing about a horoscope joke that I do actually understand, I feel stupid for doubting that I belong here. I don't need to have sex with someone like Blaire to prove it.

While Soph's inviting Phase to do a *SophieSnob* interview, I text under the table.

Hi Blaire, sorry it's taken me so long to reply. Sorry but I don't think we should see each other again. Sorry. Hope your comedy goes well. Sorry. X

Then I delete her number. While my hands are there, I dare to rest one next to Kit's knee. I swear she leans, gently, into it.

Three cocktails later, my hand has risen all the way up the side of Kit's thigh. I feel dizzy with the daring and with the heat that seems to be going directly from her leg to my cheeks. God, I'm longing to kiss her tonight. I *need* to kiss her tonight.

If Soph gets with Isobel, surely that means the Pumpernickel about Kit is off? Then all I need is to say to Kit that I'm in an open relationship – Doug's rules never said I needed to say *who* I was in an open relationship with. Then I tell her I can't do anything long-termy serious, which is exactly what she wants, right? Win-win for everyone!

Soph drunkenly shouts for us to all dance, asks for Isobel's hand, pulls her to the dance floor. Rudy laughs after them, pulling me up, severing my secret union with Kit's body. In the haze of the throbbing strobe lights, I sense Kit prowl after us.

Thank God for alcohol, which has stripped George of her inhibitions, allowing her to lose herself to the pumping music, to throw her head back, to lift her arms up, to revel in the feeling that she might be being watched. I swear I can feel Kit's eyes burning into me and just the thought of her being so nearby, her leg still warm from my hand, makes my movements more desperate. I long to feel her body behind mine, to feel her hands along my sides, to feel her lips on my neck…

In the crush of the dance floor my eyes part slightly and see flashes of recognisable bodies between the jumping masses, see Rudy's bouncing pink curls, Isobel's swaying blonde waves, the back of Soph's beaded braids. But where is Kit's short, messy—

The crowd parts and I see her at last. But she's not looking at me.

Kit's dancing with Soph.

Soph's arms are around her neck, and Kit's hands are scratching at the back of Soph's shirt, pulling her closer. Kit's kissing the side of Soph's neck, her fingers sliding under the straps of her top. And then they're kissing deeply. They look so beautiful together, Isobel, Rudy and I stop to stare.

Then I run to the toilet and throw up.

I'm in the back of a taxi with Soph and Kit. Soph's in the middle, holding hands with her. I'm squished in as close to the side door as possible, certain I smell like sick.

Soph caught me trying to sneak away and forced me to share, because they were 'going back to hers as soon as possible'.

'Did you reply to Blaire?' asks Soph.

I nod sharply. I watch Kit's thumb stroking Soph's thumb.

'You'll have better luck next time,' she says, patting my leg. 'You should obviously ask for Cara's number!'

'Cara's a great kisser,' says Kit.

My stomach writhes. It's the only thing she's said all journey. God please don't let me vom again.

'Hey,' says Soph, tickling Kit's knee, 'you trying to make me jealous?'

Kit whispers something in Soph's ear and she moans.

'Are there any sick bags in this car?' I say loudly. Soph frowns at me questioningly. I don't look back.

The rest of the journey is silent, except for the rustle of stroking fabric. I try looking out the window to distract myself, but their roaming hands are reflected in the window.

Compersion compersion compersion. Nope nope nope.

I can't tell whether I feel more betrayed by Soph or by Kit. Obviously, I am aware that really *I* was betraying both of them and completely deserve this punishment. But Kit's hand is fiddling with the fold at the bottom of Soph's mini dress and I wonder if, really, did I deserve a punishment quite *this* bad?

Probably.

After the longest twenty-three minutes of my life, I fall out of the taxi. Kit doesn't look up from Soph's neck. Soph starts to say goodnight but I slam the door in her face.

I spend the next morning in a nebulous state of dread. I dread receiving a message from Soph. I dread not receiving a message from Soph. I turn my phone off, then on, over and over.

It's 5 p.m. when my screen lights up. Soph's ringing. Despite having all day to think about it, I'm paralysed by indecision. I let it ring through. She rings again. I ignore it. She messages.

O

M

G

!!!!!

I might as well have picked up the call given how clearly I can hear her ecstasy. I leave it a few minutes then decide it's better to hear it from the horse's mouth than continue imagining it.

Tell me everything!!!!!

Unfortunately, she does.

They had the most incredible night, morning, and afternoon of lustful passion. She's physically exhausted yet never felt more alive. She's never felt closer to anyone. Kit opened up everything to her (Soph's choice of words), spoke about all her dreams and desires, and Soph says they're officially girlfriends. Great! So, even worse than I could have imagined!

im gonna start joining u guys 4 rehearsals n drinks n stuff!

it's all worked out so perfectly!

I don't think it's possible for my stomach to sink further.

*did u no flirting with isobel would work so well? great tip,
pumpernickel pal!*

Nope, there it is. My stomach finds further depths to sink
to. I start typing, but Soph sees that I'm online and she rings
me. I pick up – and she's already screaming. I scream back.
She gives me another blow-by-blow. I scream more.

Eventually a thought formulates. 'Soph you didn't... you
didn't tell Kit about Douglas?'

There's a pause.

'No, Gee, surprising as this may be, we didn't spend the
night talking about you. We were a bit busy with other things.'

I pretend to laugh. 'Cool, cool.'

'You said *you'd* tell her about Douglas.'

'Yeah, and I will, I will – it just hasn't been the right time.'

'But you have told Douglas about everything, right?'

'Yes, I've told Doug everything I've told you.'

Another pause.

'I don't like this, Gee. I can't have any secrets from Kit now
we're so close.'

I tug my hair out.

'Soph, what are you talking about? You've been my
best friend *forever*. You have a one-night stand with some
randomer and you're going to betray our Pumpernickel?'

'It's not a one-night stand and Kit's not some randomer. I
told you, we're in love.'

'Oh please, Kit doesn't *do* love. What makes you think
you're different from the others?'

There's a ringing silence.

'Gee, why are you—'

'Kit wanted an easy lay and you were throwing yourself
at her,' I say very fast. 'She'll never want to see you again.

And you'd better not come to Phase rehearsals; you'd be embarrassing yourself. I'm sorry, but I'm just trying to protect your feelings.'

I bite down hard on my hands. I'm shaking. I feel sick. I already regret everything I said, but I can't take it back now.

After a long moment she says, 'Oh, *I'm* embarrassing myself?'

The air crackles.

'*I'm* not the one embarrassing myself,' she says, her voice low and dangerous. 'Honestly? I used to think you were queer, but now I'm not so sure. You're treating it like a game, a play to dress up for. You're so desperate to fit in, you've changed every part of yourself into what you think a stereotype lesbian is. The name! The shirts! The horoscopes! The hair! Is it really *you* any more? Is any of it even true? Or are you just getting on the gay pride bandwagon now that it's more socially acceptable? Because you realize you've got nothing else in your sad little life?'

She starts mimicking my voice.

'"Ooh, I'm *George*, and I'm interesting now because I'm *queer*. I'm in a *band* which is so important I don't know what the community would do without me. Oh except that I'm only gay on Thursdays. The rest of the week I play happy families with my *boyfriend*. Did I mention I've got a super-perfect *boyfriend*? We're *so* happy. We're so happy that we cook the same batch bolognese every Sunday and do the same vanilla sex routine that we've been doing for fifty years. And when we get married and move to the country, we'll host bourgeois dinner parties and tell other straight couples that we're better than them, because we had an open relationship once where we fucked other boring people too."'

She gasps for air.

'I mean, Jesus Christ! Being a lesbian is my *life*. I dedicated my career to it. I gave up my family for it. My parents. My brother. My childhood. My heritage. You think it's all rosy for me, because I only show you that half of my life. But you have no idea. I'm not some part-timer, only queer when it's convenient. I can't leave when things get tough. You want to be a gay tourist, skipping off to The Familiar when you fancy an exotic experience. Well, holiday's over, Gina. Fuck off and stop pretending you belong with us.'

I don't know who hangs up first.

25

Alexa and I nod at each other with the recognition of two professionals trying to pretend they're not hungover or depressed. In the smoking area we stir three sugars into our teas.

'Why did I become a teacher?' she asks the universe.

'Can you roll out your lesson on the musical importance of silence?'

Alexa shakes her head. 'Already done it twice this term. They'll catch on.'

We sit in our own lesson on silence for a bit.

Alexa's sweet of the week is chocolate-coated raisins. She eats them gingerly, trying to make sure the squidgy raisin doesn't make too much noise.

'Timmy started playing the F sharp wrong again,' I complain. 'He's a lost cause. Hope's got writer's block, Percival's got "groovy" block – everyone's got a block. I wish *I* had a block – in my ears.'

I refuse Alexa's offer of a chocolate-coated raisin.

'My pupils' offerings for the end-of-term concert are going to be appalling. No, worse, they're going to be exactly the same as last year. Just a line-up of children playing "Für Elise", each, in their own special little way, playing it wrong.'

Alexa peels the chocolate off a raisin, looking at me. She pops the naked raisin back in the bag.

'Gina, is everything OK?'

I stop with my tea halfway to my mouth. We don't normally ask how the other is.

'I thought you'd actually been getting on with the rodents recently. You were all peppy about how you'd done a *Dead Poets Society* on them.'

She gestures at me with a conductor's precision.

'The hair, the clothes, the hangovers... You've changed. You're acting like I did when my marriage was failing.'

'My marriage is not failing!'

'You're not married.'

'No, but, if I *was* married, my marriage would not be failing. It would be succeeding. It would be an A-star marriage. Thank you.'

'OK... And nothing else is going on?'

'No.'

'OK...'

We both stare at the plain brick wall opposite the smoking shelter.

'Why, what happened with your marriage?'

'Oh, I was cheating on him.'

I choke on my tea.

'But what really broke us up was that he was cheating on me too.'

Alexa impassively pats my back with one hand, pops a chocolate shell into her mouth with the other.

'I think he wanted me to find out. The amount of panties he'd leave lying around. I'm sure most of them were plants.'

She shrugs.

'At least they were in my size.'

It strikes me that Alexa is currently the only person I could talk to about my mess of a life. I wonder what she'd say to my bisexual open-relationship attempts? I look at her, as she glares at the sun. She probably wouldn't bat an eyelid. Maybe she's been there herself. Maybe she'd just recommend listening to Bach.

'How was it,' I ask. 'Ending it?'

'Good,' she says. 'Good to stop pretending. And get rid of the threat of blackmail. And only have to clear up my own underwear.'

She considers.

'But I did like the secrecy of cheating. It felt like real living, like I was a protagonist.' She licks a final speck of chocolate from her finger. 'But then you realize it's not him that's making you feel anything, it's just the novelty. Tale as old as time.'

She throws her empty raisin wrapper at the bin.

It misses.

We both look at it on the ground.

'Of course it didn't work out with the other idiot,' she says. 'But it's fine, I set his car on fire.'

The bell goes. She puts the wrapper in the bin and pats my back encouragingly.

That evening, I automatically go to text Soph, then remember I can't. That's the weirdest part. Soph and I fight constantly, but we've never actually *fought* before.

I text Doug. He doesn't reply. Probably sleeping with someone else.

I text Kit. She doesn't reply. Probably sleeping with someone else.

If I had to make a bargain with the universe, that only Kit or Doug could text back today, who would I pick?

My phone lights up. Incoming call from Doug.

'Doggie!' I say, as if he was the one I chose.

'How are you, Gingerbread?'

'Fine,' I say suspiciously. He only calls me that when he's trying to win me over. 'How's the middle of nowhere treating you?'

'That's kind of what I was calling about.' He sounds a mixture of elated and sheepish. 'You know that artist who gave me the welcome drink?' He giggles. 'Well, turns out she was leaving today, so we did it again!'

Out of nowhere, I feel like he's kicked me in the lungs.

Eventually I say, 'Was it nice?'

He laughs. Another punch in my intestines.

'Obviously I'll never see her again, so, yeah, it was nice! I picked up some things for us to try...'

I remember Soph's insults about our vanilla routine. I don't have many internal organs left for him to attack.

'What happened to not liking one-night stands?' I say.

'Are you OK? I didn't do anything wro—'

'You're meant to text beforehand.'

He sighs.

'OK, well, I'm sorry about that, but the whole reason it was hot was because it was spontaneous. I rang as soon as I left. I'm never going to speak to her again. I thought this was the whole point of being open?'

He sounds so reasonable. I try to keep my tone calm.

'The *point* is for us to live happy independent lives. The

point is *not* for you to humiliate me by fucking some random woman over and over again and then gloating about it.'

I hang up and cry, then drink a bottle of wine.

Getting out of the taxi at The Familiar, I don't turn into the bar. I cross the road to Kit's van.

Doug broke the rules, so I can too. Everyone else can have meaningless sex with someone and have a great time, so I can too. I'm free. I'm spontaneous. I'm drunk.

I hear muffled music from inside: 'come undone' by Marika Hackman. I thank my lucky stars – it's perfect.

My heart beating in time, I knock on the van.

A scuffle inside. The door swings open.

Soph.

I'm paralysed and wish to cease existing. Something registers in her eyes.

Eventually I say, 'Hi!'

She doesn't reply.

'I was at The Familiar. Having some drinks. Yes, and I saw Van Morrison. I mean, Kit's van, so thought I'd see if she was in.'

Kit appears from the shadows like a sexy demon.

'Sophie was just leaving, weren't you?'

The two of them exchange a look. A nasty look. Did they just break up? Can you even break up when you were never together?

'George,' says Kit meaningfully to me, grabbing her keys. 'Let's go for a walk. Sophie, close the door behind you when you leave, please.'

Kit strides off.

Stuck in the middle of the road, I look from Kit to Soph and back again. I wish I could flip a coin, check my horoscope, make someone else choose for me. It's the worst feeling in the world, wanting to be in two places at once.

Soph's stood next to the van, arms folded, watching. My best friend. My ex best friend. Should I stay here, apologize, beg? Pumpernickel her into forgiving me?

But she thinks I don't belong. Thinks I'm not like her, because I'm not *committed*. I'm not fully gay, and I always choose the easy way out.

So if I chose Soph, logically, wouldn't I be proving her right?

Kit looks back over her shoulder for me and the summer breeze rustling her messy hair feels like fate. She was the start of George. She makes me feel like no one else does. Like I've finally found myself. The aching and blushing and butterflies in my stomach whenever I think about her have got to mean something, don't they? After everything I've changed in my life to have this chance, can I really give up on her before even trying?

The truth is, it's like when I had to choose between being in Bronze Age or being with my dad. I know that I'll regret it either way.

So I run to Kit, and I don't look back.

And then Kit and I are walking along in unison, like we're playing the same music with our stride. I swear I can feel every molecule of space between our swinging hands. Everything is right. All will be well. Thank you gods. This was the right choice.

'George,' she says, after a while, 'when did you realize you were gay?'

I watch the streetlights dance on her smooth skin. Her astonishing, chiselled face. I can hardly say, 'When I met you.'

'Pretty recently, I guess, compared to some people. What about you?'

She doesn't answer me.

'So you've never had any relationships?' she asks, hawk eyes staring at me. 'Never fucked anyone?'

I start to feel that I'm not actually inside my body, just floating somewhere above it.

'Nothing very serious,' I laugh.

Kit stops.

'What about your seven-year relationship with your boyfriend?'

The air is still. I've forgotten how to breathe. Her face is beautiful even when it's disgusted.

'Kit—'

She holds up a hand.

'Sophie told me everything. You've been lying to us from the start.'

She leans in to my face, her silver chain beating against her throat, and I can almost taste her pine cologne and her sweat. I wonder if it's the last time I'll ever be this close to her.

'Next rehearsal, you're going to tell the others,' she says. 'We'll vote on whether you stay in Phase. My vote is that you don't.'

Kit looks me up and down, in the shirt she gave me, in the haircut I got for her. She shakes her head.

'I can't believe I fell for this.'

26

I've forgotten how it feels to wake up uncrippled by dread.
In my last night of the weekend without Doug, I lie awake,
practising my Phase confession.

'Phase is *so* important to me...' I mutter to myself, glaring
in the mirror at the bags under my eyes. 'So *important* to me
accepting my identity.'

'Didn't intend to deceive you,' I tell the shower curtain.

'Open relationship,' I explain to my coffee.

'Doug – my boyfriend – partner – has been so amazing –
good – supportive in my discovery – involvement in the gay
– queer community, and I hope that you can do the same.'

It seems politically unacceptable to wear one of Kit's
shirts. But I can't face wearing one of Doug's either; we
haven't spoken since I hung up on him for acting on our open
relationship.

In the end I put on an old baggy black jumper which
used to belong to my dad. It itches like a monk's hair shirt. I
imagine him looking down on me in disgust.

There's a pregnant pause.

I don't dare to look up at Phase.

The pause gives birth to another pause.

Eventually Rudy coughs. 'I don't understand. You're apologising for being bi?'

I hesitate. Nod.

'Is this some kind of joke I don't understand?'

I hesitate. Shake.

Rudy looks from me to Kit to Isobel, then starts to giggle. Her laughter echoes around the empty room.

'Why are you being so sincere about it! George! It's fine! LGBTQ includes a B right there in the middle!'

She comes over and tickles my ribs, making bee noises.

'Just don't try and make *us* date your boyfriend! This is the silliest thing I've heard all year. We're not going to like, expel you from the band because you've got a *boyfriend*! Are we?'

She puts an arm around me and turns to look at Isobel and Kit.

'Are we?' laughs Rudy again.

'How can we trust someone who lied to us?' Kit asks her. I close my eyes. 'Our brand is gay. Our songs are about being gay. Is that all a lie now? To sell merch?'

'I'm still gay,' I mumble.

'*Half* gay,' snaps Kit.

My throat constricts.

Right. Well, it seems Kit has a knack for articulating my worst anxieties, so I should go before she finds another of my insecurities to spear. Being a terrible friend, perhaps, or an awful daughter.

I stumble towards the exit, but to my surprise Isobel stops me.

'Kit,' she says, concern on her perfect forehead, 'that was unkind and untrue. I think you should apologize.'

Colour drains from Kit's cheekbones.

'It's OK. She's right,' I mumble, and try to leave again, but Isobel's manicure grips my shoulder.

'No,' Kit mumbles. 'I *was* wrong.'

I turn to her from the door.

'That was biphobic and shit...' She grasps at the short hairs at the back of her head. 'I'm just surprised. By you... I'm sorry for being a dick.'

I look at the floor.

'Hug it out,' says Rudy.

'No,' I squirm. 'Please. It's fine.'

'Hug it out,' Rudy insists.

Kit looks up at me from under her lashes. Then Kit's arms are around my shoulders, pulling me in tight, her face nuzzled into my hair, my arms trapped between our stomachs.

'That's right,' soothes Rudy. 'Squeeze her good and proper.'

I can feel Kit's breathing, quickened and shallow.

'That's probably enough apologizing now, don't we think?' says Isobel.

We break apart, coughing. Neither of us looks at each other. We start fiddling around with rehearsal equipment. My heartbeat hasn't regulated yet.

'Glad that's all settled.' Rudy smiles magnanimously and helps herself to a doughnut. 'So who is the lucky boy? Is he nice?'

'H-he's called D-Douglas,' I stammer. 'We've been together for seven years...'

Rudy gasps. I avoid Kit's eyes.

'Is he very masculine?'

'Er, I don't know; he's got a beard?'

'Your beard has a beard,' says Isobel, cutting a doughnut into smaller portions. 'Fitting.'

I don't know what she's talking about.

'He's a musician too,' I ramble. 'Bass, like you, Ru. He's in an indie pop band. Umm, Bronze Age?'

Isobel raises an eyebrow and starts typing on her phone.

'I know them.' Rudy nods and starts to hum something unsteadily. '"Good Guy"!'

'"Shy Guy",' I correct. I'm unsure whether to be pleased or embarrassed. 'I actually played with them a bit when I was at university.'

'Oh yeah!' says Rudy jovially, waving a finger at me in vague memory. 'But it didn't work out?'

'Yeah… I quit. But,' I add hurriedly, before they ask why, 'I see them occasionally. Obviously I still have some loyalty to them.'

I notice Isobel and Kit exchange a look. I think they can do telepathy the way Doug and I can. Or used to be able to.

'With a bit of perspective, I don't think they're *amazing*, you know?' I say, trying to gauge their reaction. 'I mean, "Shy Guy" is their most famous hit – their *only* hit – but their recent ones are all a bit… naff.'

Isobel snorts. My flames are fanned.

'They do the same thing over and over again,' I gush. 'They never get any better. It's like they're *trying* to write the most bland, conventional song possible – which, to be fair, they succeed in.'

Kit snorts too this time, which heats my flames with petrol.

'They're all just there to rub the main singer's ego,' I continue. 'It's a one-man band, really.'

'A one-woman band,' says Isobel, eyeing their profile.

'Yeah, their idea of diversity is fifty shades of ginger. They're outdated. Like they really are in the Bronze Age.'

Everyone laughs again. I feel vindicated and guilty in equal measure. Why do I constantly feel like I'm trying to balance scales in my life, but both sides are weighed with crap?

'Oh, Bronze Age are going to Edinburgh for the start of August,' says Rudy, scrolling through their Instagram.

Well, isn't this nice? My lesbian friends bonding over my boyfriend's social media.

'Yeah, at Douglas's parents' place, and then they're playing at the Festival of Love,' I say, looking over her shoulder. 'I'm going to join them, actually.'

Out of the corner of my eye I see Isobel look from the phone, to Kit, to me. She suddenly moans with disappointment.

'That's such a shame,' she sighs, tucking a blonde curl behind her ear. '*I* was going to say that everyone should come to *my* parents' place in Cornwall. You know, have a break from London, practise our songs. A Summer Holiday. But my parents' place is free that same week.'

Isobel clutches her hand to her heart.

'We can't go without you, George!'

Rudy looks like Christmas is cancelled.

I get it. Isobel wants me to pledge my allegiance. Show I'm not a Bronzer, I'm a Phaser.

But she doesn't realize that I've been making decisions like this ever since that first night at The Familiar. I've been choosing Phase over Doug, over Soph, over my mum, over everyone in Gina's life. What's one more?

I meet Kit's eye and say, 'I'll make it work.'

Even though it's not pizza night, I order Doug's favourite thin crust to be here for when he returns. He's later than expected.

I'd planned to throw myself at him in a big hug, but when the key finally turns in the lock I'm bashful. He stumbles into the kitchen with his bags, including some new ones under his eyes, and my chest swells with affection and guilt.

I put on the oven to reheat the pizza, take his bags, kiss his cheek.

'Hey. Sorry I'm late.'

He's only been away for a long weekend – why does it feel like years?

'Pet,' I try to take his hand, 'I'm really sorry about how I reacted the other night.'

Doug cringes.

'It's fine.'

'No, it's not,' I say, firmly. 'I overreacted. It was just – out of the blue and it was weird to hear over the phone. But my reaction was on me. I'm sorry.'

He shrugs his hand free, ostensibly to take off his glasses and clean them on his shirt.

'Since then,' I ramble, 'I've been thinking about it, and I feel absolutely fine! I trust you. If you say that it was good and it never felt that you were jeopardising *us*, then of course it's fine. I love you.'

He squeezes my hand weakly and sighs.

'I hate fighting.'

'I hate fighting too.'

I sit on the sofa and pull him onto my lap. He puts his

arms round my shoulders, and I bury my face in his chest. He smells like travel and worry and new aftershave. I bounce him around until he cracks a proper smile.

'We're learning,' I say. 'We'll get better.'

'Do you really think it's right for us?'

I tense under him. He twists on my lap to look at me.

'I don't know if we're cut out for it. I'm starting to feel... At the weekend...' He starts again. 'We've both had our flings, and—'

'You've had more flings than me!'

He scoffs.

'Are we really keeping a tally?'

'Yes,' I say, folding my arms.

'And what's your methodology?' he says, folding his. 'It can't just be by notches in the bedpost.'

'You've had more quantity *and* more quality than me.'

'But you've got a whole new world out of this,' he says. 'The Bronzers still view me as some kind of horny hippie. Think of all the fun you've had with Phase and Soph.'

My stomach twists. Doug must see my face change.

'Hey, if you want to carry on...'

'No, it's not that. It's just... My legs are going numb.'

I push him off my lap. I should be honest with him. For a change.

'Me and Soph fell out.'

Doug does a double take.

'What the hell? How?'

'Well, she slept with Kit, you know, the drummer from—'

'I know who she is, Gina.'

'I told Soph she was kidding herself if she thought that Kit was serious about her—'

Doug breathes in sharply through his teeth.

'It's true! And then *she* said I wasn't a proper part of the queer community because I have a boyfriend!'

He raises his eyebrows at me.

'Soph? Said that?'

'Yes,' I say defensively. 'She did. She said I was only a gay hobbyist. She was textbook biphobic. So we fell out.'

'But you and Soph don't ever fall out. There must be something—'

He sniffs the air. The pizza smell has turned from cooking to burning.

'Bugger!'

I open the oven and black clouds billow out.

'Bugger bugger bugger!'

We both fan the smoke wildly, trying to avoid the—

The fire alarm goes off.

'Bugger bugger bugger!'

Doug starts poking up at the alarm with the end of a wooden spoon. I open all the windows, letting in a gale of wind that billows the curtains into my face.

When the fire alarm finally stops, we look at the charred remains of the pizza.

'It's been a busy few days for both of us,' he says. 'Let's get another pizza.'

'And chips. And garlic bread. And cheesecake.'

I wait until we're not hangry any more to say about Edinburgh.

He looks up at me from drying plates.

'So you're not coming to Edinburgh, you're going to Cornwall with Phase?'

'I'm so sorry, Isobel said it's the only time her parents'

house is free, and the others were so excited, and we need to rehearse for a-a *thing*, and...'

His face is a sad bulldog.

'I haven't seen you in ages,' he whines.

'In Edinburgh we don't spend that much time together, do we, really, in between Bronze Age rehearsals? And I'll still see you all playing at the Festival of Love.'

'But my parents already got champagne in for our first night...'

I swallow and wipe the back of my forehead with my marigolds.

'I'll ring them to apologize. I'll open a bottle on their behalf. We could do a video call.'

'It's fine,' says Doug, drying mournful circles on a plate. 'I'm sure they'll understand. They're proud of you. I sent them links to Phase's songs. I like what you've been doing with that rock one, by the way. "Mercury"?'

I drain the sink, wishing I could flush my guilt with the suds.

'I'm really sorry,' I say, for the hundredth time that day.

He kisses my forehead.

It's started to rain and puddles have formed under the open kitchen windows.

27

Liberty's Summer Concert is also the last day I need to go to work until autumn. It's a humid, sticky day, the heat mingling with the stifling anticipation in the air. It's the school term's final countdown.

The dress code for the concert performers is, as always, black, white and blue. I stick to the dress code in solidarity with the pupils and wear a new work-appropriate – but fitted – black dress, huge blue dangly earrings, and daring blue suede shoes. Sure, the heels hurt a bit, and my lipstick feels a bit tacky now that I'm used to George's chapstick, but I think I might actually look good. Gina's at her best.

Alexa is wearing all black lace, like a funeral mourner.

Students huddle in the rehearsal room to the side of the auditorium, singing warm-ups, polishing flutes, blowing spit out of trombones. The other instrument teachers bounce around, giving the kids pep talks like they're half-unconscious boxers. But mine? I think they're going to be just fine.

Timmy has blue socks on. I try to signal to him that he's accidentally got one trouser leg tucked in, but he's busy playing imaginary F sharps on his spots. Hope, wearing a cutesy polka-dot dress, is humming the refrain of her original song, 'Nobody Understands My Misery'. Percy is, of course, wearing a blue bow tie and cummerbund. He sways humming 'Clair de Lune' and taps his feet to 'Honk Honk Honkytonk', alternating queasily between the two. Matilda's mousy hair is woven with delicate blue flowers and she walks up to me so confidently I would have barely recognised her a few months ago.

'Miss Green?' she lisps. 'When I start the second half, can you stand at the back and wave at me so that I remember to play loud enough?'

God, if any child was going to make me broody, it would be Matilda. I try not to sound too intensely proud when I say, 'I don't think you need me any more, Matilda. Just play it for yourself, and you'll be brilliant.'

'Pleeease, Miss?'

'OK, OK,' I smile. 'I'll be there, I promise.'

She grins toothily at me and then peeks out to the auditorium where family and staff have assembled.

Alexa sighs to the room. 'T-minus five minutes.'

I'm about to turn my phone off when I see the Phase group chat has kicked off about GAY FEST.

The pinnacle Pride gig is tonight, and some of my absolute favourite bands are performing, plus influential industry figures 'socialising' afterwards. Deciphering Rudy's messages, between all of her exclamation marks and emojis, I read that a friend of one of her brothers has last minute got *us* onto the after-party guest list.

My heart tremors. Oh my God. This could be the coolest night of my life.

Soph would be so jealous.

george? the latest message from Kit says, *u in?*

A trendy after-party like GAY FEST wouldn't start until like, 10 p.m., right? Earliest? And the school concert usually finishes by 9.30 p.m. and I have some of George's clothes in my rucksack in the piano rehearsal room!

With shaking hands, I look up how far away the gig is. It's practically round the corner! I'll get a taxi! I'll tell Doug that Alexa wants to go for a post-concert smoking session, or something! This has all worked out incredibly!

i'm in! I type. *100%!*

George's excitement puts an extra spring in Gina's heels and I spring through the audience towards the back of the hall.

'Excuse me, Ms Green?' asks Percy, but as a middle-aged woman. I shake my head to switch from George's fantasies of dark queer rooms to smile with Gina's professional curiosity at her.

'Thank you everso for your efforts with Percival,' she says. 'You do so inspire him. The other children give him rather a hard time of it, so I'm so delighted that music has become this – this escape.'

Gina blinks. *Me?* I've never inspired anyone before... I thank Mother Percy profusely and Mother Percy thanks me profusely back, and as I walk away I try not to tear up.

Walking through the assembled families, I think that, sure, there are probably a lot of people here who don't give a damn about this concert. It's just another bourgeois chore they've set their children. But some of these kids have worked towards this for months. For some, it could even spark a lifelong passion.

I remember being thirteen, peeking into an audience like this, seeing my mum and dad waving, as giddy and excited as

I was. Afterwards they took me for a celebratory Chinese, and my fortune cookie said something like, 'You chose wisely', and I told them it was a sign.

For a moment, my memory appears to be so powerful that I conjure my mum, wearing a flowery dress and summer rain coat, waving at me. Bewildered, I turn to look at the seat next to her, hoping for a hallucination of my dad.

But no, he's not there. Instead, there's Doug, wearing a guitar tie. And it's not a Freudian figment of my imagination, because I hear a child saying, 'Look, there's a sausage dog under that seat!'

I walk over to them in wonderment.

Before I can ask what on earth they're doing here, Doug kisses me on the cheek and says, 'You've been so busy recently, what with your band and everything, we wanted to come and support you.'

'I made Doug keep the secret,' adds Mum, hugging me tightly. 'I drove up and I've got a room booked at a little B&B round the corner. Afterwards, I thought we could go and get a Chinese?'

Holding both their hands, my chest feels tight with love and gratitude and guilt. Bunny yaps affectionately at my feet.

As I stroke them all in greeting, my first thought is, I'm so lucky. My second thought is, I can't wait to eat my body weight in fried rice. Then George's voice cuts in, reminding me of my promise to go to GAY FEST. I need to cancel that, thinks Gina. Unless? thinks George. No, for God's sake, snaps Gina, I can't sneak out the back of a Chinese restaurant, get dressed up like a lesbian, and then run back in and out. This isn't *One Man, Two Guvnors*.

George suggests that I invite Mum to the gig. Are you

actually mad? snaps Gina. It's not the kind of space for an aging mother and her sausage dog. Besides, remember how she spat the word 'bisexuelles'? And how Soph's family never spoke to her again? Remember Soph's expression when she was on her old family WhatsApp?

George strops, but admits defeat. Gina, triumphant, is about to get her phone out to cancel with Phase, when Alexa walks onto the stage. She taps the microphone, glaring at everyone to sit down.

Doug and Mum pull me into a seat between them and I squeeze both their hands at once.

Apart from Bunny, who isn't allowed but is too cute to turn away, Doug and Mum fit in so well with the school concert setting. I feel intensely grateful. What if Kit, or even Rudy or Isobel had turned up here tonight? It would feel... wrong.

Is that me being repressed, or closeted, or ashamed? Is that Phase being literally too cool for school? Or are there really straight things and gay things which are fundamentally incompatible?

'Welcome,' says Alexa, with heavy sarcasm, 'to the Liberty Secondary Summer Concert. As usual, the fire exits are under the fire exit signs and, for decency's sake, turn your mobile telephones off. The first half will begin with,' she closes her eyes, 'Year 9 Music Class singing a medley of Andrew Lloyd Webber.'

As the strained strains of 'Memory' begin from the stage, George's voice pressures me into texting Phase to cancel, now. Gina blushes with guilt for being a music teacher on her phone during a *concert*.

guysssss, George types, feeling sorry for herself, *i'm rly sorry but the yawn school concert is overrunning yawn so i won't b able*

to make it tonight unless you kidnap me haha have fun but not too
much c u soon

I send it, and am about to put away my phone when it freezes. No, no, not now, you crappy piece of crap! I stroke the cracks, press a few buttons on and off, trying to get it to load. It restarts. Damn damn damn and blast – I don't know if it sent.

Year Nine finish the paradoxical finale of 'Everything's Alright', and the audience break into relieved applause. I put my phone away in my blazer. If it didn't send, I can try again in the break.

Percy galumphs to the front of the stage and announces that he's going to play 'Clair de Lune'.

Mum's head jerks to me and I meet her eyes as the first bittersweet chords echo through the hall. The music washes over us like moonlight on waves…

I'd been underestimating Percy – I'd thought he was some automaton, but the way to get him to play 'Clair de Lune' with emotion was to tell him to forget about hitting the right notes and feel his way through the chords. I made him play it with his eyes shut, like my dad used to. Percy's got his eyes shut even now. He looks completely at ease, swaying. My mind swims with memories of hot chocolates and pyjamas and Dad, playing just like this.

Mum's eyes are closed too. I squeeze her hand in my lap. Her mouth is in a tight line, her forehead crumpled, but she squeezes back, hard. Our hands stay together. I promise, next time I'm home, I'm going to finally play it for us…

Until my phone goes off. Katy Perry's 'I Kissed A Girl' blares out so loudly that it ricochets around the concert hall and back to my horror-struck face.

Scrabbling madly to get it out of my pocket – a process which has never taken longer in the history of pockets or mad scrabbling – I see it's Kit. I reject the call and try to blend back into the concert, but I can't hear 'Clair de Lune' any more, I can't see the audience any more, all I can do is listen to the blood pounding in my ears.

After the longest twenty seconds of my life thus far, horribly embarrassed, sensing Doug's, Mum's, and the rest of the audience's appalled eyes on me, I pull my slippery phone from my pocket. A voicemail, missed messages from each member of Phase, and one from Kit saying,

URGENT. RING BACK. NOW.

Mum and Doug will obviously know it's not a family emergency, so I mouth 'Soph' at them, and run out, apologising silently to each parent's knees.

Outside the concert hall, sweat congealing in the small of my back, I ring Kit.

'George,' she says. 'I'm outside.'

From round the corner, a horn blasts the rhythm of 'Mercury'.

'Kit, what? What's wrong?'

'Just come. *Now.*'

Something about the urgency in her voice makes me start running towards the gates. Something awful must have happened. To Soph? Maybe they fought and Soph collapsed from sadness. Maybe she collapsed because they were having too much sex. Whatever, Soph collapsed and her last words were for me.

The sun is trying to set, streaking red between gathering storm clouds. I haven't sprinted like this in years and I'm immediately out of breath, but urge myself on.

Percy will still be playing 'Clair de Lune'. Doug and Mum will be so confused. But Soph needs me.

I pant through the school gates into the road, and see the van. The shadow of Kit is in the front, but the headlights blind me like spotlights. I'm running up when I hear the door slide open and Isobel and Rudy jump out.

'Surprise!'

They grab me and pull me up into the van. Before I can say anything, Kit starts the van, rain starts pouring down, and we pull away.

'What the fuck is going on?'

'Something miraculous has happened,' says Isobel.

'Fate,' squeals Rudy. 'Someone pulled out of the GAY FEST line-up. Ate some dodgy burrito—'

'—so we're kidnapping you,' finishes Kit from the front, 'like you wanted. And we're taking you to perform in the best gig of your life.'

I don't reply. The others are too hyped to notice that I'm not responding.

Rain starts to tap lightly on the van roof.

I thought I loved it when people took decision-making out of my hands. But this...

'My *mum's* back there,' I say quietly.

'What?'

Kit steers us wildly round a corner.

'Text her to come join us at the gig instead. She'll have a better time.'

'I can't invite my mum to GAY FEST,' I say blankly. 'She doesn't know I'm... And Doug is there—'

'You see them all the time,' frowns Kit. 'Mate, this is a once-in-a-lifetime opportunity.'

'I promised the kids…'

'You're their *teacher*!' Rudy laughs, her eyes radiating excitement. 'Trust me, you're just some loser adult to them, they won't notice if you're there or not.'

Maybe they're right. I'm finding it hard to concentrate with the rain battering the roof.

'I could get fired.'

'So what?' says Isobel, who has never needed a job. 'You said yourself that you don't care about teaching. You won't need to be at a school when Phase is famous.'

'Pull a sickie,' says Kit. 'Say you fainted or something.'

Rudy triumphantly holds up my page on her Co-Star app. 'Your horoscope for today says you should "Stand Up For Yourself". It's in your stars that you'll ditch that concert and come to FEST!'

'OK,' I mumble.

'God,' says Isobel, poking at my shaking earrings, 'is that what they make you wear at the school? Like a uniform?'

'You look so…' I meet Kit's eyes in the rear-view mirror. 'Straight.'

This is closer to what I looked like, that first night I met Kit at The Familiar. None of the gays looked twice at me then, did they?

I quickly dunk my face in Kit's sink, the moving van swerving so that I smack my head on the tap. I wipe my make-up off on her towel, and tie up my hair into George's undercut.

'Can I borrow your jeans then?' I say picking up items discarded from her floor. 'And this jacket?'

Kit's barely answered when I'm already changed into George. Everyone's spooked.

'How the *fuck* did you do that?' shouts Rudy. 'You witch!'

Isobel's hands twitch as if wanting to cross herself.

'I said you looked straight,' says Kit, wide-eyed in the rear-view. 'I didn't say you looked *bad*. You – you look fine either way.'

She stomps on the brakes for a red light, and I fall in my half-removed heels into the side of the van. After all this worrying and changing and discovering George... Does Kit fancy me more when I look more like Gina?

I want to cry. I want to be alone. But I can't miss the Pride gig and I can't quit the concert like this. I need to go back to Alexa and the kids and, *oh God*, to Mum and Doug say... Something.

'How far away are we?'

'Ten minutes including parking,' says Kit.

'We'll actually make it in good time,' adds Isobel, checking her watch. 'I asked them to put us in the second half – that's better anyway, more memorable near the end – and—'

'Stop,' I say, very clearly.

Everyone freezes. The rain hesitates.

'Kit. I said stop the van.'

She glances at Isobel, at me, then slams her foot on the brakes. Isobel goes flying into Kit's bed.

'Drop me here,' I say calmly. 'You guys set up. I'll run back to the school, explain that I'm leaving, and get a taxi to the gig. There's time.'

It's the others' turn to stare at me in disbelief. Cars honk angrily behind us.

'George, what the actual—'

'Isobel, please can I borrow your lipstick?'

'George, we came to—'

I interrupt them and panic breaks through my paper-thin calm facade.

'I *will* be there,' I snap, opening the van door. 'And I *will* make it up to you, but I have to go now.'

I lurch out onto the pavement. Kit barely waits for my feet to land in a puddle before speeding off. The door slams shut while it's already moving.

As I run back, I try to apply Isobel's designer lipstick. Who knew? It's hard to do make-up while running through rain, dry-heaving.

I get to the crossroads, where the street meets the end of the long school driveway. I keep thinking that I can't do this, but still, some fight or flight makes me continue changing into Gina. Running, panting, stumbling, lipstick presumably smudged over my face, I untie my hair. With my left hand, I try to untie Kit's Docs. With my right, I put on the suede heels I'm clutching, and that's when I trip.

I fall forwards heavily, launching both arms in front of me to protect myself. Isobel's lipstick crumples. Kit's jacket falls into a puddle, along with the rest of me.

I really, truly *cannot* do this any more.

So I sit on the wet pavement, the damp soaking through my dress and trousers.

I need to be at the school concert right now. I need to be on a stage with Phase right now.

I know that I should just pick one and then apologize to the other. But which?

George or Gina? Which one is better? Which one is the real me? I need to choose. Right now.

Rain continues to pour. Time ticks away.

The more I think about the urgency of the situation, the more impossible it becomes.

My phone rings. Snoop Dogg's 'Doggy Dogg World'. I really need to turn my personalized ringtones off – it's deeply unfashionable.

I let the phone ring out. The puddle has completely soaked through to my bum now. Even in the humid night, I'm shivering.

Doug was probably ringing in the interval, so the second half of the concert will be starting soon. I can see it so clearly: Matilda at the front of the stage, looking for me in the crowd, her mousy sadness returning. Timmy missing that glorious F sharp. Hope's anthem to death even more... deathly. Percy playing 'Honk Honk Honkytonk' without a funky groove. It this how I'm inspiring them? By ditching them and sitting in a puddle?

But Phase. This once-in-a-lifetime opportunity. To be a musician like I've always dreamed... Surely that's worth missing some children playing Grade Three piano pieces they don't even care about? Surely it's more empowering, more feminist, more life-affirming, to choose GAY FEST?

Doug will be squeezing Mum's worried hand. Mum, who made all this effort to surprise me, who I've been neglecting and lying to for so long. God, I don't deserve her. And I don't deserve Doug, who's probably not using the opportunity to talk to her about our wedding, because he definitely doesn't want to marry me any more.

I think of what Soph said, about me only being queer when it's convenient. Being part of an underprivileged community should mean fighting for it, should mean giving back to it. Think of all that queer people throughout history have sacrificed so that there could even *be* a Pride celebration. And I can't even give up one portion of Chinese Dumplings?

I want to do both. I want to be both. I *am* both.

How do other bis do it? What am I still doing wrong?

As I remain immobile on the ground, I swear I hear the sound of distant applause.

Great, now I'm losing my mind. I'm still shivering pretty badly too. It can't be from the running because I've been sitting down for ages and I'm still hyperventilating, and it's hurting to breathe in, and I'm sweating and flushing and think I'm going to throw up and— Oh my God, what's wrong with me? I feel like I'm having a panic attack and—

Oh. I am having a panic attack.

In a moment of sudden clarity, I feel incredibly grateful to be having a tangible breakdown, because it's the perfect excuse as to why I let everyone down.

Then I remember that I'm having a panic attack right *now* and can you die from a panic attack and I'm certain I'm going to die right here right now and everyone is going to find out I've been lying to them and everyone's going to hate me even more than I already do and I don't even know what they would call me at my funeral and oh God I'm going to die and I never apologized to Soph—

With 2 per cent remaining battery, I do the only thing I can think of doing: I ring her.

'You've got to stop all this, Gee.'

When Soph arrived, I only stopped shaking when she texted Doug and Kit an excuse from her phone. But now we're in the taxi back to my flat, I can't look at her at all.

'The only time I've seen you like this,' she says, 'was when you got that phone call after your last Bronze Age gig. I was terrified then, and I'm—'

'People think panic attacks are more serious than they are,' I interrupt. 'But I was fine in the end, wasn't I? And I'm fine now. I'm sorry for bothering you.'

Soph reaches for my hand. I shake her off, trying to ignore the still-lingering dread over my whole being.

'Don't you see now?' she says. 'You're making this so much more complicated than you need to. It would help you to be honest to the people closest to you.'

'I *am* being honest,' I groan. 'I know I messed up in the past, but now Doug knows about Phase, and Phase knows about Doug. It hasn't helped things at all.'

'What about your mum?' says Soph.

I stare at her.

'You know why I can't come out to her. What if she reacts like your mum?'

She gapes back.

'The situations are completely— My parents grew up in— You don't understand. Obviously *your* mum would support you—'

'That's what *you* thought,' I say darkly. 'And I *know* it's not the same, but my mum's family was pretty bloody prejudiced too. You haven't heard the way she talks about bisexuelles.'

Soph swallows, takes a breath, tries again.

'I think you rang me to stop you. I think it was a cry for help.'

Defensiveness turns into aggression and I guffaw obnoxiously. Soph carries on through.

'You've got to stop splitting yourself up like this, Gee.

Whatever you've been doing with Kit behind my back, however much you've been taking me for granted, I still remember what it used to be like when we were best friends together. Before all this George and Gina nonsense, before your relationship calendar, before you quit Bronze Age, before—'

'Well, I'm terribly sorry,' I say coldly, 'I didn't ask for my dad to die.'

'Gee—'

'No, Soph. *You* don't understand. You made your choice. All you have is being a lesbian. But I like *both* worlds and I *want* both worlds, and now that I've *got* both worlds, I *will* keep them.'

We're still ten minutes' walk away from the flat, but I ask the taxi driver to stop.

'Sorry for inconveniencing you, but don't worry, I won't ask for your help again.'

'Listen to yourself! This isn't like you, Gee, listen to me—'

'I've had quite enough of people telling me who I am and what to do, thanks very much.'

The car slows and I open the door, taking Kit's clothes with me.

'I *am* Gina, and I *am* George. *Honest.* No one else is asking me to lose one of them, except you. So if in order to fully be myself, I have to lose you...'

I take one last look at the crumpled face of my best friend.

'That's fine with me,' I say, and slam the door.

PART THREE

PART THREE

28

In the first week of August, Kit drives us all to Cornwall. I feel like I'm in an indie film: even though *physically* we're in a big van shaking down a motorway, *emotionally* we're in a convertible and a neon-flashing tunnel.

Everyone's still being very sweet to me. The school concert was a couple of weeks ago, but I'm still reaping the rewards. Even Kit is gentle and attentive when she sets me up with pillows in the back of the van. I should have a breakdown more often.

After I'd shut the door on Soph, I locked myself in the toilet and sat on the floor until Doug and Mum arrived. Mum tucked me up in bed, blamed herself for 'surprising me', said she didn't really fancy a Chinese anyway, just a bit of toast, please, if that wouldn't be too much trouble. If Doug was upset that my emergency contact was Soph, not him, he didn't say anything.

I thought my presence was such a big deal to both events, but I guess I'd been full of my own importance as usual. Phase went to GAY FEST and didn't perform, but still made contacts out of pity for their panicky snowflake pianist. Alexa replied to my lengthy apology by saying she was jealous I'd got out of it and would throw a fit of her own next term. I forced myself to ask her how the concert went, and she said, 'Mostly abysmal. Your pupils played surprisingly adequately.'

The worst guilt came when I got a 'Get Well Soon' card through the post, clearly handmade by Matilda and signed by the others. I pinned it up above my keyboard, thinking of Dad's overflowing wall of 'Thank You' cards. I wondered about trying to send one back saying, 'Thank you and Congratulations and I'm So Sorry I Can't Cope With My Own Stupid Life Decisions', but I decided against it. I'd tell them next term.

Now, I can forget all that. *Should* forget all that. What's past is past.

Because now Isobel's in the front seat, navigating in a white linen dress and retro red cat-eye sunglasses; Kit's tanned gold in a loose black vest and Ray-Bans; Rudy's in cropped rainbow dungarees, and she's dyed her afro from bubblegum pink to Ribena purple, which appears to have recharged her energy levels to full. (We're hunched in the back like excitable children on the school run, slapping each other at every yellow car.) I'm wearing one of Kit's denim shirts and feeling like, at least aesthetically, George does belong here.

Isobel DJs, and from my recent desperate cramming of queer musicians, I recognise most of them: St. Vincent, Clairo, Liz Lawrence, Pale Waves, Claud, Mary Lambert, Melissa Etheridge, Emily Burns, Morgan Saint, Your Smith, Miya Folick, Julia Jacklin, and a string of artists in all lowercase, boygenius, k. d. lang, dodie, chloe moriondo, mxmtoon...

Then Rudy DJs: Mitski, Dorian Electra, Rina Sawayama, The Aces, Girl Ray, Keeana Kee, Lady Gaga, Tayla Parx, Sir

Babygirl, L Devine, Frances Forever, Kim Petras, Self Esteem, Goat Girl, Planningtorock, and a string of artists in all uppercase, MUNA, SOPHIE, REYNA, IDER, FLETCHER, BLOXX, MICHELLE, GIRLI...

Finally, Kit DJs. I don't recognize any of the songs.

They keep offering for me to choose, but I worry about picking the wrong thing. Instead, I make films of our karaoke covers, uploading the best to Phase's online pages. I scroll the streams of comments to see if *SophieSnob* has interacted. She hasn't.

I still don't know what's happening with Kit and Soph. I'm hoping it will become clear over this trip – that it was just a two-night stand that Soph misinterpreted. I have a recurring dream that she apologized and we're friends again. Sometimes in the dream it's me who apologized but I don't like that version as much.

Then we're rolling through a countryside of orchards, trees, and endless bright yellow canola fields. Past a 'Welcome to Cornwall' sign, through cobbled streets, whitewashed houses, tourist shops selling pasties, cream teas, fish and chips, then bumping down dappled country lanes.

'Oooh!' I point to a beautiful manor house between the hills. 'Does anyone else have a National Trust card?'

Isobel tucks a bashful curl behind her pearl earring. 'That's my house.'

Her 'house' is an elegant Georgian manor, all symmetrical neat grey brick, tall windows, and lashings of lilac wisteria. Her gravel pathway is lined with *topiary*.

'And it's a ten-minute walk to the beach,' says Isobel fondly, closing the van door.

I try not to let my mouth fall open as she gives us the tour. I gather Kit used to stay here a lot, and Ru's visited for parties, but to me it's like seeing a showroom except you're allowed to sit on stuff. My airy bedroom has a four-poster bed and tasteful floral wallpaper, it smells of the freshly cut sweet peas and has views onto the rose garden. I hide my battered old rucksack in the heritage wardrobe.

Joining the others in the artfully rustic dining room, Isobel hands me a glass of champagne. Don't get me wrong, all this luxury is lovely, but I can't help remembering the times at The Familiar when I bought Isobel's drink.

'Are you guys hungry?' says Isobel, textbook host. 'I'll start making some dinner.'

We obviously offer to help and check out the fully-stocked double-doored fridge. I've never seen so much Waitrose outside of Waitrose. We decide we'll all make one part of the meal, surprise each other. I'm given responsibility for the side – they're still being pitying.

Well, everyone loves chips, right?

Once they're in the oven, I go to the beauteous bathroom and text Doug.

We've arrived safely. Isobel's house is insane, say hi to your parents for me.

I know exactly what we'd be doing if I was there. We'd have toured his parents' vegetable patch and petted their lovely lassie dog (coincidentally also called Jasper, which Bronze Age obviously now confuse with Mickey's brother). I'd be sipping *their* welcome fizz. Soon I'd be tucking into an unwanted third helping of their meaty pie, and trying not to fart while playing Cranium.

Doug hasn't replied. Fine, then. So much for being kind to your girlfriend mere weeks after she has a panic attack.

Mum, on the other hand, has texted me again, despite the fact I haven't replied to her last two messages.

HISWEETIEHOPEYOUAREOKBUNNYHASNASTY FLEAS

I haven't told her I'm in Cornwall, and it feels too late now I'm here. I'd better wait until I'm back. I down my champagne and chuck my phone into the bedroom.

Isobel's wearing a frilly apron, and playing Shura on vinyl. When I offer to top up her drink, she fusses over telling me to relax, as if holding a Moët might set me off again. Rudy is already covered in chocolate from where she's been making her pudding and 'checking the seasoning'. Kit's outside on the patio, prodding burgers on the barbeque and smoking. I pad over self-consciously, unsure if she's watching me behind her sunglasses. But as I top up her glass, she smiles a proper, unforced smile and taps the bench next to her.

I listen to the various sizzles.

'Burgers, huh,' I say, eventually.

Good one, me.

'Yeah,' she snorts. 'Surprise.'

'I'm making chips.'

'Nice.'

We sip, smiling banally. She blows her smoke away from me.

'George. I'm sorry about the other night. And if I contributed to…'

I let the bubbles pop on my tongue. She so rarely talks of her own accord that I want to milk the experience.

'And I overreacted,' she adds. 'That night with Sophie. You shouldn't have had to… You're one of us, no matter what.'

She glances at me, rubs the back of her neck. I hope her sunglasses hide my blush.

'Thank you,' I say, when I'm sure she isn't going to confess anything else. 'I... That means a lot to me.'

I look at her profile as she flips the burgers, her skin glowing in the evening sun.

'Umm, Kit...? What's happening with you and Soph?'

'She hasn't told you?'

When I don't reply, she shrugs, turning the skewers.

'I don't know, I don't want to chat shit about your friend.'

In my mind, I beg her to chat shit.

She says, 'I swear, I try to make it clear with people that I'm only in it for the sex.'

The blush spreads further across my body.

'But for some reason they always think I'm lying. And then I'm the villain. Just cos I don't want to like, marry them.'

I don't move an inch. The smoke from the barbeque mingles with the smoke of her cigarette. My eyes are smarting as I watch her.

'Have you *ever* felt serious about someone?'

To my amazement, Kit blushes.

'Once,' she says carefully, in a wistful voice I've never heard before. 'But she doesn't want to be with me.'

She glances at me and looks away, coughing a little. My stomach backflips violently. Oh my God. She's really saying it. She's serious about *me*.

The sun throbs. Our legs are achingly close. Kit stubs out her cigarette with a grimace, still avoiding my eyes.

'But I... I can't go through that shit again, George. It's too... I just want good friends and great sex. No romance, no confusion.'

Her voice breaks, and I'm sure. This whole time, she's been hurting just as much as me. Longing bubbles up in me. I taste the champagne on my lip, and need to taste it on hers.

When Kit finally turns to me, her expression is so tentative and complicated that I can't hold it back anymore. I reach my hand out to her cheek.

Isobel's blonde head pops round the door.

'George, I think your secret chips are burning.'

Kit and I jerk apart. As I stumble up, she doesn't look at me. She just gets out another cigarette and says, 'See you in a bit, pal.'

Pal? *Pal?*

I wobble away, more confused than ever.

We sit at a dining table big enough for twelve, laid with a white cloth and an abundance of silver. Isobel made grilled asparagus with nutmeg butter, and delicately folded goat's cheese pastries. Kit's veggie burgers are piled high with chili sauce, roasted onions, gherkins and Waitrose Essentials brioche buns. My chips are burnt. For pudding, Rudy's made a – there's no more accurate word for it – lump of chocolate sponge, cream, and ice cream. Thank Christ I'm not lactose intolerant. (Or at least, not *that* lactose intolerant.)

As I'm recovering, feeling spherical, Isobel suddenly looks out the window.

'Darlings,' she says, 'I forgot. It's a supermoon tonight. We must see it on the beach.'

Isn't it a bit late to be leaving home, at bedtime?

'I'm up for a dip,' says Kit.

I'm suddenly on board. We get ourselves worked up into a

frenzy of urgency, collecting bottles, lighters, towels, torches and, in Rudy's confused hands, a game of travel Boggle.

Rudy runs ahead, Kit shouting directions, Isobel chivvying, until they reach the top of a sandy uphill path. Their silhouettes pause there. Out of breath, I join them at the peak, looking out at the view.

The moon is vast, full, and an astonishing hazy pink. The sky's a cloudy lilac, fading seamlessly into an indigo sea. The reflection is like a stick of chalk on its side, zigzagged along the sea's surface. We stand in silence, trying to take it in.

Then Rudy starts screaming. She strips her top off and runs down towards the sea. We all whoop after her, Isobel and Kit throwing their shoes into the sand. While they're splashing in the distance, I lay out the cosy towels and blankets in the sand, measure out rum and cokes into four plastic beakers, and – my chest tightening as I see her name – I play *SophieSnob*'s 'midnight mood' playlist on mini speakers: Orla Gartland, SOAK, Snail Mail, Pillow Queens, Saint Sister, Ailbhe Reddy, Catey Shaw...

Listening to the music and watching the shadow of Kit, knee-deep in the sea, I keep looping what she'd said earlier. 'But I... I can't go through that shit again, George.' She's felt the same as me, these past few months. She's scared of falling deeper, especially now she knows about Doug. So she just wants to be friends. Friends who may or may not have very casual sex.

Fine! That's cool! In fact, it's perfect! Doug's happy. Soph's happy. I'm happy. It's what I've wanted all along!

They return to me, their grins shivering violently. We huddle and toast our drinks to Sappho, looking out at the pink supermoon.

'You good, George?' asks Kit softly.

I can only nod.

'So when will you dump that beard boy of yours,' says Isobel, smoothing my hair, 'and join the lesbian coven?'

We all laugh, but I know she's not really joking.

We wake up to the dawn sun on the sea, cricks in our backs and furry tongues. Stumbling back to Isobel's house, Kit gives sleepy Rudy a piggyback. Falling into bed, my clothes are scattered with sand and my hand still tingles from where I'd woken up with Kit's fingers entwined in mine.

'George, let's rehearse *your* song.'

Gods, please forgive every time I ever insulted someone else's attempts at songwriting.

Hungover and on very little sleep, Isobel woke us with coffee and shepherded us to the drawing room – a high-ceilinged room with French windows, wooden floors, inbuilt bookcases and, obviously, a grand piano.

'Play your draft to us,' Isobel orders, 'and we'll build on it.'

They settle into their chairs, holding their mugs expectantly.

I cough. 'I haven't written the bridge yet.'

They nod encouragingly.

'And I don't have the verses like *finished* finished.'

They nod more.

'And the chorus is—'

'Sing the damn song!'

I've played it a hundred times in my head. But now I'm

trying to actually play it to an audience, I've forgotten how to move my fingers.

'*You said…*' I start to sing, but my voice breaks with nerves.

'Sorry. Sorry. I'll start again.'

I replay the introduction. Their eyes bore into me. My throat's tightening.

'*You said…*'

I'm back on that Bronze Age stage, playing my song to the crowd. But the triumphant memory's distorted with knowledge of what came afterwards. The shame stops me from singing.

Will I ever get over this? How can I call myself a musician if, every time I try to play my own music, I freeze up? God, I'm so frustrated, so embarrassed, to be blocked this badly in front of them.

I can't believe I'm back here again. Playing my stupid little songs, pretending they're worth something. Worth so much, that I'd give up anything else for them.

I'm well aware that self-pity and self-loathing are not a likeable combination. But unable to make myself dissolve, I close the piano lid and run away.

There's a knock on my bedroom door: the rhythm of 'Mercury'. Kit dances with the door, opening and closing it while balancing two cups of tea.

Cringing upright in bed, I unbury my still-pink face from my hands to accept the mug. I apologize again, but she waves it away.

'The first time I played "Mercury" to the others,' says Kit, sitting on the side of the bed, 'I played through this intense drumbeat for about ten minutes. I thought I'd smashed it. And then the others were like… where's the music? Where's the lyrics?'

I attractively snort hot tea up my nose.

'George, do you have the lyrics written down? May I…?'

It's fate. I hand over my notebook, where I've written every conversation with Kit, and all my built-up feelings, to mine them for lyrics. There might even be a page with the letter K surrounded by hearts.

Kit casually flicks through the previous pages. I scream.

'It's just *this* page.'

Sitting in bed, knees touching, Kit reads through the song I wrote about her. About us.

I nominally disguised the origins by naming it after an unrelated star sign – 'Gemini' – but *she'll* know. She's going to look at me with sudden understanding, and quote from it, and kiss me.

This is it.

My heart is pounding in my ears. I stare at her smooth face, waiting for it to react.

Finally she meets my eye.

'George,' she murmurs, 'I don't know what to say.'

Tentatively, she puts her warm hand on my leg. I moisten my lip. Tilt my head…

'They're fine,' she says. 'It's a good start. And you've written them out neatly enough that Isobel can read them.'

I blink a couple of times.

So the main thing she's taken from my love song is my handwriting? Cool.

I turn away from her, but Kit reaches her hand to my cheek, turning me back.

'George,' she says, her dark eyes soft, 'can't you see, I've fallen for all of you?'

I blush so much I stop breathing.

'I...'

'That's a good line,' she says, pointing to my notebook. 'But it could work better to change it to *you can't see.*'

I stare at her. My blush stops rising, embarrassed at itself.

'You mean in the lyrics,' I say blankly. 'So, just to get this right... *You can't see I've fallen for all of you?*'

'Yep,' she smiles. 'Nice one.'

I take the notebook back and scratch the lyrics out with a few pen strokes. While I'm here, I might as well scratch out my own eyeballs too.

'Thanks.'

'You're welcome, mate.'

Back in the rehearsal room, Rudy and Isobel are being tentatively kind again, like I've had another panic attack. When did George become such a loser?

Isobel invites me to play 'Gemini' on the piano for her to pick up the melody, and then accompany her.

I find I don't lose myself to the music the way I normally do when playing with Phase. Maybe it's because I'm concentrating too hard, or because I'm still bruised from Kit not realising it was about us, but when Isobel starts to sing my lyrics, I flinch at every word.

'*You said you're a Gemini,*' she sings,

'*No matter how hard I try*
You won't be satisfied

You're always split in two.'

Listening to Isobel singing my song feels like being in the passenger seat of my own car. Everything is slightly off. I'm not saying she's bad, obviously. It's just... not the same journey home.

'I said cool, ha ha, yeah, that's fine
You don't have to be just mine
You can't be simplified
I'll make do with half of you.'

For the chorus, her tone moves from flippant to deadly serious.

'Gemini
You're half in love with me
But you can't see
I've fallen for all of you.'

'And then there'll be a bridge,' I shout awkwardly, over the piano accompaniment. 'La la la la la. And now we're back to the verse...'

Isobel rejoins with such tender, fierce power in her voice that I almost forget to keep playing. It's like hearing her read out my diary.

'If caring is sharing then I am a saint
I won't care I'm only a side on your plate
I could be in half your heart
At least that would be a start.
Gemini
Would you still look at her
If I was prettier?
I'll change all of me for you.'

I release the final chord and close my eyes. We hold the silence.

Then I realize Isobel is blinking tears away from her crystal eyes. 'That's one for the album.'

Rudy squeals and applauds. Kit's not looking at me, she's looking shell-shocked at the ground, like she's finally worked something out. My stomach flip-flops.

In the afternoon, we take the van down to the sea. Rudy's girlfriend Amie watches on video call while she makes a sandcastle. The others sunbathe, listening to Janelle Monáe. Isobel is reading a book of the love letters between Virginia Woolf and Vita Sackville-West, and Kit's reading a queer zine, both of which make me feel like an uncultured bimbo. The only thing I've read in months is my Twitter feed.

I wander along the warm sand and ring Doug.

'Gina, hi! Sorry I didn't pick up yesterday.'

He sounds the way he does when he's forgotten to do the laundry.

'It's fine,' I say breezily. 'You don't have to be at my beck and call. I was just seeing how you were.'

God, I'm such a cool girlfriend.

'Oh! OK! Well, how are you?'

'I'm *good*,' I stretch, toes wiggling in the sea. 'How are you?'

'Happy you're happy.'

'Compersion. How's the gang?'

'Yeah, good. Jasper ate a sock this morning and threw up everywhere.'

'God, Mickey needs to stop him doing that.'

Doug laughs his barking laugh. I realize I haven't heard that in a while. I've missed it.

'Gingerbread... Umm... We *are* open at the moment, right?'

The sea comes too far up my leg.

I remember being at Doug's house for rehearsals – we wouldn't meet anyone except the geriatric neighbours.

'Yes? Why, are you getting it on with Mrs Cockburn?'

Doug laughs in horror and surprise.

'Want to find out if she lives up to her name.'

We giggle.

Then Doug asks delicately, 'Do you have a Cornwallian Mrs Cockburn?'

'Well...' I look back to where Kit is sunbathing, her bronze skin glowing next to her white vest. I must remember that I am a cool girlfriend and Doug is a cool boyfriend.

OK. Here we go. I take a deep breath.

'I do have a bit of a crush on Kit.'

I watch the waves ripple.

'Yeah, Gina,' says Doug, 'I guessed.'

Oh.

It comes out of me in a rush.

'Nothing has happened. And I don't think I even *want* anything to happen. Just a holiday crush, you know, but it doesn't, you know, mean anything, and once you and I are back together it will get packed away and...'

I am *not* a cool girlfriend.

'Yeah,' sighs Doug.

Clouds roll past.

'It doesn't change how I feel about *you*,' I say, desperately.

I imagine him pinching the bridge of his nose.

'It doesn't change how I feel about you either then,' he says.

The beach feels cold suddenly. I stumble away from the rising tide.

'Do you really think sleeping with someone in your band counts as casual?' asks Doug, carefully. 'If you keep emotions out of it?'

'Oh my God! We haven't slept together! We haven't even kissed!' I say, managing to stop myself from saying 'yet'.

'Yeah,' says Doug, 'but—'

'OK then, you're right. It'd be too much, being in a band together and sleeping together. Too hard to keep them separate. So I won't.'

Stupid mouth. The reason for ringing Doug was to get *permission* to snog Kit, not dig myself further into a hole.

'I didn't say that,' he says awkwardly. 'I'm sure it's possible, in theory, t-to be close with someone and also sleep with them, and keep that separate from *our* relationship. I'm not trying to criticise you, or forbid you or...'

He clearly doesn't believe me, thinks I've already slept with her. My defensiveness inflames further.

'No,' I repeat, half to myself. 'The rule is, nothing serious with anyone else, nothing that could come between you and me. So it's better if I don't blur the lines. No sex with friends. That's fine. Obviously. I love you.'

He's quiet for a moment.

'I love you,' I repeat.

He mumbles that he has to go.

'Oh. OK. Have fun with Mrs Cockburn.'

'Right. Ha. Thanks.'

I watch the sea.

Then I go sit with the others and start sharing Kit's cigarette.

I sleep fitfully that night. So I think I'm dreaming when I

hear soft footsteps padding down the attic stairs. But the floorboards creak by my door. A shadowy outline waits just outside.

Kit is outside my bedroom door.

Every instinct screams that this is my chance, and drowns out the sounds of my renewed (and very explicit) promise to Doug that I wouldn't sleep with her.

But after a painful, breathless pause, the shadow walks back up to the attic.

Did she change her mind? Was she sleep walking? Or... Hang on, Isobel's room is right opposite mine, and Rudy's next door – she must have thought it was too risky.

So I wee, brush my teeth, and walk up the ladder to Kit's room.

She's sitting on the side of the bed, face in her hands. The light and dark and stillness and tension make her into a Renaissance painting. I kneel in front of her.

She looks down at me in amazement, black eyes shining in the half-light, like she can't believe it's me. She tentatively reaches out her hand, traces her fingers along my cheek. My lip. Down my neck.

Then her hand is clasping my side, my hand is gripping her hip bone. Her pupils locked on mine, dilated, her body hot, her mouth a heartbeat away.

And I pause.

I want to stay like that forever. Every inch of me is raw with sensation. I've never been so turned on in my life and it's sharpened by the fear of breaking it, the knowledge that this is about to end, any second, in one direction or the other.

Is she going to close the gap between us, or is she going to pull away?

I watch her slowly bite her lip. We breathe the same breath. But *still* she doesn't reach forwards.

It's got to be me.

So, finally, unable to take the too-agonizing tension any more, I kiss her.

George has imagined kissing Kit so many times. She's imagined the exact amount of space Kit's lips would take up on her mouth. That they would be firm, even rough, and she would bite at her lower lip frantically, too hard. She had imagined, over and over, that Kit would take control. Push her against the wall, tug at her hair, tear at her clothes, scratch at her back…

Instead, this kiss is pure softness.

The tenderness tugs at me all the more for being unexpected. Every muscle in me melts into her and I hear a quiet moan from somewhere between us, unsure which of us it came from, but desperate to make it happen again. I feel intensely, completely alive, like I've been given a drug that makes me hypersensitive to her movements. The slowest slide of her finger along my ear, tracing freckles down my neck, the infinite warmth of her mouth…

George wants to take control instead. Make Kit gasp, make her look at her right in the eyes and say her name. Breathing hard, she pushes Kit down on the bed, straddling her, holding her hands above her head.

For a moment, Kit's expression is serious. Staring straight at each other brings me back to the moment and I can't think about anything except holding her gaze. But then her mouth broadens into a luxurious grin.

Composed and completely at ease, Kit laughs lightly.

'I knew you'd change your mind.'

It's like she's slapped me. I stare at her in shock and the blood rushes to my head. I stagger back from her, covering my face, sliding down the bed and onto the floor. I'm so ashamed I want to crawl into myself.

I thought that she... I thought that she felt the same way. But I lost control, and she barely gave a fuck.

I can't bear the thought that she's still there, watching me on the floor. She's going to laugh at me again. Tell me that I'm pathetic. Throw me out.

Instead, almost worse, gentle arms pull me up to the bed, under the covers. Kit tilts my chin up, wipes my eyes. I still can't look at her.

'It's fine, mate,' she whispers into my ear. 'Honestly, this happens all the time. It's fine.'

And she takes me in her arms, and holds me close to her chest.

Footsteps up the attic stairs. Panic in Kit's very close eyes. There's just enough time for us to jump off the bed.

'Good morning, Kit-Kat.'

Holding two matching coffee cups, wearing pink silk pyjamas, Isobel barely misses a beat.

'And good morning, George.' She blinks. 'Forgive me, I didn't bring your coffee up too.'

'Oh no, that's... That's fine. Thank you. I was just...' I shuffle out, not meeting anyone's eye. 'See you in a bit.'

I want to say, 'Nothing happened'. I don't know if that would be honest.

★

In the kitchen, Rudy's singing along to Queen, making a teetering pile of pancakes. She offers me some, but I can't stomach anything right now, let alone something made by her. She tells me about a time when she'd been presenting a live TV episode where children made pancakes, and one had flipped batter all over her. I try to laugh in the right places, but I'm too filled with anxiety about Isobel and Kit.

Maybe I'm overreacting. It's merely embarrassing, right? It's not going to divide the band or anything: Kit was with Marsha before, after all. Remembering this makes me feel better, until I remember that Marsha very much *did* divide the band – or at least, had to leave it, when things didn't work out with Kit. What if Kit regrets us spending the night together? Or resents us *not* having spent the night together? Which is worse?

Years off my life expectancy later, they arrive in the kitchen. Isobel bustles straight into Producer mode. Kit smiles at me inscrutably and looks away.

OK, so we're just... pretending nothing happened? Cool, cool, cool.

'Seeing as we missed out on GAY FEST,' says Isobel, loudly scrubbing frying pans, 'we should look for alternative opportunities. We need live experience outside of The Familiar.'

'Wha'bout fes'vals,' says Rudy, mouth full. 'Woz'ha'wun i' Sco'lan' nex' wee'?'

'Festival of Love,' I say.

'We can't join a festival that's happening in a week!' snaps Isobel.

'Yeah, Bronze Age are performing there,' I mumble, 'and they applied a year ago.'

'Tha's coo',' says Rudy, showing me a mouth of chewed pancake.

'Yeah, I'm going to go see them after we're finished up here,' I say casually, like it's completely normal to talk about my boyfriend in front of the woman I slept next to last night. 'I can suss it out and we could apply for next year? Though it's not very queer.'

'What do you mean?' says Isobel sharply, still not looking at me.

My heart sinks. I think she's lost respect for me now I'm a wanton woman. Her purity makes me feel sordid.

'I don't know,' I say, feeling grubby. 'I was looking at the Festival of Love page the other day and the line-up isn't very diverse. Ironic, really, given the name.'

We study the Festival of Love website together. The more Isobel looks through the list, the more irate she becomes.

'There are literally *no* out queer people. None! So few people of colour, barely any women, and extremely limited accessibility. I couldn't find anything about wheelchair access or hearing loops, or anything. How has this been allowed to go ahead?'

'We should say something,' I say, not knowing what, but wanting Isobel to approve of me.

Her icy eyes meet mine for the first time all morning, then she rolls up the sleeves of her cardigan.

'Phase should release a statement.'

Rudy and Kit agree emphatically. Before I know what's happening, we're drafting a post on Phase's social media:

@FestivalOfLove. Straight white able-bodied men are not the only musicians. Straight white able-bodied men are not the only people who love. #FestivalOfHate

Momentarily I wonder if I should give a heads-up to Doug and Bronze Age, but dismiss the thought – our band and audience circles never overlap. They won't ever see the post.

We press send.

I don't have much time to bask in my foray into activism. Isobel can't sit still this morning. She chivvies us into the rehearsal room to rework 'Gemini'.

To be honest, it's unrecognisable from the song I wrote. I'd imagined it as a song that was better bare: just a piano and a broken heart. Not… this. Ironically for a song about being torn in too many directions, all of us are fighting over different parts. Isobel twists my lyrics into a different kind of unrequited love. Rudy tries to sugar-coat it with a sweet bass, and my piano melodies – which were meant to be the main feature of this song – are completely lost in Kit's ostentatious drums.

'It's not quite there yet,' admits Isobel, 'but we'll keep working on it. Add some more Phase sparkles in.'

I bite my tongue. I want to say we should simplify, take some stuff out. But I'm probably wrong. Maybe more *is* more?

When we stop for a break and check our phones, we've been flooded by notifications. We look up at each other in alarm.

'Our post's going pretty viral…'

Pretty viral? Hundreds shared it instantly, including, I see with horror, *SophieSnob*. Her thousands of fans have loyally joined the fight and now #FestivalofHate is trending.

We drop rehearsing and pace like a four-headed robot, replying, liking, sharing, watching the numbers go up and up and up. Comments from ticket-holders saying they'll boycott.

Donation chains to outreach charities. Trolls telling us to go fuck ourselves. Isobel methodically reports them and pastes screenshots onto the original thread, dousing it in petrol.

Will Bronze Age think this is my fault? Is 'fault' the right word when we're doing something good?

By the evening, our songs have been featured on hundreds of fan-made playlists with an inclusive #FestivalofLove theme; our Spotify listens have skyrocketed. Our following has quadrupled, tickets for our Familiar gigs have sold out and journalists are asking if we'd accept a slot at the festival if it was offered.

'I think it's likely,' gloats Kit. 'If I was in the Festival's comms team, *I'd* give us a slot to make the problem go away.'

I know I'm meant to be righteously angry, but I have a sudden surge of sympathy for the people on the other end. They're probably not actively bad people…

'Oh my God!' says Rudy, holding her phone up. 'Stormzy has said he won't play his headline slot if there isn't better representation!'

The others scream in delight, but my stomach lurches. How on earth have my fewer than 150 characters had any impact whatsoever on someone like Stormzy? And if *he* doesn't play, who else might pull out? What if the festival gets cancelled?

I text Doug.

Hey bae how are you? I don't know if you've seen about the Festival of Love stuff on Phase's account? Basically we're pointing out it isn't inclusive, but it's gone bigger than I expected. I'm sure it will settle soon xo

He reads the message. His typing dots sit there.

'Guys,' Rudy calls from the living room, 'we're on TV!'

It isn't a major channel but still, there we are, our social media accounts blown up and cycled through.

'Self-labelled queer pop band Phase have made a public statement against the Festival of Love, the Scottish music and arts event, claiming bias against minority groups...'

They're using images from a photoshoot Rudy did of us at The Familiar. There's George, on national television. Her shaved undercut, hipster glasses and earrings, suit shirt and Docs, leaning on the piano like she belongs there.

Rudy, Isobel and Kit are hugging, but I just feel dizzy.

I guess I can't really claim I've been 'outed' when I've been part of a queer band for months, but that was only ever in front of other queer people. Now it's being said out of some stranger's lips. I know I should be loud 'n' proud, but... I'm not used to being a public queer representative. Another bi privilege, I guess.

Now everyone will know... All my pupils and their parents. Alexa and the staff at Liberty. My mum.

Oh God! I should have used a stage name. I should have performed in a mask. It's out of control.

Resting my head against the cold bathroom tiles, trying to breath slowly, Doug replies.

What are you trying to do?

Heart racing faster, I type back *?*

Are you trying to get the festival cancelled, he types, *or just get handed a slot yourselves?*

I reread the message, gut churning.

do u think its ok that a major music festival has zero queer people on its line-up

I feel my loyalties hanging in the balance. I imagine Libra scales in the air. The Gina side has been weighed down with

Doug, passively accumulating interest through years of lucky pennies and Hobnobs. But the George side has been showered with shiny gold bars: creative fulfilment, exciting friendships, an intense crush...

I'm not saying it's right, types Doug. *Can we please remember I'm not the bad guy here, Gina? But this is Bronze Age's biggest-ever opportunity. We've all been looking forward to it for years, remember? Feels like you're throwing us under the bus just because it suits you. You're meant to be our supporter.*

Gina's side of the scale comes crashing down.

yeah, well i thought you were meant to support me too so guess we were both wrong. maybe we should finally stop pretending we're the same people we were seven years ago and move on

Then I turn my phone off, go back to the room with Rudy and Isobel, and kiss Kit squarely on the mouth.

29

Today's horoscope: *the worst day of your life is the best of someone else's.*

Do: *Expect collisions / Flee / Stay hydrated*
Don't: *Push / Pull / Panic*
Well, that's encouraging.

Best bit about performing at a festival? Access to the performers' loos.

Yes, the Festival of Love begged us to come, and we kindly agreed. From the moment we arrive our experience is cushier than an upholsterers. Chauffeured to Scotland, we're greeted by fawning officials promising to 'improve their diversity even more significantly next year'.

They show us to our two private yurts. (Rudy and I whisper 'Yurt!' to each other like a game of Bogies.) It's unrecognisable from the sodden camping tent Doug and I stayed in when we attempted cool Glastonbury (in the end it was all too loud for us). These have actual beds, welly boxes, and charging sockets. We don't discuss who is sleeping in each one, but I deliberately put my rucksack on top of Kit's.

We also have a Phase trailer to ourselves. We included stuff on our rider as a joke, but it's all there: champagne, rum, four types of coke (Original for Kit, Diet for Isobel, Cherry for Rudy, Zero for me) and Rudy's favourite waffles.

Looking at our Performers' Schedule, I see we've been bumped to a slot way beyond our experience. Phase is in the third row from the top on the official billing posters, alongside actual celebrity bands. (Bronze Age is in a tiny font, three lines up from the bottom.) We have requests from journalists, scouts, and agents wanting to meet us.

This all feels really... real. Phase could make it? And then, I'd be a musician. Like Dad said I would.

It might be financially necessary for my musical career to take off, because I think Liberty are going to fire me.

My first thought is that it's weird for them to email me during the summer holidays. My second thought is 'Maybe they're making sure I'm OK after missing the concert'. My third thought is 'Oh shit'.

Dear Ms. Green,

Liberty Secondary cares for the well-being of its pupils. It has come to the Headmaster's attention that you participate in a 'Queer Pop Band'. The nature of this activity has led to discussion of your future at the school. However, we do not wish to make rash decisions. Prior to the Michaelmas term, we will therefore schedule a meeting for how best to proceed.

Sincerely.

I can't believe they're bringing me in for a disciplinary hearing for being gay. I've been a terrible teacher for so many years, and it's only *now* they want to discuss their pupils' well-being? OK, sure, I abandoned them during their performance in order to sit in a puddle of my own misery, but apart from that I'd been better – helping, even *inspiring*. Now I've failed them, again, by being in a 'Queer Pop Band'.

Yet again, my bi worlds are incompatible. Yet again, I've failed my dad.

'George, are you OK?' asks Rudy.

I try to hide my puffy face. The others turn to me, worried.

'Boyfriend being shit again?' asks Kit.

I shake my head, still in my hands.

How am I going to make money? I don't have savings. Piano teacher is hardly a high earner. Mum doesn't have money to lend me. What if the school gives me a bad reference? Will I have to scrounge off Doug? But what if Doug and I...

'Can we help?' asks Isobel.

I look up at them all. Isobel with her family wealth, Rudy with her TV salary, Kit who always lands on her feet.

'I'm fine, really, just– just eaten too many waffles.'

Rudy gasps. 'You've been eating my waffles?'

'I'm so sorry,' I say, and burst into tears.

Rudy, devastated, assures me she was only joking and I can have as many waffles as I want. Isobel pours me rum with a splash of coke. Kit massages my shoulders. I start perking back up.

After all, if Phase makes it big, I won't need the school job any more. We could rehearse during weekdays. We could go on tour. I don't need some homophobic school, cramping my style. I'm finally proud to snog women, specifically one very sexy woman, and Liberty will regret it when they want to use my famous musician name to advertise the school to prospective pupils.

Fuck 'em, right?!

I think of Matilda, Timmy, Hope and Percy, signing my 'Get Well Soon' card.

I need something to expel the doubt. Fortunately, I have a perfect distraction right here.

I grab Kit's hand to go exploring.

Kit and I have been happily friends-who-sometimes-snog ever since Cornwall. Since Doug and I haven't been speaking and Soph and I haven't been speaking, it's been much easier to keep the parts separate. Ironically, I can now see how open relationships work better when it isn't all secret. But there we go.

Striding towards the shared Performers' Tent, still holding hands and sharing a cigarette, I swear people check us out. Whether that's because they recognise us, or are homophobic, or just fancy Kit, I don't know. Kit's revelling in the attention, tanned shoulders back, stride long and nonchalant, tousling her hair, helping herself to food. I try to copy her.

Other acts are sitting around, also trying to look casual. I recognise some of them and feel my imposter syndrome knocking – until Kit puts her hot arm round my shoulders, her skin brushing my neck, steering us to a corner sofa. I forget everything as she turns my face to hers, playfully tapping my nose, stroking the frame of my glasses to the tip of my ear, a cat with a new toy. I drink in her dewy brown skin, her soft lips, her dark eyes sparkling in the tent lights. Maybe I should get a nose ring too, or maybe then they'd get tangled up when we...

Kit leans forwards and kisses me, and every part of me fizzes, like sinking into a scorching bath.

She pulls back, bites her reddened lip. I'm trying not to faint when, over her shoulder, I glimpse a group of people walking into the tent.

A group of redheads wearing bronze jackets.

I nearly *do* faint. Shit fuck. I can't bump into Doug while Kit's tongue is literally in my mouth.

I gag, get off Kit's lap, grab her hand, and pull her behind the tent.

I'm breathing heavily in a claustrophobic limbo space between the outer and inner marquee. She grins at me, thinking that my face of horror is one of lust.

'So many convenient spaces to hide away,' she says, into my neck.

'Good for eavesdropping,' I twitch. Condensation builds on my glasses.

Kit's lips reach mine, and she kisses me again. My brain thunks out, like when we play music together.

It's dreamy for about ten seconds. But then Kit's hand starts to rove underneath my shirt. Well, *her* shirt. But you know what I mean.

I subtly twist to stop her access. Instead, she fiddles at my belt. And sure, it's hot. And sure, I don't want her to be mad at me for being a prude. But what if someone sees us? Not just someone, but my own boyfriend? Compersion is one thing, but I don't think compersion is walking in on your girlfriend being fingered.

I shrug Kit off. She starts up again, but I say it's too clammy. It's all too much. I can't breathe. I need to get out.

We walk out, straight into Douglas.

★

Thank God we weren't holding hands. Or indeed, other body parts.

'Gina?'

'Doug! Hi!'

We stand in sphincter-tightening silence for a moment.

'Er. Kit, this is Doug. Doug, Kit.'

Neither moves. They stare at me. I have no Bridget Jones-style fun fact to introduce them except 'You have similar taste in women'. When I see Poppy coming over, carrying two coffees, I almost swoon with relief. Apart from her bronze jacket, she's wearing all black: ripped jeans, thick eyeliner, and a beanie, all of which emphasises her bursting red waves. Kit and Poppy size each other up. The thought of Poppy getting with Kit brings up bile.

Kit reaches out a hand. To Poppy. Slowly handing the coffees to Doug, Poppy takes it. It looks like they're trying to gauge their comparative drumming skills by how hard they squeeze. Neither one flinches.

'Kit Tsuki,' says Poppy. 'I've listened to your work. You have a tendency to rush. You should watch that.'

'Poppy O'Flanagan. I've listened to you too,' Kit replies. My stomach twists. 'Though most of the time you can barely tell you're not just a drum machine.'

They let go of each other's hands. I swear the entire tent has gone silent.

'You'd be better off in a band that used your talents,' says Kit.

Doug's glasses have steamed up.

'My talents are used fine, thanks,' says Poppy.

Kit shrugs.

'Ok, if you're happy settling.'

Kit turns to me at the same moment Poppy turns to Doug.

'We'd better be—'

Doug and I look at each other instinctively, then quickly away.

'We've got a soundcheck,' lies Doug, to the floor.

'Cool,' I say to the same patch. 'We've got an interview.' I'm not trying to boast, but I realize that's how it sounds.

'Oh,' he says, rubbing the back of his neck. 'Cool. It's not in your calendar.'

My cheeks burn.

'N-no, I h-haven't been updating it recently…'

Poppy and Kit share a glance. Unbearable.

'We'll chat later,' I say, at the same time that Doug says, 'See you around then.'

When we walk away, I look back. Doug doesn't.

We arrive at the yurts to find Isobel and Rudy have disappeared. We're alone. I'm about to mention how cripplingly awkward that whole interaction was, when Kit starts snogging me again.

I agree, now that we have access to each other's mouths, it's a waste to leave them unattached. We really are phenomenally good at snogging. I guess I bring *depth* of experience from Doug, but she brings *breadth*. She's more varied, more daring, with biting, tongues…

She slides her fingers round the elastic of my bra.

Look, I'm not a complete nun. I get the hints. And on the one hand, I'm obviously like *yes please*, I've been fantasising about this moment ever since I first laid eyes on Kit. On the other, I'm self-conscious about how many people she's slept with. In my head, she's on triple figures, whereas I'm only on triple figures in the sense that the number of people I've slept with is three.

On the *other* other hand, I'm feeling weird about seeing Doug. Either I want to discuss this with Kit as a 'friend' or be left alone to think about it, because I'm still feeling guilty about breaking our rules even though Doug and I are clearly in an anarchic rough patch. On the *other other* other hand, I'm worried Kit will get bored with me if we don't fuck.

I've got way too many hands and my confusion is preventing me from losing myself to Kit's advances.

She gestures towards the bed.

'Shall we...?'

I don't respond. She tilts my chin to look into her eyes.

'You're in control,' she says, though it doesn't feel like that. 'Yes, or no?'

She gently kisses my neck. Half of me loosens, the other half tenses.

'What's stopping you?' she asks.

She has a point.

'I want you,' she whispers.

I want to reply something along the lines of 'Wow, that's cool, and I think I'd like us to do more at some point, but I don't think I can do it right now.' But that would be pathetic, and of course I do want this... surely?

'Could you get me some water?'

She pulls back from me. Frowns.

'Look, mate, if you're not feeling it—'

I flinch.

'It's just... a bit fast.'

She laughs, which is not exactly the noise I want my lover to make in the bedroom.

'This is the least fast I've ever gone,' she says.

I blush up to my hairline.

'I'll bring you some water, but honestly, it's cool. Let's just hang out.'

When Kit leaves the room, I collapse onto the bed, face down in the pillows, screaming in pent-up sexual tension and self-loathing.

Come on, George. Live a little, for God's sake!

Right. I'm going to do it. *We're* going to do it.

Resolved, I take my clothes off. Then put them back on. Then take off just my shirt and bra. Then think about how my boobs look weird and put them back on.

As soon as Kit comes back into the bedroom, I'm going to say something seductive, like...

It'll come to me in the moment.

The minutes tick by.

Where is Kit getting that water from? Directly from the minerals?

Finally, noise from the yurt next door. I position myself, shirt on, but half-unbuttoned. Seductive.

Through a gap in the doorway, I see Kit, kissing Soph.

They're touching each other everywhere, groaning. Thankfully it covers up my own.

What is she *doing* here? Did Kit know Soph was coming and not tell me? How *dare* they be snogging right now?

I back away from the gap and weigh up my options: go out

there and break them up, or hide until they leave? I feel so embarrassed, snubbed, shocked, guilty, all at once, that I want to do the latter. But if I stay in here, they'll sleep together in the other bed, like a horrible farce. George, the warm-up act for Soph, headlining.

No way.

I wriggle back into my clothes like an angry snake, then clomp my (Soph's) Docs theatrically loudly, and rip open the fabric of the other yurt. Like a pantomime audience have shouted 'she's behind you!', they both turn from their embrace to face me.

I try to gauge whether Kit looks guilty, caught out, or genuinely nonchalant about having two girls in neighbouring rooms. Am I meant to find this normal?

Kit raises her eyebrows at me, significantly, but I can't understand her at all. It's very difficult to give her the benefit of the doubt when her hands are on my ex-best friend's bum.

'Look, Sophie's arrived,' smiles Kit. '*And* she's interviewing us this afternoon.'

Soph looks at a point a metre to my left. Now I notice the colourful 'critic' lanyard round her neck. *SophieSnob*, finally interviewing Phase, the only queer band at the Festival of Love. Of course she is.

'Hey,' says Kit, elbowing her playfully, 'you'll give us a nice review right? Mates rates?'

'My reviews are honest,' says Soph.

Well, there goes my career in music. Kit can't pretend not to sense the chill in the air.

'You guys are friends again, right?' says Kit.

Silence.

'Come on, we're all adults here,' she chides. 'Now everything about George's boyfriend is out in the open, you're both here to enjoy the music and be part of the Festival of Love... Let's all be friends.'

Yeah, because both being 'friends' with Kit is the problem.

Soph and I don't look at each other. I think of her calling me a 'part-timer'. That I was only queer when it was convenient. 'Do I belong *now*?' I want to say. Now that things are *really* inconvenient?

But we just stand in awkward silence, until I say pointedly, 'Kit, I'll see you at the soundcheck in a few minutes, right?'

'Soundcheck's this afternoon,' she says, fiddling with Soph's dress.

'Right. I must have got the timings wrong.'

As I leave, Soph pointedly turns her back on me. I hear Kit murmur to her, 'Is there *anything* I can do to get us a good review?'

Running away, feeling sick and pissed off, I check my phone to see ten missed calls from Doug.

I ring him back.

'We haven't even had sex, OK?' I snap. 'Why were you being so—'

'Gina,' he interrupts, 'Jasper has broken his hand. Can you play in the Bronze Age gig? Now?'

30

Bronze Age's rider is a couple of crates of Heineken. No one offers me one.

We run through their music in their cramped trailer. Maybe it's the chip on my shoulder talking, but I swear they're surprised at how easily I pick it up. Compared to Phase, it's so simple: basic chord progressions, all of it's written down – and the benefit of them having such a static repertoire is that I know most of them from our uni days anyway.

It's weird to think how much I used to imagine this moment. Fantasies of Bronze Age asking me back, where I'd miraculously overcome all my built-up blocks about performing and relive that perfect golden university gig, erasing the aftermath.

But now it's real, everything is wrong. Doug is sweating. Poppy won't meet my eye. Mickey is being even more prima donna than usual. Are they *that* jealous about Phase getting a good slot?

Maybe I'm overthinking. They're just nervous and worried about Jasper.

'How did he break his hand, anyway?' I ask Mickey.

He glares at me from tuning his guitar.

'Sat on it.'

'Sorry?'

'Jasper was sitting on it and then moved into a different position. Suddenly he's screaming in agony.'

I blink at him.

'People sit on their hands all the time,' he says defensively.

'He broke his hand with his bum?'

'Technically it's a Grade Two Sprain.'

I look at Doug, who just fiddles with his guitar strap, his back to me. Festival of Love, indeed.

'Here,' says Mickey, throwing me what seems to be an orange furball.

It's a ginger wig. Cheap, synthetic, unnaturally neon, presumably bought from a costume shop, though I'm not sure what it's meant to be: Orphan Annie?

This must be a joke. I put it on and do jazz hands. They don't laugh.

'Obviously I can't wear this.'

'We need to keep up appearances,' says Mickey. 'Our *thing* is that we're all ginger.'

'But there's no gain in trying to pretend everything's normal? Just say at the top that I'm a step-in because your keys player sprained his wrist. You don't even need to say that he did it by removing it from his own arse.'

'This is our one chance to get taken seriously!' Mickey snaps. 'We can't have reviewers write us off because it's not the usual line-up.'

'They're not going to take you seriously if I'm dressed like the Johnny Depp Mad Hatter.'

'Can't you wear a hat?' barks Doug.

'I don't *have* a hat,' I say. 'Why can't I just—'

'Poppy, give your hat to Gina to wear over the wig.'

We all look at Poppy's beanie.

'No,' she says.

'Thank you!' I say, pulling the wig off.

Poppy frowns at me.

'You could gel it down,' she says.

This is actually insane.

'Look, guys, I'm happy to help, but I am doing you a favour here.' I throw the wig at Mickey. 'I'm not wearing this. It makes me look stupid, and you guys look even worse.'

'Well, *sorry*, Your Royal Highness,' says Mickey, bowing, 'we know that you're one of the Gay Lords of the Festival, and thank you for *lowering* yourself to our level...'

He sneers at my George undercut, my shirt, my Docs.

'But you wear a costume for your *lesbian* band. Barely recognise you from the Gina we used to know.'

I gape at Doug and Poppy, expecting them to come to the gay's defence like they did at Great Dane's. They just look away.

Like a horrible furry boomerang, Mickey throws the wig back at me.

'Mickey, you're a bigoted, entitled piece of shit sometimes.' I say, gesturing with the orange furball. 'And you guys shouldn't let him walk all over you. This isn't a freshers' gig any more. Grow up.'

I throw the wig on the floor and grind it into the dirt.

'I don't *need* to help you. I'm sure you'll find some other pianist to replace me – after all, you did it so effortlessly when my dad died.'

I slam the door behind me. It's crap to end the nostalgic

Bronze Age spell like this, but I'm in Phase now. They should finally treat me like an equal.

After a moment, Doug catches up with me and grabs my hand. I flinch it away.

'Gina, I'm sorry about Mickey. He – he's not in a good place right now, mental health wise.'

Oh great, now *I* look like the bad guy.

'Jasper was the only person who could keep him grounded and I know it's not an excuse, but it's an explanation. I'm sure he'll feel terrible later.'

'It's not just Mickey,' I say. 'You and Poppy clearly don't want me here.'

Doug blushes, looks away.

'No, no. I…'

He pinches the bridge of his nose.

'Please, Gina, we need your help,' he says. 'No one else would be able to pick up our piano parts like you. I know this isn't the best timing in the world, but we'll sort it out between the two of us, won't we? Please do this for us. For your old friends? For me?'

Seven years together should count for something, I guess.

'Just this once,' I say.

'"One shot",' he smiles weakly back.

After I go back into their trailer, the others disappear somewhere, leaving me alone with the dirty ginger wig. I send an unimpressed selfie to the Phase chat.

Y r u dressing up as a clown???!! types Rudy.

I'm going to wear it on stage I reply.

hahahaHA ur boyfriend is such a joker :P she replies.

Good messages Isobel. *Means you won't get recognised from Phase. Take it off for our interview.*

Kit doesn't see the message.

'Festival of Love! Are we well?'

The cheer that comes back is dulled somewhat by distance. A fence and bouncers create metres of separation between us and the audience. I've never played a stage this big before. There's so much space even between me, standing at Jasper's keyboard, and the others. Mickey's getting in his Fitbit steps, bounding up and down the stage.

'We are Bronze Age! I'm Mickey and it's a pleasure to be here.'

I'm willing myself not to let myself get déjà vu. I want to recreate the final Bronze Age gig, sure, but I cannot let myself remember the rest of that night while I'm up here. I cannot get blocked in front of all these people, not even when a part of me is still telling me I should be ashamed for being here again. The same self-obsessed attention-seeker. The same terrible daughter, breaking her promise to quit forever.

Mickey's face is projected onto three screens at the back. He's covered a spot in foundation that doesn't quite match his skin tone.

'That's Poppy on the drums.'

Poppy slams a solo on the drums, tossing her red waves, the screens looking like an inventive shampoo commercial.

'And my man Doug on the bass.'

Doug's crinkly smile is projected on the screen. My stomach squeezes. I know how much he's always wanted to play on a stage like this. And here we are, doing it together. Like we planned, years ago. We'll make up after the gig. I know we will.

'And...'

Mickey's about to introduce me. I arrange my face into a candid smile, force myself not to fiddle with my wig. Raise my hand in a wave.

'... thank you for having us!' says Mickey, and counts into the first number.

I pretend I was just stretching.

Contrary to my advice, we're starting with 'Shy Guy'. Mickey thinks it will 'get them on side'.

'I guess I'm just a shy guy'

I remember the first time I heard this song's recording: on someone else's phone, with Jasper at the keys. I didn't even know that Jasper existed. It was only a week after I'd quit the band.

Stop it, brain, just play the notes.

The audience are loving it. They're bopping around, singing along, throwing their pints around. People are already dancing up on each other's shoulders.

And you know what? I start to love it too. 'Shy Guy' *is* catchy. It's *easy*. It's *fun*. The old chords come effortlessly to my fingers. And playing its chorus, I feel a release of tension deep in my stomach, tension I think might have been there for years. Maybe I can replace my old memories of this song with new ones?

We sing the last '*Shh*' together and the crowd explodes. For a perfect moment it's like that last student gig. The gold lighting shining on us, my oldest friends grinning back at me like they used to, and I half convince myself that we're back in the student bar, about to go out for post-exam parties, rewriting the rest of that night. No phone calls. No quitting the band. No shame.

'Thank you, Festival of Love!' calls Mickey. 'Now we're going to sing some of our newer songs. This one is called "One Shot".'

A strange noise comes from the crowd.

'*Shhshhshh.*'

The sound is like waves of white noise. Are they shushing him?

'*ShhhShhhGuyShhhhGuyhhh*'

They're all still singing the chorus to 'Shy Guy'.

Mickey fiddles with the sweaty microphone on his cheek.

'If you're really good to us,' he laughs, 'maybe we'll do "Shy Guy" again as an encore!'

But the audience shush louder. They're unified now, singing together like a football chant.

'*SH-SH-SH-SH-SH SHY GUY SH-SH-SH-SH SHY GUY.*'

Mickey pretends he's in on the joke. Shouts the count-in to 'One Shot'.

It's like when music starts playing on two websites at once. The constant clashes are the musical rendition of a migraine. Poppy's tempo races faster, Doug slips into the wrong key, even Mickey starts singing the wrong lyrics. A drip of gel dribbles stickily down the wig onto my forehead.

By the end, Mickey's stage make-up has completely sweated off.

'OK, you want "Shy Guy"? We'll give you "Shy Guy"!'

So we play 'Shy Guy' another three times, and then leave.

'Blue Da Ba Dee,' says Mickey, counting on his fingers.

'Somebody That I Used to Know,' adds Doug.

'The Ketchup Song,' sighs Poppy.

'I'm just saying, there's nothing wrong with being a one-hit wonder,' says Mickey, again. 'It's still got "wonder" in the title.'

He's drunk on disappointment and a lot of beers.

'Who cares about the Festival of Love, anyway?' he says. 'It's an outdated shitshow.'

I agree brashly, helping myself to a Heineken.

'Heard anything from Jasper?' asks Doug.

Mickey checks his phone again.

'Nah. He's still in bed. He's devastated because the one he's sprained is his wanking hand.'

Poppy looks sick.

'So we *do* have some goss these days, don't we?' leers Mickey. 'How's the open relationship for you, Gina?'

Everyone tenses.

'Fine,' I say casually. Change the subject. Why can I think of zero subjects? Mickey's cheeks are ruddy. His eyes have a nasty glint I don't recognise.

'Are you guys in a mange a trois?'

I look at Doug for backup, but he's spooked.

'It's called a *ménage à trois*, Mickey,' I say, crossing my arms. 'And no, we don't hang around in threes. We just sometimes see other people.'

'Very open-minded,' sneers Mickey. 'So Doug like, shacks up with you during the week and then shags Poppy while we're on tour?'

The world freezes.

Mickey nudges Doug's stiff elbow. 'I always thought doing it doggie style meant something else, but maybe you get some of that in too, eh? Eh? Eh?'

He raises a hand for Doug to high five. But Doug's become a statue. As has Poppy. As have I.

Mickey looks blearily round this museum of effigies and finally reads the signs.

'Oooh,' he says, trying to put his hand over his mouth and missing. 'Was that meant to be a *secret*? But I thought you were all so *open*?'

I'm about to say 'Is this true?'. But there's no point. I can see from the way Poppy and Doug are looking at each other.

It all makes sense. His interest in Poppy's sexuality, his asking me on the beach about whether it's OK to sleep with someone in your band... He wasn't thinking about me and Kit. He was thinking about him and Poppy.

How long have they been seeing each other, behind my back? Has Doug *always* liked her? Was I his second choice?

I watch them now, looking at each other in despair, and picture them in bed together. Tender, urgent, desperate, Poppy's hair on our 'his' and 'hers' pillows, Doug writhing in positions completely unlike our routine.

I peel off the orange wig and leave it on the table.

31

I'm lost in front of a Festival of Love tat stand when Doug finds me. I look at his crushed face over the Festival of Love rainbow rubbers.

'Gingerbread – Gina, I'm so sorry. So, so sorry. This isn't how I planned to tell you...'

I click a Festival of Love pen on and off.

'Did you like Poppy before me?'

He gapes at me. 'Of course not! We've always just been mates. I even thought she was gay, remember? I— Please could you stop clicking that pen?'

I carry on clicking the pen. He pinches his nose.

'When I told her we were open, she started asking these hypothetical questions about whether that meant she and I could... and it was just bants but her *asking* it opened this – this new way of looking at each other. I don't know, things changed really fast, and I needed to talk to you, but you were spending so much time with Phase—'

'Don't blame your actions on me,' I say, clenching a Festival of Love bear.

'I'm *not*, but don't you agree that...' Doug sighs and folds his arms. 'Look, I was worried about talking to you and

344

ruining things, so I kept putting it off. I was worried you'd hate me, Poppy was worried you'd hate her, so...'

I can't believe what I'm hearing.

'Poppy was worried, was she? What a *good* friend. How nice! Just a shame she wasn't worried enough to stop fucking my boyfriend!'

A browser in the tat shop looks round interestedly.

Doug winces, then speaks low under his breath.

'I followed all of our other rules. Sh-she knew about you, obviously, and knew we couldn't be anything more serious – and it did always feel completely different to *us*.'

I look up from the Festival of Love snow globe I'm shaking.

'Always? How many times have you two slept together?'

Doug rolls his eyes in exasperation.

'Quantity of times doesn't matter. There was no rule about—'

I had been about to throw the snow globe at him. But now I'm limp.

'Doug? Do you love her?'

He closes his eyes and rubs them behind his glasses, like he used to when he'd been revising late in the library.

'I'm not going to dignify that with an answer,' he says.

Doug. *My* Doug...

I can't look at him any more. The falling white confetti in the Festival of the Love snow globe blurs in my vision.

I turn to run away, but he grabs my hands.

'Ginger, please, talk to me.'

'What *about*?' I shout. 'The weather? Or how long you've been screwing someone else?'

The eavesdropping shopper shuffles closer.

'You must have been delighted when I quit Bronze Age.

You could know I was doing our recycling while you and Poppy fucked backstage.'

Doug throws his hands up.

'I tried a million times to get you to come back to Bronze Age. I never stopped saying how welcome you were, how much we missed you, but you kept pushing us away.'

'Oh sure, you invited me to your weekly show-off at Great Dane's,' I scoff. 'Did you never think about how shit that felt, to be in the audience, watching you guys having an amazing time without me?'

'It was your *choice* to quit,' Doug shouts. 'It was *you* who texted us, out of the blue, after we'd just played that amazing gig together, saying you didn't want to be in Bronze Age any more. It was *you* who said that you never wanted to play our songs again. *You* who said that you were giving up performing forever. It was *your* choice.'

And he's right. It *was* my choice. I had chosen to be at that gig, instead of with my dad. To play some stupid little pop song, instead of be by his side. To be a pathetic, self-indulgent, egotistical show-off, whose pointless ambition was more important than her family.

After I left that stage, high on adrenaline and attention, I picked up my phone to tell him all about it, only to see missed calls from my mum. I knew exactly what I'd done. Even before I saw that text one from her, in her stupid all capitals.

IAMSOSORRY.

How could I have carried on playing the songs that I'd been singing when he died? I had to try to apologize somehow, try to tell him, too late, that I regretted my choice. So of course I quit Bronze Age. I promised to give up playing forever. But I couldn't even do *that* right.

'You quit the band and said you were never playing piano again,' Doug says. 'What were the rest of us meant to do, give up our dreams too? It was all so sudden. We'd been having such an amazing time playing together, we thought you might change your mind. We *hoped* you'd change your mind. It felt like such a waste! But just in case you… we thought it would be nice for you to have a reminder. A memento. A recording of our single. We thought it was lucky that Jasper was visiting Mickey and played keyboard well enough to substitute you. We didn't send the recording to you *then* because it didn't feel appropriate while you were—' He swallows but pushes through. 'While you were obviously grieving. And you'd told us explicitly not to come to the funeral…'

I start clicking the Festival of Love pen again. It's already broken. Doug's gesturing but I can't bring myself to look at him.

'It was just a random YouTube video,' he begs. 'It was complete chance that there was that "Shy Guy" meme, and then it was on those playlists, and suddenly we were getting requests, and we just thought, well, if Gina quit anyway then what does it matter if—'

'Meanwhile,' I say brightly, 'not even knowing about the recording, I hear "Shy Guy" playing on a stranger's phone, with someone else at the piano. On the day before my dad's funeral.'

We meet each other's eyes for the first time in this whole argument. His face is crumpled in pain, his eyes clouded.

'I'm sorry. I *am* sorry, Gina, you know how sorry I am. I loved your dad.' He laughs ruefully. 'And his terrible jokes.'

I want to cry and sleep and be left alone.

'How am I supposed to trust anything you say?' I sigh.

'How am I supposed to believe any of this, when you've been lying to me?'

Doug pinches the bridge of his nose, breathes out.

'I *haven't*,' he says, then corrects himself. 'Or – barely. I haven't been lying to you as much as you've been lying to me. About your sexuality, about Kit – about who knows what else.'

He gestures, frustrated, with his glasses, using the arm of them to point at me accusingly.

'I changed *everything* to make you happy. I wanted things to stay how they've always been. Like we'd always planned. I was about to—'

My eyes land on those novelty rubber rings which light up when struck. I lash out at them. It attempts a flash and then, reading the room, dies.

I wonder how much Doug can still read my mind. Surely he knows I guessed about him proposing?

Quietly I say, 'I think I would have said yes.'

Douglas looks up from a Festival of Love dog keyring he was fiddling with.

'Would have?' he asks. 'Not any more?'

I can't meet his eyes.

'I… I don't know.'

Suddenly a menacing voice booms from the back of the shop.

'If you're going to touch all my stuff you need to pay for it.'

Doug and I jump out of our skin. He buys the dog keyring he was fiddling with.

I stand around awkwardly, waiting to resume our conversation/fight/proposal/break-up.

Returning, he offers me the keyring. It's so badly printed

348

that the dog's eyes are bulging into its ears. I stare at it until he puts it away.

We wander aimlessly through merchandise stands, sidestepping happy festival-goers, and carefully avoiding any physical contact with each other.

'What next?' asks Doug eventually.

'I don't know… Are you going to keep seeing Poppy?'

He squirms.

'I guess, at rehearsals and stuff. Are you going to keep seeing Kit?'

'I guess,' I parrot, 'at rehearsals and stuff.'

He and Kit have the same habit of touching the back of their necks when they're uncomfortable. He says, 'It's hardly the one-night-a-week we were going to see other people.'

I think of our shared calendar, which I haven't looked at since Cornwall. Since kissing Kit. I remember Gina's feeling of being boxed in by our co-dependent schedules, our curfews, our set-in-stone date nights. And, when I joined Phase, how often I had clashes I had to secretly move, how anxious I felt, permanently disappointing one side or the other.

'I don't know how to divide up my calendar any more,' I say.

Doug turns to me in disbelief and walks into a pile of sick.

Gagging in revulsion, he hops to some grass and wipes his shoe, looking up at me with a similarly disgusted expression.

'Are you honestly saying I take up too much of your time?'

Righteous anger bubbles in me so that I stride around him in circles while he cleans the chunks off.

'Before Phase, my entire life revolved around you!' I explode. 'I was like some Victorian housewife, waiting for the master of the house to return from *his* career and *his* friends so that we could eat *his* favourite pizza.'

'We *agreed* that thin crust is—'

'This isn't about the *pizza*, Doug, this is about the pizza *night*. And the other labelled little nights. The soul-destroying, mind-numbing routine that you've set up for the past seven years of our life!'

Doug's suddenly a kicked puppy again.

'I thought you liked our routines,' he whimpers. 'You're the one who didn't want us to break it.'

'*You're* the one who started it,' I snap.

'Because you were depressed!'

I keep walking onwards, past the hippies and peace signs, trying to find somewhere to breathe. Doug tries to stop me, but can't touch me; instead, he jogs to keep up.

'When we first moved to London, you barely left the bed,' he's saying, breathless. 'You couldn't make any decisions for yourself. I was so scared. I'd leave for work and you'd think I wasn't going to come back. You panicked all the time. I thought if you could see my calendar, you'd feel safer, connected to me, and – and you'd remember what you were missing, out in the world.'

He grabs my arm and I let him spin me round into his chest. He crushes me in a hug.

'I thought putting those little things in your calendar helped you? And it did, didn't it?'

He's right. Watching his calendar unfold from bed, seeing the days pass without surprise or fear, it *did* help. And when he put those notes in my calendar, like telling me to go for a walk, or text my mum, or just drink water, I know it sounds stupid, but they helped make things seem possible again. I needed someone to help me make decisions I wouldn't regret. Everything I'd planned for had crumbled apart and Doug was there to help me rebuild my life from scratch.

Doug's been nothing but kind, and I've been nothing but selfish and greedy. Like always.

'Once you were back on your own two feet,' Doug's saying, 'I kept saying to you that the calendar was optional. I kept moving stuff. I kept trying to balance—'

The self-loathing cuts away at my insides like a knife. And then, because I'm a terrible person, I turn that knife on Doug.

'Well done,' I say, and start clapping. 'My knight in shining armour, saving the princess from her turret of paternal grief with a calendar notification to drink water. Let me give you a medal.'

Doug tries to clamp my hands, embarrassed. I shout louder.

'But first you'll have to put it into the calendar, won't you? Because I can't do *anything* without your permission. Couples are meant to be *equals*, Doug, they're meant to *share*, but I gave you *everything*.'

I look him, dead in his lovely blue eyes, and say, 'I think you liked the control. Liked having a girlfriend with nothing else in her life but you. To idolise you. To never question you. Bet it made you feel like a big strong man, didn't it? Well, guess what? There's more to me than you, Doug. There's more to my life than half your calendar.'

We stare at each other for a moment, breathing heavily. Then he snaps. He grabs his phone out of his pocket, has to enter his password because his thumb is too sweaty for ID, and fiddles into the calendar app.

'Fine. Then I'll just get rid of all this.' He jabs at the screen. 'Date nights. Delete. Sunday walks. Delete. Sex. Delete.'

The notifications are lighting up my phone now, coming through one after another. Cancelled event. Cancelled event.

'Text your boyfriend. Delete. Drink water. Delete.'

The sky-blue squares disappear until there's none left. Then his name disappears completely. He's removed my access to his calendar.

'You're completely free, just like you wanted. Happy now, *George*?'

Doug looks at me with more disdain than at the stranger's vomit.

'I'll pick up my half of our stuff from the flat when you're out. Don't message me.'

32

Breaking up with Doug is the best thing that could have happened. I can finally be George, 24/7. Be *myself*.

I buy a vegan salad, like lesbians do. I use the wet hand-wipe they give me with the food to wipe off my Bronze Age stage make-up. The acrid synthetic lemon burns.

No, I'm not so lacking in self-awareness that I don't understand that all of this is my fault. I know I've burned bridges. I know people hate me. Rightly so. Believe me, it's not a fraction of the amount I hate myself.

But I have one last chance. One last fresh start. This time, it's all going to be OK. Because I've finally picked the right one.

Gina is dead, long live George.

'How was the circus?' winks Rudy. Isobel and Kit snigger.

'Fine,' I say coolly. 'Doug and I broke up.'

I crack a coke into the silence. The pop fizzles. I take three large gulps and start hiccupping.

'You broke up with Dog?' says Soph. The surprise must have made her forget she hates me for a moment. We make eye contact for the first time in weeks and her familiar concerned expression is almost enough to make me crack.

Our limbs twitch. Our muscle memory is telling us to hug.

'It was mutual, I guess,' I hiccup painfully.

'Are you OK?' asks Rudy, starting to cry on my behalf.

'Yeah,' I say very breezily. 'It was overdue. Time for a change.'

I almost believe it.

'Best thing that could have happened,' says Kit, putting her arm around me. 'Might not feel like that right now, but you'll see. And you know, the best way to get over someone is to get under someone else.'

Bit forward, I think, to come onto me here, in front of everyone, especially Soph, but I can't say I'm not pleased.

'I met a cute girl earlier,' says Kit. 'A fan. I think she's your type. Blonde. I can give you her number.'

I lean slowly away from Kit's shoulder. Squint at her. She smiles.

The *audacity*.

My hiccups become violent.

'Kit,' I say, 'tell me. Do you think of *everyone* as an interchangeable sex object?'

Kit's smile vanishes. She's about to reply when Isobel claps her hands.

'Remember girls, *Sophie is here to interview us*.' She raises her plucked eyebrows threateningly. 'We're going to show her what Phase are really like, aren't we? So let's get it together. Sophie, how's this light for you?'

★

Isobel scrapes us through with her consummate professionalism. Rudy provides the otherwise lacking cheery energy. Kit provides bad boy vibes. I hiccup angrily throughout.

'So,' asks *SophieSnob*, checking her last cue cards, 'what next for Phase?'

'We have big ambitions,' sings Isobel, to the camera. 'We want to continue to surprise people.'

'As long as we still enjoy playing together, and our audiences still like listening to us, I'm happy whatever happens,' grins Rudy, her children's television presenter skillset shining through.

'We don't have it all planned,' says Kit, leaning back against the sofa. She seems to have already forgotten my attack on her honour. 'We're just hanging out, jamming, seeing what happens, making our own rules.'

Her stoner parody pisses me off.

'We're not like some old boys club—'

'You need *some* rules,' I interrupt, 'otherwise' – hiccup – 'things fall apart.'

'We need to keep experimenting,' says Kit, to the camera. I guess she's hoping *SophieSnob* will edit me out. 'Never say no.'

'Sounds like you,' I mutter.

'Whatever happens,' says Isobel, calmly cutting over us and fluttering her delicate eyelashes, 'it's all mapped out in our stars. If listeners really want to know our future, they can check our horoscope. Or our social media.'

Everyone except me giggles together. I pour yet another rum, slouching on the bed in contempt of the court.

'Final question,' says Soph, in her camera voice. 'What does Phase *mean* to each of you?'

'Friendship,' says Rudy, with a sincere smile.

Oh bless her. I feel bad for being an arse. Now I think about it, it's not a great policy for me to burn bridges with the only friends I have left.

The others look at me next, but I'm not sure what to say. How can I put the last few months into words?

'Change,' I hiccup. 'Community. Creativity.'

Soph catches my eye. Yes, I glare back, that's my pretentious way of saying it helped me come out.

Isobel and Kit have been musing. Then they say at the same time, straight to the camera, 'Fate.'

They look at each other and smile. It's the perfect closing clip for the video interview, as I'm sure they're both aware.

'Well, thank you so much Isobel, Kit, Rudy, and,' Soph swallows my name, 'for your time.'

'Thank you *SophieSnob*,' we intone. I put an emphasis on the 'nob'.

'And we all look forward to seeing what the future holds for Phase,' she finishes.

She turns off the record button.

'Thanks, guys. I'll record your set later and then edit everything together. Shall I send you the video before publishing?'

'Oh, we trust you,' says Isobel, shaking Soph's hand. 'Post whenever it suits your scheduling.'

Soph shakes hands back, freaked out by her formality. I think Isobel's trying to keep Soph in her place.

'You girls hungry?' asks Soph, still in her posh *SophieSnob* accent.

Isobel looks surprised, like a plumber has just offered the houseowner a cup of tea, but the others agree.

'Cool. Come on, baby,' says Soph, reaching for Kit's hand. I throw up in my mouth.

'Kit, could I talk to you for a second?' I say, reaching for her other hand. 'Alone?'

Isobel looks from Soph to me to Kit.

'We'll be by the vegan salads,' says Isobel, smoothing a ruffle on her dress. Soph tosses her braids and leads them away, deliberately not looking back.

As they leave, I hear Rudy muttering, 'Vegans can still eat chips, you know.'

Kit waits until they're out of earshot to round on me.

'Look, I'm sorry you got dumped or whatever,' she says, 'but that's no reason for you to be a dick to me.'

'We were about to have sex, and then you had sex with my best friend in the room next door. Kit, *you're* the dick.'

'No, you made it pretty clear you didn't want to fuck. And that's cool, obviously. But you can't make me into the bad guy for hooking up with someone else who *did* want to.'

I blush with confusion.

'B-but what about *us*?'

Kit shrugs as if she doesn't know what 'us' means. I blush deeper.

'Kit,' I say, 'can we be completely, unequivocally honest with each other for a moment? Cards on the table? Now I don't have a boyfriend...'

My brain flashes up an unhelpful image of Doug's face, crumpled in disgust. I shake it away.

'Now that I'm single, and you're single, we don't have to just be friends with... We could get together. Officially.'

Kit looks away from me, out towards the open trailer door.

'I don't even mind if you still want to be open,' I add

hurriedly. 'In fact, I want to be open too. I'm great at open relationships.'

The silence stretches.

'It could be like you were with Marsha.'

The silence does yoga.

'My only rule would be that you stop seeing Soph.'

The silence completes an intense session of Pilates.

'Please say something.'

Finally Kit sighs, reaches into her jacket for her roll-ups and lays the parts on the yurt table.

'Look, being girlfriends isn't going to work, mate.'

Mate?

'I thought we understood each other? No feelings, just good friends, great sex. But now it's clear to me that you can't do that. So we should step away.'

She opens up the tobacco, pinches a clump out, starts to pull it apart. She gestures, asking if I want her to roll me one. I stare at her.

'What do you mean?' I say, throat tight. 'Are you saying you don't feel *anything* for—'

'I don't want to break up the band,' she says.

My mind flashes back to when I said that to her, outside her van, when she was about to kiss me. Kit impassively lines tobacco across paper.

'The dynamic in Phase got weird when Marsha wanted us to be a "couple". I think Isy... I don't know. Maybe it's cos she's such a prude herself. She thinks it's unprofessional, or something.' She shakes her head, rolling her cigarette back and forth. 'She's already been off, right, since she walked in on us?'

I had noticed Isobel's terseness, but I'd figured she was just embarrassed, like a mother would be finding her daughter's condoms.

Kit sighs and puts the cigarette to her lips. I hate how relaxed she is. It's so embarrassing how little she cares how important this is for me. Her disinterest in my desperate need make me suddenly furious.

I grab the cigarette from her mouth and slam it on the table.

'So break up the band. So what? It's been going for less than a year. We can't decide on a direction anyway. Anything could happen. Rudy could get some big TV job, Isobel could become a nun, you could go off travelling.'

I grab her face in my hands, forcing those falcon eyes to look at me. 'Why couldn't it be travelling with me?'

'You've got too many ties here,' says Kit, pulling away.

'No,' I say seriously, yanking her back, 'I don't. No boyfriend, no friends, and soon, no job. I can't come out to my mum, so it's even better if I don't see her...'

I think of Mum alone in Greengables cottage. The garden withering again. Bunny growing older.

I add, 'I can still call her, even if we're in Uzbekistan.'

Kit breaks free, stepping away from me, rubbing her face.

'This is not about me having too many ties,' I say quietly. 'This is about you not being able to have any.'

She doesn't answer.

I remember that night when we met. Kit on The Familiar Green Room floor, shaking my hand, calling me George. George wouldn't exist without her.

Right now, I don't know whether I'm grateful to her or hate her.

I pick up her cigarette, and hand it back to her.

'I changed everything about myself, you know. Just so that you'd notice me.'

'I'm sure you didn't actually change,' Kit says awkwardly, failing to light up. 'Maybe I just helped you discover new parts of yourself.'

Is she right? Would I have found George eventually?

'Maybe,' I say. 'But if it weren't for the increased possibility of flirting with you, I'm pretty sure the old Gina wouldn't have shaved most of her head.'

The cigarette catches. Smoke twists around Kit's face and her mahogany eyes glitter at me as though she's not sure whether I'm serious or joking. I'm not sure either.

'I'm sorry, George,' she says, exhaling. 'It's complicated.'

Aha, the famous line! The line that people only use if they really don't care about you at *all*!

And you know what? It doesn't even hurt any more. It's a strange sort of relief, to realize your feelings are completely and utterly unrequited.

'No,' I say with abandon, 'you're not sorry, and it's not complicated.'

I pinch her cigarette and take a long drag, then exhale, taking in the surprise on her face.

'I can tell you *exactly* what the problem is here. You simply don't like me the way I like you. If two people really want to be together, it doesn't have to be complicated.'

Kit looks away with a weird expression on her face. I'd like to think she was in shock at my cutting remarks, but I'm finally realising that most things Kit does don't have anything to do with me.

When she eventually looks back at me I feel, for the first time since I met her, that I'm seeing the real Kit. Not some fantasy I'd projected onto her. Just another human, with her own stuff going on.

I pass back the cigarette for her to take a last puff. My hopes of being with her fall to the ground amongst her ash.

'Friends, then?' she asks, reaching out her hand to shake, like that first night we met. 'No hard feelings?'

I look at the hand between us, and back up at Kit. God, it's tempting to leave it hanging. But a morsel of closure would be nice.

I shake her hand, and say, 'OK, mate.'

'Festival of Love!' sings Isobel.

The crowd roars approval. It's like being at The Familiar, but with the usual ninety screaming fangirls replaced with thousands.

'We are Phase. We were not invited to the Festival of Love until we pointed out the lack of representation for music like ours. For love like ours.'

The crowd scream long and hard. Isobel clutches her earnest hands to her heart and looks to the sky.

'Thank you! Thank you so much. We're going to start by playing you a song called "Virgo in June"…'

I should be enjoying this, George's face projected onto the big screens at the grand Phase stage. George, finally allowed to perform, guilt-free. This should be a new best-moment-of-my-life. Instead, I'm still just thinking about Kit. For my own sanity, can I really be friends with her? How do the lesbians do it? But if I can't be around her, do I have to quit Phase?

Then we start playing 'Virgo in June', and I slip into that

blissful barely conscious flow, my brain unspiralling for the length of the song.

'*Another lonely afternoon,*' sings Isobel,
'*I'll sing my same old tune,*
Virgo in June'

I'm barely aware of the stage lights fading around us, from blue to pink to purple and back, and the crowd swaying with their lighters. Kit's free tempo supports Isobel's emotional singing, Rudy's supportive bass complements my nostalgic spread chords. For the length of a song, our differences harmonize.

But the song comes to an end.

The crowd goes wild and I'm jolted awake. They're screaming, cheering, throwing their bras around.

Please, please don't make me give this up again. We're so in sync when we play. Surely that means we could smooth over our off-stage frictions?

But it's not only me and Kit. It's becoming clear that the equilibrium of Phase is increasingly fragile. Even before coming onto the stage tonight, we fought about running order. Isobel said that for this, our biggest ever performance, we should choose a strategic running order. I agreed. But Kit said we shouldn't change just because of the crowd, should do what we always do, and play whatever feels right at the time. Rudy said she was happy either way. In the end, the compromise was that we'd start with 'Virgo in June', and Isobel would shout the next song from the front.

Isobel makes a signal from the mic, which I read as 'Supermoon', a new song we created in Cornwall, and I start playing my piano introduction. But Rudy starts playing the sugary opening to 'Co-Star', and Kit slams hard on the punk rock beat of 'Mercury'. We all realize what's happened in a millisecond. Now, hearts in mouths, we all instinctively switch to 'Mercury'.

I don't know whether anyone from the audience would have noticed much, but for the four of us, it's like a ravine has cracked the stage open.

We're all suddenly too conscious of trying to stay in tune and in time with the others, scared of another rupture. We've lost trust. We're not synchronised swimmers any more, just four people splashing around the same pool.

For the next songs, Isobel carefully announces them. The crowd are still cheering, but I get no rush of joy, just nausea.

We've used up all our safe repertoire, but we still need at least one more song – a finale. We could play 'Gemini', but it was still sounding too cluttered the last time we played it. We should have saved something. Rudy and I look at each other across the stage, trying to hide our panic.

Kit starts counting in on her drums. 'Cusp'. Isobel turns furiously.

'No,' she hisses.

The crowd laughs. We look out at them with paper-thin grins, as if this is part of the show.

'Let's improvise,' says Kit. Is she making a weird joke? 'That's what we're best at.'

Isobel's perfect veneer is cracking under the pressure. I spot a rainbow lanyard in the front row: Soph's camera pointing towards us. This is the show we'll be remembered for.

'OK,' says Isobel, to Kit, 'I trust you.'

And so Kit counts us in, and Rudy shouts the key, and we improvise a song, live on stage, at the Festival of Love.

It's a disaster.

Rudy and I lock eyes, trying to keep things simple and stable. But Kit's trying too hard, pushing the tempo. Isobel starts singing lyrics we discarded months ago – discarded with good reason. They're about first love being eternal, even in heaven. Not exactly a crowd-pleaser. Some of the particularly pissed or high members of the audience carry on dancing, but the atmosphere's gone. People start to leave.

The song ends with a whimper.

On the big screen behind us, even Rudy can't pretend to smile and Isobel swallows down tears. Kit throws her drumsticks down like she's about to walk off.

No one knows what to play next, or whether to just leave.

What would my dad have done, I wonder, if he was here in this crowd, watching us give up? He'd have probably heckled some terrible joke, and told us to get on with it because he wanted to boogie.

I snort at the thought. Feeling a bit delirious, I carry on giggling, pushing past the guilt and the shame of performing without him. I remember, instead, all the times he encouraged me. How he taught me to keep going when I messed up. How he said how proud he was of me, for spending my life doing something I loved. I remember him and mum, watching me at awful gigs, cheering wildly.

Sure, my silly little pop songs can't bring him back. But maybe I don't have to give them up to show how much I miss him.

'Festival of Love!' I shout into my microphone.

The audience claps uncertainly. It's enough.

Kit, Isobel and Rudy turn to me, but I don't look at them. I find Soph's eyes in the front row.

I push back the piano stool. I loosen the tight top buttons on my shirt. I untie George's bun, and shake my hair over to one side, where it finally sits comfortably.

'This song is called "Gemini",' I say. 'It's about trying to have everything, but ending up with nothing. Or maybe the other way around. And I'd like to dedicate it to my dad.'

I start to sing 'Gemini', just me and the piano, the way it should be. My doubts fade away.

'What the *actual* fuck?' spits Isobel, up in my face. 'What were you playing at?'

I'd skipped off stage, waving at the cheering crowd, and walked into the backstage area.

But seeing Isobel and Kit's furious faces, my mood crashes like an asteroid. Rudy tries to stand as a peacemaker in the middle.

'I'm not going to apologize for saving the gig,' I say. 'You gave up, I carried us over the finishing line. That's what teams do. Oh, also, I quit.'

I grab my bag, and head towards the door.

'Thanks for the mems,' I say. 'See you around.'

Isobel's manicured claws grab me back.

'You can't quit,' she snarls. 'We've been on the *news*.'

'Kit and I had a long talk and agreed we're not working together,' I say. Isobel glares at her. 'This band is out of balance. Maybe there's something in our stars—'

'Don't try and use horoscopes as an excuse,' says Isobel warningly. 'You don't even know what they mean.'

'You're so right!' I say, throwing up my hands. 'I *don't* understand astrology. I don't understand a whole bunch of lesbian stuff! Slam poetry. Strap-ons. Cat babies. I'm new to this. I was constantly double-guessing everything to fit in, to try to make you like me.'

'We *do* like you!' wails Rudy.

'Thanks Ru, but it's not you, it's me. Well, it's not me, actually, I think it's a kind of distorted persona I inhabit to escape repressed parts of my psyche – but whatever, that's not—'

'You're being selfish,' says Isobel. 'So what if there's been some little "thing" with you and Kit? You'll get over it and she'll get over it.'

She's turned to Kit now.

'You will, won't you?'

'I always have in the past,' says Kit, uncomfortably.

'Please… I don't want Phase to be over, Kit-Kat.'

Kit looks up at Isobel with a start. Isobel suddenly has tears in her crystal eyes.

'I don't want us to be over.'

Kit strides over instinctively, grabs her shoulders.

'Isy, listen to me. We will never be over, OK? Whatever happens with anyone else, whatever happens with Phase, *we* will always be together.'

'But what if you're *lying*,' Isobel gasps, mascara running down her face in stylish strokes. 'What if everything comes apart and you fall in love with someone and—'

'I am not going to—'

'You will! You will! And you won't waste any more time with your prissy, uptight, prudish little school friend!'

Kit shakes Isobel's shoulders.

'I will *always* want to be with you, you stupid idiot!' She takes Isobel's cheeks in her hands. 'Because I love you. I've always loved you.'

Isobel blinks.

I blink.

I don't know what she's thinking, but I'm thinking, '*What the hell?*'

Kit slides down Isobel's shoulders to grip her hands, staring down at them as she strokes her long fingers, twists her rings.

'Don't worry, I know you don't feel the same way. You made that very clear, back in school. And yes, it's hard, not being everything to you, the way you are to me. But you're still the most important person in my life. The only person I *need* in my life. For the rest of my life.'

'But,' Isobel sniffs, 'I told you at school that I liked you.'

Pain flashes across Kit's face.

'Yes, I know, thank you. You "like me more than any of your other friends".'

'I meant,' says Isobel, slowly, 'I like you *more* than any of my other friends.'

Kit freezes, eyes wide, unblinking.

'I thought it was obvious,' says Isobel, through beautiful sobs. 'I've always loved you. Always. I've been waiting for you to choose me my whole life.'

And finally it all falls into place. The times I thought Kit was trying to make me jealous with other girls, she was doing it for Isobel. The times I thought she was trying to say something to me in code, or through Phase's songs, she was saying it to Isobel. God, even in Cornwall, listening to Isobel singing my love song... No wonder Isobel hated me after she found us in Kit's attic. It was *never* about me. It was always about Kit and Isobel. I was just a minor character in their love story.

The backstage door swings open and Soph stands there, holding a bouquet of roses.

But Kit and Isobel don't notice. She's another cameo character for them.

We all watch as Kit and Isobel kiss, a perfect Hollywood kiss. Isobel's neck swooning backwards like a dancing swan, Kit leaning down like a victorious hero. You can practically hear the violins.

When they eventually pull apart, Soph, Rudy and I remain open-mouthed.

'Let's take it slow,' Kit whispers to Isobel, who gazes devotedly up at her.

'We've waited long enough,' Isobel laughs breathlessly. 'Let's move fast. Let's move back in together. Let's go travelling. Let's get a cat. Let's do everything, together.'

They kiss again, deeply.

'Sorry, but what the fuck is going on?' says Soph.

The romantic soundtrack scratches.

'Well,' I say, 'I tried to have a big break-up moment, and then those two stole my thunder.'

'*You* were trying to have a big break-up moment?' says Soph. 'This is *my* big break-up moment.'

'*I'm* not having a big break-up moment,' says Rudy placidly.

'Yes, we all still love you very much, Ru,' says Isobel, flushed, tucking a loose curl behind her ear.

'Let's stay friends,' says Kit, smiling more broadly than I've ever seen her smile before. 'But for now...'

Kit picks Isobel up, bridal style, and, both giggling madly, they stride out onto the stage.

Soph, Rudy and I stare at each other. Then we watch from the wings as Kit shouts into the microphone.

'Festival of Love, I'm in love with my best friend—'

'And I'm in love with her too!'

There's a wild, raging, rollercoaster of a cheer from the crowd. Isobel and Kit laugh, holding onto each other.

'Isy?' she asks. She's no longer speaking into the microphone, but from backstage we can still hear her tender, can't-believe-my-luck voice.

Oh God. This can't be—

'Kat?' asks Isobel.

And in unison, like a perfectly timed final line of a duet, they say, 'Will you marry me?'

They smile into each other's kiss, and Rudy starts screaming, bouncing out onto the stage to join them. The Festival of Love crowd goes crazier than I'd ever imagined possible.

Even if we're enemies, I know Soph and I are thinking the same thing: *What. The. Actual. Fuck.*

'I'm leaving.'

I try to storm out. But it's a pull door, not a push. As I walk away I hear Soph say, 'No, *I'm* leaving,' and try to slam the door behind her, but it's also got one of those safety catches on which slows it down. She wrestles with it and kicks it in frustration.

I have so much pent-up anxiety and surprise in my stomach that the sight of her bent over her injured foot in her preposterously high heels makes me choke out a laugh. She glares.

'Soph, come on,' I say. 'It's all over now, we can go back to—'

'No,' she says, and the laugh dies in my throat. 'Kit ditching both of us does not absolve you of all the ways you've been shit. I've done nothing but help you. When you called me from a puddle because you were panicking about the mess you got yourself into, I even *forgave* you for breaking our promises, to try to stop you from hurting yourself. But you *still* weren't honest with me. We're obviously not the friends I thought we were.'

'Soph. Please. I've changed. Again. Please. Listen to me. Pumpernickel. Pumpernickel!'

But she just shakes her head and limps away.

33

Unable to stand the thought of seeing Doug and Poppy unleashed, Isobel and Kit on their honeymoon, Rudy's pity face, or Soph's lack of pity face, I get on the sleeper train to London.

This term is false advertising, obviously. As is my ticket for the cheapest option, a 'Comfort Seat'.

I've never cried on public transport before. After the initial horror that your body is letting tears out in front of strangers, the experience is quite liberating. But then it becomes that guttural kind of crying, you know, when you realize how much you've had stored up and you make inhuman rattling sounds and all the snot starts trying to come out of every orifice at once.

None of the other passengers say anything to me, or even acknowledge my presence, which makes me feel proud to be British.

I wonder if I'm going to have another panic attack. That would be terrifying and boring, but maybe it would make people like me more?

Mmm, no. I feel the opposite sensation to that night of the school concert, or even that night of the Bronze Age gig in finals. Then, I'd felt overwhelmed with choice and possibility; had too many things to do, too many lives to lead; so torn in two that I was ripped apart and stopped functioning altogether.

Now, my Libra's scales are completely empty.

No Gina. No George. And no one to miss them.

Yet another fresh start should feel exciting, shouldn't it? A blank slate. A fresh notebook. But I can't help feeling I've used up all my chances.

I check my phone, half to see if anyone has messaged and half to see if my calendar or horoscope have an answer to my meaningless little life. But the internet connection isn't working.

In a rush of abandon, I delete the horoscope app. After all, I only used it to try to convince myself that Kit liked me. It could at least have given me a heads-up about Isobel. Bloody NASA.

I click onto my empty calendar to delete that app too. Now that there's no Doug, no Soph, no Phase, no Liberty, there's no point having it.

But there's still one green event in there. A recurring event on a Sunday, long postponed: *Ring Mum.*

I look at it for a long time. Then I click onto my mum's contact image. She and Bunny look back at me, their tongues sticking out.

I read our one-sided text conversation, Mum patiently asking how I am, my series of excuses back. I take a deep breath and type out a message. *Mum, can I come home? Like, now? Arriving tomorrow morning? No worries if not!*

Seconds later, Mum's typing cursor starts blinking. But then it's there for a very long time. I imagine her painstakingly pressing the space bar between every letter of a message disowning me.

IWILLMAKEALASAGNEDOYOUWANTCHIPPIESO RROASTIES

Once my brain has uncoded the punctuation-less crossword, this, obviously, makes me cry again.

I message back, *Both. Please.* And, after a moment, a smiley emoji.

I may have no friends, but at least Bunny still loves me. He leaps around on his back legs, a pogo stick of delight, wets himself a bit in excitement.

Mum envelopes me in a huge hug, which I definitely don't deserve. She bundles me into the front seat, and tells me off for having clearly not been taking my vitamin supplements.

As we pull up the driveway at Greengables, I see Mum's newly repainted our cottage's emerald door, and the flower beds are blooming with white carnations, lilies, and chrysanthemums. I admire the fruiting trees and try to take a deep breath of clear country air.

But then Mum turns off the ignition, and says, 'I'm going to make us a cuppa, and then you're telling me everything.'

My stomach plummets again.

'Mum, please, nothing is wrong, honestly. I just want to sleep in something that isn't vertical—'

She slams the car door behind her, lets Bunny out, and twists the house key. I'm still struggling with my seatbelt.

'Go to your room. Put on your jim-jams and slip-slaps. I'll see you on the sofa in five. Come on. Pork-pork, chop-chop.'

She bustles off to the kitchen, Bunny at her heels.

Oh fresh hell. I'd hoped I'd be able to avoid actually *talking* to her. If I was going to tell her anything, I'd need to come out.

I can't even run away – I'm trapped here, enclosed by sheep fields.

In my childhood bedroom, trying to give myself a pep talk in my sticker-covered mirror ('You Go Girl!', 'Busted 4 Eva!'), I wonder if all this would have been easier if I'd realized my sexuality when I was younger. If there were more role models, if the world was more accepting, if I'd never felt the need to repress that. If there was no pressure to even label yourself at all, because everyone was chill with the thought that everyone might be a bit bi, a bit 'bisexuelle'…

Oh God. Remembering the way Mum pronounced that, so cuttingly, over the phone, I bury my head in my pillows.

Mum raps on the door, telling me my tea is getting cold.

So I put on my childhood pyjamas and warmest slippers. They're decorated with cows playing the piano. 'Moo Maestro'. I breathe in their heady lavender fabric conditioner smell, and think of them as protective armour.

Sitting on the edge of my usual position on the sofa, I look guiltily at the family portrait of the four of us. Mum, Dad, teenage me, and Bunny all stare back like it's an inquisition.

Real Mum sits in the same spot on the now more worn-down sofa, expectantly sipping.

I don't think I'll ever know the perfect words to say. So I decide to go for it. Avoiding every photographic and living pair of eyes, I say, 'Doug broke up with me, Soph hates me, I'm about to lose my job, and I made my band fall apart.'

She nods at me to go on. When I don't, she says, 'And why is that, then?'

I take a deep breath, and say, 'I think it's all because I'm bisexual.'

Mum chokes a bit on her tea. She avoids my eye.

'Oh,' she says, eventually, then covers her mouth with her hand. 'Oh dear.'

I stare at the worn patterns in our carpet, my vision blurring. I was right all along. I should never have come out. Why didn't I learn from Soph?

But then Mum chuckles.

'I'm sorry, Ginny, I'm so embarrassed. I've been pronouncing it wrong, haven't I?'

She starts cutting into a freshly baked fruit cake.

'So, why are your friends cross at you for being bi-sex-you-al? I don't *really* understand all those different modern terms, and I'm sorry if I say the wrong thing but… it doesn't change who you are, does it? You're still the same little Ginny to me. Big slice or small slice?'

I blink at her. She cuts me a vast slice of fruit cake and passes it to me.

I look from her to the cake and back again.

'But,' I say, 'I thought you'd be cross.'

'Why on Earth would I be cross?'

She sounds genuinely confused.

'Because… Because…' I look around the room, trying to vocalise the ambient homophobia I'd thought she'd displayed in our conversations. 'Because I thought you wanted me to get married and have children and a sausage dog with a sausage-themed name.'

She flops back into her cushions. 'These days, you can do all of those things with a girlfriend, can't you?'

'I... Well... Yes, you're right,' I admit.

'Or not,' she shrugs. 'I suppose that's what I'm used to, and, well, I just assumed you and Doug would do that – but only because he seemed to make you happy, Ginny. But of course it doesn't matter if you don't do any of it. I'll still be here. That's what mum's are for.'

She takes a huge bite of cake. 'Mmm, that is good, if I do say so myself.'

As I watch her carefully tear off a bit to give to Bunny, my chest hurts with love.

'I've been a moron,' I say.

'Oh, well,' she says kindly, patting my hand, 'we all have our moron moments. Go on, tuck in. Have your cake and eat it.'

'That's not what that phrase means, Mum.'

'Is it not?'

So, as we head out into the garden to walk off the cake, I tell her everything. Well, everything apart from the sex stuff. She might be OK with her daughter being queer in theory, but her daughter in bed with a woman in a banana costume is another thing entirely.

Bunny waddles along behind us, smelling the roses. And as we make slow loops of the cascading flower beds, I do feel better. Except...

'I have no idea what to do next,' I say, stroking the petals of a sweet pea. 'I don't know whether I'm meant to try and put my broken pieces back together, or whether I was doing everything wrong and need to start over. I still don't know whether I was happier being Gina or George.'

'Why can't you just be yourself?'

'That's a nice motivational quote,' I sigh, 'but I don't know who myself *is*.'

'Oh sweetie,' she smiles, 'no one knows who they *are*! Everyone is contradictory. Everyone's lived a bit of a double life sometimes, even if only in their imagination. You're so worried about how the different parts of you don't belong together that you're ignoring the obvious. They must belong together. Because they're all a part of what makes you *you*. Our overthinking, talented, hopeless, loving, lovable Georgina Green.'

The summer evening lights Mum's milk-chocolate eyes.

'Now, you might be surprised to hear that I don't know much about what it's like in the LDBZ hashtag—'

'LGBTQ+!' I laugh.

'Yes, your alphabet club,' she says, 'but aren't there other people with your B one? You won't be alone in feeling like this.'

I can't believe I'm receiving advice on queerness from my mother, but she's right.

I've been so worried about proving to others that I belong in Straight World and in Gay World that *I've* been boxing myself. I viewed other people's identities as criticisms of my own. But, duh, there's no one way to be queer, just as there's no one way to be straight. Doubtless I've met people who swing in all sorts of different directions, but I couldn't see their variety outside my own insecurity. And I belong in the Alphabet Club, just as much as all of them do. I'm not only 'half-gay' or 'half-straight'. I'm fully bi, *all* the time. And finally, I think that's an OK thing to be.

Woo, self-acceptance! Give me a medal!

But looking around at the Greengables garden, at the flowers my dad planted before I was even born, I can't help but worry if he would have felt differently. Is this just yet another way I've let him down?

Mum and I sit on his bench under the apple tree and I wonder if she's remembering him too.

We've never talked about the day my dad died. We've never even properly talked about him since, only in tentative asides or accidental anecdotes. But now the emotional floodgates are open, I can't seem to close them again.

I take a breath of lily-scented summer air and ask very quietly, 'Do you think Dad would have been disappointed in me?'

'Oh, Ginny…'

Before I lose my nerve, I press on. 'He loved Doug, but I've ruined that. He loved Soph, but I've ruined that. He loved teaching, but I've been such a terrible teacher, Mum. I dread to think how many children I've put off piano for life. And now they're going to fire me and I think he would have agreed with them. He taught me to love music, but – but I ruined *everything*.'

I stare at the apples on the ground, not trusting myself to look at Mum, scared of seeing blame and disappointment in her eyes.

'That night, when I left the Bronze Age stage and I saw the missed calls from you, I kept thinking… If only I'd been here. Maybe if I'd been here, he wouldn't have…'

'You're not a magician,' says Mum, bluntly. 'You're not even a doctor. You can't work miracles. It wasn't your fault that your father was ill.'

'But it *was* my fault to not know that he was so…' I shake

my head hopelessly. 'He seemed back to normal. Didn't he? He seemed... I remember, that day I left, only a week before, and I'd been here with him, and he was out of bed, and we were in the music room, and we'd played "Clair de Lune" like a duet, and he *told* me to go back to do my finals. He—'

I choke suddenly at the memory. I'd forgotten the detail until now.

'He joked that he'd paid so much to bribe the examiners, the least I could do was turn up.'

I'm not sure if Mum laughs or sobs. Bunny yaps for reassurance and Mum strokes his tender ears.

'But I should have – I shouldn't have... If there was even the slightest doubt, I should have chosen him. We could have... At least we could have had a bit more time together...'

I swallow painfully.

'But I wasn't there. I went off to prance around at my fucking student concert.'

I sink my toes into the grass, wishing it could swallow me completely.

'I'll never forgive myself for that. Never.'

'Ginny,' my mum says thickly, brushing her greying fringe out of her eyes. She takes my hand.

'Ginny, I don't know if it's the right time to tell you this. But... Your father knew he was at the end. He knew, and he knew that he didn't want you there.'

The world blurs. I snatch my hand away and get up, stumbling away from her.

I can't understand.

'B-but why—'

Bunny starts howling.

'Ginny, Ginny.'

Mum follows me, holding my face in her hands.

'Listen to me. He loved you *so much*. You were his star. And he was determined not to let his death get in the way of your life.'

I try to struggle away, but she holds me steady.

'He thought, if you were away, doing what you loved, it would help you to... To move on without him. He was so proud of you. He was so smug that you'd become a musician...' Her laugh catches in her throat. 'And he was so, so sorry that he wouldn't get to hear you play again.'

Mum's resolve breaks and she crumples. She drops her hands from my face. I clutch desperately at handfuls of her cardigan, pulling her into a hug.

'He would have been devastated,' she sobs into my shoulder, 'to think that you'd stopped playing because of him. That you'd been blaming yourself. That not only were you missing him desperately, you were punishing yourself too.'

She pulls away and brushes the hair from my face, her tear-stricken eyes searching mine.

'Oh Ginny, I had no idea. Please forgive me. I thought you really had changed your mind – thought you *wanted* to be a piano teacher. To be closer to him.'

I shake my head and nod at the same time. She pats at her pockets and pulls out some crumpled tissues, passing me one. I'm pretty sure it's already been used, but I blow into it anyway.

'I'd always hoped...' She blows her nose loudly. 'I'd thought if you were still happy with Doug, you might go back to Bronze Age, and you might remember how much you loved it, how good you were at it.'

She puts her sodden tissue back into the depths of her pocket and sniffs deeply.

'When you said you were in a band again, I was so thrilled for you. I wanted to come and cheer you on. But then you stopped telling me anything.'

Absently, she fiddles with my hair, feeling the shaved layers underneath. She tucks a loose strand behind my ear.

'Of course, I understand why, now. But... Oh, Ginny, I'm sorry you didn't feel you could share that with me. I'm sorry I wasn't there for you, when you needed me. I'm sorry I let you down.'

'No, no, Mum, please, *I'm* sorry,' I say. 'I'm sorry.'

'I think we've both been having a bit of a moron moment,' Mum says contemplatively.

I catch her eye. Our sobs become painful giggles. Then hysterical hiccups that send us giggling and sobbing again.

The sun is setting, turning the sky into a watercolour of indigo and gold.

Mum wipes my eyes with another old tissue and smiles.

'I hope you can see now,' she says. 'You can miss him and still let yourself be happy. That's all he would have wanted. Of course he would be proud of you. Of all of you. He always was and he always will be. *We* always will be. Nothing can stop us.'

We hug tightly for a long time.

Then I say, into her shoulder, 'Let's have some Prosecco.'

Hungover the next morning, eating Sheila's eggs for breakfast, I finally dare myself to check my phone.

Piled up lists of notifications from the Phase social media accounts, missed calls and messages from unknown numbers – and a single message from Soph with a YouTube link.

SophieSnob posted the Phase interview video.

I must look panicked because Bunny starts yapping.

'Deep breaths,' says Mum, over her eggs. 'Find your balance. Good things will start again.'

'But what if they don't?' I say.

'But what if they do?' sings Mum.

I glare at her.

'But what if they—'

My phone lights up on the table between us, silently ringing from an unknown number. Mum presses the accept button onto speaker.

'Hello? Is that George Green?'

'Er, yes, I think so?'

'*Finally*. I've been trying to get hold of you since your Festival of Love set. Do you have representation yet?'

Mum drops her piece of toast. Bunny has a field day.

'No,' I say, baffled, to the phone, 'Phase doesn't have an agent, but—'

'Not Phase,' says the agent. 'You. As a solo artist. We loved "Gemini", and we want to hear more. Can you send us your portfolio?'

'B-but… I don't…'

Mum gestures menacingly with her yolk-encrusted knife.

I stutter, 'By the end of the week.'

After we hang up, Mum and I stare at each other, listening to the sounds of Bunny licking the floor clean.

'Mum, I don't *have* a portfolio. I only have that one song I wrote with Phase.'

'You have hundreds of notebooks full of songs, gathering dust by the piano.'

'Those songs are old and awful!'

'So keep the good bits and write new better bits.'

'Muuuuum…'

She whips me with a teacloth.

'Get onto that piano,' she says. 'You're only allowed to leave when you've got the start of your next song.'

We glare at each other. Then grin. Just like the old days.

In the music room, I pull out the box of notebooks. The top one is covered in peeling university stickers.

My chest tightens when I open it – not just because of the dust, but because there's Doug, Poppy, and Mickey's handwriting… A draft of 'Dance With Me,' covered in beer stains. Pages reworking 'Shy Guy' in different coloured pens. Mickey's drawn a penis.

Turning to halfway through the notebook, where the writing stops, is a song called 'I Choose You'. The last song I wrote back then, while I was at home with Dad. The only time I ever played it in public was at the end of that last Bronze Age concert.

How did it go again?

I play for a while, transported by the smells of laundry and lavender and dog hair.

And you know what? Mum's right. There are a few bits worth keeping.

A while later, I'm scribbling edits when I notice the last page of the notebook is carefully folded over.

I turn to it and forget how to breathe.

It's my dad's handwriting.

Ginny,

I wanted to write to say thank you. Thank you for being here with me and playing for us. It's been the best part of my wonderful life, listening to you. I'm even humming one of your songs to myself right now – it's pretty good! Who's your teacher?

I hope you'll understand why I told you to leave me. It was the hardest decision I ever made. But I realized it would have been too selfish to keep you here. I didn't want that to be the way you remembered me. I want you to get to live your life. I know your future will be filled with bright lights, beautiful music, and crowds of people who adore you. Whatever happens, I'm there with you. I'm cheering you on, louder than anyone.

Keep practising. Look after your mum. And give In-A-Bun a belly rub from me.

You'll always be my favourite daughter.

Love,

Dad

What could be minutes or hours later, I notice Mum, watching me from the doorway.

I don't show her the letter. But I do close my eyes, and play 'Clair de Lune'.

After the final chords have echoed around the music room, I leave the piano seat untucked, one side out at a jaunty angle.

34

I'm at Soph's door, holding a giant bread basket.

I knock and take a deep breath, then another; not so much to calm my nerves as to smell the sweet, sweet Pumpernickel.

The door opens. Soph looks at me and shuts the door.

Well, that went well.

The door opens again a second later, to Soph, returned, also holding a giant bread basket.

We stand looking at each other, trying not to smile. Then we eye each other's bread baskets.

'Yours is smaller,' I say. 'You're less sorry than me then?'

'I didn't want to inflict as much flatulence on you,' she replies. 'Also, I got you a card, and you didn't, so...'

'But I've prepared a speech, so...'

We catch each other's glance and can't help but grin.

'Oh Soph, you're the love of my life! I've been a truly terrible friend, and you've been impeccable, and I don't deserve you, but I really miss you. I'm desperate for us to slob around again.'

Soph nods. After a pause, I gesture that it's her turn for a heartfelt speech.

'Just read the card,' she says, 'when you have a few hours to appreciate it. I even used gel pens.'

Optimistic birds are flocking around us, so we go into her flat. We're awkward for a second. Then we crack open some wine, rip up some bread, and cuddle up on the sofa. Thank God.

'I watched your Phase interview video,' I say. 'I don't know how to say this properly, but… you made us sound amazing. Despite everything. I thought you were going to edit it into a hate-tape exposé.'

She laughs.

'I was tempted. But no, the more I watched it back, the more I was sure. *SophieSnob* tells the truth.'

The video was called *Not Just a Phase: the Rise and Fall of a Queer Pop Band*. Soph interspersed clips from our interview with Familiar performances, the Festival of Love gig, her own commentary, and talks with fans. She made us look like how I remember seeing Phase that first time. Inventive, fresh, bittersweet, *fun*. I was proud to be part of it. And George really does look like she belongs on that stage. *I* really belong.

'Have you been in touch with any of them since?' Soph asks, removing a seed from between her teeth.

'Only Rudy. You?'

'Same. Don't know what I'd say to Kit.'

'Yeah… I keep thinking I'll get a wedding invite through the letter box.'

'That's what I said to Jenny.'

'Oh,' I smirk, 'someone's back with Jenny, are they?'

Soph rolls her eyes, but she's grinning.

'I'm feeling good about it this time. She even agreed to be

in a couple video, as long as she can still wear Arsenal merch. Which, to be fair, she looks hot in, so…'

'Can't wait to hear all about it,' I say. 'Blow by blow.'

'What about you and your, er, fiancé?'

'I don't know,' I sigh. 'He told me not to message him. But all his stuff is still in the flat, and I know how much he loves some of those board games, so…'

She kisses my cheek.

'Well, I'll be here no matter what.'

'Pumpernickel?'

'Pumpernickel.'

We toast each other's bread.

'I have more news for you,' I say, with a knee drum roll. 'I've got an open mic slot booked next weekend. As a soloist.'

'*Finally*,' she squeals. 'I'll be there.'

Then her face clouds. 'What's your artist name?'

'I think if I worry about another new name for myself, I'll probably shatter into little pieces,' I reply. 'So I'm just going to be Georgina Green.'

Soph affectionately cleans crumbs from my shirt.

'And when Georgina Green's a pop star, what are you going to do about teaching?'

'Oh, yeah! The school's about to fire me.'

'Did you finally strangle Timmy?'

'Alas, no. The Head heard about Phase and, I don't know, thinks it's inappropriate for me to teach? I'm not sure. The email wasn't specific. But I've got some big meeting before term.'

'I mean, it's literally illegal for a UK workplace to discriminate against gays,' says Soph, 'but you wouldn't be the first. Let me know if you need me to lead a revolution. I'd love to throw a brick at a homophobic school.'

'Thanks,' I sigh. 'It's a shame, I was weirdly starting to enjoy it. And making a bit of a difference. Guess you only appreciate what you've got when you lose it, and all that.'

Soph makes emphatic sounds of agreement. But then her nods turn more contemplative. She swallows her wine and looks at me over her glass, opening and closing her mouth a few times, like a femme goldfish. The mood in the room has suddenly become serious.

'What's wrong?' I ask. 'Has the pumpernickel already hit your digestion?'

But she doesn't slap my elbow the way I expected.

'I have more news too,' she admits, biting her lip. I try to analyse her expression: Surprised? Vulnerable? Tentatively pleased?

'Joshua called me.'

It's my turn to goldfish.

'Joshua as in your brother?' I ask, choking on my crust. 'Joshua as in your brother who disowned you forever?'

Soph just nods shyly.

'He apologised and said he wants to meet up. I dunno, it's still complicated, but he – Mum—'

She coughs and takes a wobbly sip.

'He said he thinks Mum and Dad miss me too, but are too stubborn to get in touch.' Soph warily catches a tear from her duct before it gets a chance to smudge her eyeliner. 'The problem is... I'm too stubborn to say anything to *them*. Guess it must be genetic.'

She tries to laugh, but misses. I squeeze her hand and pull her to me. She shrugs me off at first, but I refuse to let her go. I crush her tighter and tighter until she gives in and has a full-on weep.

It's been a long time since Soph has let herself let go like this. As I rub her back and make soothing sounds, I wonder if it's wrong of me to be glad my best friend is crying? If it's in like, a supportive way?

When, finally, all the feelings and mucuses have been released onto my shoulder, I fetch her environmentally friendly make-up remover, and dab gently at her face.

'Thank you bab,' she says between strokes.

I shake my head lamely and mumble something pointless about being happy she's happy and sad she's sad.

'About that,' she says. 'I've been wondering... If you're not going to stay living with Doug, would you like to move in with me?'

My hand slips and pokes her in the eye.

'You serious?'

'Deadly,' she says, winking painfully. 'I could move the camera stuff out of my spare room.'

'Then we wouldn't have to schedule in time together—'

'—because we'd be in each other's space all the fucking time, and—'

We start to push each other manically.

'Obviously I want that!' I shout.

'So maybe you should move in some time then,' she yells back.

'Maybe I bloody will!'

We push each other onto the sofa, exhausted.

'But for now,' I say, 'let's have a takeaway and watch a cheesy romcom.'

In affirmation, Soph happily farts.

*

Alexa eats another Revel, and passes one to me.

We sit in companionable silence for a while, listening to the sounds of children gossiping in the alleyway they think is soundproof.

'Thank you, Alexa.'

She shrugs.

'It's fine. The bag only cost a quid.'

'I meant with the promotion.'

'Oh. That's fine too.'

'I thought they were going to fire me, not invite me to lead an LGBTQ club.'

Turns out the headteacher didn't know how to say 'We want to ask a newly outed member of staff to lead an after-school club for queer and questioning kids, but we don't know if it's homophobic to ask.'

I did also assume the worst, to be fair.

'Am I really the only queer member of staff here?'

'You're the only one who makes a song and dance about it. And they literally want someone to sing and dance about it, so…'

I think of Matilda coming out to me in our music lesson. How many of the pupils I teach might be looking for a role model? Could I really live up to that?

'Do you think many kids will come?' I ask.

Alexa raises an eyebrow.

'The *only* pleasure of teaching in a performing arts department is that it self-selects the gay children. I could basically hand you the list of the attendees already.' She passes me a Malteser. 'And an LGBTQ club means the bullies can know exactly who to target.'

'Alexa!'

'Oh, it'll be fine. Kids these days are better at acceptance than our lot are. And if not, I get to expel them.'

I grin at her, and swear I see just the faintest glimmer of an upturned curve at the edge of her lips.

We're interrupted by a scuffle behind us – the sound of a group of children pushing one forwards to knock.

'Miss?'

Alexa and I, startled, look around to see Matilda, Hope, Timmy and Percy, standing with the awed awkwardness of pupils peering into a Staff Room. I try to subtly wipe my chocolatey fingers on my skirt.

'We just wanted to say hello,' smiles Matilda. No trace of mouse.

'Oh! Thank you! Hello! And, umm, thank you all very much for my card!' I'm flustered. They're flustered. But we push through. 'And I'm so, so sorry that I wasn't there to see you all perform last term. I heard you were *amazing*. I knew you would be.'

'We thought you did it on purpose,' laughs Hope. 'Didn't we, guys?'

'Yeah, we thought you were teaching us another lesson,' mumbles Timmy. 'Showing us we didn't need to rely on you anymore.'

'That even though you weren't there, physically,' says Percy, hand on his chest, 'you were still there. In our hearts. In the music.'

'In a puddle,' coughs Alexa.

'And you were still proud of us,' says Matilda simply, 'even if you weren't there to tell us.'

'Well,' I say after a moment, trying very hard not to cry. 'Yes. Yes, I suppose that's… That would have been a good lesson. I'll try that next time.'

We all smile bashfully at the shelter floor, except for Alexa, who picks a bit of caramel out of her teeth.

'Miss, there was one other thing,' says Mighty Matilda. 'We wanted to sign up for your new club.'

'Wow,' I reply, without thinking. 'All of you?'

Hope and Timmy nod, not quite meeting my eye. Bless them!

'I don't think I'm a homosexual,' muses Percy. Alexa chokes. 'But I do love extra-curricular clubs. And I'd like to be able to better support my lesbian, gay, bisexual, transgender, questioning, intersex, asexual and queer friends.'

Alexa and I exchange a look. Since when did Percy have *friends*?

'That's… That's great, Percy. It's for allies, too. I'll put up posters with more information, and we'll have our first meeting next week. Sound good?'

They all nod their little heads, and go off chattering amongst themselves. Gay Club is going to be great.

I try to hide my affectionate sniffles from Alexa, who looks at their retreating backs and says, 'The bullies are going to have a field day.'

I shush her, but can't help snorting.

Alexa pats her blazer in a practised motion, flourishing her dogeared box of cigarettes.

'To celebrate?' she offers.

'No thanks, I don't smoke.'

'You know what?' says Alexa, after a moment. 'Neither do I.'

Overarm, she throws the packet into the bin.

It hits the rim and bounces back out.

I quickly go and slam dunk it so the moment isn't ruined.

Alexa sifts the rest of the Revels between us and we chomp contentedly.

I'm madly excited to move in with Soph, but I don't know what to do about Doug's stuff. It's been nearly a month since we broke up and I still haven't heard from him. Soph accuses me of living in a shrine.

I know I'm meant to have gained self-acceptance and I'm a feminist who don't need no man, and etc. But honestly? There are moments I just want to go back to having a night in with Doug.

Then, completely out of the blue one Sunday, I get a calendar notification.

Douglas Grant has invited you to an event: Apology chat from your moron boyfriend.

Douglas? Apology? Chat? Moron? *Boyfriend?*

Should I flip a coin?

Oh, don't overthink, for God's sake. I want to see him, so I accept the invitation.

A few seconds later, the doorbell rings. Doug's outside, looking tired but lovely and holding a pack of Hobnobs.

I suggest that we go for a walk, thinking it would be more neutral territory, but our feet automatically walk our old route to Hampstead Heath.

When we get to a fork in the road, I lead us down a different path. It's muddy, hidden-away, surrounded by trees which can't make up their mind about whether it's still summer or the start of autumn. Fresh green, fiery gold, and deep pink leaves mix in dappled waves.

'The weather's getting colder,' I say, eventually.

'Yeah, the nights will soon be drawing in.'

'I like these autumn trees though.'

'I'm sorry I slept with Poppy.'

His eyebrows jump, startled, like he hadn't planned to say that.

'Cutting the small talk then,' I say cheerily. 'Well, I'm sorry too. I messed up our whole relationship.'

He shakes his head. 'It was mutual. In sync till the end.'

We traipse through an assortment of crunchy, soggy, and new leaves.

'Are you and Poppy together now?'

He rubs the back of his neck. 'No, no. That would never have worked. Anyway, I haven't been feeling very, you know... Sexy.'

'Me neither,' I admit. 'Like we glutted ourselves on new relationships and now we're detoxing.'

'Does that mean,' he says tentatively, 'you want us to stay apart?'

Through a gap in the trees, I spot a snuffling golden retriever. Doug sees it too. I almost shout Bingo, just out of habit, and my hand tingles with the memory of squeezing his.

I think I could reach out now and we'd get back together. It could be like nothing ever happened. Doug extends his hand.

'I miss you, Gina,' he says, blue eyes misty behind his glasses. 'I miss our old life. I think we could make it work again if we gave it another chance.'

The Libra scales appear back in my mind, weighing up different possibilities. The sides swing back and forth. I feel like I'm back where I started.

'I don't know,' I say honestly. 'I really don't know.'

'Well, I know something that helps make decisions,' says Doug, and gets his wallet out. A two-pence coin lies in his palm.

'You flipped this to help decide whether to be with me, those seven and a bit years ago. So...' He twists it in the air between us. 'Shall we try it again?'

We both watch the coin, glimmering gently, trying to work out which side looks heavier.

I fold his hand over the coin, leaving my hand around his.

'I think that this is something we should decide for ourselves, pet.'

He puts the coin away, smiles weakly.

'Even if we got back together,' I say, 'it wouldn't be the same relationship we had. Any change makes you feel nostalgic, but it's inevitable, right? I think if we tried to recapture it, we might end up ruining the memories *and* the future possibilities, you know?'

I stroke his familiar cheek. 'But I don't want to lose you. I know it's a cliché, Doug, but you're my best friend.'

'Apart from Soph?'

I snort. 'I'm moving in with her, by the way, so... so you can stay in our flat, if you want. We'll sort out the rent and the who-keeps-which mugs.'

He chuckles and looks away, wiping a hand over his eyes. I put my arms around him.

He doesn't smell like how I remembered him, or like the clothes I may very occasionally put my face into when I'm feeling lonely. The loss of that old smell tugs at my chest, but, I try to remind myself, he still smells *nice*. Just different.

'I'm sorry, pet, I know this isn't exactly the next step you'd planned…'

He pulls back.

'What next step?'

I look to see if he's joking, but his eyes are clear.

'You know, the *thing* you were planning, a few months ago?' I nudge. 'That you spoke to my mum about? The secret thing I'm not meant to know about but worked out? The thing we said in the heat of our Festival break-up?'

He finally clocks.

'Oh! Yes! Well, to be honest, I was going to still do it by myself.'

I stop. A leaf crunches under my boot. He's going to marry himself? Like, self-partnering? Is he OK?

'I feel like I'm ready,' he continues, eyes crinkling. 'I have more than enough love to give. But if you want to get involved, that'd be nice too.'

'Umm… I don't know. I could be a bridesmaid?'

He frowns at me. I frown at him.

'What are you talking about?' he asks.

'I thought you were proposing.'

His eyes pop out.

'What? Why would I propose to you?'

I blink at him.

'Bit harsh.'

'I mean, not that it hadn't crossed my mind, for one day in the future. But that isn't what I'd been planning!' He grabs my hands. 'Gina, I'd been planning to get us a puppy.'

A puppy.

'A sausage dog,' says Doug, slowly. 'That's why I asked your mum for advice. And permission. I know how protective she is over the breed. It was meant to be a surprise, but I thought you'd already guessed.'

All of this. All of this because I thought my boyfriend was proposing to me. Change and mess and ups and downs and double lives, and all he was proposing was a dog...

I start laughing. I sound like I've lost it – I *have* lost it – but Doug joins in, and we startle the squirrels from the area, and a final weight falls from my shoulders.

If this is what it took for us to realize that we had to change our plans – if it took all this for me to realize that I'm not defined by my partner, or by my past – then so be it. Now I know that I'm whole, just by myself.

But it *would* have been nice to hang out with another sausage dog...

'I was thinking we could call her Frankie,' says Doug.

'Short for Frankfurter?'

He nods bashfully and I pinch his cheek.

'That's perfect. Even my dad would have been impressed.'

'I think I'm still going to adopt a Frankie for myself,' says Doug, his cheek still pink. 'I hope that's OK? And I'd love it if you came to visit us. Whenever you want.'

I take his hand, and squeeze it like the hardest Bingo in the world.

'I'd really like that. Really.'

He smiles at me and squeezes back, and I think that, maybe, everything is going to be OK after all.

Whatever the fuck *that* means.

Epilogue

Even in my weirdest cheese dreams, I never thought I'd see my mum wearing a witch's hat in a gay bar, ordering Prosecco. Yet here we are.

'And...' she counts the group around our booth, 'eleven glasses please.'

Piled around neighbouring tables at the back of The Familiar are three groups: Soph, Jenny, Rudy and Marsha around one, Doug, Poppy, Mickey and Jasper around another, and my mum and Alexa at a third, looking different levels of bemused at the camp decor.

I thought my mum and Alexa would get on as badly as a house on fire, but they seemed very happy discussing garden slug removal.

'Better make that two bottles of Prosecco, actually,' my mum says to Cara.

Getting them ready, Cara winks at me over her shoulder. My already fizzing stomach explodes.

'Thanks, Mum,' I say, helping carry them over, and nudging her. 'Celebrate the small things.'

'And celebrate the big ones too,' she says sternly, handing

out the glasses. 'My precious baby girl's first professional solo performance! Sheila is going to be so jealous.'

I pop the corks. Under the table two dogs yap delightedly.

Though, ironically, The Familiar doesn't usually allow pets, they're turning a blind eye to two well-behaved sausage dogs.

Bunny and Frankie fell in love at first sight and have been nuzzling ever since. Romance has given Bunny new vigour. Could there be puppies on the horizon? Little chipolatas? Could I keep one? Call him Chip?!

Spilling Prosecco into everyone's glasses, my heart's overflowing too.

Georgina Green wears her hair loosely parted, undercut visible on one side. Shirt unbuttoned, earrings of various dangles, gold glasses framing the make-up she actually likes, and her own newly worn-in pair of bouncing Doc Martens – yes, with laces in the pink, purple and blue of the bi flag. Finally, I feel like myself. For now.

'To Georgina Green!' Mum toasts.

'Georgina Green!'

I bury my happily blushing face into Mum's cardigan and she whispers, 'He would have loved to see you performing tonight. He'd be so, so proud.'

I breathe in her lavender washing powder and let myself remember him: teaching me those first scales, listening patiently through my mistakes, showing me that anyone could create their own melodies. Me, racing back from school to practise. Him, leaning contentedly back in his chair as I sang him my first song.

Remembering him hurts, of course it does, but I don't shove the pain away. I don't need to any more. Because now, as I imagine what my dad would have thought of me and what I'm doing with my life, I don't feel ashamed. So I let the grief in – and the love and pride and joy flood back too.

Bunny dances up on his hind legs, trying to join in the hug. Mum and I pull apart, laughing as we wipe our faces, and give Bunny some well-deserved attention.

I'm rubbing two sausage-dog bellies at the same time (glad I've ticked that one off the bucket list) when I see Doug watching me, his expression indecipherable.

It hasn't been easy, changing from being Doug's girlfriend to just friends. We broke down dividing our nick-nacks into separate 'his' and 'hers' boxes. I felt crazy, leaving our flat that day – no longer our flat, but his – knowing how kind he is, how much he'd supported me, how well we'd suited being each other's other half.

But just because we're not right together forever, doesn't mean we weren't right for each other for a time. We had seven happy years together and I don't regret a second. Well... OK, I regret quite a few things, like my lies and terrible anniversary gift to him, but you know what I mean. I don't think there are many couples who could go through all we've been through and come out friends at the end of it, but I reckon Doug and I have got a shot.

I raise my glass to him and his eyes crinkle as he does the same back. Frankie leaps into his lap, spinning contentedly.

I follow her path to the Bronze Age table.

'Hey, guys,' I say, bashfully, 'what's the goss?'

Four variously out-of-place gingers turn to me. For a second, I'm terrified it's going to be awkward, but they break out into enthusiastic praise.

'Gina, I always knew you were good on the old ivories,

but…' Mickey shakes his head. 'I wish we'd asked you to write *all* Bronze Age's songs.'

Now Mickey's found the right medication for him, he's back to being the friend we knew at uni. Still a cocky little sod, obviously, but he was supremely apologetic about acting out, and he and Jasper have been bonkers supportive while I've been starting as a soloist.

'Don't do yourself a disservice,' I smile. 'You've written some real bangers.'

'*And* you've written "One Shot",' says Poppy, sticking her tongue out.

'OK, OK,' he says. 'We'll never play "One Shot" again.'

As we all laugh, I catch Poppy's eye. I know this will sound mad, but her sleeping with Doug brought us closer together. On a walk with Frankie, Doug tentatively asked how I'd feel about going for a coffee with her, as she was apparently pulling her hair out with guilt. We met and I told her it was me who should apologize, for having pushed them all away since that last Bronze Age gig. I could see that Doug was right – I'd been believing my self-doubt-fuelled narratives that they didn't want me. They'd felt just as betrayed by me as I did by them, for not letting them share my grief. And even though Jasper is the right person for Bronze Age now, it doesn't mean I'm not their friend, or not part of their lives. So I told Poppy bluntly that I'd always wished we could hang out again. We've been for coffee every week since.

So it feels completely natural for me to gesture to Poppy and lead her to the neighbouring table where I've overheard Rudy, Marsha, and Soph complaining that they miss performing.

In her natural Brummie accent, Soph is saying, 'I stopped playing guitar cos I couldn't stand not being 100 per cent perfect at something in public.' She twirls Jenny's Arsenal scarf around her neck. 'I love being a critic with *SophieSnob*, but seeing Gee perform like that makes me realize how much I miss playing for the fun of it, you know?'

Rudy and Marsha are nodding when I butt in, arm around Poppy's shoulders.

'Rudy, Marsha,' I say, 'I'd like you to meet Poppy. She's a bloody good drummer, who plays excellently in the Bronze Age, but she's been looking to branch out too…'

I look from Rudy, to Marsha, to Poppy, to Soph, shrugging innocently.

'Hang on!' shouts Jenny, pointing around the table. 'You all want to be in a band. Rudy plays bass. Marsha plays piano. Poppy plays drums. Soph, you play guitar and sing… That's a full team, isn't it?'

I look smugly round at the table, as they all start giggling uncertainly at each other. I feel like I'm Cupid, shooting my entire quiver at once.

'I'm in if you are,' says Marsha. I swear she and Poppy are already eyeing each other up. 'What's our name? Our logo? Our colour theme?'

'Woah woah woah, let's just have a go!' laughs Rudy, tossing her cloud of curls (recently dyed mint green) and pulling up a loose strap on her matching dungarees. 'And if we sound *awful*, we can always still hang out and support each other and go to gigs, even if we aren't in a literal band together.'

'Mind *blown*,' I say. 'Is that really possible?'

'Yeah,' Soph winks at me. 'And did you know, you don't even need to change your name or whole way of life to be friends with someone?'

'But George, *you* should be in our band too,' says Rudy,

remembering not to leave any child out. 'Write for us? You and Marsha could share the piano between you?'

I grin round at the table. It's so unlike how I used to feel with Bronze Age, where their successes made me feel like more of a failure. I'm genuinely, unreservedly excited at the chance to hear these four make music together, but I shake my head at Rudy's offer.

'Thanks, Ru, but it feels right to be a soloist for now. Maybe one day we can do a collab.'

After a moment, Marsha sips her Good Witch and muses, 'I wonder what Kit and Isobel would say?'

'Mmm,' says Soph, sipping her Bad Witch, 'maybe they'll invite our new band to play at their wedding?'

We all turn to her in astonishment for a moment, then spit out our drinks, spluttering with laughter. We start riffing opening lyrics to anti-love songs we'd dedicate to our heartbreakers on their special day.

Let's be honest, it was very weird to receive those slips of fancy card in the post, inviting us to Kit and Isobel's wedding. At Isobel's parent's holiday home, in Venice. No one has heard much about what they're up to, except that they went for a honeymoon beforehand, holidaying all across the globe. And sure, the night we received those invitations, Soph and I got very drunk and traded complaints about Kit. But in a way, it was fun to have something else to add to our in-joke arsenal, and a relief to know that we could go to The Familiar without fear of seeing Kit's van.

With a bit of distance, I'm secretly glad that something good came out of all that mess. Romance isn't completely dead. At least *their* love story had a perfect happy ending.

I wonder if mine ever will?

My eyes are drawn back to a flash of platinum hair behind the bar...

I'm roused from my reverie by Soph pushing me off my chair.

'Hey!'

'You're staring at her again,' she says, 'just go do it already.'

I take a sheepish breath, cross all of my fingers, and walk towards the bar.

Cara's there, as always, smiling lopsidedly at me. Under her cropped vest, I see the edges of her colourful tattoos, the rainbow heart, the terrible *Friends* sofa, the sunflower growing down her side, and feel that familiar blush spread across my cheeks. But I don't feel ashamed of it any more.

'What can I get you?' she teases. 'The usual doubles?'

'No, not tonight. Umm, I'd actually really like to ask you for something I've been wanting to get for months.'

Her hazel eyes don't flicker from mine. In the changing lights of the bar, they're like kaleidoscopes, flecked with gold and green.

'Your number?'

She blinks at me. And then sniggers.

Shit. I read the vibe wrong. I knew she was out of my league.

I start apologising, but she holds out her hand, clutching her stomach with the other.

'That was so corny!' she gasps. '*Love* it. I always hoped you'd say something like that.'

I let out my breath in a big raspberry, too thrilled to play cool.

'Thank Christ for that.'

Still laughing she gestures for my phone.

'Maybe you could get *me* some double cocktails somewhere.'

'Yes, great idea. My turn to serve you.'

'Sounds fun,' she says significantly, biting her lip.

Cripes...

Then Cara laughs, and I realize she's blushing as much as I am.

'That doesn't even make sense, does it?' she says in a rush, rubbing the shaved hair at the back of her neck. I wonder if it feels soft or bristly. 'I'm being weird. I just really fancy you.' She covers her mouth in shock. 'See what I mean?'

'I always hoped you'd say something like that,' I say, grinning. 'Don't you have a day off on Thursday?'

Cara nods delightedly and hands my phone back, her warm fingers brushing mine. I feel my face naturally mirror her lopsided smile.

'It's a date.'

And I don't need to flip a coin or check my horoscope to know that right here, right now, this feels wholly, truly, right.

'I'll put you in my calendar.'

Thank You!

Umm, obviously, thank you so much for reading this book. I hope you enjoyed it. If you did, please do tell everyone you know. (If you didn't, for God's sake don't.)

I'd like to thank the people who got this book into your hands: thank you booksellers, reviewers, bloggers, word-of-mouth-spreaders and anyone attractive who reads it in public. Thank you also to the authors and reviewers who generously said nice things about it – bit surreal, to be honest. Special mention to Laura Kay, whose quote literally bought my friendship.

Thank you to the people without whom this book wouldn't exist:

To my agent Hellie Ogden (Hello!) for indispensable guidance, edits, and making me feel like an official writer. Also to Allison, Emily, Maimy, Ma'Suma, Nathaniel, and the rest of Janklow & Nesbit.

To the team at Head of Zeus, especially Anna (before you tried to escape), Bianca and Kate, who each had to put up with me a lot. Also to Amy, Ayo, Christian, Dan, Jessie P, Jessie S, Jo, Kati, Lottie, Nikky, Nina, Paige, Steve, Yas and everyone else whose work helped to make this book more readable, and/or read. Special thanks to my editor Laura Palmer, not only for championing Double Booked but for the excellent editorial work which made the story impossibly better. I'm hugely grateful. And massive thanks also to Rachel Faulkner-Willcocks, for filling Laura's big boots to publish it in perky paperback.

To Marianne for the attentive sensitivity read. To the disgracefully multi-talented Cecile Pin for my headshots. To Meg Shepherd for the fun new paperback design.

To the international publishers who are translating this story in other countries. It's an honour that my characters are better-travelled than I am.

To Urban Myth, for so brilliantly envisioning Double Booked on the screen, and to Claire, for crying when I said you were in the acknowledgements.

To everyone who was encouraging about early drafts of this book (back when it was called Gay on Thursdays!). And especially to the incomparable Ana Fletcher, for the most affirming, valuable, and downright enjoyable voice notes of advice about the whole process – apologies for my astrological butchering, and any unintentional offence I've caused to Libras.

To Amy, Antonia, Lucy, Martha, Max, Riss, and the other aspirational queers who made me feel like I was welcome in the Alphabet Club.

To any acquaintance who thinks they recognise themself in one of my fanciable characters... Text me x

To the friends and family who were supportive of my clandestine writing career and haphazard coming out. To Haydn – I swear I asked them to make the dude on the cover look less like you. Special mentions to my sister Holly for staying up late to read my manuscript and listening to my neurotic spirals about potential titles! To my mum, for being my one and only supermum, and making me so much impeccable knit-wear. And to my dad, to whom this book is dedicated, for first teaching me C major scale on the piano.

About the Author

Lily Lindon is a writer and editor living in London. She studied English Literature at Cambridge University, where she was also involved with the Footlights comedy group. She was an Editor at Vintage, Penguin Random House, before joining The Novelry. *Double Booked* is her debut novel.